VOYAGE
Of The
BLACK HORSE

VOYAGE
Of The
BLACK HORSE

Helena Poortvliet

To order additional copies of this book, contact:
Xlibris
1-888-795-4274
Orders@Xlibris.com
www.Xlibris.com
714423

DEDICATION

Dedicated to Cyndi Baird, friend and encourager for many years
through trials and happy trails alike. Looking forward to many more
years in the saddle with friends like you.

CONTENTS

CHAPTER 1

The Letter

January 15, 1852
Dearest Jeanette,

I barely know how to begin there is so much to tell. First of all, how much I miss you and love you! How much it pains me to be away from you! I thank God for you and pray we'll be together soon.

I am amazed every day at God's hand on my life. I found the Durans' who invited me to stay with them, as it turns out, five days waiting out bad weather. But God had a purpose. The Durans listened to God's Word and immediately became believers. The next day, their employer's daughters came and one of them believed. The next day her maid came and believed and the next day their butler.

On the way to Birmingham an escort of Romani invited me to their camp south of Birmingham. I stayed there two days and many believed, and there were miracles! The Romani have escorted me all the way to Birmingham.

I found Pierre Mirande in Birmingham, not doing well. Again, the weather held me there for two days. Pierre, after listening to the Word, believed. I found an orphan boy on the street, cold and hungry; his mother died on the street. After feeding him and getting him some new clothes, I realized I could not leave him, so he is going to Canada also. His name is Harry; he is only eight years old but seems much younger, he is so small. Pierre also decided to go with me; he plans to sign on the ship's crew. God says to "feed my sheep." I hope you don't mind, but I feel I had no choice.

The Durans were shocked and saddened to hear of your father's passing. They are now praying also for your brother's recovery, as I am.

I miss you so, my love. I look forward to the day we are together again. Thinking of the future with you gives me hope. There is an empty place in my heart without you.

I send my greetings to Antoine and Ellienne. I hope all is working out with them being there with you. Please let them know I miss them. They are such good friends. I hate to think that I may never see them again. I also send my greetings to your mother and to Darren.

As I post this letter, we are leaving Birmingham, headed for Liverpool. Jules Duran told me of a ship captain who specializes in transporting horses. His ship is the *Bucephalus*. I will look for it when I get to Liverpool.

So, my dearest, I look forward to being in Canada in a few weeks and pray you will be there soon as well. I miss you terribly, but look forward to our future together.

All my love, until we are together,
Jacques

E MOTION WAS FLOWING as Jeannette looked up from the letter, to see the other two women open-mouthed, waiting. "Well, what did he write?" Her mother spoke first.

Jeannette opened her mouth to speak, overcome with emotion constricting her throat. She could not stop the tears.

"Oh, sweetie, what is it?" Her mother reached to embrace her and Ellienne rushed over to embrace them both.

"Oh, I miss him so," she choked out, leaning on both her mother and her friend.

While the three were still embracing, Madam Newall asked again, "What did he say?"

As they separated, Jeanette started to answer their questions.

"Well, he posted the letter from Birmingham, but they were leaving for Liverpool, so I suppose by now he's already on the ship. He visited the Durans and read to them and they all believed, and some of their neighbors also."

"Oh, that's wonderful!" her mother exclaimed.

HELENA POORTVLIET

"The Romani escorted him all the way to Birmingham." She looked at Ellienne. "Did you know they were going to do that?"

Ellienne shook her head. "I didn't know that was planned, but I'm not surprised. The Romani look out for their own," she said smiling.

"What else?" Madam Newall pushed for more.

"Mother, you remember Pierre Mirande?" Her mother nodded.

"Well, Jacques found him in Birmingham and now he's a believer." "But that's not all," Jeannette went on, as she glanced back at the letter.

"What else?" her mother asked again.

"He found a little boy in Birmingham on the street. It looks like he's adopting him.

Now both Ellienne and Madam Newall were open-mouthed with amazement.

"He says he hopes I don't mind," Jeannette continued, shaking her head. She knew Jacques enjoyed being around children, remembering how the Romani children would try to be close to him, even climbing in his lap, the week they stayed in the Romani camp.

"And he says he misses you and Antoine," she said to Ellienne. "He says he's afraid he'll never see you again. She looked back at her mother. "He sends greetings to you and Darren and hopes Darren is better.

"That's nice," her mother responded. "He's such a good boy." Then with a sober look, turned, "I'd better go check on your brother."

Jeannette put the letter in her pocket, turning to Ellienne, "I guess we better get this place cleaned up for dinner. Antoine should be back soon with supplies."

La Petit Fleur was the French-styled café and inn Madam Newall operated in Southampton, England, with the help of her daughter Jeannette. Ellienne and Antoine Merlot were the Romani couple who worked for them, and were also their good friends. Darren, Jeannette's brother, was still recovering from a beating he received a few weeks ago. They still did not know who had done it.

Jeannette made one last trip to the dining room to be sure it was ready for the dinner guests. After replacing some soiled table linens and picking up the last dirty plate, she went back to the kitchen where Ellienne was taking a huge beef roast out of the oven and replacing it with a pan of fish to bake. The aromas were tantalizing; Jeannette knew the effect on the diners would be positive.

Just then the back door opened and in came Antoine, arms full of bags of supplies. Jeannette went out to help unload the wagon backed up to the door, but took a moment to go up and pet the two bay mares hitched to the wagon. She loved these horses. One belonged to her and the other to her brother Darren. Before leaving for Liverpool, Jacques bred both of the mares to his black Percheron stallion, Tounerre. Jeannette was anxious for the foals to come, hoping the care of the foals would help to heal her relationship with her brother.

When Antoine came back out for another armload, Jeannette left the mares to help him, feeling guilty for her moment of pleasure. By now she was feeling the chill of the evening which was closing in. It was still January, a hard winter so far. She pulled bags of vegetables from the back of the wagon and headed for the door.

Madam Newall was back in the kitchen and Jeannette was surprised to see Darren sitting at the table. She went over and sat next to him.

"Darren! I'm so glad to see you up!" She put her arm around his shoulder "Can I get you anything?"

"No, Sissy. That's okay." He spoke slowly, still showing the effects of bruises and broken facial bones.

Jeannette went back out to help unload the wagon, getting the last packages, which she knew were fresh fish from the terminal, so Antoine led the team into the stable. When she went back in, there were guests in the dining room, so she went out to greet them.

There were several regular customers, men who worked at the boat terminal, a family who had just come across the channel, and some late shoppers, mostly women. As Jeannette went around greeting them, many she knew well, two men came through the door. Looking around, they went toward an empty table near the front window. As she approached the table, Jeannette felt uneasy. The men were strangers; but it wasn't that. Many strangers came through here. But these men had a defiant, insolent look which made her uncomfortable.

In her usual cheerful voice, she asked them, "Would you like soup while you're waiting for dinner?"

HELENA POORTVLIET

The two looked at each other, smirking. One smiled at his companion and repeated, "Do we want soup?" in a mocking tone.

The other leered at Jeannette and said, "Beer," and after a pause, "and you."

Jeannette felt herself reddening, and backed up. The man reached out and grasped her wrist.

"Not so fast, darlin'," he laughed, "I was just tryin' to be friendly. You must be Darren's sister. He talks a lot about you."

Jeannette wrenched her arm free, moving away.

"Wait now, darlin'," the man continued. "While you're gitten' that beer, tell your brother we've come to see him."

By now, others noticed the exchange and some of the shoppers were getting up to leave, the women looking indignant. Jeannette turned to the kitchen, walking fast, becoming aware that she was shaking. The shock was clear on her face as Ellienne looked toward her.

"What is it, honey?" Ellienne dropped what she was doing to go to her.

"There're some men out there asking for Darren and they're not nice at all. I think they're looking for trouble."

Darren started to get up from the table. His mother protested. "Now, sweetie, you're not up to seeing anyone. She reached for his arm, but he pulled away from her.

"I'll go see what they want."

"I'll go with you," Antoine offered.

"Oh, that's not necessary," Darren protested.

"I'll go anyway," Antoine was firm.

Madam Newall said, "You stay here; I'll go see what they want." She started for the dining room. "Where are they?" She looked back at Jeannette.

"Over by the window. Mother, be careful."

As Madam Newall went into the dining room, Antoine followed her only to where he could see. She walked up to the men, asking why they wanted to see Darren. "He's too ill to see visitors."

"Oh, that's too bad." The tone was still mocking, impudent. The other man was snickering, watching his companion.

"We really must see him."

"Well, not today." Madam Newall was firm.

"I guess the little boy has to hide behind his mama's skirts," the man said, sarcastically.

"I think you should leave now," Madam Newall warned. People all around were stirring now. Antoine, watching from the doorway, started walking toward them.

The men started to get up. They were not laughing now. As he came closer, Antoine asked, "Is there anything I can help you with?"

As they started for the door, one turned back to say, "A man who don't pay his debts might find trouble where he least expects it," as they went out the door.

Madam Newall was shaking, both indignant and frightened. Antoine put his arm around her shoulder, guiding her back toward the kitchen. Now diners were getting up all over the dining room.

In the kitchen Madam Newall, confronted her son. "What do you owe money for? Those men were very threatening, saying you owe debts."

Darren shrugged. "I don't know what they're talking about. I don't owe anything." He looked apprehensive.

Jeannette went back into the dining room. There were no diners remaining now. She went to the front to lock up, noticing money left on most of the tables. She started gathering up dirty dishes as she headed back toward the kitchen. Darren and her mother were gone. To her questioning look, Ellienne answered, "She took Darren back to his room."

Jeannette looked at her two friends. "I think we need to pray. This may not be the best neighborhood, being so close to the waterfront, and the Dolphin Tavern so close, but we've never had trouble here before." She reached her hands toward Ellienne and Antoine. As they joined hands she began to pray, "Oh, Father, we pray for thy protection and peace. We want this to be a safe place for travelers to find shelter. We pray for your hand on my brother, Darren. I rebuke fear in Jesus' name."

And they all said, "Amen," together.

Later, when Jeannette went to her room, she took the letter from Jacques out of her pocket and read it again. She missed him terribly. Sometimes it all seemed like a dream. *Will I really see him again? Canada seems so far away.* There were times when she considered she would not hear from him again, that he would get on the road and forget her. She held the letter to her breast, wanting to hold him. Now he had written, confirming his promise to her.

She reread all the parts about all the people he encountered who were receiving God's Word and becoming believers, feeling admiration for this man she loved. *He really seems to be growing spiritually and learning to do God's will.* Jeannette longed to be with him.

She wondered about the little boy he found. She realized this meant they would be starting out as a family. *Harry, his name is Harry. I'll remember to pray for him.'*

Jeannette put the letter away and put out her lamp, climbing into bed. Laying in the dark, she felt too agitated to fall asleep. As she lay there, the face of that man came to her, the one who grabbed her wrist in the dining room. She shuddered, trying to erase his face from her memory, but the memory taunted her. She pondered over what he said. *Were these the men who had beaten Darren?* She prayed, rebuking the fear, and as her prayer changed to the heavenly language, she fell asleep.

Waking with a start, she sat straight up. *What was that?* She thought it was a dream at first, riding her mare Katy, galloping like the wind. Then it seemed like a loud explosion behind her, and she felt herself falling. Realizing it was a dream, she still thought the explosion might have been real. Then she heard footsteps, and was out of bed, pulling on her dressing gown. She opened her door to run into Antoine heading down the hall toward the kitchen.

"You heard it too," he confirmed as they hurried into the kitchen to find smoke coming from the dining room. By now Madam Newall and Ellienne were right behind them.

Jeannette was the first to dining room. It was smoky, but she could see no flame. Cold wind was coming through the smashed front windows. Choking, she turned back.

"We've got to get some buckets of water." She turned to Antoine. He nodded, turning back to the kitchen.

The family, who had just come across the channel last night, were now coming down the stairs, still looking sleepy, pulling robes around themselves. Ellienne led them all to the kitchen, where the man assisted Antoine to carry buckets of water.

Madam Newall was looking dazed, in shock. Jeannette turned to her and spoke sharply. "Mother, where is Darren?"

Madam Newall turned back toward Darren's room. Jeannette called after her, "Better get him to the kitchen, in case we have to get out."

Jeannette went back to the dining room, where the smoke was beginning to clear. Broken glass was all over the room. The wood mullions of the multi-pane front window were broken and splintered, pieces strewn all over the room. Water soon doused smoldering bits of wood and areas of the floor that were emitting smoke. Neighbors awakened by the explosion were arriving to help. Damage was extensive, but fortunately, fire never had a chance to get started.

After a while, when it was clear any fire danger was past, they all gathered around the kitchen table. They were all silent at first; Madam Newall looked in shock. Darren had a strange, distracted expression. Jeannette and Ellienne just looked at each other, speechless, Antoine started to get up.

"I'm going out to check the stable," he said as he turned toward the back door. The man whose family had just come across the channel got up to follow. Madam Newall turned to the man's wife and daughter to apologize for their interrupted sleep.

Jeannette turned to Ellienne, reaching for her hands. "Pray with me; I need your prayers. I'm not coping with this." The hands Ellienne took were shaking. She closed her eyes, praying, "Father, restore peace to this home. We thank you for your protection. I rebuke fear in Jesus' name." Ellienne put her arms around Jeannette, whispering, "It's going to be all right, sister. We have to trust God."

The café was closed for several days while Antoine repaired the window wall, and women thoroughly cleaned the dining room, walls, floor, and linens of dust, smoke and water damage.

On Sunday, Antoine rode up to the Romani camp to minister God's Word, but Ellienne stayed behind. When he returned Sunday evening, he brought Fidel Balansay with him. "I hope you don't mind, Madam; I thought it might be good to have an extra man here for a few days."

"Oh, thank you," said Madam Newall, as she greeted Antoine's friend.

HELENA POORTVLIET

The local constable and port authority agents were there this week to question them about the attack, and also the incident the night before. They all talked to Darren, who seemed to have no memory of knowing the two men. Through it all Jeannette thought of how she coped by her anchor in God and the words Jacques had written.

She was glad Fidel Balansay came back with Antoine. She remembered Fidel from the week she had spent at the Romani camp ministering God's Word with Jacques. Fidel and his wife Elena became believers on their last night there. In fact Elena was transformed from demon possession and a crippling infirmity, a transformation so astounding she was barely recognizable as the same person. She was able to stand straight for the first time in her life, and was all smiles. Before, she was described as "the meanest witch there" by her campmates. Now she and Jeannette were becoming good friends. Seeing Fidel made Jeannette miss Elena, wishing he had brought her along.

Fidel shared with them that he and his son Roman rode almost to Gloucester with Jacques on this way to Liverpool, and other Romani from his camp rode all the way to the Romani camp near Birmingham to tell them Jacques was on his way. They intended to make sure he arrived in Liverpool safely. This welcome news deeply touched Jeannette how the Romani cared for Jacques.

Monday morning when they reopened, the window wall looked better than before, with much of the wood replaced, as well as the glass. The wood mullions were freshly painted white. The floor was refinished and a new rug installed. The walls were freshly painted, and the paintings cleaned and replaced on the walls. With new table linens, they were ready for breakfast service. They congratulated each other, feeling proud of their work.

The reopening of the dining room was a huge success. Many of their friends and regular customers heard about the attack, and came by the day of the reopening to show support. The day went well and business continued at that momentum all week. Several families had come across the channel during the week so most of the guest rooms were occupied. The men were kept busy with all the extra horses in the stable.

When Sunday came again, Antoine went back to the Romani camp, leaving Fidel to help out and offer some protection in case of problems. He was sleeping in the stable, just in case that might be the focus of further mischief.

When Antoine came back Sunday evening, Roman and Elena Balansay came with him. Jeannette was overjoyed to see Elena. At first, Madam Newall offered them all rooms, but the men insisted on staying in the stable. So Jeannette asked Elena to share her room.

While the Romani men were there, Darren mostly kept to his room. When he did come out, he was barely civil to them, speaking very little. Jeannette usually made an effort to make conversation with him, but with Elena there, she was giving much of her attention to the Romani women.

When Antoine and Ellienne first visited the Newalls, Darren verbally attacked them in an angry outburst, insisting his family should not associate with "Gypsies." Jeannette and her mother disagreed with him, apologizing to the Merlots for his behavior. His feelings may not have changed; he just wasn't vocal about it. He knew the Romani were there to help and protect them, so his argument was weak.

In the intimate way women often like to share with their closest friends, Jeannette shared most of the contents of Jacques' letter with Elena. "He found a little boy on the streets of Birmingham. He didn't know his father, and his mother had died on the street. Jacques took him in, fed him and bought new clothes for him. I guess he couldn't leave him then, so he's taking him to Canada with him. He asked if I minded. Can you imagine? Should I mind."

Elena responded, "He's such a good man! I can see why you care for him. I could tell he loves children. They were all over him when he visited us. You like children, too, don't you?"

"Oh, yes," Jeannette answered, "I hope to have many."

CHAPTER 2

Out of the Ashes

F IDEL AND ROMAN made beds for themselves in the straw of one of the box stalls. There were several horses in the large roomy stable which was part of *La Petit Fleur*. Two bay mares which belonged to the Newalls were well-bred English thoroughbreds. There were five horses which belonged to the Romani, as well as four other horses belonging to guests. Father and son would retire early to be as inconspicuous as possible while they kept watch on the stable and horses.

This was the first time Roman had been away from the camp environment. Staying in the stable may have seemed strange, but staying in that inn would have been even stranger. He was always close to his father. His mother was sick and crippled and mean for as long as he could remember. But now she had changed. She was no longer sick and crippled; she was happy all the time. Roman did not know how to react. He kept expecting the real Elena to return.

Fidel settled right down, and soon Roman could hear him snoring quietly. The horses were fairly quiet. Some were still munching their evening meal. Now and then he could hear hooves pawing in the straw. He was nearly asleep when he heard a picking, squeaking sound. He lay very still, barely breathing; then, when he heard it again, he tried to dismiss it as mice. He glanced toward his father in the darkness. Fidel was sound asleep. Roman heard the sound again, a little louder now. It was in the direction of the door they had locked behind them. The very faint snapping of metal now did not sound like a mouse. Then a tiny shaft of light began to grow, as the door began to open, admitting the lantern light from the alley. Roman sat straight up.

As Antoine lay in bed, holding his wife with her face buried in his shoulder, he was still wide awake. He tried to relax. It still seemed strange, sleeping in this huge bed in this beautiful room. He thought *it's really perfect for Ellienne; she is so beautiful.* But he felt out of place; he was so used to living in the open, sleeping in a wagon. *Was that it? No, it's something else. Something is wrong?* He stiffened, holding his breath.

"What is it, dear?" asked his sleepy wife, barely awake.

He tried to consciously relax his body. "It's okay; go back to sleep." But he was still tense. Now he could also feel the tension in Ellienne. She rolled over and sat up.

"You're nervous as a cat," she said. "What is it?"

"I don't know; I just feel like something is wrong," he answered.

"Maybe we ought to get up and look around," she suggested.

He was already pulling his trousers on, heading for the door.

The floorboards in the hall creaked as Antoine headed for the kitchen, trying to step quietly. Ellienne was right behind him. They went through the kitchen and looked into the dining room first. All was quiet.

Elena was so happy to be with her friend she found it hard to sleep. She looked over at Jeannette; in the dim light of the window, it appeared she was asleep. Elena shut her eyes and lay still, expecting sleep to come, but she could not relax. Then she heard creaking floor boards in the hall. She sat up and listened carefully.

"Papa," Roman tried to whisper as quietly as possible to get his father's attention. The snoring continued. The door opened a little more, and then Roman could hear the whispering voices.

"I've seen him riding that fancy horse of his, but he can't pay us what he owes us."

"You mean he won't pay us!" the other corrected. "You know he could. These folks are loaded. It's ter'ble to see some folks got so much more than the rest of us!"

"Hey, hurry up and git that lantern lit. I can't see a thing!"

"I am; don't git riled. I've almost got it now."

The lantern came on, a splash of light in the darkness, and Roman stifled a gasp. He put his hand on his father's shoulder and again whispered, "Papa!"

HELENA POORTVLIET

The snoring stopped as Fidel looked at him. Roman put a finger up in front of his mouth to warn his father. Then Fidel was aware of the lantern light and knew someone else was in the stable. Moving carefully and quietly he got up. As Roman watched his father move he could feel his heart pounding so loud he was afraid the intruders could hear it.

"Here's that fancy horse of Newall's," one of the men remarked on finding Dani in her stall.

"Naw, here it is." The other one was looking at Katy.

"There's two of 'm; they look alike."

"Yeah, well why not just take'm both."

"Yeah, we kin handle both of 'm."

Roman and Fidel looked at each other. They suddenly understood the two were determined to steal the two mares. That's when Fidel opened the stall door and stepped out. The man holding the lantern whirled to face him, startled. As he turned, his arms flew out, and the forgotten lantern went flying. It landed in the stall where Fidel and Roman had been sleeping, shattering, releasing the burning fluid, which quickly ignited the straw. The two intruders bolted for the door.

"Oh, my God!" came from Fidel, in shock, as he saw the flames fill the stall. He yelled at Roman, "Get the horses out!"

Turning from the empty dining room, Antoine hurried through the kitchen to the back door. Looking out the window just in time to see the two intruders dash from the open stable door, he also saw the flash of light as the flames ignited.

"Fire!" he yelled. "The stable's on fire! Fidel and Roman are in there!" He snatched the door open.

Ellienne took one look then turned back, saying, "I'll get the girls up and get water poured!"

Antoine raced across the stable yard as Fidel and Roman came through the door leading Dani and Katy. They let go of their leads to race back in behind Antoine to get the other horses out. They opened all the stall doors, leading out some horse and chasing others, while the flames spread to an inferno.

The four women were coming out the door with buckets of water. Jeannette handed her bucket to Roman and turned to go back to the kitchen when she looked down the alley and saw Dani and Katy trotting loose toward the road. She ran after them, her dressing gown flying around her. Two of their neighbors appeared at the end of the alley, seeing the mares, reached for their leads. The other horses, which were inclined to follow them now stopped, milling about. Jeannette took the leads from the men and led them back to the hitching rail by the back door. The men were catching the other horses, and the ones that were still loose crowded close to the others in their fear.

The women were all now taking turns pumping water. Several more neighbors arrived, awakened by the commotion and the flames which lit up the sky. With more help the fire was soon under control, but it took much longer to make sure it was completely out. Most of the central part of the stable was ruined, even much of the roof. Miraculously, the fire did not reach the hay storage or the tack room and carriage shed.

The smoke laden sky was lightening with the early morning by the time the men were sure the fire was completely out. The men were all filthy with soot and sweat, and the women were all in dressing gowns, now soaked with the light rain that had begun to fall. As panic subsided, they realized how cold it was and headed for the kitchen door.

Madam Newall insisted the neighbors who came to help should come in for breakfast. Some did, but some opted to go home and clean up. The women just took time to get dressed quickly while the men got the fire in the big cook stove started. Soon they were all back in the kitchen.

Madam Newall called everyone together to pray and give thanks nobody was hurt and the horses were all safe. Then she looked around at the men and asked, "What happened? How did it start?"

Antoine answered first, "We couldn't sleep and we thought something was wrong so we got up to look around. When we got to the back door we saw two fellows run from the barn, and we could see fire inside. The first thing I thought of was Fidel and Roman inside. Then they came running through the door with Katy and Dani. We all went back inside to get the rest of the horses out."

Madam Newall looked at Fidel, "What can you tell us?"

"I was asleep," he began. "My son woke me. Those two fella's were in the stable with a lantern. We heard them talking about stealin' your two mares. When I came out of the stall we were sleepin' in, the one man turned around and threw the lantern. That's when the fire started. It broke out in the stall where we'd been sleepin.' That's when they ran off. The first thing we thought of was to get the horses out.

"I'm so thankful for that," Madam Newall said.

The guest who owned the other horses in the stable agreed.

Ellienne and Elena started passing out cups of hot chocolate which they had prepared, to everyone's welcoming hands.

Jeannette looked around. "Where's Darren?" she asked. He was not in the kitchen. Her mother, looking around, answered, "I'll look in on him."

Then Jeannette said, "I think we all need the benefit of God's Word right now," as she turned to reach for her Bible. As she opened it Psalm 34, she announced, "This is a Psalm of thanks for deliverance. We need to give thanks for God's protection." And she began to read:

> "I will bless the Lord at all times; his praise shall continually be in my mouth.
> "My soul shall make her boast in the Lord: The humble shall hear thereof and be glad.
> "O magnify the Lord with me, and let us exalt his name together.
> "I sought the Lord and he heard me, and delivered me from all my fears.
> "They looked unto him and were lightened: and their faces were not ashamed.
> "This poor man cried, and the Lord heard him, and saved him out of all his troubles.
> "The angel of the Lord encampeth about them that fear him, and delivered them.
> "O taste and see that the Lord is good: blessed is the man that trusteth in him.
> "O fear the Lord, ye his saints: for there is no want to them that fear him.
> "The young lions do lack, and suffer hunger: but they that seek the Lord shall not want any good thing.
> "Come ye children, hearken unto me: I will teach you the fear of the Lord.
> "What man is he that desireth life, and loveth many days, that he may see good?

"Keep thy tongue from evil, and thy lips from speaking guile.

"Depart from evil and do good; seek peace and pursue it.

"The eyes of the Lord are upon the righteous and his ears are open to their cry.

"The face of the Lord is against them that do evil, to cut off the remembrance of them from the earth.

"The righteous cry, and the Lord heareth, and delivereth them out of all their troubles.

"The Lord is nigh unto them that are of a broken heart; and saveth such as be of a contrite spirit.

"Many are the afflictions of the righteous: but the Lord delivereth them out of them all.

"He keepeth all his bones: not one of them is broken.

"Evil shall slay the wicked: and they that hate the righteous shall be desolate.

"The Lord redeemeth the soul of his servants: and none of them that trust in him shall be desolate." (Psalm 34, KJV)

As Jeannette finished reading, she began to pray, "O Father, thank you for your protection, both for ourselves and for our friends, but also for our horses. We thank you for good friends and we pray for your peace."

Darren awakened to many footsteps in the hallway. He expected his door to open at any moment and his mother coming in to check on him or to tell him what was going on. He felt himself withdrawing, wishing she would leave him alone. It seemed like they were always telling him what to do, or asking him questions he could not answer. He felt uncomfortable most of the time, not so much for the bruises and broken bones, but for the thoughts he imagined his family was thinking about him.

Even worse was the self-loathing. It began when his father had died in his arms, and he could not stop it. At the funeral, he heard people say God had taken Ed Newall, and he had cried out to God, "Why?" No answer had come. *It was not fair. Why should God take my father when I needed him so much?* Then, to the self-loathing, he added his hatred of God. The more his hatred grew, the worse the pain became.

He could not talk to his mother and sister. *They just don't understand. Jeannette was always quoting the Bible and talking about God. And they'll listen to anyone. Like that French guy Jeannette was so crazy about. He came here acting so great and now he's gone and she's by herself. And now they've let those Gypsies move in here. They're just asking for trouble. They would not listen to him.*

He started going to the Dolphin after his father died, because he could not talk to his sister or mother anymore. They just did not agree about anything. Those men seemed to understand about the pain. They gave him medicine which seemed to make the pain go away. Then the confusion started. Now they wanted a lot more money for the medicine just when he really needed it.

Someone came up with the idea of intercepting that Frenchman on the road to Andover for those big black horses. That part was really clouded in his memory. What he did remember was that big black stallion attacking him. He was sick for a long time after that. The worst part was that Frenchman hung around here for a month, acting so nice, his mother and sister were all over him. Then the Gypsies moved in. Now men were looking for him, saying he owed money. He was jumped and beaten one night after leaving the Dolphin, but he did not see the men. Now he was afraid all the time, and his mother kept asking him questions he could not answer. There was a brief knock on his door, before the door opened. Darren knew it would be his mother.

"Darren, sweetie, are you all right?" It was his mother.

"Of course, Mother," he answered, "Why wouldn't I be? I haven't been anywhere. What's going on out there?"

"Now don't be upset, sweetie," she began. "There was a fire in the stable. But the men got all the horses out and everyone's safe now. We're all having breakfast together. Don't you want to come out?"

Anger seized Darren as he jumped out of bed, despite wrenching pain in his ribs. "It's those Gypsies! I told you they would be trouble."

Madam Newall stood still in shock at this outburst. Darren continued. "Don't you know those people are no good? You wouldn't believe me the first time I told you. Now you've let more of them in here." Now he was shaking, he was so angry, heading toward the door.

Madam Newall reached for his arm. "It's not like that. They got the horses out. They saved the horses and they could have been killed." She was pleading with him. "Now please, sweetie, calm down, and don't make a scene. Several of the neighbors are here. They all came over to help and we're having breakfast. Please come out and be civil and have breakfast with us."

Darren appeared to calm down, but he was seething inside. He was getting better at hiding his feelings. "All right, Mother, in a few minutes. Go ahead; I'll be right there." He urged her toward the door.

Madam Newall returned to the kitchen just as Jeannette finished reading the Psalm, and listened to the short prayer. Then she went over to start preparing breakfast. Jeannette quietly got up and went to her. She could see that her mother was shaken. She put her arm around her mother as she pulled the letter from her pocket.

"Mother, I think it's time to leave here. You know how much I want to be with Jacques." She held up the letter. "And now I know he still wants me to come."

For a brief moment, her mother looked stricken. "You mean you would leave us now when all this is happening?"

"No, Mother, I mean all of us," she answered. "I want to be with Jacques, but I don't want to leave you. Let's all go to Montreal. You know you've had offers on this place. You could sell it for a little less with the damage to the stable, but still get plenty for fare and to start a new place in Montreal."

Madam Newall looked even more shocked. "But your grandfather worked so hard to build this place. How can I let him down?"

"You wouldn't be letting him down, Mother," Jeannette countered. You've worked hard here, but there's only so much you can do. If we stayed, we would have to rebuild the stable. We can't keep guests horses out there the way it is."

Ellienne and Antoine were listening to this exchange, looked at each other, catching each other's expression at the same time. "Are you thinking what I'm thinking?" Antoine asked his wife, who replied, "I think so." They both got up from the table at the same time, and joined mother and daughter.

"Madam," Antoine began, "we are at your service to escort you and your family to Montreal," and he paused, "if you'll have us."

Madam Newall was speechless, even looked dazed. Things were happening too fast for her to comprehend.

Fidel spoke up now, "We could provide an escort to Liverpool." Elena grinned at Jeannette, "It'll be such fun on the road; but I'll miss you terribly when you're gone. Montreal! How exciting! It's a whole new world!"

Madam Newall was still looking back and forth at her friends, her mouth open. "I don't know."

"Mother, I think it's a good idea." The voice came from the doorway, where Darren was standing, listening.

Jeannette turned to her brother, "Oh, it's good to see you up, Darren. Then you agree it's the thing to do."

"Yes, I think it's the only thing to do. But we don't need all these people to go with us. I can look after you and Mother. That's my job." Darren looked straight at his mother, his gaze avoiding Antoine and the other Romani.

Jeannette went to his side. "Of course you can, but they're our friends. It's wonderful they want to go with us. I'd miss them so much, otherwise." She smiled back at Ellienne and looked at her mother, the question showing on her face.

Madam Newall was still shaking her head, not sure; but a smile began to show. "Do you think we could do this in Montreal? We'd have to start all over."

"Yes, Mother." Jeannette was adamant. "It's a new and growing city. It's a chance for all of us." She glanced at Darren, smiling.

Antoine and Ellienne were smiling at each other, as they embraced.

CHAPTER 3

Bucephalus

TOMORROW THE *BUCEPHALUS* would be leaving Liverpool for Montreal. Some of the horse cargo would be loading this afternoon, but most would be loading tomorrow morning. Jacques had thirty stalls, fifteen on each side, facing each other, cleaned and ready with fresh bedding, including the three occupied by his own horses. The stalls were roomy, but each had a moveable partition of heavy timber that could be swung in place in rough seas to crowd each horse into a tight area, to help it keep its balance. Jacques' own horses, two mares, weighing over a ton each, and a young stallion, weighing almost a ton, barely fit into the cramped space which resulted when the partition was in place.

The three were purebred Percherons from Jacques' family farm in the La Perche district of France. He brought the three with him to England in December with the intention of immigrating to Montreal and eventually to the frontier of Canada West. The two mares were bred to his father's best stallion and due to foal in April and May, now only a few weeks away. The stallion, Tounerre, barely four years old, was a product of one of his father's mares and the top stallion at the National Stud at Argentan in France.

As big as he was, Tounerre was gentle, proven by the small boy who as completely unafraid to play in his stall, around the huge feet, but was happiest sitting on his broad back. Harry McKeller was the boy Jacques found on the street in Birmingham, an orphan who never knew his father, whose mother died on the street only weeks ago. He found his way into Jacques' heart so securely Jacques was willing to give up his beloved stallion for the boy when he was kidnapped. Miraculously, both the boy and the stallion were returned to him.

Since boarding the ship this morning, Harry followed Jacques as he cleaned stalls; then, tiring of that he wandered up on deck to follow

Pierre, who was following Captain Palmer as the captain showed Pierre around the deck, imparting general instructions to the newly hired sailor.

Although Pierre Mirande came to England several years earlier, he was not faring well when Jacques encountered him. His family, close to the court of King Louis Philippe, lived a privileged life, with servants to do most menial tasks, so he applied himself at school and sports, but never knew much hard work. When Louis Philippe's government fell, Pierre's parents were executed, and he literally escaped with his life to England.

Once in England, he found life not so easy. His family meant nothing now, especially when his money ran out. His previous life did not prepare him for work. Expecting respect for who he was, nobody seemed to care. After frequent rejection and getting fired from several job attempts, he hit bottom, even becoming homeless. Then Jacques Boudreau looked him up in Birmingham at the request of the Newalls. Jacques shared God's Word with Pierre and his life changed. He made the decision to go to Liverpool with Jacques and sign on as a sailor. He was determined to learn how to work.

Traveling from Birmingham together, the two young men and the child became fast friends, even calling themselves brothers. They were fortunate to make the connection with the *Bucephalus,* but this morning, on the way to the ship, Harry was kidnapped. Fortunately, the boy was found, and the three became even closer. Now they were all going to Montreal together.

Jacques' attention turned to the boy running down the ramp toward him, squealing, "Horses coming, Jacques, horses coming," in English, while jumping up and down in front of Jacques, who was learning more English since Harry had been with him than in the two months he had been in England. Now Pierre was coming down the ramp toward him, laughing at Harry's antics.

"Captain Palmer sent me to tell you there're four horses boarding now, but it looks like Harry's beat me to it. If I'm not sharp, that boy will have my job!" Pierre tried to look worried, but his affection for Harry was obvious.

Jacques did a quick check of the four stalls next to his mares, before turning to go up the ramp to the main deck. By that time, the horses were already coming up the ramp from the pier. The first was a magnificent chestnut stallion. Jacques thought he looked like a thoroughbred. The other three looked like yearlings of the same breed, two fillies and a colt. The stallion was agitated, his head held high, looking all around him. There were leads snapped to both sides of his halter, with a chain running beneath his chin, and two handlers, each holding onto a lead. Each of the yearlings had one handler, but they were all showing a great deal of excitement.

Captain Palmer was shaking hands with a well-dressed man who looked about forty years old to Jacques. As Jacques approached, Palmer turned to introduce the two. "This is Victor Ashton, Jacques. He's the Earl of Godolphin's son-in-law. The Godolphin Stud is shipping these four thoroughbreds to a buyer in Ottawa. I've guaranteed their safe arrival." He turned back to Ashton. "Jacques is my stableman for this trip. I hired him based on the condition of his own horses. I trust him to handle your horses as if they were his own."

Jacques shook hands with Ashton and directed the handlers to follow him down the ramp to the lower deck. A quick look confirmed the first stall was ready. Jacques took the leads from the two handlers, talking softly to the stallion as he led him carefully into the stall. There was already hay in the rack in the corner, so the stallion went right to it, while nervously looking around. The yearlings were put in adjoining stalls.

Ashton told him the stallion was Sun Flair, probably the most valuable horse the Godolphin Stud ever exported, a direct descendant of the great Eclipse (clearly shared with pride). When he saw all four horses were settled, he walked over to the end of the stable area, noting the cleanliness, stopped to stare at the three Percherons.

"They do look well cared for," he commented. "What do you do with horses like that in Montreal?" Captain Palmer, following them, translated, and Jacques responded. "I hope to breed them for farming and logging in Canada West. Some folks like to breed their thoroughbreds to the Percherons for nice carriage horses." Jacques watched Ashton's expression as Palmer translated back to him. Ashton nodded, confirming his confidence his horses were in good hands.

Just as Ashton and Palmer were walking back up the ramp, Harry came running down, shouting, "More horses coming!" Jacques started back up the ramp, thanking Harry, who was jumping up and down beside him in his excitement. This time it was a coach with four-in-hand, all geldings, a good example of the thoroughbred-heavy horse cross just mentioned. He was relieved to see geldings, hoping there would not be many more stallions, to add to the stress in the relatively close area.

The coach belonged to a young family who were immigrating to Canada, Roger and Andrea Breakfield, and their two children, Andrew and Julia. Andrew appeared to be slightly older than Harry and Julia a year or so older than her brother.

Before the afternoon gave way to darkness, six more horses arrived, all of them shire mares. Shires were a heavy draft breed of England as big, and maybe even a bit taller than Jacques' Percherons. They were all dark bay or black with lots of white markings. The curious thing about them was the heavy hair on their legs, not just their fetlocks, but all the way around, starting from the knees and hocks. They looked as though they were all wearing bell bottom pants, like the sailors. They were also being shipped by the breeder to buyers in Canada. Once the shires were all settled, Jacques saw Palmer securing the ship for the night, so he knew they would not be receiving any more horses until tomorrow.

Tomorrow, January 21st, after loading more horses, plus other cargo, and a few more passengers, they would be embarking from Liverpool, bound for Montreal. With God's help and protection, they should arrive in Montreal around the first week of March.

Jacques made one more trip to each stall to make sure each horse was as comfortable as possible. The coach was stowed in a compartment in the hold beneath the horse deck. He then headed up the ramp to look for Harry. The first person he saw was Sean McRae, the first mate, directing two men at some routine tasks. He met all three this morning at breakfast. Deral McDonald and Dirk Mallory looked about as old as Jacques. They both greeted him in English and Jacques nodded in return. Then he saw Harry running toward him, ahead of Pierre who was walking fast to keep up.

"My brother," Pierre greeted him, "Captain Palmer showed me where we can eat, and Cooks got it ready now. Come on!" Harry was jumping up and down in his excitement, urging Jacques to hurry.

The galley was toward the rear of the ship, just ahead of the officer's quarters. Since most of the crew would be coming on early tomorrow morning, there would only be a few of them eating together this evening. Leon Mackay, the cook, had sailed several trips on the *Bucephalus.* He was a jovial man, used to teasing and harassment from the crew, in spite of the fact that he was probably better than average, as far as ship's cooks go. As he served a sumptuous meal, he warned the diners, "Enjoy this while you can, 'cause by the time we reach Montreal, most of the food that's left will be pretty boring. Not too many veggies last a whole trip, and the fruit only last a coupla' weeks."

The Breakfields, the only passengers on board so far came to dinner, and were very friendly with Jacques and Pierre, asking him questions about Harry. Their son Andrew already made friends with him. The two boys seemed delighted to find companionship. Andrea Breakfield was curious that Jacques spoke French, while Harry spoke English; but it was clear that Harry was completely attached to Jacques. With Pierre's help with the translation, they explained how Jacques found him on the street. Pierre even told them how Jacques bought clothes for Harry, then how he was kidnapped, and how Jacques gave up his horse to get him back. Everyone laughed how Tounerre came back to him, because the kidnappers could not handle him.

After dinner, Pierre was off duty until tomorrow, so he returned to the horse deck with Jacques and Harry. As the dark settled in, the fog rolled in with it, blanketing the ship, but the water was remarkably calm. Jacques suspected the calm would not last for long, but he was hopeful it would remain as they left port tomorrow.

Jacques was now anxious to get back to his quarters. He had not read from God's Word for a couple of days now, and recalled that Jeannette encouraged him to get into the Book of Acts. He remembered how on the trip back to Southampton from their week at the Romani camp, she read to him, the account of the Holy Spirit coming on the disciples, like "tongues of fire," and that gift of the heavenly language. She said he should read the Book of Acts, since it was the story of the beginning of the Christian church. Now he was anxious to get started. He mentioned to Pierre what he was thinking and asked him if he'd like to listen to him read. Pierre quickly agreed, grinning happily.

When they got to the little cabin Jacques settled on one bunk and Pierre on the other. Harry snuggled up to Jacques, as he began to read:

> "The former treatise have I made, O Theophilus, of all that Jesus began, both to do and to teach,
> "Until the day in which he was taken up, after that he through the Holy Ghost had given commandments unto the apostles he had chosen:
> "To whom also he shewed himself alive after his passion by many infallible proofs, being seen of them forty days, and speaking of the things pertaining to the kingdom of God:
> "And being assembled together with them, commanded them that they should not depart from Jerusalem, but wait for the promise of the Father, which saith he, ye have heard of me.
> "For John truly baptized with water, but ye shall be baptized with the Holy Ghost not many days hence.
> "When they therefore were come together, they asked of him, saying, Lord, wilt thou at this time restore again the kingdom of Israel?
> "And he said to them, It is not for you to know the time or the seasons, which the Father hath put in his own power."
> (Acts 1:1-7, KJV)

Jacques read only these few verses when he realized Harry was sound asleep curled up next to him. He stopped reading to move the boy lengthwise on the bunk, pulling his coat off and drawing a blanket over him. Then he looked at Pierre, who just urged, "Read more," so Jacques continued reading:

> "But ye shall receive power after that the Holy Ghost is come upon you: and ye shall be witnesses unto me both in Jerusalem, and in all Judaea, and in Samaria, and unto the uttermost parts of the earth." (Acts 1:8, KJV)

This reminded Jacques of his experience at the Romani camp, when the presence of the Holy Spirit was so evident, and many people experienced the heavenly language. He felt amazed at how his confidence in God increased after that, how much stronger he was spiritually. He spoke of that experience to Pierre.

"I don't think I even realized it at the time, but now I realize after that I had much more confidence to talk to others about Jesus."

A look of sudden recognition came to Pierre now. "I can see now, that I too, since we left Birmingham, have felt more confidence. I think it's because of my trust in God. I never felt that way before." Pierre was grinning broadly. "My whole life is changed now. Oh, read some more."

So Jacques continued to read:

> "And when he had spoken these things, while they beheld, he was taken up; and a cloud received him out of their sight.
> "And while they looked stedfastly toward heaven as he went up, behold, two men stood by them in white apparel:
> "Which also said, Ye men of Galilee, why stand ye gazing up into heaven? This same Jesus, which is taken up from you into heaven, shall so come in like manner as ye have seen him go into heaven." (Acts 1:9-11, KJV)

Jacques stopped his reading at this point, reacting to what he just read with silence. *What did this mean?* Pierre's words echoed his own thoughts. "What does that mean? Did he disappear into the air and then come back? Or is he coming back still?"

"I don't know," Jacques answered. "I don't think he's come back, but I don't know that much. I think I've heard that people believe he's coming back at the end: I guess this is what it means." Jacques was shaking his head. Then Pierre urged him, "Read more," so he went on:

> "Then returned they unto Jerusalem from the mount called Olivet, which is from Jerusalem a Sabbath day's journey.
> "And when they were come in they went up into an upper room, where abode both Peter and James, and John, and Andrew, Philip and Thomas, Bartholomew, and Matthew, James the son of Alphaeus, and Simon Selotes, and Judas the brother of James.

"These continued with one accord and prayer and supplication, with the women, and Mary the mother of Jesus, and with his brethren." (Acts 1:12-14, KJV)

Jacques thought again of the gatherings in the Romani camp. It seemed that powerful things happened when believers came together in prayer and worship. The times when he felt the Lord's presence the most were the times in group worship. He longed to be in that presence.

CHAPTER 4

Embarkment

JACQUES AWOKE TO the dead weight of Harry asleep beside him, and saw Pierre sound asleep in the other bunk. He got up quickly to dress, already hearing hungry horses moving impatiently outside. He expected more horses to be boarding early in the day and as well as another load of hay. He thought, *I'd better make sure the horses already on board are taken care of first.*

Leaving the small cabin he was first greeted by nickers from Tounerre, quickly drowned out by the shrill whinnies from Sun Flair and the yearlings. The yearling colt was the loudest, with angry, distressed sounding squeals, twisting, even rearing in his stall.

Jacques apportioned out hay to all the horses, starting with Sun Flair and ending with Tounerre, thankful that most had quieted down. But the colt was still fractious, grabbing a mouthful of hay, then whirling around in his stall. Jacques thought to himself, *this fellow will have a little behavior adjustment before we reach Montreal.*

Just as Jacques began cleaning Tounerres stall, a sleepy-eyed Pierre appeared. He looked a little guilty, seeing Jacques at work. "Did I sleep too late? You should have wakened me."

Jacques laughed. "No, you're just in time for the good stuff. You can start down there with Sun Flair's stall. You know what to do?"

Watching Jacques scooping up forkfuls of soiled straw from Tounerre's stall, he nodded. "Unfortunately, yes," he answered, heading for the far end. Both worked quickly, meeting in the middle, among the coach horse geldings, when Deral McDonald came down the ramp.

"Wow, this is just like a regular stable down here," he said, looking from one horse to another. Jacques could tell most of what he was saying, but Pierre translated anyway. Then Deral remembered, "Oh, Cook sent me to get you guys for breakfast." At this announcement, a sleepy-eyed Harry appeared, saying, "I'm hungry," which brought laughs from all of them.

Breakfast was an opportunity to share fellowship with both the passengers and the rest of the crew. Since this was both a cargo and a passenger vessel, there would not be separate areas for each. There would be few passengers other than those who would be moving horse cargo. Captain Palmer, unlike many captains, did not refrain from mingling with both crew and passengers, but this did not mean he expected anything less then respect and dedication to duty. After witnessing Palmer's display of anger yesterday in firing his former stableman, Jacques had no doubt.

They arrived in the dining room just as the Breakfields came in. Harry and Andrew were overjoyed in seeing each other. They wanted to sit together, but couldn't decide whether it would be with Andrew's family or with Jacques, and for a time they were bouncing back and forth, until both Jacques and Andrew's father got firm with them.

Captain Palmer came in while they were eating, but did not sit down and eat. Instead, he walked around nervously, asking questions and giving directions to the crew.

"Have you got stalls ready for more horses?" he asked Jacques.

"Yes, sir, they're all clean and ready, with feed in all of them," Jacques answered.

"Good, I expect more horses will be arriving anytime." He directed his next comment at Pierre. "You check with Jacques to see if he needs any help. Anytime he doesn't need you, you are to report to Sean McRae. I don't want to see you just hangin' out 'less Sean lets you off. Understood?"

"Yes, sir," Pierre answered seriously.

Then Palmer helped himself to a plate of food and left the dining room with it. Jacques and Pierre looked at each other for a moment, not saying anything. Pierre, at first, looked a little indignant, before Jacques spoke. "I think he just wants to make sure it's clear he means business. There's a job to be done and it could be crucial if it's not taken seriously.

Pierre was silent for a moment, and then he seemed to relax. "I guess you're right. I really don't want to mess up here."

"I think we better make ourselves available," Jacques said, getting up from the table. "It would be good if you stayed around to help as long as we're loading horses. If several come at once, I'll need your help."

Pierre nodded in agreement as they headed for the horse deck. Then Jacques remembered Harry, who was eating with the Breakfields. As he turned to call to him, Andrea interrupted.

"Oh, why not leave him with us," she suggested. "He's really no trouble, and he's good company for Andrew." Her smile was infectious, making it easy for Jacques to agree with her.

Jacques made the rounds once more to be sure the remaining stalls were in good shape, before Deral McDonald came down the ramp to tell them horses were arriving. This time it was two teams, all geldings, to Jacques relief. One was a heavy work team, called Suffolks, both chestnuts, much shorter than his Percherons, but very stocky. The other team was light carriage horses, both bays, which reminded him of Dani and Katy, the two horses belonging to Jeannette and her brother. The horses were all well-behaved, but it took some time to get them all settled. The owners of both teams would be passengers immigrating to Canada along with their horses.

They barely finished with the horses when a load of hay arrived. There were several tons, and several of the crew came to help unload it and stow it in the compartment above the stable area. Then, Jacques was surprised to see another smaller wagon was been attached behind the hay wagon, pulled on board to deliver its cargo: a dozen goats. While Jacques stared open-mouth, Pierre began to laugh, still laughing when Captain Palmer appeared.

"I'm usually confidant my stableman knows what to do with them," he began, "but if the stable assistant thinks they are so hilarious, maybe he should learn the art of milking goats."

Pierre stopped in the middle of his laugh.

Palmer turned to Jacques, "They're your responsibility. It's okay by me if you want to delegate that responsibility," then walked away, stifling a laugh.

Jacques and Pierre just looked at each other for a moment, then Jacques laughed.

The goats fit neatly in the two box stalls next to the Godolphin thoroughbreds. Jacques was hopeful they might have a calming effect on the yearling colt. He soon learned this would be a source of fresh milk for the voyage, so the milking was to be taken seriously.

Another group of draft horses arrived shortly after the goats were settled. These were also shires, four mares and a stallion. The breeder was shipping them to a buyer in Canada West who would be there to meet them in Montreal. They were all mature animals and seemed to be quite docile.

Now there were only two stalls left. Much of the other cargo was already loaded, so it looked like departure was close at hand. Jacques was standing close to his charges, wanting to be ready for any problems which might develop when the ship began to move. Just when he thought he was hearing sounds of the ramps being dismantled and brought in, there seemed to be some commotion on the pier. Jacques listened intently from the bottom of the horse ramp, trying to hear what was going on without leaving his charges. Then Harry came running down the ramp.

"Jacques, more horses," the boy was shouting. Jacques started up the ramp, with Harry jumping up and down beside him, tugging his hand. When he reached the main deck, he saw the sailors lowering the ramp to the pier again. Captain Palmer was leaning over the rail, shouting in French to someone on the pier, who also was speaking French.

When Jacques got to the rail he looked down to see a man, somewhat older than himself, very tanned and rugged in appearance, riding one horse and leading another, which was carrying packs. What was odd was the striking appearance of the two horses. They were both piebald, that is, black and white in an uneven pattern over their bodies. They looked a little like Arabian horses, which were sometimes seen in France; but Jacques had never seen Arabians colored like that.

The man looked frantic. He was imploring Captain Palmer. "But I must embark on this ship. I must get to Montreal immediately. Please, do you have room? I have gold for fare."

Captain Palmer looked around to see Jacques just as he reached the rail, and asked, "Do you have any more stalls available?"

"Yes sir, there's two left," Jacques answered.

Palmer turned back to the men who were handling the ramp. "Go ahead, let him on."

As the man rode up the ramp, Jacques realized the piebald the man was riding was a stallion and the other, carrying the packs, was a mare. From the looks of her rounded sides he surmised she was in foal. Once on deck, the man dismounted, and at Palmer's direction, handed over his horses to Jacques and Pierre, before going off with Palmer to negotiate his fare.

As Jacques took the stallion's reins, he admired the fine, rather exotic shape of the stallion's head, much like the Arabians he had seen, but the horse was bigger than most Arabians, and much more heavily muscled. The arched neck was heavily crested, even for a stallion. The mane was long, covering one side of his neck, part black and part white. The tail was so long it probably reached the ground, but the stallion carried it high, arched over his hindquarters.

As they led the horses down the ramp, Jacques remarked to Pierre, "I've never seen horses colored like this."

"I have," answered Pierre, "in the royal stables. They come from Morocco, I believe. The sultan of Morocco sent some of them to the king."

"Well, we don't know if these came from Morocco," Jacques was skeptical. "But they're nice horses, wherever they came from. Looks like that mare's about to foal. I'll bet she doesn't wait to get to Montreal."

Jacques put the two piebalds in stalls next to the Breakfield geldings, noting the four stallions were pretty evenly spaced apart. He hoped the spacing would discourage bickering. The piebald stallion was nervously moving around in the stall, head high, looking around. The mare was quite docile. Jacques took the pack and saddle off her first, and Pierre followed his direction and unsaddled the stallion, finishing when the owner of the two piebalds came down the ramp. At the same time they felt a great shudder underfoot as the ship began to move. Finally, they were underway.

"I am Ramon Claudel," the man announced to Jacques and offered his hand. "It is good to find a countryman when far from home, no?"

Jacques returned the friendly greeting and introduced Pierre, then continued with, "I can put your saddles in the tack room, and Pierre can help you with your luggage if you like." He gestured to the packs he had taken off the mare. "I need to stay here with the horses until I'm sure they're adjusting to the movement." He looked around at the horses, seeing some of them seemed startled that the deck under them was moving.

Claudel answered with, "If you don't mind, I stay with my horses for a while. I think they won't be as frightened if I am here. They are like children, you know?"

Jacques smiled and nodded in agreement, then commented, "Your mare hasn't long to go. She'll probably foal before we get to Montreal."

"Oh, yes," Claudel agreed. "We were almost too late, but at least we are out of France." He was inspecting the stalls. "If baby comes here, it will be all right; there is room. Better if they are strong to travel when we get to Montreal."

"When do you expect her to foal?" Jacques asked.

"No more than a week now," was the answer. "I'm surprised we made it to Liverpool. I was afraid she would foal on the road." Claudel was shaking his head. "We have come a long way this year, all the way from Morocco in North Africa. I was afraid we would not make it, but we did."

Jacques quickly looked over at Pierre, who was looking smug. Then his attention was diverted to the rumbling, shuddering of the deck beneath his feet. He quickly scanned the rows of stalls to see how each horse was reacting to this new movement. He could hear Sean McRae above, shouting orders, and racing footsteps, as ropes were cast off and sails were raised to catch the wind. The ship was rocking side to side as it began to gather speed. Jacques staggered down the row of stalls, trying to get used to the motion as he checked on each horse. His own assumed the crouching stance he remembered them doing when they came across La Manche. Some of the others were over-compensating for the motion by moving around more. As long as the movement was no more than this, he wanted the horses to get use to it. The swing partition, now off to the side of the stalls, were only to be used in extreme conditions. The trip was too long for the horses to be that confined continually.

Jacques was glad Claudel chose to stay with his own horses. He now realized this was a lot of horses to keep an eye on all at once. His own were the least problem. Most of the draft horses adapted pretty quickly. The Breakfield's warmblood geldings were showing a lot of fear and one of them seemed near panic, so Jacques stayed near that one for a while. The worst were the thoroughbred yearlings. Jacques was glad to see Pierre staying close to them and to Sun Flair. Claudel was in the stall with his piebald mare, holding her head and talking to her. Jacques could see this man cared for his horses as he did.

Jacques was kept busy with the Breakfield's geldings and did not get back to his own horses for some time. The motion smoothed out to a steady rocking, and then suddenly, they hit the race tide going out, and Jacques could tell they had rapidly gained speed as the rocking became more regular.

He left the geldings and started up the row toward his horses, making sure there was plenty of hay in each stall, hopeful it would be an inducement to keep them occupied. As he got to the end, Tounerre's head came over the door, begging attention. His eyes were moving all about, but he was calm.

Jacques could hear the yearling colt squealing in panic and anger, and glanced in that direction to see Pierre in the stall with him, holding his halter, stroking his neck, moving around the stall with the colt. Jacques considered this was the extreme condition that needed the partition for a while, until the colt calmed down. Jacques went to assist Pierre in swinging the partition in place, squeezing the colt into a narrow space, and tying his head up short, next to his feed box.

Things started to calm down, and the three men looked at each other in relief. Claudel commented, "We are lucky; it is a calm day to start out. It probably won't last for long, this time of the year."

All this time Harry watched the activity, staying a safe distance away from the horses, but always somewhat near Jacques. Now that the crisis was past, he came to hold onto Jacques' hand, his eyes wide with apprehension at all he was seeing, needing reassurance, so Jacques picked him up and carried him over to the stall where Tounerre welcomed the boy's attention, his head over the front of his stall to accommodate Harry's petting.

Now Claudel was willing to leave his horses to take his packs to his cabin, so Pierre left with him to help carry the packs.

Jacques made one last check to be sure all the horses were okay, then with Harry hanging onto his hand, headed up the ramp to the main deck. They got to the rail in time to see the southwest coast of England slip by as the ship sped toward the open water. The Breakfields were all at the rail, watching the last of England as it disappeared into the fog. No one was talking, all dealing with private feelings about leaving England, so the silence was broken with Harry's quiet voice as he waved to the fading shape of England and softly spoke, "Mama, bye…"

Jacques looked down to see tears on Harry's face, for the first time recognizing the boy's grief. He picked up the boy, who sobbed into his shoulder. Jacques thought of what he left behind: the security of his family in France. His grief at that loss had temporarily softened during his stay with Jeannette's family in Southampton. He wished she was here now to help fill the gap that made Harry's loss so painful. Could he give the boy what he needed? He wanted to do everything he could to make the boy feel safe.

.

CHAPTER 5

Exodus

ANTOINE AND FIDEL had the two mares in harness, backing them to the wagon. The women were getting the last of their personal belongings together and ready to load into the wagon. It was a big wagon, but still space was limited, so only the most essential items could be taken.

The past month went unbelievably fast. Jeannette had been right. There were several good offers on the property, so they received a good price, despite the fire damage. The new owners were happy to take all the furnishings and equipment, adding to the sale.

Darren was still recuperating from his injuries, but was packing the saddles and equipment from the tack room, with Roman's help. Roman Balansay spent the past month at the inn with his parents. Even though Darren voiced his dislike for the Romani in general, it appeared he and Roman were becoming friends. About the same age, living in close proximity seemed to bring them together, finally. Roman's friendly personality seemed to be overcoming Darren's prejudice. And Roman's experience with horses finally impressed Darren, gaining his respect.

Antoine and Ellienne were immigrating to Canada along with the Newalls. The Balansay family, along with some of their friends from the Romani camp, would be riding to Liverpool with them, providing an escort. But first they would stay a few days with the Romani, allowing the Merlot's to make their farewells, and have some time of fellowship and worship with the Romani. They would then visit the Duran family on the Montgomery estate between Bristol and Bath. The Durans stayed with the Newalls for a year when they first came to England from France many years ago. Jeannette and Darren were just children then, and the Duran's daughter, Marielle was born that year.

Nearing March, it had been a hard winter, but now the weather was cooperating with their travel plans. Although it was overcast, precipitation was not imminent; the air was chilly, but not as cold as it had been.

With both their mares in harness, all three of the Newalls were riding in the wagon. Darren felt good to be driving, feeling like the man of the family, with his mother and sister on either side of him. The Romani rode ahead, cheerfully talking and joking as they led the way.

Jeannette was excited about spending time with the Romani, even though she was anxious to get to Jacques. With the horses' quick pace and all the banter from the Romani, it seemed no time before they were on the ridge overlooking the camp. Memories came flooding back to Jeannette as she saw many of the Romani riding up the hill to meet them. It was here, while visiting the Romani, that Jacques first professed his love for her. One of the approaching riders was Augusto Gavino. Jeannette, looking past him, saw his wife Rosa standing by their wagon, waving enthusiastically to them. It was many weeks since Jeannette had stayed with Rosa and Ellienne in Rosa's wagon during her stay. Jeannette taught them many of the songs and choruses she knew from church; and with Rosa's guitar accompaniment, they shared their music with the camp.

Royal Roland was riding up with Augusto, and when they were alongside, Antoine introduced him to Madam Newall and Darren. They were led down into the circle of wagons where there was a space pointed out to them. While the men were unhitching the mares, Ellienne took Jeannette and her mother to her wagon, where they would be staying. Roman convinced Darren to stay in his family's wagon.

As dusk became imminent, the smells of cooking came from many campfires and the travelers were invited to the Gavino's campsite for dinner. There was a good time of fellowship as they ate, and Jeannette was not surprised when someone asked if she would be reading from God's Word.

As she stood up, she was recalling the wagon trip home to Southampton with Jacques and the Merlots after their last visit to the camp, when Jacques asked her questions about the heavenly language. As she shared this with the people, they responded with nods of agreement as they whispered and murmured to each other.

So she began, "I'd like to read to you some of the Book of Acts, which is the next book of the Bible after the Gospel of John. It is the story of the early believers after the death and resurrection of Jesus: so it is the story of the beginning of the Christian church.

"After Jesus rose from the dead, he spent time with his disciples, in the presence of many and showed himself alive to many people for forty days, speaking to them about many things about the future." Then she opened her Bible to the first chapter of Acts and began reading:

> "And, being assembled together with them commanded them that they should not depart from Jerusalem, but wait for the promise of the father, which, saith he, ye have heard of me.
> "For John truly baptized with water; but ye shall be baptized with the Holy Ghost not many days hence." (Acts 1:4, 5, KJV)
>
> "But ye shall receive power, after that the Holy Ghost is come upon you: and you shall be witnesses unto me both in Jerusalem, and in Judaea, and in Samaria, and unto the uttermost parts of the earth." (Acts 1:8, KJV)
>
> Then she turned to Chapter Two, and began again to read:
>
> "And when the day of Pentacost was fully come, they were all of one accord in one place.
> "And suddenly there came a sound from heaven as of a rushing might wind, and it filled all the house where they were sitting.
> "And there appeared unto them cloven tongues like as of fire, and it sat upon each of them.
> "And they were all filled with the Holy Ghost, and began to speak with other tongues, as the Spirit gave them utterance.
> "And there were dwelling at Jerusalem Jews, devout men, out of every nation under heaven.

HELENA POORTVLIET

"Now when this was noised abroad, the multitude came together, and were confounded because that every man heard them speak in his own language.

"And they were all amazed and marveled, saying one to another, Behold, are not all these which speak Galilaeans?"

"And how hear we every man in our own tongue, wherein we were born."

(Acts 2:1-8, KJV)

Looking up from her reading to Antoine to finish translating, she smiled while watching the people's reaction before commenting. "So you see, this is not the first time such a thing has happened. And, honestly, I don't think it's only the second time either."

After Antoine translated, he added, "I think it must be a tool God uses whenever people of various languages come together, to worship and fellowship in God. And I sense such a presence of God when I hear those unknown words in the group."

Roman and Darren were sitting together, both looking very serious watching the exchange. Jeannette turned to see her mother with tears showing, so she walked over to embrace her.

Ellienne approached her husband to say to the group, "Isn't it wonderful, to know God loves us so much he would bring such a thing to our camp."

There were nods of agreement, as many now raised their arms. Some were praying, others singing, as the violins began to play softly.

It was a long day and the travelers were anxious to retire. They all were made to feel comfortable and welcome, despite the sparse accommodations. Even Darren seemed to be comfortable with Roman's companionship.

CHAPTER 6

The BusyBody

T HE DAY WAS overcast, but still calm, with just enough wind to fill the sails. Jacques was grateful for the calm, sensing, as Claudel said, it would not last. As they moved further from land, he noted a few other ships moving toward the land mass of England which was rapidly disappearing. The feeling of isolation was increasing as the watery world surrounded them. He was in England for seven weeks, but in some ways, it seemed almost a lifetime. Now he thought of how they would be surrounded by nothing but water for almost that long.

With Harry still on his shoulder, he headed back for the horse deck. He took the boy to Tounerre's stall, where the stallion eagerly received his petting. Being near the stallion seemed to comfort the boy.

Hearing the sounds of metal, he turned to see Deral McDonald coming down the ramp with his arms full of milk cans and pails. "Cook sent me down to bring this stuff. I guess you've got goats to milk?" The question in his voice made it sound incredulous. Jacques smiled at him, understanding enough of the English to pick up on the joking reference to the goats. The creatures in question were now bleating for attention, whether it was for food or milking yet to be determined.

At the mention of goats, Harry ran over to the goats' stalls, and now was climbing up on the rails. This seemed to encourage their bleating, especially when Harry began to imitate them by bleating back at them. This set off hysterical giggling, through which Harry was asking Jacques, "Can we milk the goats now?"

"Wait a bit, son," Jacques responded in a mix of English and French, as he stowed the milking utensils in the tack room. He wanted to release the thoroughbred colt from his confinement, now the motion of the ship was not so extreme. He also wanted to spend some time with the yearlings, to improve their manners, especially the colt. He knew he would not be able to count on it everyday, but he intended to take advantage of every calm day.

After leading the colt the length of the row of stalls, several times, continually insisting on good behavior, the colt was much calmer to return to his stall without being tied or confined.

Later, while milking the goats, Harry was so interested in the procedure Jacques began to show him how it was done. He picked up the technique easily, beaming with pride at his accomplishment. Harry was so enthusiastic, Jacques let him do several of the goats, watching him carefully, making sure each was done correctly. After a while, Harry confessed he was tired, so Jacques finished the milking while the boy stayed close by. Then he sent Harry to find Pierre to help them carry the milk cans back to the galley.

With twenty-eight horses and a dozen goats he would never run out of work cleaning stalls, so he got busy with a few of them before dinner. He reflected that the routine was almost as if he was at home on his parents' farm. At this rate, maybe the voyage would go quickly.

At dinner, he met two of the families who brought horses on with them this morning. Willis and Patricia Caldwell, from Kent County, east of London, owned the Suffolks. Willis told Jacques the team was a wedding gift from Patricia's father. Hoping to homestead in Canada West, they were very interested that Jacques had similar plans. Their conversation was somewhat intense with effort on both parts to understand each other, but Jacques was starting to see how much English he picked up just in the few weeks he was in England. And now he was trying even harder through his efforts to communicate with Harry.

The carriage team of bays belonged to Richard and Elizabeth Tennison from London, who were immigrating to Montreal to open a bank branch there. With them were their twin daughters, Deidre and Daphne, who were thirteen, and their son, Roland, who was seventeen. When they came into the dining room, they paused to look around, then sat at the end of the table with the Breakfields.

Jacques and Willis Caldwell were in conversation over the relative comparison of Percherons and Suffolks when Andrew Breakfield came over to ask if Harry could come over to their table. Jacques nodded okay, and the happy boys ran for the other table.

Patricia Caldwell now leaned forward to say, "He acts like he's your son, but he doesn't look like you."

Jacques tried to explain how he found Harry on the street in Birmingham, but the language difference made it hard to understand. Or she just couldn't believe such a thing could happen. She continued to ask questions, but Jacques was feeling frustrated trying to answer. Willis interrupted, "Let it be, Trish; it's not our business." He tried to apologize to Jacques. "Women think they must have a hand with everyone else's children. Pay her no mind."

But Jacques still felt uncomfortable, as though his relationship with Harry might be threatened. Pierre came in to sit down with them, just in time to catch the last bit of the conversation. He said nothing.

Jacques finished his dinner in silence and got up to go back to his quarters, calling out to Harry with a wave. Pierre followed, asking if he would read from God's Word. Jacques nodded, thinking to himself how he needed to hear from God, with questions rising in his head. When they reached the cabin, Jacques reached for the Bible and sat on the bunk. Harry quickly snuggled in next to him, as Jacque began to read:

> "And in those days Peter stood up in the midst of the disciples, and said, (the number of names together were about an hundred and twenty.)
>
> "Men and brethren, this scripture must needs have been fulfilled, which the Holy Ghost by the mouth of David spake before concerning Judas, which was guide to them which took Jesus.
>
> "For he was numbered with us, and had obtained part of this ministry.
>
> "Now this man purchased a field with the rewards of iniquity; and falling headlong, he burst asunder in the midst, and all his bowels gushed out.
>
> "And it was known to all the dwellers at Jerusalem, insomuch as that field is called in their proper tongue, Aceldama, that is to say, The field of blood.
>
> "For it is written in the book of Psalms, Let his habitation be desolate, and let no man dwell therein: and his bishoprick let another take.
>
> "Wherefore of these men which have companied with us all the time that the Lord Jesus went in and out among us.

"Beginning from the baptism of John, unto that same day that he was taken up from us, must one be ordained to be a witness with us of his resurrection.

"And they appointed two, Joseph called Barsabas, who was surnamed Justas, and Matthias.

"And they prayed, and said, Thou, Lord, which knowest the hearts of all men, shew whether of these two thou has chosen.

"That he may take part of this ministry and apostleship, from which Judas by transgression fell, that he might go to his own place.

"And they gave forth their lots; and the lot fell upon Matthias; and he was numbered with the eleven apostles." (Acts 1:15-26, KJV)

It was quiet for several moments as Jacques ended the reading. Harry had fallen asleep. Jacques thought about the community of believers, who stayed together and prayed together and solved their community problems through their shared prayers. It reminded him of the close knit relationship of Jeannette and her mother, sharing their problems with shared prayer. Later that family prayer circle included Jacques and the Merlots. He missed that relationship. These people seemed not of that spirit, and he felt like an outsider. He felt threatened this evening by Patricia's questions about Harry.

Pierre broke the silence. "My brother, you are concerned about these people and what they might think."

Jacques agreed. "I'm not sure they think I should have Harry with me. I don't think Mrs. Caldwell approves."

"But it's not her business."

"But I think she may try to make it her business."

"My brother, just like those people you were just reading about, we are God's community here. We should pray."

Jacques gave a hearty, "Yes!"

"Father, I thank you for my brothers, both Harry and Pierre. I know that you brought Harry to me to take care of, so I put him in your hands. I pray you watch over him and protect him, and guide me in caring for him."

"Amen," Pierre added.

Jacques, feeling relieved, was ready to settle in for the night.

CHAPTER 7

Sleeping With the Enemy

W HEN DARREN AWOKE in the Balansay wagon, his consciousness was flooded with confusion. The first time in his life he slept anywhere but his own room, it seemed he awakened to a nightmare. Where was he, and who were these people? Bits and pieces were coming back. Roman was asleep in the narrow bunk across from him. Gypsies! What was he doing here? He sat up with a start, and then remembered—he encouraged his mother to sell the inn. It seemed to him the only way to get away from those men. More confusion. Why did they want to see him? That part was still not clear. At first he thought the Gypsies started the fire, but they all said it was those men trying to steal his horse. So confusing! But after a month of getting ready to move, that Gypsy boy, Roman, seemed sort of okay. At least he was pretty smart about horses.

Darren shook his head. He could not believe his whole family was staying at a Gypsy camp. Ugh! Everyone else in the wagon was still asleep, so he got up as quietly as he could and slipped out of the wagon. Finding his family's wagon, with the two mares tied to it, he went to his mare, Dani. Lost in confused thoughts, leaning on the mare, he became aware of someone close by—that Gypsy his mother hired.

Antoine greeted him jovially, "It's good you're up early. As soon as you get your horses fed, you can come and help me with the fire. The women will be up soon and wanting to cook breakfast."

Darren put on a polite smile and nodded. "Okay, I'll be right there." He knew better than to not be agreeable. When he heard singing voices coming from another wagon, he realized it was his mother and sister singing with those Gypsy women. He tried to tell himself, "Ugh!" but realized they really did sound nice.

Rosa Gavino came early to the Merlot wagon with her guitar. She was anxious for what would probably be her last opportunity to sing and play her guitar with Jeannette. Her friend was going to Canada forever. She was even sadder because Ellienne was going too.

Feeling at loss for what to do, thinking of being in the enemy's territory, Darren found where Antoine was cutting wood, and began to stack it with his one good arm. Antoine smiled and nodded at him, and bent to feed the campfire he had just started.

Activity was starting all over the camp now. Women were coming with food to be shared with the visitors as well as their neighbors. The weather was chilly, but the spirit of the people was warm. After breakfast, the four women began to sing for the group, and soon others joined in as well, some with violins and other instruments.

Jeannette knew they would want her to read and knew it was critical she pick the right material, since she would have to turn all further teaching over to the others. She wanted to leave them with tools to continue to learn from God's Word. She gave Elena a copy of the English Bible and was teaching her as much as possible in the last few weeks. After a period of singing, she recognized the expectant silence, and stepped up to begin reading.

"I will be leaving soon, and am so sorry to say I probably won't get to see most of you again. I've been teaching Elena Balansay to continue to lead you in the study of God's Word. I would like you to learn of the Acts of the Apostles, since it will tell you so much about the Holy Spirit's influence in the beginnings of the Christian church. And then Paul's letters to the churches are God's instructions for us to know how to live as Christian believers. So, today I'm going to read just a little from Paul's letter to the Roman believers:

> "There is therefore now no condemnation to them which are in Christ Jesus, who walk not after the flesh, but after the Spirit.
> "For the law of the Spirit of life in Christ Jesus hath made me free from the law of sin and death.
> "For what the law could not do, in that it was weak through the flesh, God sending his own Son in the likeness of sinful flesh, and for sin, condemned sin in the flesh:

"That the righteousness of the law might be fulfilled in us, who walk not after the flesh, but after the Spirit.

"For they that are after the flesh do mind the things of the flesh; but they that are after the Spirit the things of the Spirit.

"For to be carnally minded is death; but to be spiritually minded is life and peace.

"Because the carnal mind is enmity against God, for it is not subject to the law of God, neither indeed can be.

"So they that are in the flesh cannot please God.

"But ye are not in the flesh, but in the Spirit, if so be that the Spirit of God dwell in you. Now if any man have not the Spirit of Christ, he is none of his.

"And if Christ be in you, the body is dead because of sin; but the Spirit is life because of righteousness.

"But if the Spirit of him that raised up Jesus from the dead dwell in you, he that raised up Christ from the dead shall also quicken your mortal bodies by his Spirit that dwelleth in you.

"Therefore, brethren, we are debtors, not to the flesh, to live after the flesh,

"For if you live after the flesh, ye shall die: but if ye through the Spirit do mortify the deeds of the body, ye shall live." (Rom. 8:1-13, KJV)

Jeannette paused to wait for Antoine to finish translating from the English to Romani. The expressions of some were perplexed, while others eagerly absorbed the teaching. She saw her brother, seated on the ground near Roman Balansay, looking uncomfortable. Roman was listening intently. She went on:

"For as many as are led by the Spirit of God, they are the sons of God.

"For ye have not received the spirit of bondage again to fear; but ye have received the Spirit of adoption, whereby we cry, Abba, Father.

"The Spirit itself beareth witness with our spirit, that we are the children of God:

"And if children, then heirs, heirs of God, and joint-heirs with Christ; if so be that we suffer with him, that we also may be glorified together."
(Romans 8:14-17, KJV)

Now as Jeannette again paused, she began to see more looks of understanding, and now a few hands raised in worship. She flipped a few pages and continued:

> "I beseech you therefore, brethren, by the mercies of God, that ye present your bodies a living sacrifice, holy, acceptable unto God, which is your reasonable service.
> "And be ye not conformed to this world, but be ye transformed by the renewing of your mind: that ye may prove what is that good, and acceptable, and perfect, will of God." (Rom. 12:1, 2, KJV)

As Antoine finished the translation, many hands were raised in worship, and violins played softly. Jeannette gave the invitation, "If there are those of you who would profess your belief in Jesus as your Savior, I would love to have you come forward so I may pray with you."

Several moved toward her, but there were many also praying with each other. Prayer and worship continued for a time. Gradually the people were hugging and continuing to talk. Jeannette and her mother moved from person to person to pray, until most were just talking and enjoying the gathering. She looked around for her brother, but did not see him.

Darren and Roman walked away from the group after the last part of the reading. Roman had little to say, so Darren just walked with him. Finally, Darren asked, "Do you believe all that?"

"I don't know. My parents, I think, believe it. And my mother has really changed. I keep thinking the old Elena is coming back, but I don't know. Papa is really happy now. But I'm not sure yet." Roman was shaking his head. "It all seems too good to be true."

Darren thought to himself, smugly, *well, not everyone believes all that.* A brief picture again flashed through his mind, of his father, dying in his arms, and he felt pain stabbing him in the chest. Pain in his throat was so intense he could not speak.

CHAPTER 8

Education

WHEN JACQUES AWOKE, the motion of the ship was a rhythmic rocking. He knew they were moving well with the wind, but the sea was still relatively smooth. He slipped out of the cabin quietly, but as soon as the horses saw him there was a relay of whinnying and pawing. Soon the horses were joined by the bleating of the goats. Jacques hurried to get the feeding started. Plenty of fresh hay would help keep the horses occupied and calm.

Hearing the clanking of the metal, he wasn't surprised to see Deral McDonald with milk cans and buckets. At the same time his sleepy-eyed cabin mates appeared. This time Pierre didn't wait to be told. He picked up the fork, pushing the cart toward the first stall to be cleaned.

Jacques knew Cook would be waiting for the fresh milk, so he waved to Harry as he headed for the goats stall. Harry was anxious to help, and was getting more skilled at the task since his earlier attempts. Jacques watched him carefully, surprised he did not tire of it as quickly as yesterday. Soon they had the cans ready to carry to the galley. As they headed up the ramp, Jacques realized they were so busy with all the work, he had not given a thought to the things Patricia Caldwell said last night at dinner.

At breakfast the three sat down with the Breakfields, to the delight of Andrew and Harry. Roger gave a jovial smile and a "Good Morning," as he glanced from Jacques to Pierre. Andrea greeted Harry with a smile and asked him several questions about his short experience on the ship. Harry chatted happily about the horses, and even more excitedly about getting to milk the goats. Andrew listened with almost envious attention. Andrea, noticing her son's response, said, "Well, maybe Jacques wouldn't mind showing you around the stable, if you mind him and do everything he says." She looked sidelong at Jacques, as Pierre translated to him.

Jacques agreed enthusiastically, "Oh, yes, that would be fine!" and watched the boys expressions as Pierre translated back. Then Roger began asking what Jacques was planning to do when they reached Canada. He explained, as again, Pierre translated, how he planned to homestead in Canada West, and raise the Percheron horses his family had bred for generations. As Pierre was translating, he added, "And Jacques has a bride coming from England to marry him, --a beautiful wife!" with a grin.

The Breakfields both responded with raised eyebrows in their surprise. "So Harry will have a new mother," Andrea responded.

Jacques thought he knew what was being said, but showed some apprehension. Pierre explained to him. Jacques just looked at Pierre, then said, "I pray that day comes."

The Breakfields were planning on joining the business of family friends in Montreal, who had been there for several years, prospering enough to ask their friends to join them. Roger was confident it would be a good life, but thought Jacques' future looked much more adventurous.

Breakfast was cut short as Jacques realized the time had flown and he was uneasy to leave his duties for too long. As he got up to leave, Andrea again encouraged him to leave Harry with them so the two boys could keep each other company. Jacques nodded in agreement and turned to go, with Pierre following him.

The sea was still relatively calm, so Jacques worked more with the yearlings, starting with the colt, walking him several laps of the space between the two rows of stalls. When the colt tried to raise his head high above Jacques, he talked quietly and calmly, as he gave short tugs on the lead, until the colt's head dropped down to Jacques elbow. Jacques rubbed his neck and spoke in an approving tone, "Good boy." After putting the colt back in his stall, he gave each of the fillies a similar workout. It seemed to Jacques the three young horses had little or no training, other than very minimal halter breaking.

Sun Flair was another story. He probably had a season or two of racing. A racehorse's behavior, as a rule, was pretty much forgivable, as long as he was winning. Sun Flair had been in his stall now for several days, so was ready for some exercise. However, a walk around the deck was nothing like a gallop around the track. Jacques took him several laps, insisting on the stallion's good behavior every step of the way. He was firm with the stallion, always speaking in a low tone, always calm in responding to the stallion's behavior.

Jacques would continue taking each of his twenty-eight charges, one by one, for walks around the deck between the stalls, as long as the sea and the weather allowed. He was determined each animal would arrive in Montreal in good condition.

Jacques was just returning Sun Flair to his stall when he heard footsteps on the ramp from the main deck, and looked to see Harry and Andrew running down the ramp ahead of Roger Breakfield.

"We've come to see your stable," was the cheery announcement from Roger. Andrew was looking around in wonder. "Where's our horses, Papa?"

Roger looked around, and quickly caught sight of his four bay geldings, just beyond the Percheron mares. He walked over and peered into the stalls, which he could see were spotless. Pierre had cleaned stalls while Jacques was working with the thoroughbreds. Roger paid special attention to one of the bays, obviously his favorite. When Jacques approached, Roger expressed his approval.

"You've got everything so clean."

Jacques understood most of it, so he attempted a reply in a mixture of French and English, which mainly meant, "If I don't keep it up now, when the weather gets rough, it could really be bad." Roger got most of the meaning, and laughing, agreed.

Harry was following Jacques with a piece of paper, waiting patiently to show him. Jacques finally realized the boy was trying to show him something and took the paper. It showed Harry's name, Harry McKeller, in carefully formed letters.

"I did it," he said, shyly, "I wrote my name."

Jacques was surprised, and after a moment of silence, picked up the boy and swung him around. "Wonderful! I'm proud of you!" It was a mixture of English and French, and the boy corrected his words in English. Jacques laughed, but suddenly realized he had not even thought about the boys learning. He was eight years old and proud he had just written his name for the first time.

"I hope you don't mind," Roger began. "Andrea showed him how when she realized he could not read. She would like to teach him more, if you don't mind," Roger said, sounding apologetic.

Jacques was stunned. He had not even considered these things, since the events of the last few days had evolved so fast. Jacques paused for a moment, even a bit embarrassed. He had no better answer than, "Oh, yes, merci!" Roger had no trouble translating.

"Great! Andrea will be happy to hear that." Roger turned to Andrew, "Come on, boy, let's get back." And the two headed back up the ramp.

CHAPTER 9

Prophecy

ON THE ROAD since early this morning, leaving the Romani camp just as faint lines of dawn began to appear, the three wagons, the Newalls, with their two mares in the lead, were followed by the Merlot's wagon and the Balansay wagon, each pulled by a two horse team. Roman Balansay, along with Augusto Gavino and two other Romani men were all riding horses, hoping to reach the Duran's between Bath and Bristol. The colorful Romani wagons brought stares as they passed through Andover, even a few jeers. Darren, driving his family's wagon, embarrassed at being associated with the Gypsies, was glad to leave the city behind. Finally stopping for lunch along the road to Bath, they all shared food which they brought along, sharing conversation as well, a mixture of English and Romani.

As they started on the road again, all the Romani except the Merlots turned north. Darren was relieved they had gotten through Bath with no incident, even though there were stares at the colorful wagon following their wagon. He continued to feel a seething, hidden anger that they were traveling with these people for whom he had so much contempt.

In the little cottage, brightened by all the lamplight, the windows were now black as darkness had closed in. Jules and Teresa knew wagons approached, because there always seemed to be eyes peeking out into the darkness at the sounds. Looking at each other with the questions on their faces, Teresa spoke first.

"Well, who would it be, this late?"

Jules started for the door with at least four of his six children trying to peek past him into the darkness. He lit a lantern before he opened the door. In the darkness, he could barely make out two women and a young man in the first wagon. But he was startled to see the second wagon in the lamplight. It looked like a little cabin on wheels. His first thought was *Gypsies!* But the two didn't go together. *What is this?*

Then Madam Newall spoke, "Jules, is that you?"

Recognition out of the past came slowly. It was only a few weeks ago that young man Jacques was here. And he just received a letter from him, about a month ago, posted from Birmingham. By now, Teresa came through the door, scolding the little ones to "stay inside!" It started to sink in. *It's the Newalls, Jeannette and her brother Darren and their mother.* Teresa ran past her husband to greet them. There was laughing, crying and hugging all around.

"Well, come in, come in. Get in here out of the cold!"

But Jeannette stopped them, to call attention to the Merlots, still on the seat of their wagon. "These are our friends, Antoine and Ellienne." She was waving to them to join them.

Then Jules remembered the couple Jacques told them about. Jules at first was shocked there were Gypsies staying with the Newalls, but later understood when Jacques told him about them. He reached out his hand to Antoine and introduced himself.

"Welcome, my brother. I am Jules Duran. I hear we are countrymen from France." He could see relief on the faces of both Antoine and Ellienne. Teresa came past him to give Ellienne a hug and invited them all to come in.

Darren was still seething. *How can they be so friendly to those— Gypsies!?* But he said nothing.

Dinner was a joyous time of catching up on old times. Madam Newall was completely amazed at all of the Duran children, and how grown up was Marielle. She was just a baby back in Southampton, all those years ago. And the Durans were just as amazed to see Jeannette and Darren now grown. Of course, they expressed sadness at the death of Ed Newall.

Darren stayed quiet through all this talk, but inside his mind was racing between anger and confusion. Much was said about his father, but none of it came from him. The pain in his chest became intense and his confusion deepened. But he smiled politely whenever anyone looked his direction or spoke to him.

Then Teresa asked, "But what are you all doing here?" Then looking at Jeannette, she continued, "That young man Jacques told us he was expecting you to marry him. Are you on your way to meet him now? But, why are you all here? What about your place in Southampton?" The questions came one after another, while Jeannette waited to speak.

"Yes, I'm going to marry Jacques." Jeannette was beaming as she spoke. "And all of us are going to Montreal. We sold *La Petit Fleur.*"

Teresa looked at Antoine and Ellienne, questioning. Ellienne smiled, "Yes, we are going to Montreal, as well."

Then everyone was talking at once. There were more questions. Jeannette held the letter in her hand she had been carrying in her pocket. There was some talk of the incidents of the bombing and the fire, and their decision to sell the inn and move. Jeannette spoke of how much Jacques helped them through the winter, and about their trip to the Romani camp.

The Durans shared how Jacques read to them out of the little book and how they all became believers. The Merlots also shared how that little book had such an impact on their lives, and on their camp. So, finally, the Durans asked if they could all read together.

Jeannette was ready, anxious to share God's Word with them. However, she felt in her spirit she should go in a different direction in her reading. She silently asked for God's confirmation on what to read as she went to get her Bible. Obediently, she opened up in the Old Testament, and began to read:

> "Now the Lord had said unto Abram, Get thee out of thy country, and from thy kindred, and from thy father's house, unto a land that I will shew thee.
> "And I will make of thee a great nation, and I will bless thee, and make thy name great, and thou shall be a blessing:
> "And I will bless them that bless thee, and curse him that curseth thee: and in thee shall all the families of the earth be blessed." (Gen.12:1-3, KJV)

Jeannette paused to see the expressions of the others. All looked interested, waiting for her to continue. She started to explain:

"I thought the Lord was leading me to go to the Old Testament. I think the story of Abram is about his obedience to the Word of God. He doesn't question why; he just obeyed. He just picked up and moved when God told him to. Not knowing what was ahead; he just trusted God."

Teresa replied, "And you're going to a new country, much like Abram. You must trust God to take you on the right path."

Jeannette continued, "I wanted to go to meet Jacques. But Mother wasn't so sure. She wasn't sure it was the right thing to leave Southampton, when she knows nothing about Montreal. I convinced her, and Darren agreed."

Darren looked up, startled when she said his name. Yes, he had agreed. *But,* he thought to himself, *we all have our reasons.*

"And when Antoine and Ellienne decided to go with us," she continued, "it seemed even more right."

Teresa commented, "I'm so glad you're all going together. You're much safer."

Jeannette continued reading:

> "So Abram departed as the Lord had spoken unto him; and Lot went with him: and Abraham was seventy and five years old when he departed out of Haran.
> "And Abram took Sarai his wife, and Lot his brother's son, and all their substance that they had gathered, and the souls that they had gotten in Haran; and they went forth to go into the land of Canaan; and into the land of Canaan they came.
>
> "And Abram passed through the land unto a place of Sichem, unto the plain of Moreh. And the Canaanite was then in the land.
> "And the Lord appeared unto Abram and said, Unto thy seed will I give this land: and there builded he an altar unto the Lord, who appeared unto him." (Gen. 12:4-7, KJV)

Jeannette paused. After a moment, Jules spoke up, "That was the beginning wasn't it? That was the beginning of it all."

Jeannette agreed. "Yes, that was the beginning. God called Abram out, made him a promise, and the promise had to do with Abram's children, even when he had none yet. So it was a prophecy.

Jeannette's mother spoke up, "But my dear, what do you think this has to do with us?"

Jeannette thought for a moment. "I knew Jacques was special when he first came to us. You know I've given out so many of those little "Gospel of John" pamphlets. But do any ever read them. Not many, I'm afraid. But he did, and look what happened when he shared it with the Romani."

Then Antoine broke in, "Oh, yes, our whole camp was changed. They've not been the same since. And look how it's changed us." He was looking at his smiling wife.

"That Jacques was a man with a message, and I don't think he even knew it right away." Ellienne looked admiringly at Jeannette. "I think these two have a great destiny in that new land. It's only just beginning."

Jeannette looked at her friends, "And you two are part of it. You know that, don't you?"

They both looked back at her, smiling, and said no more.

Darren's mind was full of confusion and fear. These things were out of his control. It was all he could do to control his anger. Biting his tongue, he said nothing.

CHAPTER 10

Stormy Voyage

"And when the day of Pentecost was fully come, they were all in one accord in one place.

"And suddenly there was a sound from heaven as of a rushing mighty wind, and it filled all the house where they were sitting.

"And there appeared unto them cloven tongues like as of fire, and it sat upon each of them.

"And they were all filled with the Holy Ghost, and began to speak with other tongues, as the Spirit gave them utterance.

"And there were dwelling at Jerusalem, devout men, out of every nation under heaven.

"Now when this was noised abroad, the multitude came together, and were confounded because that every man heard them speak in his own language.

"And they were all amazed and marveled, saying one to another, Behold, are not all these which speak Galilaean?

"And how hear we every man in our own tongue, wherein we were born?

"Parthians, and Medes, and Elamites, and the dwellers in Mesopotamia, and in Judaea, and Cappadocia, in Pontus, and Asia,

"Phrygia, and Pamphylia, in Egypt, and in the parts of Libya about Cyrene and strangers of Rome, Jews and proselytes,

"Cretes and Arabians, we do hear them speak in our tongues the wonderful works of God. (Acts 2:1-12, KJV)

JACQUES LOOKED UP from what he had just read. Pierre was open-mouthed. Jacques exclaimed, "That's what I was telling you. That's the way it happened at the Romani camp. With all the different languages, we could understand each other! It was so amazing!"

Pierre said, "Read more," so Jacques continued:

> "Others mocking said, These men are full of new wine.
>
> "But Peter, standing up with the eleven, lifted up his voice and said unto them, Ye men of Judaea, and all ye that dwell in Jerusalem, be this known unto you, and hearken to my words:
> "For these are not drunken, as ye suppose, seeing it is but the third hour of the day.
> "But this is that which was spoken by the prophet Joel:
> "And it shall come to pass in the last days, saith God, I will pour out my Spirit upon all flesh: and you sons and your daughters shall prophecy, and your young men shall see visions, and your old men shall dream dreams:
> "And on my servants and on my handmaidens I will pour out in those days of my Spirit, and they shall prophecy:
> "And I will show wonders in the heavens above, and signs in the earth beneath; blood, and fire, and vapour of smoke:
> "The sun shall be turned into darkness, and the moon into blood, before that the great and notable day of the Lord come:
> "And it shall come to pass, that whosoever shall call on the name of the Lord shall be saved." (Acts 2:13-21, KJV)

"Whoa!" Pierre interrupted. "When is all that supposed to happen? …I mean the part about wonders and signs in the sky and all that? And what's the day of the Lord?"

Jacques looked up to answer, "I think it means the end of time, when Jesus comes back. But remember, I'm just reading this too. It's all new to me, so all I can do is keep reading and try to learn."

"Okay, okay, go on and keep reading."

Jacques paused to give Harry some attention, pulling the blanket over the sleeping boy, and then resumed his reading:

> "Ye men of Israel, hear these words: Jesus of Nazareth, a man approved of God among you by miracles and wonders and signs, which God did by him in the midst of you, as ye yourselves also know:

HELENA POORTVLIET

"Him, being delivered by the determinate counsel and foreknowledge of God, ye have taken, and by wicked hands have crucified and slain:

"Whom God hath raised up, having loosed the pains of death; because it was not possible that he should be holden to it.

"For David speaketh concerning him, I foresaw the Lord always before my face, for he is on my right hand, that I should not be moved.

"Therefore did my heart rejoice, and my tongue was glad; moreover also my flesh shall rest in hope.

"Because thou will not leave my soul in hell, neither wilt thou suffer thine Holy One to see corruption.

"Thou hast made known to me the ways of life; thou shall make me full of joy with my countenance.

"Men and brethren, let me freely speak unto you of the patriarch David, that he is both dead and buried, and his sepulcher is with us unto this day.

"Therefore being a prophet, and knowing that God had sworn with an oath to him, that of the fruit of his loins, according to the flesh, he would raise up Christ to sit on his throne;

"He seeing this before spake of the resurrection of Christ, that his soul was not left in hell, neither his flesh did not see corruption.

"This Jesus hath God raised up, whereof we are all witnesses.

"Therefore being by the right hand of God exalted, and having received of the Father the promise of the Holy Ghost, he hath shed forth this, which ye now see and hear.

"For David is not ascended into the heavens: but he saith himself, The Lord said unto my Lord, Sit thou on my right hand,

"Until I make thy foes thy footstool.

"Therefore let all the house of Israel know assuredly, that God hath made that same Jesus, whom ye have crucified, both Lord and Christ." (Acts 2:22-36, KJV)

"Who is this David?" Pierre asked. "It sounds like we should know who he is, like a prophet or something."

"Yeah, it sounds like someone the Jews knew about, the way it refers to him. I wish I could ask Jeannette. I know she would know." As Jacques mentioned her, he felt a flood of longing. Then he added, "I guess we just have to keep reading to learn more."

"Yeah, keep on reading," urged Pierre, so Jacques continued:

> "Now when they heard this they were pricked in their heart, and said unto Peter and to the rest of the apostles, Men and brethren, what shall we do?
> "Then Peter said unto them, Repent, and be baptized every one of you in the name of Jesus Christ for the remission of sins, and ye shall receive the gift of the Holy Ghost.
> "For the promise is unto you, and to your children, and to all that are afar off, even as many as the Lord our God shall call.
> "And with many other words did he testify and exhort, saying Save yourself from this untoward generation." (Acts 2:37-40, KJV)

Jacques caught a glimmer of meaning in what he just read. "There, he's talking about us. We're the ones God calls 'afar off,' and our children and the ones we talk to about Jesus."

"Oh, yes," Pierre agreed, as Jacques turned back to continue:

> "Then they that gladly received his word were baptized, and the same day were added unto them about three thousand souls.
> "And they continued steadfastly in the apostle's doctrine and fellowship, and in breaking of bread, and in prayers.
> "And fear came upon every soul, and many wonders and signs were done by the apostles.
> "And all that believed were together and had all things in common, and sold their possessions and goods, and parted them to all men, as every man had need.
> "And they, continuing daily in one accord in the temple, and breaking bread from house to house, did eat their meat with gladness and singleness of heart,
> "Praising God, and having favour with all the people. And the Lord added to the church daily such as should be saved." Acts 2:41-47, KJV)

Pierre was shaking his head. "Wow, three thousand souls. That's amazing. That's what we should be doing."

Jacques looked up, surprised. "You mean here, on this ship?"

"Yes," he answered. "Or anywhere. Isn't that what you were talking about at that Gypsy camp? Why not here?"

Jacques felt surprised at Pierre's words. But he was right. God had been good to them. They should be sharing his word.

Jacques thought he was having that dream about falling, as he woke to the reality of what was happening. Their little cabin was rising and falling to the motion of the ship, and they were all sliding back and forth on the bunks. Jacques gripped the edge of the bunk as he jumped down. Slipping quickly into his clothes and boots, while still gripping the bunk, he knew he had to get the horses secured. He saw the fright on Harry's face as the boy was awakening to the tossing motion.

"Stay here, son. You'll be safe in here."

Now Pierre was up and dressed and ready to follow him. They ran to the nearest stalls together, in an uneven side-to-side pace, attempting to compensate for the rocking motion of the ship under their feet, and began to close the safety partitions in each stall, squeezing each horse into a tight space. They split up to move faster, alternating from horse to horse, then coming together for some of the more difficult ones. Horses were trying to compensate for the motion, moving around in their attempt to keep their balance, many whinnying and squealing in fear. The noise of the ocean was becoming louder and louder, and noise from men on deck, running and yelling, added to the din.

The last two stalls they reached were the two piebalds. They got the partition closed on the stallion first, and then as Jacques moved quickly to the mare's stall, his heart sunk when he saw her. She was down, almost on her back, rolled into the corner of the stall. There was no way to get her into the partition. He went to her head, grasped her halter to try to steady her and roll her onto her side. In his effort, he found himself on the floor, with his feet against the wall, holding her head in his arms. He could feel her straining, and suddenly realized what was happening. She was having her foal.

Pierre slipped into the stall, holding onto the rail. "What shall I do? I can see its head and feet."

"Good, then it's coming out in the right position." Jacques was trying to brace his feet against the wall so he could hold her head still. She was straining to give birth, not trying to get up. "Just be ready to grab it and keep it out of her way, so she doesn't kick it or roll on it."

Pierre leaned back against the gate and braced his feet against the mare's hindquarters, out of the way of her hind hoofs. He grasped her tail, pulling all the long hairs away from the slowly emerging foal. Both were sliding around on the floor to the rocking of the tossing ship. The mare would slide away from the wall and then roll back into it. Now the foals head was emerging, along with two tiny hooves, on long, thin legs. There was a slimy film encasing the foals head. Pierre managed to pull off his shirt, wrap it around the emerging foals head and neck, wiping the slimy membrane away from its nose and mouth.

Jacques could only get a glimpse of what Pierre was doing, but shouted, "Good, make sure it's breathing." With a last great effort from the mare, the foal slipped out, landing in a slimy pile on Pierre's lap. The mare finally relaxed. Pierre crawled backward to the far side of the stall with the foal in his lap. Even though they were still rocking, Jacques got the mare to roll over so she was now upright. Her ears pricked up when she saw the foal in Pierre's lap. With a great effort, she lunged forward and managed to get on her feet, pulling Jacques up with her as he was still holding her head. With the mare on her feet, Jacques moved fast, swinging the partition in place to crowd the mare to the side of the stall. Pierre was rubbing down the foal, freeing it from the slimy membrane. And in the process, he was able to report she was a filly. He slid back close to the mare, so she could put her head down to lick her daughter, still in Pierre's lap.

Now another face appeared at the stall: Ramon Claudel. "So she picked a storm to deliver her baby!" He slipped into the stall and made his way to the mare's head.

Pierre, feeling a little strange, just sat there, the filly still in his lap, but he was close enough so the mare could get her nose to the foal. It seemed like hours to Pierre that he held the filly, with the hard rocking of the ship now making him nauseated, even though it was just minutes.

With Claudel in the stall with his horses and Pierre, Jacques thought of Harry back in the cabin. He made his way to check on him, but when he reached the cabin, Harry was not there. Jacques felt panic, then turned from the door, calling, "Harry!"

A search of the ship ensued. The storm was gradually calming, but Harry was nowhere. No one had seen him. Jacques' fear was overcoming, and he could feel his heart breaking. He went to Tounerre's stall, where the stallion was crowded tightly within the partition. As Jacques climbed into the stall to his horse, there was a movement in the straw under the hay rack. There was the frightened boy, cowering in the corner. Relief flooded over Jacques as he dropped down under Tounerre's neck to where Harry was crouching. He stayed in the corner with the boy as the hard rocking of the ship continued to decrease to a more normal motion.

Jacques pulled Harry out of the corner, saying, "Come on, boy, let's go see what you missed."

By the time they arrived at the stall of the piebald mare, there were several others now peering into the stall. Harry looked in to see the filly now standing next to her mom. Pierre was still sitting on the floor of the stall looking ill. Harry spoke, "That little horse came in the middle of a very stormy voyage." Everyone looked around at Harry with surprise.

Claudel responded, "That's her name, Stormy Voyage." There were some laughs, but also nods of approval.

CHAPTER 11

Friendship and Flirtation

R ACHEL MONTGOMERY JUST turned eighteen. Her parents, Lord and Lady Montgomery were planning an event, really a ball. In England in 1852, nobility related to nobility. At their social level, the people attending would have the same social standing or higher. Rumor was at least one of Queen Victoria's sons would be attending. Rachel's mother was very excited. She was proud of her beautiful daughter and anxious to see her connect with a young man of high-born status. Rachel's beauty and skill at the hunt brought her a lot of attention. All the best young men noticed her, tall and slim with her jet black hair beautifully complimenting her dapple-gray hunter. But now, Lady Montgomery hoped her "event" would draw attention from some young man of even higher status.

Rachel's sister Peggy doted on her older sister. She admired and envied her for the coming celebration. There were dress fittings, hair stylings, makeup, etc., and Peggy wanted to be in on all her sister's plans.

Now something different was going on. Their neighbors, the Durans, who worked for the Montgomerys, that is, Jules Duran, the Montgomery's stable manager, had company. There were two wagons. One looked like a plain cargo wagon. But the other, that was the strange thing: a brightly painted wagon that looked like a little cabin on wheels. Rachel never saw anything like it before, but somewhere she heard those were Gypsy wagons. She could not imagine that the Durans had Gypsies visiting.

Rachel was friends with Marielle Duran, until recently. That Frenchman came to visit with those big black horses, so the Durans invited Rachel and Peggy to come and hear him read from a little book—about Jesus?! Now they were all religious, even her sister Peggy! But Rachel was curious.

Peggy burst into the room excited, "Rachel, Mother has more gowns for you to try on!"

Rachel stopped her short, "I think I'd like to ride Misty in the arena this afternoon. I think he needs some work, and I want to be sure he's sharp for the hunt on Saturday."

Peggy stopped to stare at her sister. Where did this come from? Rachel even acted as if she wasn't going to the hunt. "So you want me to ride with you."

"Would you? Maybe Marielle and Nicole will ride with us."

"Rachel, you know they have a lot of company."

"I know, but don't you want them to ride with us?"

"Sure, if they want to."

"Great. I'll get Father to tell Jules to get our horses ready." With that, Rachel left to find her father.

The three men, Jules, Antoine and Darren went to the barn to take care of the horses, leaving the women in the cottage, with the children. Jules admired the Newall's two bay mares, asking Darren about them.

"Father got them both almost two years ago," he answered. "Dani is mine, and since Father died, Katy belongs to Jeannette." Mentioning his father's death brought that all too familiar stab of pain in his chest. After a moment he added, "But we use them as a team."

Jules acknowledged they were an exceptional pair. Then he turned his attention to the Merlots' team. They were a small, compact draft type. Antoine told him, "The breed comes from the Tyrol Mountains in Eastern Europe; they're called Hafflingers. They're a great team, but we like to ride them if we don't need to take our wagon. They're really easy riding, smooth-gaited, but strong enough to pull the wagon."

Their attention turned to the tall, well-dressed man who entered the barn, breathing hard, pausing to catch his breath before he spoke. "The young ladies wish to ride in the arena this afternoon, so Lord Montgomery says you should have their horses ready." It was Morton, the butler, from the big house.

Jules greeted him cheerily, "Sure thing, Morton. How's it going?"

"Good," came the answer, still somewhat out of breath. "Got to get back." Then he stopped and turned back. "The young ladies want to know if your girls will come out and ride with them, that is, if they're not busy."

"Sure, I'll ask them," Jules answered.

As it turned out, they did, but Marielle wanted Jeannette to come with them. "I heard you say, one of those bay mares is yours. Don't you want to ride her?"

Jeannette thought about how long it had been since she had ridden just for fun. It had been months. She looked at her mother.

"Go ahead, dear," Madam Newall urged.

"But I really don't have riding clothes."

Marielle broke in, "I have some you can wear. It's much easier to ride with a divided skirt. I have an extra."

Madam Newall raised her eyebrows.

"Rachel and Peggy wear them too," Marielle quickly added.

So Jeannette followed Marielle to get dressed for riding.

Darren and Antoine were helping Jules get horses saddled when all the girls arrived at the barn. Darren was surprised to see Jeannette in the divided skirt she borrowed from Marielle.

"They talked me into riding too," she grinned. "Do you think Katy is up to it?"

Darren was open-mouthed.

"Come on, brother, ride with us," Jeannette laughed.

Darren answered, "All right! If you will, I will." His whole demeanor changed. He even temporarily forgot about his barely healed broken arm, and still painful ribs.

"Where are those new bridles we got for Christmas?" Jeannette asked. "Are they still in our wagon?"

"I'll get them," Darren turned to go.

Antoine looked at the two, brother and sister, and smiled. *What a change,* he thought.

When the Montgomery girls came in, Jules made introductions to the visitors, which brought warm response all around. Rachel and Peggy greeted Jeannette with friendliness, if some curiosity.

Jeannette could barely contain her excitement to ride Katy. She hurried to get the mare out of her stall, spending some time brushing her before Antoine came over to help her saddle the mare. Katy lowered her head to Jeannette, making it easy to slip on the fancy bridle Jacques had given her for Christmas. Antoine gave her a boost up on the tall mare. What a thrill! She was actually riding Katy! Darren was already on Dani, following the others to the arena. Jeannette turned Katy to follow him.

By the time Jeannette and Darren arrived in the arena, the others were already moving around the course at Jules direction. After a couple of laps of warm up, Rachel was the first to take her gray horse over a series of jumps. Darren and Jeannette stayed on the clear track, avoiding the jumps, but were amazed to watch the others taking the jumps. Rachel pulled up her gray next to them, laughing.

"Do those horses jump?"

Jeannette felt a brief panic, looking at Darren, seeing the look of excitement in his eyes. "Oh, no, Darren, don't try it. You've not jumped her before. Remember, your arm is just healing."

He remembered then, keeping Dani under control. In Southampton, riding was different than here in the country. He'd heard about the hunt, but had never seen horses jumping fences. He thought horses needed to be trained for it. But he was fascinated by this beautiful black-haired girl on her dapple-gray hunter, taking one jump after another. She was amazing.

"She really is quite a sight, isn't she?" Jeannette commented to her brother, as she watched him watching Rachel.

Darren reddened as he looked back at his sister. "That really does look like fun. Wouldn't you want to try it?"

Jeannette shook her head, laughing. "Not without a good teacher to start out with small jumps. I don't think our horses would know how to do that, or even us." Darren began to canter with Dani, so Jeannette followed him, content just to be with her brother, riding her horse.

After riding, the younger girls were talking and giggling as they put their horses away. Marielle and Nicole wanted the Montgomery girls to come back to the cottage with them. Marielle missed her friend Rachel, and hoped for some of the former companionship. Now Rachel surprised her by agreeing to come. Peggy was also happy her sister might want to join the other girls. So after getting permission, they were back at the cottage for dinner, with an already full house.

The dining room was the biggest room in the cottage. Good thing, especially when a crowd like this comes all at once. The Newalls and the Merlots were all on one side of the table; on the other side were the Duran children and the Montgomery girls. Jules was on one end of the table, and Teresa on the other.

Darren felt so relaxed after riding, much of the recent tension fell away, at least for the moment. His sister sitting next to him was comforting. After riding together, they were both more relaxed with each other. Darren looked directly across to meet eyes with Rachel Montgomery. *What a beauty!* He couldn't help but smile, which brought a smile from her. Her hair and eyes shone in the lantern light. In his mind, he could still see her flying over jumps on her gray horse, with that black hair flying.

"It was such fun to ride with all of you today." Jeannette spoke first.

Peggy was quick to answer, giggling, "I love riding. I've been hoping Rachel would want to ride."

Rachel looked directly at Darren, glancing briefly at Jeannette, "Those are nice horses you have; they could be great hunters."

Darren's eyes lit up. "You think so?"

Jeannette broke in, "But they've never been jumped before. They probable don't know how."

Rachel looked back at Darren, "They could be trained. It's probably in their blood." She looked at Jules. "Don't you think they could jump? You could train them."

Now Madam Newall broke in. "But we are traveling. We're going to Canada. Those horses are our team."

His mother's voice brought Darren back to reality. For a moment his imagination swept him away. Just for a moment he thought, *Rachel is more exciting than anyone I've ever known.*

As food was passed, and everyone began eating, conversation dwindled, but Darren's mind was still going, imagining flying over fences with Dani, with this fascinating girl riding next to him on her spirited dapple-gray.

Teresa and Marielle began carrying away the food. Jules said he was interested in hearing from God's Word and Antoine and Ellienne enthusiastically agreed. Jeannette also agreed and Madam Newall was nodding her head. Darren said nothing, glancing at Rachel just as she rolled her eyes. He thought of Roman Balansay expressing his doubts about his parents' new faith. Darren was quick to pick up on anyone who might be sympathetic with his view.

Madam Newall questioned her daughter, "What are you reading this evening?"

Jeannette glanced from the Durans to the Merlots. "I have an idea, but what do you think?"

Jules replied, "I'd like to hear more about this Abram fellow."

Jeannette laughed, "That's just what I was thinking. I think it's good to know about the beginnings." So she opened her Bible and began to read:

> "And he removed from thence unto a mountain on the east of Bethel, and pitched his tent, having Bethel on the west, and Hai on the east: and there he builded an altar unto the Lord, and called upon the name of the Lord.
> "And Abram journeyed, going on still toward the south.
>
> "And there was a famine in the land: and Abram went down to sojourn there; for the famine was grievous in the land.
> "And it came to pass, when he was come near to enter into Egypt, that he said unto Sarai his wife, Behold now, I know that thou art a fair woman to look upon:
> "There it shall come to pass, when the Egyptians shall see thee, that they shall say, This is his wife: and they will kill me, but they will save thee alive.
> "Say, I pray thee, thou art my sister: that it may be well with me for thy sake: and my soul shall live because of thee."
>
> "And it came to pass, that when Abram was come into Egypt, the Egyptians beheld the woman that she was very fair.
> "The princes also of Pharaoh saw her, and commended her before Pharaoh; and the woman was taken into Pharaoh's house.
>
> "And he entreated Abram well for her sake: and he had sheep, and oxen, and he asses, and menservants, and maidservants, and she asses, and camels.

"And the Lord plagued Pharaoh and his house with great plagues because of Sarai Abrams wife.

"And Pharaoh called Abram and said, What is this that thou has done unto me? Why didst thou not tell me that she was thy wife?

"Why saidist thou, She is my sister? So I might have taken her to me to wife: now therefore behold they wife, take her, and go thy way.

"And Pharaoh commanded his men concerning him: and they sent him away, and his wife, and all that he had." (Gen.12:8-20, KJV)

When Jeannette looked up from her reading she saw startled looks from some and anger flash in Rachel's eyes. Jules was indignant.

"What are we hearing here?" he asked. "The man threw his wife to the wolves!" Antoine and Ellienne both looked on in disbelief. Darren's expression was smug, as though he'd won some point.

Jeanette's mother just looked at her daughter, waiting for an explanation. Jeannette started in, "This is an interesting story with more than one lesson. Why don't we just think about it for a bit." She looked around, waiting for comments.

She started to explain, "There was a real threat. Men in power, in that culture, such as Pharaoh, had no problem taking beautiful women from others." She waited again.

Antoine was looking perplexed, "But how could he lie about his wife?" He looked unsure of himself, even offended.

Rachel and Peggy were both wide-eyed, waiting.

Jeannette started again, "Just because God called Abram, doesn't mean he was perfect. Just like us. We may be called by God, but we don't always do what's right. We all make mistakes, but God still looks after us."

Jules and Teresa suddenly looked at each other as if a light had just come on. "Oh," he began, "even though Abram acted like a dolt, God still protected them, and really protected Sarai."

Jeannette nodded, "That's good. Sarai was special. The family line all the way down to Jesus would come from her. God would not allow Pharaoh to defile her, no matter how badly Abram handled the situation."

HELENA POORTVLIET

Antoine then spoke up, "Maybe some of us are offended that we might ever do something like that, but we're all human. But God looks after us despite our shortcomings. Abram came out richer than ever."

Jeannette nodded and said, "Let me read a bit more. I think you'll see that to be the case."

> "And Abram went up out of Egypt, he, and his wife, and all that he had, and Lot with him, into the south.
> "And Abram was very rich in cattle, in silver, and gold.
> "And he went on his journeys from the south even to Bethel unto the place where his tent had been at the beginning, between Bethel and Hai;
> "Unto the place of the altar, which he had made there at the first; and there Abram called on the name of the Lord."
> (Gen. 13:1-4, KJV)

"See, Abram left Egypt a rich man, blessed of God. But I think he recognized where he'd gone wrong. He went back to the place where God directed him in the beginning. And there he worshipped God." Jeannette closed her Bible.

CHAPTER 12

Ship of Faith

"**S**O THIS IS the 'Black Horse of God'!"

Jacques turned around, startled, to find Ramon Claudel peering into the stall, where Jacques was brushing Tounerre. He was open-mouthed, his question still unspoken.

Claudel had a sly grin. "Oh, he is well-known, within certain circles, that is!"

Jacques was still speechless.

"Oh, yes," Claudel continued. "I wondered about your black horses, but when your friend Pierre started talking about our Jesus, I started to make the connection. When I brought up the 'Black Horse of God,' he told me it was your stallion."

Jacques finally regained his composure to ask, "Do you know the Romani?"

Claudel's laugh was hearty. "I was born Romani. My father was French, but my mother was Hispanic Rom. Her family fled to Morocco to escape the Spanish Inquisition of the Catholic Pope. My father came to Morocco with Napoleon's Legion. When we travel through foreign lands we always know we are welcome with the Romani. We are not always welcome with the English. I hope the future holds more promise in Canada. France is not a good place for foreigners now."

Jacques' mind was racing, connecting all he was hearing. "So you are a believer?"

"Oh, yes," Claudel laughed, "thanks to you and your stallion."

"How is that?" Jacques asked.

"They told me all about your little book. Then when your friend came to the camp on Sunday, he read to the people from the same little book. I could see that Gods' presence was there when the people worshipped. And it was what I was searching for all my life. And your friend gave me one of the little books." Claudel reached in his pocket to hold up the little book, which Jacques recognized.

Jacques was shaking his head, amazed at what he was hearing, but Claudel went on. "Your friend Pierre tells me you read from God's Word every night."

Jacques nodded. "Yes, we've been reading in the Book of Acts. Some of the things we are reading about sound just like what happened at the Romani camp."

"I pray you would allow me to join you when you read, if I may be so bold," Claudel implored.

Jacques remembered what Pierre said to him, the night before the storm, concerning talking to others about Jesus like the apostles were doing. He then realized Pierre had followed through, in talking to Claudel.

"Sure," he answered, "we usually read when we come back down here after dinner. The cabin's pretty small, but we could sit outside down here and read."

Claudel grinned enthusiastically, "Oh yes, that would be great!" Then he changed the subject. "I am so grateful for what the two of you did for my mare and her baby. They might not have lived, but for you and Pierre. Thank you!" And he extended his hand in a hearty handshake, before he turned to cross the aisle to his own horses.

Pierre spent the afternoon working in the galley and Harry was with Andrew and his mother, so Jacques spent the time walking horses around the area, taking advantage of the calm day. He just finished walking his own horses when Claudel appeared. Now Pierre was coming down the ramp with milk cans clanking and behind him were Roger and Andrew Breakfield with Harry, who was happy to arrive in time for the milking. Andrew was delighted to get to watch. Harry was now so skilled at milking he managed to milk just as many goats as Jacques. When they were done they had lots of help carrying the full cans back to the galley.

At dinner Jacques and Harry sat with the Breakfields, much to the delight of the two boys. Jacques felt good seeing Harry interacting with the other boy, thinking how happy and healthy he looked now, compared to the orphan he found on the streets of Birmingham. Harry had grown, gained weight, and looked much fuller-faced now. His hair, which Jacques at first thought was dull brown, now looked shiny reddish gold. He often showed Jacques more examples of his writing efforts, and now the boys were writing notes to each others.

After dinner Jacques headed back to the stable area with Harry. Once there, he dragged over some hay bales in front of his cabin, just as he saw Ramon Claudel coming down the ramp. Behind him was Pierre, followed by Deral McDonald and Dirk Mallory.

At Jacques look of surprise, Pierre explained. "I hope you don't mind; these guys wanted to hear you read. I'll translate, if that's okay with you."

Jacques laughed, "Oh, you were serious. You meant what you said."

"Of course, I was!"

So now there were five, six including Harry. Jacques got his Bible out of the cabin and began:

> "Now Peter and John went up together into the temple at the hour of prayer, being the ninth hour.
> "And a certain man lame from his mother's womb was carried, whom they laid daily at the gate of the temple which was called Beautiful, to ask alms of them that entered into the temple
> "Who seeing Peter and John about to go into the temple asked an alms.
> "And Peter, fastening his eyes upon him with John, said, Look at us.
> "And he gave heed unto them, expecting to receive something of them.
> "Then Peter said, Silver and gold have I none; but such as I have give I thee: In the name of Jesus of Nazareth rise up and walk.
> "And he took him by the right hand and lifted him up: and immediately his feet and ankle bones received strength.
> "And he leaping up stood, and walked and entered with them into the temple, walking and leaping and praising God.
> "And all the people saw him walking and praising God.
> "And they knew that it was he which sat for alms at the Beautiful gate of the temple: and they were filled with wonder and amazement at that which had happened unto him.

"And as the lame man which was healed held Peter and John, all the people ran together unto them in the porch that is called Solomon's, greatly wondering."
(Acts 3:1-11, KJV)

As Jacques paused often between verses to allow Pierre to translate, he watched the expressions of the other men. Ramon Claudel had a jovial, joyous expression, nodding and agreeing as he heard the Word. As Pierre translated to the young sailors, they sat wide-eyed, listening, fascinated. They both had questions about the healing, and Pierre was quick to assure them this was not the first example. They looked amazed, but urged him to go on. Now Harry, who normally fell asleep when Jacques began to read, was listening intently to Pierre's English translation.

Jacques read on:

"And when Peter saw it, he answered unto the people, Ye men of Israel, why marvel ye at this? or look ye so earnestly on us, as though by our own power or holiness we had made this man walk?
"The God of Abraham, and of Isaac, and of Jacob, the God of our fathers, hath glorified his Son Jesus; whom ye delivered up, and denied him in the presence of Pilate, when he was determined to let him go.
"But ye denied the Holy One and the Just, and desired a murderer to be granted unto you:
"And killed the Prince of Life whom God hath raised from the dead, whereof we are witnesses.
"And his name through faith in his name hath made this man strong, whom ye see and know: yea, the faith which is by him hath given him this perfect soundness in the presence of us all.
"And now, brethren, I wot that through ignorance ye did it, as did also your rulers.
"But those things, which God before had shewed by the mouth of all his prophets that Christ should suffer, he hath so fulfilled. (Acts 3:12-18, KJV)

Again, as Pierre translated, Jacques watched the faces around him. Claudel was obviously enjoying what he was hearing. To the two wide-eyed sailors he exclaimed, "It is so good to hear how God's Spirit is guiding the apostles. We can see Jesus is alive and still with them."

Deral McDonald looked at him, amazed, "Then you believe all this?"

Claudel grinned back, "But of course! Can't you tell? His Spirit is here with us as well!"

Jacques noticed Harry was wide awake, listening to all that was said. He looked at Jacques, and said quietly, "Jesus is here," and he put both hands on his chest.

Jacques mouth dropped open, "What do you mean, son?"

Harry repeated, "Jesus is here; He's here." He was still holding both hands to his chest.

Claudel laughed joyously. "That's the best profession of faith I've ever heard! Why should we make it more complicated than that?!"

Pierre looked at the two sailors. "What about you two guys? Do you believe Jesus died for you?"

Deral answered, "I want to believe. There's something going on here I've not seen before."

Pierre explained more to Deral and Dirk about Jesus dying on the cross for our sins and being raised from the dead. Deral melted, agreeing with everything Pierre told him. Dirk was a little more doubtful, not quite ready to accept what he heard. But he was interested in hearing more, so Jacques agreed to read on:

> "Repent ye therefore, and be converted, that your sins be blotted out when the times of refreshing shall come from the presence of the Lord:
> "And he shall send Jesus Christ, which before was preached unto you:
> "Whom the heaven must receive until the times of restitution of all things, which God hath spoken by the mouth of all his holy prophets since the world began.
> "For Moses truly said unto the fathers, A prophet shall the Lord your God raise up unto you of your brethren, like unto me: him shall ye hear in all things whatsoever he shall say unto you.
> "And it shall come to pass, that every soul which will not hear the prophet, shall be destroyed from among the people.

HELENA POORTVLIET

"Yea, and all the prophets from Samuel and those that follow after, as many as have spoken, have likewise told of these days.

"Ye are the children of the prophets, and of the covenant which God made with our fathers, saying unto Abraham, And in thy seed shall all the kindreds of the earth be blessed.

"Unto you first God, having raised up his Son Jesus, sent him to bless you, in turning away every one of you from his iniquities." (Acts 3:19-26, KJV)

As Jacques looked up for the last time to allow Pierre to translate, he saw a big difference in Dirk's demeanor. The resistance was gone. His hands were raised in acceptance of what he was hearing. Ramon's hands were raised, praying in the heavenly language. Jacques felt overwhelmed as he remembered those meetings at the Romani camp, and found himself wiping away tears.

Patricia and Willis Caldwell came into the dining room and hesitated, looking around. Andrea Breakfield looked up and met her eye. Andrea had an engaging smile that could set anyone at ease. She waved to the Caldwells in invitation, while moving over to make room. Andrea was quick to ask questions meant to draw out conversation. Roger smiled at Willis, his usual jovial smile. With them also were their children Andrew and Julia.

Jacques and Pierre delivered the fresh milk to the galley, then headed for the dining room. Harry was jumping up and down, urging them to hurry. When he saw Andrew with his parents, he happily ran to join him. Jacques hesitated, but Andrea gave him that same engaging smile and waved him over, so all three went over to their table.

Willis Caldwell got up to offer his hand to Jacques with a cheerful greeting. Andrea greeted Harry with questions about his activities on the horse deck. Jacques could see that Harry liked her, and saw that he chattered back easily with her. Patricia Caldwell watched all this quietly. The conversation was lively around the table, and Jacques realized that much of the English was getting easier for him to understand.

After sitting quietly for a while, Patricia spoke up, looking at Jacques. "How is it you can take someone else's child off the street and transport him on a ship to another country?"

There was a moment of shocked silence around the table. Jacques understood some of what she said, but not all. But there was no confusing her accusing tone. He felt a moment of panic, before Pierre cut in. Pierre understood clearly her accusation.

"If Jacques hadn't found Harry, he probably would not have lived another night. It was freezing and the boy hadn't eaten in days, and he was in rags with no coat. His mother was dead. I was there with him. Jacques wanted to find if he had relatives. There are hundreds of children like him on the streets of Birmingham, and they die every day—especially in the winter."

He paused for a moment, and Patricia started to speak, but her husband interrupted. "Trish, I told you to leave them alone. It's not your business."

Patricia argued back, "I don't believe that. He's not a street urchin. Who are these men, anyway? It's only their story!"

"Trish!" Willis exclaimed.

Now Harry looked frightened, moving closer to Jacques, who was too shocked and confused with the English to reply, but Pierre was his champion.

"That boy was starving, in rags and covered with bruises when Jacques found him. It was so cold, he wouldn't have lasted the night. Jacques wrapped him in a blanket he was so cold, then took him to get him some food, and me too. We were both in a bad place if it wasn't for Jacques!

"He tried to find out where he lived. Harry told us his mother died in an alley. Jacques took in both of us. He bought Harry new clothes, shoes and coat and hat. And fed him. And when some men snatched Harry, Jacques was devastated. He gave up his stallion to get him back."

Pierre was out of breath.

Patricia was not done yet. "How can you take care of a child? He needs a family!"

She was looking directly at Jacques, trying to ignore Pierre. "You can't even speak English!"

Jacques was getting up to leave, but Harry was hanging tightly to his arm. Willis was already pulling Patricia away from the table, as he looked back at Jacques, saying, "Sorry!" As Willis escorted his wife out of the dining room, Andrea reached out to Jacques and Harry. "I'm so sorry; I didn't know she would do that." She looked imploringly at Jacques. "We know you just want the best for Harry. Please stay and have breakfast with us."

As Jacques and Harry sat down again, Pierre still stood up as if he was standing guard over them. Roger sat back down, looking at Jacques, "So that's the story. It's a good thing you have a witness. And it's pretty clear you've done the best you can for him. But let me make a suggestion. My partner in Montreal has an excellent solicitor. When we get to Montreal, if you want, we'll go see him and he can make the adoption official. And we'll vouch for you." He looked at his wife, and she nodded, agreeing with him."

Then she added, "And maybe you'll name us as his godparents— if you want to, that is!" She looked hopeful. "We really like him, but it's clear he's your boy."

Pierre was nodding in agreement, but still looking defensive.

Jacques was aware of the time, and felt he had to get back to his chores. Andrea suggested Harry stay with them, but he was still clinging to Jacques' arm.

When they got back to the horse deck, Harry ran to Tounerre's stall, squeezing through the rails, and reached for the stallions head which was lowered to accommodate him. He wrapped his arms around the stallions head. When Jacques reached him, he asked to be boosted up on the stallion's back, which was done.

Jacques got a fork and began cleaning the stallions stall. Harry was content to stay on Tounerre's back while Jacques worked. When he was done, he started down the line, cleaning his mares' stalls before going on to the others. As he went on, he noticed Ramon was across the aisle, cleaning his own horses' stalls. Pierre started at the other end with the Godolphin thoroughbreds. About the time they reached each other, they saw Claudel opening the gate of the mare's stall. He had a halter on the filly and guided her out of the stall.

The filly showed some resistance, but Claudel used both strength and gentle encouragement to show her what to do. By now, Harry managed to slide off Tounerre's back and came out of the stall when he saw the tiny horse baby, but still refrained from going close to her.

Claudel worked with the filly for only a few moments before he put her back with her mother. Now Harry went over to look in the stall at the filly. Claudel greeted him with a wide grin, "God is good to give us such calm seas to keep our horses calm. Isn't it good to know God cares so much for us?"

Harry's face brightened with the recollection of the feelings he experienced the previous night. This morning he felt fearful of that woman's words. Now he remembered last night he felt the assurance Jesus was with him. He was comfortable with this jovial man who seemed to understand about Jesus.

By now Jacques and Pierre both arrived to look at the filly. Claudel greeted them, "God is good, my brothers!"

Jacques thought to himself, *What a difference. This man made him feel so comfortable.*

Harry was next to him, hanging on to his arm.

"So you're halter-breaking already!"

"Oh, yes, she will have to grow up fast once we are off this ship," Claudel answered. "It was so good to have fellowship in the Word. Would it be imposing if we did it again?"

Jacques felt amazed he should ask. "Oh, no, it is better to have more believers involved. Pierre has been saying we should have more people hearing God's Word."

"Oh, yes, it has such an affect on people!" Claudel agreed.

Jacques wanted to spend time walking horses so he and Pierre took out two of the Shire mares to walk around the horse deck. They were quite docile and seemed to enjoy the activity. At last, he took the Shire stallion out to walk, finding him to be just as docile as his own stallion.

The time passed quickly as he kept busy and only realized how late it was when Deral appeared with milk cans and pails clanking. Harry was excited to begin milking the goats. As they began, they realized again they had company. Roger Breakfield appeared with his son Andrew.

"Andrew missed having Harry to spend the day with. So he wanted to come down," Roger explained.

"Oh, that's okay," Jacques answered, "You can come down anytime." Jacques was surprised it was so easy to talk to Roger, understanding more of his English.

"Your friend Pierre told us you read from the Bible after dinner and several people have been coming. Sometimes we hear Harry talking about Jesus to Andrew. I think Andrea misses going to church. Would you mind if we join you?"

Jacques felt surprised he could understand almost everything Roger said. He answered, smiling, "Oh, yes, feel welcome!"

Dinner was uneventful. Jacques did not see either of the Caldwells, even though he felt apprehensive after the confrontation at breakfast. He noticed Captain Palmer came out and walked around the dining room, saying a few words to almost everybody before taking his plate back to his own cabin.

When Jacques and Pierre went back down to the horse deck, they pulled out more hay bails out to the area in front of the little cabin. Deral McDonald appeared with two other young sailors who were looking apprehensive, but curious. Ramon Claudel came down the ramp with all of the Breakfield family, smiling and talking, including his attention to both Andrew and Julia. Harry was jumping up and down with excitement at seeing Andrew.

Jacques got his Bible out of the cabin and sat down on a hay bale, motioning Harry to sit down next to him. Every one settled down, expectantly, waiting as he began.

> "And as they spake unto the people, the priests and the
> captain of the temple, and the Sadducees, came upon them,
> "Being grieved that they taught the people and preached
> through Jesus the resurrection of the dead,
> "And they laid hands on them, and put them in hold unto
> the next day: for it was now eventide.
> "Howbeit many of them which heard the word believed;
> and the number of the men was about five thousand." (Acts
> 4:2-4, KJV)

Jacques stopped to allow Pierre to translate, looking around at the listeners. When he heard Pierre say "five thousand," someone else repeated it and there were some looks of astonishment. He went on:

"And it came to pass on the morrow, that their rulers, and elders, and scribes, and Annas the high priest, and Caiaphas, and John, and Alexander, and as many as were of the kindred of the high priest, were gathered together at Jerusalem.

"And when they had set them in the midst, they asked, By what power, or by what name have ye done this?

"Then Peter, filled with the Holy Ghost, said unto them, Ye rulers of the people, and elders of Israel,

"If we this day be examined of the deed done to the impotent man, by what means is he made whole;

"Be it known unto you all, and to all the people of Israel, that by the name of Jesus Christ of Nazareth, whom ye crucified, whom God raised from the dead, even by him doth this man stand before you whole.

"This was the stone that was set at naught by you builders, which is become the head of the corner.

"Neither is there salvation in any other; for there is none other name under heaven given among men, whereby we must be saved." (Acts 4:5-12, KJV)

Jacques paused after each verse to allow Pierre to translate, but after this last verse, Claudel began to clap and as others looked at him in surprise, several others began to clap. Jacques looked over to see Andrea Breakfield with her hands in the air and her eyes closed. The two young sailors were looking around at the reaction of the others, with looks of amazement. Pierre looked back at Jacques expectantly, so he went on:

"Now when they saw the boldness of Peter and John, and perceived that they were unlearned and ignorant men, they marveled; and they took knowledge of them that they had been with Jesus.

"And beholding the man which was healed standing with them, they could say nothing against it.

"But when they commanded them to go aside out of the council, they conferred among themselves,

"Saying, What shall we do to these men" For that indeed a notable miracle hath been done by them is manifest to all them that dwell in Jerusalem, and we cannot deny it.

"But that it spread no further among the people, let us straitly threaten them, that they speak hence forth to no man in this name.

"And they called them and commanded them not to speak at all nor teach in the name of Jesus.

"But Peter and John answered and said unto them, Whether it be right in the sight of God to hearken unto you more than unto God, judge ye,

"For we cannot but speak the things which we have seen and heard.

"So when they had further threatened them, they let them go, finding nothing how might they punish them, because of the people, for all men glorified God for that which was done." (Acts 4:13-21, KJV)

Again Jacques watched the others as Pierre finished translating this last verse. Pierre looked at the two sailors with a questioning look. One shrugged, while the other just said, "Read more."

Jacques looked over at Roger and caught his nod, "Yes, read more." Andrea had a heavenly expression, with her hands raised, praying. Jacques began to read again:

"For the man was above forty years old, on whom this miracle of healing was shewed.

"And being let go, they went to their own company, and reported all that the chief priests and elders had said unto them.

"And when they heard that, they lifted up their voice to God with one accord, and said, Lord, thou art God, which hath made heaven and earth, and the sea, and all that in them is:

"Who by the mouth of thy servant David hast said, Why did the heathen rage, and the people imagine vain things?

"The kings of the earth stood up and the rulers were gathered together against the Lord, and against his Christ.

"For a truth against thy holy child Jesus, whom thou has anointed, both Herod and Pontius Pilate, with the Gentiles, and the people of Israel, were gathered together.

"For to do whatsoever thy hand and thy counsel determined before to be done,

"And now, Lord, behold their threatenings; and grant unto thy servants, that with all boldness they may speak thy word.

"And by stretching forth thine hand to heal; and that signs and wonders may be done by the name of thy holy child Jesus." (Acts 4:22-30, KJV)

Jacques was amazed to realize he had read the last two verses very loudly, almost shouting, as if the Holy Spirit was speaking through him. He was even more amazed to hear Pierre translate in the same loud tone as if someone else was in control of his voice. He looked around at the others. Roger had his arm around his wife and the other arm raised. Ramon Claudel had his arms raised, praying. Pierre walked over to talk to the two sailors, and Jacques soon saw him praying with them.

Harry looked up at Jacques to say, "Jesus is here!" as he patted both hands on his chest. Andrew was next to Harry saying the same thing, also with his hands on his chest. Then Jacques felt a great wind rushing through the horse deck, and for a few moments the ship began to rock as if a storm was starting up, but then settled back done to the normal rocking motion. Everyone looked around at each other in wonder.

Captain Ernest Palmer noticed calm dominated most of the voyage so far, producing just enough wind to fill the sails, keeping the ship moving on course toward its destination. This was one of the easiest trips he experienced in years. He was almost afraid to think about it for fear that calamity was imminent. *The calm before the storm,* he thought. He was pleased with his crew; even the new members seemed to be good workers. He had a full cargo which promised to be profitable. He made a big gamble refusing steerage passengers, depending instead on horse cargo and cabin passengers. The hold was full of inanimate cargo which was well anticipated in the markets of Montreal and Quebec.

Those two young Frenchmen were zealous in their care of the horses, their actions even heroic in that storm. What luck to have them! Palmer turned from the rail and started toward his cabin.

"Captain Palmer," began the voice behind him. "I want you to arrest that man!" He turned to recognize Mrs. Caldwell.

"Arrest what man," he asked her, gruffly, "and for what reason?"

"That Frenchman," she answered, indignantly, "for kidnap!"

Palmer looked at her incredulously, perceiving she was serious. "Perhaps you should come to my cabin and explain to me what you're talking about."

"What do you mean—go to your cabin?" She sounded even more indignant.

"Oh, lady, go get your husband if you're afraid of me. But I think we need to talk about this," he said impatiently, as he started to walk away.

Patricia Caldwell followed him.

He opened the door, waiting as she reluctantly entered. He pointed to a chair in front of the desk, then sat down on the chair behind the desk.

"Now what is this all about?"

"That Frenchman kidnapped that child off the street and is taking him to Canada. You can't just take someone else's child!" Palmer detected an indignant, self-righteous tone to the accusation.

"Well, Mrs. Caldwell, just how much do you know about the situation?" Palmer raised one eyebrow, waiting for the explanation.

"Well, he says he found the boy on the street in Birmingham. But that boy is not a street urchin. He's somebody's son!"

"Mrs. Caldwell, how long have you been married?"

She looked startled at the question. "Almost two years now. What's that got to do with anything?" Her tone was even more indignant.

Palmer pressed on, "And no babies yet?"

Patricia's mouth dropped. "How is that any of your business?"

Palmer went on, "You and your husband drove all the way from Kent County to Liverpool. Hundreds of orphans on the streets of Birmingham and Liverpool and every other city between here and Kent County, many of them dying every day, and you never saw any of them on your way to Liverpool?" He waited for her response.

"Well, I suppose we saw the street urchins," she said slowly.

"You never thought of helping or feeding any of them?"

Patricia felt uncomfortable, and defensive. "Well, those aren't my children!"

"Well, whose children are they?"

She was afraid to say any more.

"Little Harry doesn't look like a street urchin because he's clean and well-fed and has new clothes. Give the man credit for taking care of him."

Patricia was silent.

Palmer continued, "In the last five, six years, thousands of starving Irish families traveled by steerage to Quebec City and Montreal to escape starvation on potato farms of Ireland. Many of the babies died enroute, and even worse, parents died enroute. The streets of Montreal are crowded with homeless children. Can't you leave a good thing alone? If it's a child you want, find your own orphan. You'll have plenty of opportunity in Montreal."

Now Patricia sat speechless with tears running down her cheeks. Palmer pulled out his handkerchief and offered it to her as he walked over to open the door. He watched from the door of his cabin as she walked away toward her cabin. Just as he was thinking to himself of the emotional storm he just witnessed, a sudden wind came up, rocking the ship so hard he hung onto his cabin door to steady himself. The rocking lasted only a few moments and was gone as quickly as it came. Palmer walked toward the ramp down to the horse deck, thinking he heard singing. As he started down the ramp, he saw the group with hands raised, singing and praising God. The child, Harry, was holding tightly to Jacques' arm. The whole Breakfield family was there with their children. And there were others, all men, and even some of his sailors. *Well, I'll be*—he thought to himself. *Just what we need on this—ship of faith!*

CHAPTER 13

Lessons

RACHEL WAS LYING in bed next to Marielle who was sound asleep. Her sister Peggy was across the room, sharing Nicole's bed. It was very quiet. Rachel had too much on her mind to sleep. Her mother's event—she knew it was her mother's way to get her married off to a prince or somebody of higher status than she knew now. Everyone was excited except her. She dreaded the thought. *And these people all just talked about the Bible now. Except that boy Darren. He didn't seem to agree with all that.*

The more she thought, the more restless she felt. She was afraid if she moved she would wake up Marielle. She carefully slipped out of bed, changed into her riding skirt and boots and coat and quietly slipped out the door. She was so restless she could not bear to stay in the house with all these people. She thought she would feel better to be with her horse.

Darren lay awake in the room with Simon and Andre Duran. He liked Simon, who seemed pretty smart, but the younger brother followed them everywhere like hero-worship. He thought, *it would be easy to be in this family. Jules reminds me of Father.* At that thought he felt that all too familiar stab of pain. *But they're all so religious. I don't get it.* Then he thought of that girl Rachel. *She's a beauty. And she sure knows horses. Watching her riding is like a dream.* He could imagine riding with her on and on endlessly. He was smitten. He kept thinking of her talking about training Dani to be a hunter. But then his mother's words came back to him. Yes, they were traveling. The horses were their team. But yet—that picture was in his mind—*flying over fences, side-by-side with Rachel.*

The sky was clear and the moon full as Rachel walked toward the barn. She did not need a lantern in the moonlight. Slipping through the small side door without opening the large door, skylights in the loft allowed the moonlight to light her way to Misty's stall. She noticed the two bay mares of the visitors in the next two stalls. *What a shame,* she thought, *those horses should be hunters, not "cart horses."* In Rachel's world they would be hunters. She did not see much beyond her world. And she was not looking forward to her mother's event. *But the prince was coming!* Rachel wanted to run— literally! *Peggy's so excited. Let her marry the prince!*

Misty welcomed her with his usual horsey noise. She picked up a brush as she entered the stall. She was greeted with an affectionate head rubbing as she began to groom the gray, comforting both of them. Time stood still and other events faded as horse and girl enjoyed each other.

As Darren slipped outside he was awed by the clear sky and full moon. The early March air was unseasonably balmy, yet still chilly as a result of the clear sky. It felt warm to Darren, to what the winter had been. Tension lifted as Darren felt free of the pressure of so many people in that house. He was perplexed at the mixture of the people. *The two daughters of Lord and Lady Montgomery staying with the stable help—and those Gypsies! Confusing! Rachel and Peggy don't seem so high minded. Rachel even seems to admire my horse.*

As Darren approached the barn, he noticed the small door to the side of the large door was ajar, so he entered, apprehensively, feeling as though someone else was in the barn. As he headed for Dani's stall, he could see a shadow moving in the adjoining stall, which he knew held Rachel's gray, so he approached carefully, unsure what to expect, before he realized someone was brushing the horse, so he was not surprised it was Rachel. As he approached quietly, she was startled, dropping the brush and crying out.

"It's just me," he said quickly, "I didn't mean to scare you." He felt self-conscious, surprised to see her in the stall. "I just couldn't sleep with all those people." As he stood facing Rachel, Dani put her head over the stall door to reach for him. He rubbed the mare's head, but continued to face the girl. "What are you doing out here?"

"I couldn't sleep. I was afraid I would wake up the other girls. It's a good thing it's not so cold out, like it was." She looked down, feeling

HELENA POORTVLIET

nervous, alone with Darren. She liked him; he seemed to agree with her a lot. *He doesn't seem as religious as those other people.*

"I saw you roll your eyes when everyone started reading and talking about God. Don't you believe all that?"

She looked around, shaking her head. "I just don't get it. That Frenchman was here a few weeks ago, reading that stuff. They all fell for it, even my sister. But I just don't get it. I think it's foolishness. Peggy talks about Jesus all the time, driving everyone crazy." Rachel paused, feeling a little embarrassed. Thinking about her mother's event, she said no more.

Darren spoke up, feeling more relaxed now. "I know what you mean. My mother and sister are like that, and now those Gypsies are the same way."

Rachel responded, "And you're going to Canada with all of them. You're not like them at all."

"Well, you're lucky then, if it's just your sister."

Not so lucky, Rachel reflected on her mother's event, which she dreaded more than her sister's religious opinions. She looked down, saying nothing.

"It's something more, isn't it?" Darren prodded. "What else is troubling you?"

"You wouldn't understand."

"Maybe I wouldn't, but maybe I could listen."

"You're a man, though. You just don't get it. Women have no choices." She blurted it out, angry and frustrated.

Darren looked surprised. "Your parents are rich and important. Can't you have about anything you want?"

She looked indignant. "You just don't get it! I've got no choices. It's all about my mother's plans. Father goes along with all of it. It's got nothing to do with what I want. My parents want to marry me off to the most important man who'll have me. I've got about as much choice as my father's favorite mare. She's planning a great ball. She's even inviting some of the princes. Some of the men who are invited are as old as my father." New Rachel felt embarrassed. She wished she hadn't said anything.

"Well, what do you want?" Darren asked.

"I don't want to get married!" she exclaimed. "I don't want things to change. I just want to ride my horse and go to the hunts. But girls never get to choose. There's always someone else to make the choices and tell us what to do."

"What if you could choose for yourself who you wanted to marry," Darren asked. He felt strange, talking to this girl about her issues. It seemed that for so long, everyone was talking about his problems.

Rachel thought to herself about some of the men she met. She was attracted to that Frenchman with the big black horses, until Jules told her he was engaged. Now, she knew it Darren's sister Jeannette. Then that Frenchman was reading about Jesus, and everyone was getting religious, including Rachel's sister Peggy. There was that other Frenchman, Pierre, a couple of years ago. He said his parents were close to the king, and she liked him, but her father got very angry and ran him off the property. But it was always someone else's choice.

Darren saw her eyes twinkle in the moonlight. "If I had to choose right now, I'd choose you," she smiled. His mouth dropped, then she laughed.

While he was still speechless, she explained, "It just seems like you're the only person I know who isn't religious, or trying to make my choices for me. And I can't fault your looks." Now she was giggling, and he began to laugh with her.

Darren's mind was spinning. This girl was even more beautiful in the dimly moonlit barn. His imagination was racing with thoughts of her. Nothing was logical. It was all a fantasy, more real than anything he had ever known. When he reached for her, she opened her arms to him.

Jules was accustomed to early rising most of his life and appreciated when others did the same. He was up before dawn to get the fire started in the big cookstove. The fire was not yet going when Antoine joined him.

"Good morning," was the cheery greeting from the latter.

"Ah—it's good to be up early! There is always so much to do!"

"Oh, yes," agreed Antoine. "At your service!"

"Well, our fire is about ready. Then we can get in some more wood." Jules looked around. "Well, where's our young friend?"

Antoine looked around. "I guess you mean Darren? He can be a bit reclusive?" It was stated almost like a question, followed by a shrug.

"Well, oh well," was the response, as the two men headed for the door.

Teresa came into the kitchen, rubbing her eyes. She was still tired, but happy to have all the company. She wished for more energy to deal with it, but happy to be with her friends. *It was so much fun to have all the young people together last night.* She was so worried since Jacques told them about the trouble with young Darren. Now she was glad to see that he appeared to be doing all right, even if he was a bit quiet. It did not escape her that he noticed Rachel Montgomery. *She did seem to attract attention.*

She was thankful Jules started the fire so the kitchen was warming up. She got a kettle of water going to start breakfast, then headed for the parlor for a quick check to be sure things were in order before everyone started getting up.

The girl curled up on the settee moved a little, but did not quite wake up. Teresa gave a little start. "Oh dear," she cried. Rachel jumped up, rubbing her eyes. Teresa said, "Oh, I didn't mean to wake you, but what are you doing here. Aren't you cold, my dear?"

"Oh, I'm sorry, I couldn't sleep, and I was afraid I'd wake the other girls. But I'm awake now. Can I help you with anything?"

"Oh, sure, honey. Come to the kitchen. I've got some hot water ready for tea. You can help me get breakfast started. I'm so sorry you couldn't sleep. We've quite a crowd here. I hope it's not too much for you."

Rachel followed Teresa to the kitchen. "Oh, I don't mind. It's really fun to be here with everyone. I really like your friends."

Teresa smiled at Rachel. "Well, you know you're always welcome here—you and Peggy both." Then she continued, "Now, I hear your mother is planning a big party. Are you excited?"

"Yes, yes, it's just wonderful!" Rachel gave her a wide smile.

Jules and Antoine had the great wood box next to the stove in the kitchen well filled. Then they headed for the barn. Once out of the house, Jules asked Antoine, "I guess young Darren doesn't like to get up early. Is he like that at home?"

"Well, he's had a lot of problems," Antoine grinned. "I think he's missing his father."

Both men were shaking their heads as they entered the barn. Horses were greeting them noisily as they headed for the lower hay storage where they found a horse blanket covering a lump on top of the stack of hay bales.

"Well, what is this?" Jules looked at Antoine as the blanket moved and Darren sat up, rubbing his eyes.

"What's going on here, young man?"

Darren shook his head. "I couldn't sleep and I didn't want to wake all those boys, so I came out here to be with my horse. Then I got sleepy, so I just lay down on the hay." He did not say anything about Rachel being in the barn. "I guess it's time to start feeding the horses. I can help with that."

The other two men just looked at each other and started piling hay in the carts, so Darren followed suit. No more questions were asked.

By the time the men got back to the house, everyone was up and breakfast was at hand. Marielle, Jeannette, and Rachel were all helping Teresa get everything on the table. Madam Newall and Ellienne were busy at the stove with the baking and cooking they were so accustomed to doing.

When Darren came in with the men and saw Rachel, he again was thinking, *she's the most beautiful, exciting person I've ever seen.*

When the travelers were with the Durans a little more than a week, Fidel Balansay arrived at the door. Elena and Roman were staying at the Romani camp near Birmingham. Fidel had ridden all the way to Liverpool to check on the arrival of the *Bucephalus.* The ship left Liverpool on the 20th of January. It was estimated to would arrive in Montreal the first week of March. It would leave Montreal after a week in port and arrive back in Liverpool late in April.

At hearing this news, Jeannette and her mother just looked at each other in despair.

"That's another six weeks," exclaimed Jeannette.

"Oh dear," Madam Newall looked anxiously at her friends.

Teresa immediately interjected, "Oh, you'll stay here; you're welcome here. We'll enjoy your visit."

Then Fidel said, "Our brothers at the camp near Birmingham are begging you to come and spend time with them teaching God's Word."

Jeannette's face lit up, "Oh, yes, that would be wonderful."

Darren, hearing this, felt chagrinned. *Another week with the Gypsies!*

The Montgomery girls were planning to ride in the arena this afternoon. Rachel wanted to work her horse in preparation for the hunt on Saturday. Darren looked forward to seeing her again. He could not stop thinking about taking Dani over jumps. It was becoming an obsession with him, but he said nothing about it. He was secretly happy their travel was delayed, because it would extend his time to be near Rachel.

When they all entered the arena on their horses, the jumps in the center lane all had their rails laying flat on the ground. Jules was walking in the center, waiting for them. He raised his arms to get everyone's attention. Then he called out Darren and Jeannette.

"I've been hearing the talk. Now if you're going to jump with a novice horse, you'll do it right. Then he waved to Peggy and Rachel to trot their horses over the rails. Then he waved to Darren.

"Now you do the same."

Darren took Dani at a trot over the series of rails. Dani trotted with her eyes down, looking at the rails. Jeannette followed on Katy with equal results.

"Good, good," Jules called out. "Okay, do it again." He looked at Rachel. "You first, again." Then he nodded to his own children, starting with Marielle, "Go ahead, keep it to a trot."

Darren and Jeannette went last. Jules clapped. "All right, not bad. Than wasn't hard, was it?" Then he went back and put the rails up on the lowest peg, crossing two rails in the center, with one end on the ground, so that it was only about 6" off the ground in the center where the rails crossed.

Then he nodded to the Montgomery girls. "Go ahead; keep it to a trot."

All of the riders followed, one at a time.

"Again, keep it to a trot."

Several times to follow, all doing the same, Darren and Jeannette both did fine, then Jules waved to Rachel and Peggy and his own children, to go ahead with the low jumps around the outside circle. He waved to Darren and Jeannette to come to him.

"All right, that's enough with the rails today. Take the clear lane and alternate between walk, trot, and canter. Keep each of them well collected at each gait. No mad running. Make sure you are the one who has control. We'll do a little more with the rails next time." Darren was so happy to have Jules coaching he was willing to do anything. He looked back at his sister, who was grinning broadly.

After the riding lesson, the Montgomery girls were invited to come back to the cottage for the evening. By now, news had gotten around that the visitors would be staying a few more weeks.

Dinner with all the company was even friendlier than before, since everyone was getting more acquainted. Fidel Balansay would be staying for the night. But he agreed to stay only if he were allowed to sleep in the barn, before returning to the camp the next day. On hearing that, there was a quick meeting of eyes between Rachel and Darren. Rachel was in high spirits because Jules was willing to coach Darren and Jeannette to jump their horses. She was also hopeful hearing about their extended visit, happy that she would have more time with Darren.

As dinner was ending, Jules and Teresa both expressed their hope of hearing Jeannette read from God's Word. Antoine and Ellienne quickly agreed they too looked forward to the reading. Fidel jovially expressed his agreement. Darren glanced at Rachel in time to see her roll her eyes, but Peggy was grinning excitedly.

Madame Newall asked her daughter, "What are you reading tonight, dear?"

Jeannette looked around. "Shall we continue with the story of Abram?" This brought general approval, so she went to get her Bible, and began to read:

> "And Abram went up out of Egypt, he, and his wife and all that he had, and Lot with him, into the south.
> "And Abram was very rich in cattle, in silver, and in gold.
> "And he went on his journeys from the south even to Bethel, unto the place where his tent had been at the beginning, between Bethel and Hai;
> "Unto the place of the altar, which he made there at the first: and there Abram called on the name of the Lord."
> (Gen. 13:1-4, KJV)

Jeannette paused to wait for comments. The first one came from Jules. "Well, it looks like he's right back where he started. But now he's richer, and he's paying attention to God."

"Yes. I think God would have provided for him, even if he had not gone to Egypt, but he didn't hold the mistakes against him." Jeannette gave her opinion, and then began again to read:

> "And Lot also, which went with Abram, had flocks and herds, and tents.
> "And the land was not able to bear them, that they might dwell together: for their substance was great, so that they could not dwell together.
> "And there was a strife between the herdsmen of Abram's cattle and the herdsmen of Lot's cattle: and the Canaanite and the Perizzite dwelled then in the land.
> "And Abram said to Lot, Let there be no strife, I pray thee, between me and thee, and between my herdsmen and thy herdsman; for we be brethren.
> "Is not the whole land before thee? separate thyself, I pray thee, from me: If thou wilt take the left hand, then I will go to the right; or if thou depart to the right hand, then I will go to the left.
> "And Lot lifted up his eyes, and beheld all the plains of Jordan, that it was well-watered everywhere, before the Lord destroyed Sodom and Gomorrah, even as the garden of the Lord, like the land of Egypt, as thou comest into Zoar."
> (Gen.13:5-10, KJV)

Jeannette looked around at the others, waiting for comments. Madam Newall looked at her two children. She hoped to keep the family together, but sensed a separation was coming. The story of Abram and Lot was like a prophecy to her. But she kept the thought to herself.

Antoine started to speak. "This lesson may be about separation." He was hesitant. Ellienne listened attentively as he continued, "Sometimes the present association is no longer appropriate. The Romani are my brothers and sisters, but it seems as though this is the time for us to move on." He looked at Madam Newall. "It wasn't easy for you to leave Southampton. Up till now, that was your life work." He hesitated, then added, "but it was time for you to break that connection and move on."

Darren and Rachel's eyes met. The same idea was coming to both.

Jeannette started with her explanation. "God told Abram to leave his country and his people. But Lot tagged along. I think Lot was holding Abram back, because Lot was not in God's will. But Abram loved Lot, and wanted to part on good terms." She waited for more comments before continuing:

> "Then Lot chose him all the plain of Jordan; and Lot journeyed east: and they separated themselves from one another.
> "Abram dwelled in the land of Canaan, and Lot dwelled in the cities of the plain, and pitched his tent toward Sodom.
> "But the men of Sodom were wicked and sinners before the Lord exceedingly." (Gen. 13:11-13, KJV)

Jeannette paused to comment on what she just read. "There's a difference between these two men. Any ideas?" She looked around. Peggy spoke up. "It looks to me like Abram was trying to do the right thing. But Lot was looking at the best land for himself. And he seemed to be interested in the people that were known to be wicked."

Teresa smiled at her. "That's good—very good observation. How would you apply that in your life." She was looking at Peggy, but then looked around at her own children.

Simon answered, "When it's time for us to separate and go on our own, it's not always about us. We need to be open to God's will and consider how the change affects everyone.

"That's good, Simon; I'm so glad to hear that." Teresa was beaming proudly as she looked back at Jeannette. Jeannette read on:

> "And the Lord said unto Abram after that Lot was separated from him, Lift up now thine eyes, and look from the place where thou art northward, and southward, and eastward, and westward:
> "For all the land which thou seest, to thee will I give it, and to thy seed forever.

"And I will make thy seed as the dust of the earth: so that if a man can number the dust of the earth, then shall thy seed also be numbered.

"Arise, walk through the land in the length of it and in the breadth of it; for I will give it unto thee.

"Then Abram removed his tent, and came and dwelt in the plain of Mamre, which is in Hebron, and built there an altar unto the Lord." (Gen. 13:14-18, KJV)

Jeannette looked around at the others. "It seems to me as soon as Abram let go of Lot, then God released to him his destiny. Can any of us see that as a lesson?" There were many looks exchanged, but no more comments. Jeannette closed her Bible.

Rachel and Peggy did not plan to stay over with the Durans, so Morton arrived shortly after Jeannette finished reading to walk back to the big house with the girls. Rachel was so excited about Jules' coaching, the Bible reading went quickly. But she thought about the lesson on separation. Her dissatisfaction with her own life choices had her thinking more about what she heard. She thought she understood Darren's thoughts when their glances met. *Were they really the soul-mates she was starting to think they were?*

"Well, what did you think of the reading?" Peggy's question broke into her thoughts."

"It was good," Rachel surprised her with the reply. "Something to think about."

"Oh, really?" The words came simultaneously from Peggy and Morton, both surprised.

When Simon and Andre heard Fidel would be spending the night in the barn, they decided that sounded like great fun, so they asked their father if they too could do so. They both looked to Darren for support. Darren was in a good mood, with all the excitement of learning to jump, so he agreed. Jules thought it would be okay, since Fidel would be out there with them. Then Darren thought, *Fidel is a Gypsy. He would be sleeping in a barn with a Gypsy? Well, Fidel is Roman's father, and Roman maybe isn't so bad.* So he went along.

Teresa found blankets and pillows to take to the barn, fussing with her need to be sure all the boys (and men) were comfortable.

She tried to apologize to Fidel for the boys, hoping he did not mind. He laughed, obvious that he enjoyed the boys.

Once settled, Andre asked Fidel, "Are you really a Gypsy?" Simon was embarrassed. "Andre!"

Fidel laughed, "Oh, that's okay. That's what most of the English called us for years, because they first thought we came from Egypt. But we are Romani. Our ancestors came from India many generations ago. But our people have lived in many countries and intermarried with many people in all those countries. For instance, my father came from Eastern Europe, in the Tyrol Mountains, but he met my mother in Spain. I was born in England and my wife Elena was born in England. I've been in England all my life, but heard many stories about my parents' travels."

Simon and Andre were wide-eyed listening to Fidel. Darren began to think he was a bit interesting. He knew Roman felt very close to his father, which made Darren feel envious.

Simon wanted to ask more questions but felt embarrassed, but his younger brother did not hesitate. "I heard people say that Gypsies steal horses."

"Andre!" Simon was really embarrassed now. Darren tried to refrain from laughing.

Fidel laughed the loudest. "I've heard that too!" he exclaimed, still laughing. "I don't know of any that steal horses, and I never have, but that doesn't mean that nobody ever has." Fidel had a broad grin and a twinkle in his eye. "But I suppose there may also be Englishmen who steal horses." Darren thought to himself about Dani being stolen, and later found at the Gypsy camp. They told him Jacques had gotten her back. Then, later, he knew Fidel and Roman helped rescue their horses when their stable burned. Maybe they weren't so bad after all."

HELENA POORTVLIET

CHAPTER 14

St. Elmo

A S SOON AS Jacques awoke he was aware something was different. The movement of the ship was rough and irregular, but not really a storm. He knew work had to be done quickly, so he was out of his bunk and into his clothes. Harry and Pierre caught on to the urgency of his mood and were up almost as quickly. As soon as they fed the horses, they started cleaning stalls, just finishing when Deral arrived with the milk cans. Everyone seemed to be anxious to act while they could. Jacques did not have to tell Harry what to do. He got right to the milking while Pierre was still disposing of the soiled refuse from the stalls. They worked quickly with the willing cooperation of the goats. The three were ready to carry the fresh milk to the galley, leaving behind the animals eagerly eating. As they carried the milk up the ramp to the main deck, they shifted their balance constantly to compensate for the heavy motion of the ship.

Leon McKay greeted them with relieved approval at the arrival of the milk. "It looks like we're in for some rough seas, so the earlier we get everyone fed the better. We may not have another opportunity for a while. Go ahead and get your food now, while you still can!"

The three headed for the dining room to find the Breakfields and the Caldwells together. Both Roger and Willis stood up to greet them. Andrea greeted them enthusiastically, especially Harry, who was happy to see Andrew. Patricia smiled at them, but remained quiet.

There was excited anticipation with the rough seas, but not a great amount of fear. Roger commented, "This could be a good thing, if it gets us to Montreal faster." Andrea gave him a disbelieving look, as she turned to Jacques.

"You may have your hands full with the horses today. Harry's welcome to stay with us. He'll be safe in the cabin with us." She was grinning at Jacques, waiting for an answer.

Jacques looked at Harry. "What about it, son? Do you want to stay with Andrew today?"

Harry was exuberant, showing his excitement to be with Andrew.

Jacques got face-to-face with Harry. "Okay, if you stay with Andrew and his mother today, will you do everything they say and stay in the cabin with them?"

Harry looked back at him and nodded, "Yes, sir!"

"I don't want him to come looking for me and be out on the deck alone," Jacques explained to Roger and Andrea, as he remembered the fear he felt when he could not find Harry after the last storm. They both nodded in agreement.

After breakfast, Jacques and Pierre headed back for the horse deck. Jacques hoped to get some of the horses walked before it got any rougher. The Breakfields' coach horses had not been worked for several days and they seemed the most skittish, so he started with them first, two at a time with Pierre's help. The walking helped to calm them, so he hoped they wouldn't be too fearful as the motion increased. Jacques was glad to see Ramon coming down to walk his stallion.

They put the last of the Breakfields' geldings back in their stalls and were taking the Caldwells' two Suffolk geldings out. He left them for last knowing they were very docile. While they were walking the two, the motion of the ship began to increase and Jacques was amused at the horses' response. They seemed to crouch somewhat as they walked to keep their balance, but did not seem to show much fear. While they were walking, Jacques became aware of two visitors coming down the ramp, Roger and Willis, who was surprised to see them walking his horses. Jacques explained.

"I try to walk each horse at least every few days as much as possible. It helps to keep them calm, especially if the sea is rough."

Roger added, "Jacques takes his job seriously. He really cares about the horses."

Willis looked a little guilty. "Maybe I should be coming down and walking them."

"Well, you could, if you want," Jacques answered, "and then I could work more with the others."

"All right, I will," Willis answered.

The motion of the ship was getting stronger, so they put the two horses back in their stalls. Jacques explained to the other men about how the swing partition worked. "But we won't use it unless it gets much worse than it is now. I'd rather they have room to move around most of the time." The men nodded their understanding.

Harry and Andrew were happy to anticipate their day together, and were in high spirits on their way to the Breakfields' cabin, giggling as they staggered with the motion of the ship. Andrew's sister, Julia, rolled her eyes at the boys' antics. She was more fearful of the rough seas, fearing a worse calamity, with little patience for the boys' behavior. When they got to the cabin, Andrea got out books and writing tablets, hoping to keep the children occupied with learning projects. They barely started when there was a knock on the door.

It was the Caldwells. Roger greeted them, "Come in, come in!"

"We hope you don't mind the intrusion," Willis began. "I was thinking of going down and checking on our horses, and I didn't want to leave Patricia alone."

Andrea smiled as she reached out to Patricia, "Oh, you're welcome here."

Patricia looked apprehensive, but began to warm up to Andrea's compassionate welcome.

Roger reached for his coat, saying, "That's a good idea; I'll go with you." Then he turned to the boys. "You boys stay here in the cabin and keep the door closed." He looked at his own children. "Do whatever your mother says." Then he looked at Harry. "Remember what your father told you. Stay here with Andrew, and don't go outside."

Harry nodded, "Okay, I will."

The three children were seated together, with books in front of them. But the atmosphere was charged; they just looked at each other. Harry was aware of Patricia in the room and was uneasy, filled with foreboding, fearful of what she would say at any time. *But he had promised he would not leave the cabin.*

Andrea led Patricia to the settee and directed her to sit down. Then she turned to face the children. "I want you to practice writing from the book, starting were we left off last time." Then she stooped down to face Harry. "Don't worry, everything will be okay. You're safe here."

She turned back to Patricia. "I have a feeling this hasn't been a happy trip for you. Do you want to talk about it?"

Patricia looked around, evasively. "I don't know what there is to talk about. If we make it to Montreal, we shall go to Canada West to build our home and raise our family. Our future is promising."

Andrea faced her. "But you're not happy."

Patricia looked to one side, then to the other, then down. "You don't know what it's like. You have two beautiful children. And you could have that one too." Her head jerked toward Harry.

Andrea moved closer and took Patricia's hands. "We love Harry, and he can stay here whenever he wants, but he is Jacques' boy, just as if he was his natural son. The boy needed his help and Jacques was there for him. There's a bond there as strong as a blood tie. But that's not really the issue, is it? You're afraid you won't have children aren't you?"

Patricia could not hold back the tears any longer. When she started to shake and sob, Andrea moved closer and embraced her. "That's it, you just have to cry about it sometime," Andrea consoled her. After a moment, she asked, "What about Willis? Is he okay with it?"

"He's just mad because I asked about Harry." She was sniffling.

"Well, you did more than just ask about him. You accused Jacques of kidnapping him. You don't really believe that, do you?"

"But he doesn't look like a street urchin!"

"Of course, he doesn't. Jacques takes good care of him. But look, he's just now learning to read. Jacques is letting me teach him. Now do you believe us?"

"Well, maybe I was wrong."

"That's a hard thing to say! But what do you think you should do about it?" Andrea felt compassion for her.

"Well, Captain Palmer says there are a lot of orphans in Montreal. But I don't know. It's not like having your own baby. Those street urchins look so rough. They're scary."

"Does Harry look scary?" Andrea asked.

"No, but that's different," Patricia protested.

"Well, how is it different? He's only been with Jacques for a few weeks. Do you think maybe some of those children seem scary because they're so scared themselves?"

"I'm starting to see what you mean."

Andrea reached out to embrace Patricia again. "I think you're able to resolve this. Sometimes we have to recognize the good things we know. Harry is a lucky boy, and I think he's good for Jacques, too. Now, your Willis seems awfully nice. Am I wrong?"

"No, he's a good man."

All the time they were talking the rocking motion was steady, but it seemed to be increasing now. The children were looking around, not really interested in their books. Andrea moved over closer to reassure them.

The action of the sea continued to increase throughout the day. The horses were getting more restless, but the biggest protest came from the Godolphin thoroughbreds, especially the yearling colt, early in the afternoon Jacques decided to close them in the swinging partitions, tying them close to their feed boxes. As soon as he accomplished that, he did the same for the Breakfields' coach horses. By that time, Deral arrived with the milk cans. The goats were having trouble keeping on their feet; some of them actually fell and rolled over. Jacques tied them on short leads to the surrounding rails of their stalls as he milked them the best he could. The animals were panicked, not giving nearly as much milk as usual. Jacques missed Harry's help, realizing how much help the boy usually gave him. Pierre helped him carry the cans of milk to the galley, both of them staggering and weaving to keep their balance.

At dinner they joined the Breakfields and the Caldwells in the dining room with the children. When Harry saw Jacques he left Andrew to run to him. The boy stayed by Jacques' side, all through dinner. The food was simple fare, bread and sliced ham, and cups of milk. As long as the storm was imminent, the cooking would not be any more complicated than that.

After dinner, Jacques, Pierre, and Harry headed back to the horse deck. The motion of the sea was still increasing, so they determined to confine the rest of the horses in the movable partitions. When they got to the piebald mare, Jacques closed the partition to confine her, but was concerned for the safety of the filly. If she was thrown by the storm in the stall, she might not survive. He put on her halter and tied her close to the side of the stall. Then he was relieved to see their owner.

"I will stay with them as long as the sea is bad," said Ramon.

"Oh, good; I wasn't sure what to do with her." Jacques sounded apologetic.

Harry climbed into the stall with some of the goats, now concerned that they were all tied. Some of them were bleating in panic, so he was trying to comfort them. When it seemed all the animals were secure, Jacques thought, *We could be up all night.* He thought, *no reading tonight.* He regretted that. Then he heard footsteps on the ramp, looked up to see the Caldwells, all of the Breakfields and several others including the Tennison family, coming down the ramp, all hanging onto each other to keep their balance.

Roger Breakfield spoke for the group. "We all felt we needed to hear God's Word, and to pray together."

Jacques was astonished. He began, "There's nothing to sit on. I stowed the hay bales."

That's okay," spoke up someone. "We can stand, and hang onto these posts and each other."

Others were adding comments of agreement. Jacques looked around—the animals were all secure. *All right!* He looked up, seeking God's guidance, then reached for the little book, still in his shirt pocket. He sat down on the deck, close to the stall where Ramon was holding the filly on his lap. The ship was rocking, rising and dropping with the motion of the high sea. Most of the others sat down also, hanging onto each other in a tight circle. Jacques opened the little book and began to read, stopping with each verse, for Pierre to translate:

> "When Jesus therefore perceived that they would come and take him by force to make him a king, he departed into a mountain himself alone.
> "And when even was now come, his disciples went down unto the sea.
> "And entered into a ship, and went over the sea toward Capernaum. And it was now dark, and Jesus was not come to them.
> "And the sea arose by reason of a great wind that blew.
> "So when they had rowed about five and twenty or thirty furlongs, they see Jesus walking on the sea, and drawing nigh unto the ship: and they were afraid.
> "But he saith unto them, It is I; be not afraid.
> "Then they willingly received him into the ship: and immediately the ship was at the land whither they went."
> (John 6:15-21, KJV)

As Pierre finished translating the verses, Jacques began to pray:

"Our Father, we know you are with us, holding us in your hands. Though the enemy wants us to be afraid, we know you as our protector. Give us strength in the face of the storm. We know we have a destiny in this new land we are traveling to, so this storm will not keep us from our destiny. We trust you with this prayer and our lives in Jesus name. Amen."

The "amens" were repeated all around the circle. Jacques even heard an enthusiastic "amen" from the stall of the piebald mare.

Everyone staggered to their feet, hugging each other, and expressing their faith, before the group started back up the ramp. Now hail, mixed with snow and sleet was enveloping the ship, with much of it blowing down the ramp into the horse deck. There were many warnings of "careful" and "watch your step" as they all staggered up the ramp, hanging onto each other. As they reached the top of the ramp, the fireworks began. All hands were on the deck, racing to adjust the sails, gathering up the largest to minimize the effects of the gale. Suddenly there were blue-white flames touching each of the three tall masts, silently burning with sulfurous aroma, the sparks falling with the snowflakes.

They saw Sean Macrae hit the deck with his knees as his arms crossed his chest, crying out, "Thank you, St. Elmo, for your protection!"

As the group looked around them in stunned silence, many of the sailors crossed themselves in prayer, despite the extreme rocking of the ship. The colors of the flame which danced around them, from the tips of the masts on down, ranged from blue-white to blue-green. Sparks were flying all around them, but the heavenly show seemed to comfort more than scare them. The passengers, hanging on to each other, quickly moved toward their cabins.

Below, on the horse deck, sparks were flying with the blowing hail and snowflakes, and the eerie glow from the deck above. The show was a fearful sight, but Jacques felt a warm sense of God's presence as he held onto the stall of the piebald mare, with Harry tightly holding on to him. Ramon braced himself in the corner of the stall holding onto the filly, cushioned in his lap. Jacques pushed Harry through the rail into the stall with Ramon, and squeezed through the rails behind him. The three continued to brace themselves inside the stall, as the storm went on and on, the noise of the sea growing louder and louder. He could hear many of the horses squealing in fright. He thought he recognized specifically the squeals of the thoroughbred colt. It seemed like a bad dream that went on and on. The mare, miraculously, stayed on her feet, but was thrown alternately against first the partition and then against the side of the stall.

They were there for hours, seemingly an endless night. Sometimes the motion eased a bit, only to intensify again. Jacques felt nauseated, also concerned for Harry's fear, as the boy continued to clutch him tightly. Ramon had little to say, holding onto the rail with one arm, and holding onto the filly with the other arm. Jacques wondered where Pierre was. He had not seen him since the others went up the ramp. He said a prayer for his friend's safety.

As they first began to catch hints of the light of day, the heavy rocking finally diminished. The storm eventually passed and miraculously, the *Bucephalus* was still intact. As the storm finally abated, the two men and the boy fell asleep in the stall. Hours later, as they awoke the filly had escaped from Ramon's grip and made her way to her mother, who was still confined. Ramon was on his feet, opening the partition to examine his mare, who had some obvious bruises.

Jacques climbed out of the stall and headed for his own horses with Harry following him. They were greeted with Tounerre's impatient head nodding and nickering. The hay, given out almost twenty-four hours ago, was gone. The mares looked patiently from their confinement with their ears pointed forward, looking expectant. While Jacques made his way down the row, inspecting each of the horses, Harry ran toward the goats' stalls. The Breakfields' geldings all had bruises and scrapes which would need attention. The shires were pretty much unscathed, but obviously hungry. Suddenly, Harry screamed, burst into tears, and ran back to Jacques, crying, "Goats are dead!"

Jacques hurried to the goats stall, fearing the worst. Most of the goats were bleating, hungry and desperate for milking. One was laying still, her head and neck twisted in a grotesque position. Two others lay still with no visible signs of trauma. Jacques could see milk seeping from the teats of overextended udders. Harry climbed in to the goat with the broken neck, sobbing. It was the boy's favorite, the one he always milked first. Jacques went in to embrace the boy, petting the lifeless form sadly, wordlessly.

Finally, the words came, "It's okay, son. She's in a better place, with green pastures." He left the child, momentarily, to inspect the other two casualties. He picked up the bodies and carried them out of the stalls.

Harry was trying to pick up the dead goat, so Jacques picked her up and put her with the other two. "Come on son, we have to take care of the rest of them," he said, gently. They untied the rest of the goats and Jacques left Harry with the task of cleaning out the soiled straw while he continued to inspect the rest of the horses.

Jacques found Pierre in the stall with the thoroughbred colt where he spent the night. The colt was finally calm, but bruised and scraped from his ordeal in the enclosure. There were no other serious injuries, so Jacques and Pierre got busy apportioning out hay to all the animals. They barely finished when the sound of clanking metal alerted them of Deral arriving with the milk cans. Jacques was glad to have the diversion for Harry to help him through the loss of the goats. The goats were desperate for relief, but so stressed they were unable to produce as abundantly as usual. A few of them produced only a little.

With the milking done, the three carried the milk to the galley, where they learned dinner would be ready soon, so they took the time to look around the deck. The sea was still high, but the storm had passed. Sailors were unfurling the sails to take advantage of the wind to pick up speed again. The deck was littered with debri, some of it blown in from the storm, and much of it broken parts of the rigging. Exhausted sailors were working steadfastly on the repairs. It was very cold, with hail pellets rolling on the deck in open areas, but in some areas had piled up forming protuberant slabs of ice.

They arrived back at the horse deck in time to get started on chores there, such as the long overdue stall cleaning, and attending to the wounds of some of the horses with the worst of bruises and scrapes. Jacques was grateful that Ramon was there to take care of his own horses.

"Well is there still life down here?" It was Roger's attempt at cheer, despite the worry in his voice. Andrew and Willis were with him. Andrew and Harry were thrilled to see each other, and Harry hurried to show him the dead goats.

Willis was relieved to see that his calm, stolid, Suffolks were relatively unscathed. But unfortunately, Roger's warmblood geldings all had many bruises and scrapes, so Jacques set him to work applying medication to their wounds. Being able to do something for his own horses was therapy for Roger as well.

Deral came hurrying down the ramp to announce that dinner was ready, welcome news since it was the first time in almost twenty-four hours. Everyone was happy to drop what they were doing at the offer of food. Leon McKay had outdone himself to prepare a meal to compensate the crew and passengers for the last two days of worry, discomfort, and finally hunger. With dinner, it was obvious that many had bonded even more closely through the ordeal. Patricia and Andrea were now fast friends and Patricia was no longer showing hostility toward Jacques.

Many expressed thankfulness the storm passed without serious damage to the ship. Roger stood up and asked that everyone bear with him in asking God's blessing on the meal and giving thanks for their protection. When someone asked if Jacques would be reading from God's Word after dinner; he agreed he would. Many asked if they could come, many Jacques did not even know. Pierre was very pleased.

So, as soon as dinner was over they went back to the horse deck to pull out the hay bales again, and more, so there would be plenty of seating. Before long, many began to arrive, so many they had to pull out even more hay bales. Jacques began to read to them from the Book of Acts:

> "And when they had prayed, the place was shaken where they had assembled together; and they were all filled with the Holy Ghost, and they spake the word of God with boldness.
> "And the multitude of them that believed were of one heart and of one soul: neither said any of them that ought of the things which he possessed was his own; but they had all things in common.
> "And with great power gave the apostles witness of the resurrection of the Lord Jesus: and grace was upon them all,
> "Neither was there any among them that lacked: for as many as were possessors of lands or houses sold them, and brought the price of the things that were sold.

"And laid them down at the apostles' feet: and distribution was made unto every man according as he had need.

"And Joses, who by the apostles was surnamed Barnabas (which is, being interpreted, The son of consolation) a levite, and of the country of Cypress.

"Having land, sold it and brought the money and lay it at the apostles feet."

(Acts 4:31-37, KJV)

It was a perplexing passage, and Jacques was interested in the expressions he observed while Pierre translated. A man Jacques did not know volunteered the first comment which started a lively dialogue.

"It sounds like what we just experienced with all the shaken' an' rockin'."

"But what about this selling of land and giving it all away?" The speaker was Richard Tennison, the banker. "Does that mean if we are believers we should give it all away?" The question sounded a bit incredulous.

Pierre translated back to Jacques.

"Well I don't know about that. But I don't think we should leave someone in need, if we can help them. What about it? Someone else?"

"I think it just means that group of believers. They were so touched by God's power most felt bonded to the community of believers, and were thankful for the word of the apostles." Roger commented.

Pierre spoke again, "I understand about the boldness. Believing in the power of the Holy Spirit brings boldness. It makes it much easier to speak out about Jesus—even imperative to speak about Jesus."

Ramon Claudel began to clap and said, "Amen to that!"

Then Jacques heard someone say, "Read more!" so he went on:

"But a certain man named Ananias with Sapphira his wife, sold a possession,

"And kept part of the price, his wife also being privy to it, and brought a certain part, and laid it at the apostles' feet.

"But Peter said, Ananias, why hath Satan filled thy heart to lie to the Holy Ghost, and to keep back part of the price of the land?

"While it remained, was it not thine own? and after it was sold, was it not in thine own power? Why hast thou conceived this thing in thine heart? Thou hast not lied unto man but unto God.

"And Annanias hearing these words fell down and gave up the ghost: and great fear came upon all them that heard these things.

"And the young men arose, wound him up and carried him out, and buried him.

"And it was about the space of three hours after, when his wife, not knowing what was done, came in.

"And Peter answered unto her, Tell me whether ye sold the land for so much? And she said, Yea, for so much.

"Then Peter said unto her, How is it that ye have agreed together to tempt the Spirit of the Lord? Behold the feet of them which have buried thy husband are at the door, and shall carry thee out.

"Then she fell down straightway at his feet, and yielded up the ghost, and the young men came in, and found her dead, and carried her forth, buried her by her husband.

"And great fear came upon all the church, and upon as many as heard these things." (Acts 5:1-11, KJV)

Jacques paused several times, throughout the passage, watching the expressions of the listeners while Pierre translated. These ranged from surprise to shock and almost disbelief. As soon as the translation was complete, the comments started.

"So you mean God killed them just because they held onto part of their money?"

"Not because they held it back, but because they lied about it."

"They thought they were looking good to the people." This came from Andrea. She continued, "They were concerned about what people thought about them. That's hypocrisy. When Peter pointed out to them their lie was to God, I think their fear killed them. I think the lesson for us is to be very transparent in our lives. Deception will eventually harm us."

Roger looked proudly at his wife. "It really seems it put fear into the other believers. While we are so thankful for coming through the storm, I think that we should realize how dependant we are on God's grace. If we really have faith in God's provision, we realize that we have no reason for deception."

One of the newcomers whom Jacques did not know said, enthusiastically, "Read more," so he went on:

> "And at the hands of the apostles were many signs and wonders wrought among the people; (and they were all within one accord in Solomon's porch,
> "And of the rest durst no man join himself to them; but the people joined to them.
> And believers the more were added to the Lord, multitudes—both men and women)
> "Insomuch that they brought forth the sick into the street, and laid them on beds and couches that at least the shadow of Peter passing by might overshadow some of them.
> "There also came a multitude out of the cities round about Jerusalem, bringing sick folks, and them which were vexed with unclean spirits: and they were healed every one." (Act 5:12-16, KJV)

As Jacques watched the reaction of the people as Pierre completed his translation, he observed a different attitude, an attitude of worship and thankfulness as hands were raised and singing began.

As he finished the translation, Pierre gave an invitation, "If any of you here would like to profess your belief in Jesus Christ as your own Savior, we invite you to come forward so we can pray for you."

As several moved forward others were praying or singing with their hands raised. From the top of the ramp, Captain Palmer observed this last and said quietly to himself, *"Praise God!"*

CHAPTER 15

In Love

QUESTIONS CONTINUED AS the boys fascination with Fidel's stories went on. It was clear he enjoyed their company and loved telling stories. He noticed even Darren joined in with questions and laughter. They talked and laughed so long it was very late when they finally quieted down and fell asleep. When Antoine and Jules entered the barn early in the morning to feed the horses, they found all of them still sleeping.

"Some people come to the barn to work, while others, only to sleep." Jules was laughing at the sight, bringing a laugh from Antoine at his remark.

Fidel was the first to sit up, as the others continued to sleep. Looking a bit guilty, he concurred quickly with the others' humor. Their laughter succeeded in waking Darren, but the other two boys took longer to awaken.

"The boys worked hard, learning the history of the Romani last night." Fidel laughed, remembering all the boys' questions. Now Simon and Andre were sitting up, yawning, but not yet moving quickly.

Jules laughed, "Come on, boys, the horses are hungry," as he began to pile hay into the cart. The horses were making noises that seemed to agree with him.

Warm humor enlivened breakfast, as many of the stories of the night before were repeated to the rest of the household. The bonding deepened as they all became better acquainted.

It was decided Fidel would report to the Romani at the Birmingham camp that the Newalls and the Merlots would arrive in a week to spend a week there to teach from God's Word. Darren's chagrin at the prospect of spending another week with the Gypsies was quickly dispelled when Morton arrived to announce the Montgomery girls would be coming to ride their horses, and they hoped the rest of the young people would ride with them, bringing an immediate cheerful response.

As they were all entering the arena together on their horses they found Jules waiting for them, on foot, in the center of the arena. The rails were still at the low crossed position. Jules waved to Rachel and Peggy to trot their horses over the rails, followed by the Duran children, and then Darren and Jeannette, who did as well as the rest. They all took the course at a trot several times, then Jules instructed Rachel and Peggy to increase to a canter and nodded to the rest to follow. Dani and Katy hopped over the low jumps easily. Jules again nodded for them to repeat the course at a canter.

Jules' bay gelding was standing patiently just outside the arena. After a few more repeats of the course, he called them all back to him. "Today's a good day for some cross country. We'll get these horses used to some off road work." He grinned at Darren and Jeannette. They both reciprocated with grins, showing their excitement. As the group headed out of the arena, Antoine and Ellienne were both waiting, ready with their stocky chestnut mares. Jeannette's excitement increased to have her friends coming with them. She pulled up Katy to wait for her friends as they joined up at the rear of the group. As she dropped back, Darren took the opportunity to urge Dani into a trot to catch up with Rachel, who reined up to wait for him.

All of the Duran children followed their father in the lead. When Peggy saw her sister rein up to wait for Darren, her mouth dropped open. She waited for just a moment, then pulled her chestnut around and kicked him into a canter to catch up with Marielle.

To Darren, it was the picture he had seen in his dreams over and over, riding side by side with this beautiful girl on her gray horse. His mind was racing. *How could he make this picture last? He wanted to leave Southampton. He urged his mother to leave. Now he realized that moving to Canada would bring an end to this picture. How could he make it last longer?*

Jeannette looked at her friends. Antoine smiled. "In the spring, a young man's heart…" He did not quite finish the quote. His wife smiled back at him, her knowing expression agreeing with his.

The ride lasted most of the afternoon, so when they returned to the barn, the Montgomery girls were invited to come back to the cottage for dinner. The talk around the table was mostly about the ride, about the horses, and how wonderful was the weather. There was no more shyness; the atmosphere was warm and friendly. Rachel talked enthusiastically about the horses, both hers and the Newalls'. Darren's mother was amazed he was no longer quiet, talking freely about his horse and the ride. Madam Newall looked back and forth at Antoine and Ellienne. They just looked at each other, nodding and smiling.

Jules spoke up, "I'm looking forward to hearing from God's Word this evening." He looked at Jeannette. "Are we working you too hard?"

Jeannette smiled back, "No, not at all. I look forward to reading from God's Word. She got up to get her Bible as the others headed for the parlor. When Jeannette came back into the room with her Bible, she noted that Rachel and Darren were seated together on the settee. She opened her Bible and began to read:

> "And it came to pass in the days of Amraphal king of Shinar, Arioch king of Ellasar, Chedorloamer king of Elam and Tidal king of nations;
> "That these made war with Bera king of Sodom, and Bersha king of Gomorrah, Shinab king of Admah, and Shemeber king of Zeboiim, and the king of Bela, which is Zoar.
> "All these were joined together in the vale of Siddim, which is the salt sea.
> "Twelve years they served Chedorloamer, and in the thirteenth year they rebelled.
> "And in the fourteenth year came Chedorloamer, and the kings that were with him, and smote the Rephaims in Ashteroth Karnaim, and the Zuzims in Ham, and the Emins in Shaveh Kiriathaim.
> "And the Horites in their mount Seir unto Elparan which is by the wilderness.
> "And they returned, and came to Enmishpat, which is Kadesh, and smote all the country of the Amalekites, and also the Amorites, that dwelt in Hazezontamar.

HELENA POORTVLIET

"And there went out the king of Sodom, and the king of Gomorrah, and the king of Admah, and the king of Zeboiim, and the king of Bela (the same is Zoar) and they joined in battle with them in the vale of Siddim.

"With Chedorloamer, the king of Elam, and with Tidal king of nations, and Amraphal king of Shinar, and Arioch king of Ellasar, four kings with five.

"And the vale of Siddim was full of slimepits: and the kings of Sodom and Gomorrah fled, and fell there, and they that remained fled to the mountain.

"And they took all the goods of Sodom and Gomorrah, and all their victuals, and went their way." (Gen. 14:1-11, KJV)

Jeannette paused to wait for comments. They were all speechless, listening to the tale of war, so she went on:

"And they took Lot, Abram's brother's son, who dwelt in Sodom, and his goods, and departed. (Gen. 14:12, KJV)

"Oh, no!" The exclamation came from Andre, which brought everyone's attention. Jeannette paused for a moment, then continued:

"And there came one that had escaped, and told Abram the Hebrew; for he dwelt in the plain of Mamre the Amorite, brother of Eshcol, and brother of Aner: and these were confederate with Abram.

"And when Abram heard that his brother was taken captive, he armed his trained servants, born in his own house, three hundred and eighteen, and pursued them unto Dan.

"And he divided himself against them, he and his servants, by night and smote them; and pursued them into Hobah; which is on the left hand of Damascus.

"And he brought back all the goods, and also brought again his brother Lot, and his goods, and the women also, and the people." (Gen. 14:13-16, KJV)

There was a collective sigh of relief. Everyone was interested in the story. Jeannette waited for comments.

"It sounds like they were really outnumbered." Simon was wondering, "How did they do it?"

His father replied, "With godly wisdom, and God's grace!"

Jeannette laughed, "Abram rescued his nephew, so he had great incentive. But I think you're right, God gave him wisdom, and favor, but no more than we can expect." She read on:

> "And the king of Sodom went out to meet him after his return from the slaughter of Chedorloamer; and the kings that were with him, at the valley of Shaveh, which is the kings dale.
> "And Melchizedek king of Salem brought forth bread and wine: and he was the priest of the most high God.
> "And he blessed him, and said, blessed be Abram of the most high God, possessor of heaven and earth:"
>
> "And blessed be the most high God which hath delivered thine enemies into thine hand. And he gave him tithes of all. (Gen. 14:17-20, KJV)

Jeannette paused again. Darren and Rachel were both silent, but were both listening intently. Andre spoke up again, "Who was Mel—Mekezed…?"

Jeannette corrected, "Melchezedek—the priest of the Most High God. Some think this was a precarnate appearance of Jesus Christ."

Everyone looked startled at this announcement. Jeannette was turning the pages of her Bible. "In the Book of Hebrews it says in Chapter 6 and verse 20, 'Whither the forerunner is for us entered, even Jesus, made an high priest after the order of Melchezedek.' Then in Chapter 7, the Book of Hebrews tells us more about the comparison of Melchezedek and Jesus:

> "For this Melkezedek, King of Salem, priest of the most high God, who met Abraham returning from the slaughter of the kings and blessed him.
> "To whom also Abraham gave a tenth part of all; first being by interpretation king of righteousness, and after that also King of Salem, which is King of Peace.
> "Without father, without mother, without descent, having neither beginning of days, or end of life; but also made like unto the Son of God; abideth a priest continually.

"Now consider how great this man was unto whom even the patriarch Abraham gave a tenth of the spoils." (Heb. 7:1-5, KJV)

Jeannette explained, "No one seems to know where he came from or where he went. He just appeared to Abram, who recognized him as a man of God. Melchezedek blessed Abram and prophesied over him and shared communion with him, long before communion was taught by Christ. He referred to himself as the King of Salem, or King of Peace."

Antoine commented, "Very mysterious—sounds like an embodiment of the Christ." Others around the group nodded in agreement. Jeannette turned back to Genesis:

"And the king of Sodom said unto Abram, Give me the persons, and take the goods to thyself."

"And Abram said to the king of Sodom, I have lift up my hand unto the Lord, the most high God, the possessor of heaven and earth.
"That I will not take from a thread even to a shoelatchet, and that I will not take anything that is thine, lest thou shouldst say, I have made Abram rich:
"Save only that which the young men have eaten, and the portion of the men which went with me, Aner, Eshcol, and Mamre: let them take their portion." (Gen. 14:21-24, KJV)

As Jeannette finished the chapter, she looked around for reaction and comments. Rachel and Darren's attention was rapt, but they both remained silent.

Antoine was excited. "This Abram was quite a man! What a hero! But he gives all the credit to God!"

Ellienne looked admiringly at her husband and agreed. "Who would guess that the Bible could be so exciting?"

Darren grinned slightly, and just barely nodded. Rachel looked at him, surprised.

Morton came to the cottage to walk Rachel and Peggy home. Peggy asked Rachel what she thought of the reading. Rachel answered, "Well, it was more interesting than that Jesus stuff."

Peggy and Morton both looked at her, as she continued, "That Abram seems like quite a hero—kind of unbelievable."

Peggy paused a moment, then commented, "I think it is God's favor on his life, because he loves God, and God has called him out."

"Well, Lot left him and got into trouble, but Abram rescued him. He didn't have to. Do you think our father would do that?"

Peggy and Morton both looked at her, bewildered. Morton spoke, "Your father would do anything for you!"

"I don't know about that." Rachel was serious. "As long as I do what they want."

"Rachel!" Peggy exclaimed.

The next day was another day of riding. They all met in the arena to practice over the rails. Jules had Rachel and Peggy go first, which they did in perfect form, followed by the others. After repeating the low jumps, Jules raised the bars so they were straight across about a foot high. Then he instructed them all to try it, led by Rachel and Peggy. They all accomplished it successfully several times. The bar was raised to a foot and a half, and they all repeated the task, again perfectly. After two more turns, Jules walked to the gate of the arena where his bay gelding was waiting, with Antoine and Ellienne on their two chestnut mares. The young people were all in high spirits at the prospect of a ride outdoors.

Jules opened the gate into the meadow to let all the riders through, then rode to the lead with his own children following. Rachel looked back at Darren and he urged Dani to catch up with her. Jeannette was following with the Merlots.

About a furlong down the trail was a rail fence crossing the meadow. Jules cantered his bay up to it, dismounted, and removed the top two rails. The bottom rail was approximately a foot and a half off the ground. The spring meadow grass reached almost to the rail. Jules remounted his horse, circled around and galloped toward the raid and easily cleared it. As he slowed to a stop, he waved to the others to follow.

Darren was right behind Rachel as she cleared the rail and Dani eagerly cleared it, Darren feeling as if his heart was in his throat. Behind him, his sister cleared the rail on Katy, laughing joyfully. They both turned around in time to see the Merlots stocky chestnuts hop over the rail, much to everyone's surprise.

Jules was waiting for them, clapping his hands. "Now you've all got hunters! That's what it's all about." He was laughing heartily. "Just don't overdo it too fast!"

They rode the rest of the afternoon with no more jumping, but Darren's heart was flying, a combination of the exhilarating ride and the company of the beautiful girl with whom he had fallen in love.

CHAPTER 16

Newfoundland

"LAND! LAND HO-O-O---!"

The voice reverberated from high above the deck near the top of the foremast. Most everyone on the deck looked up and toward the bow of the ship but could see nothing as yet. Captain Palmer came out of his cabin with a long telescope. He went forward to the bow and looked toward the horizon with the glass. He watched for a long while, but it was not until a high wave lifted the bow of the ship that he acknowledged he saw it too. He turned around to the rest and announced, "Gentlemen, I believe we are approaching Newfoundland!"

A cheer went up from the weary crew and a few of the passengers who were on the deck. It was early in the day, the sky was clear and the sun was behind them. It was not long before the rest of those on the deck began to see the faint dark shape in the distance. More cheers went up, which could be heard even down in the horse deck.

Jacques pulled harness out of stowage to spend some time cleaning. This past week the sea was relatively calm, so he spent most of the time walking horses. Ramon, Roger and Willis were coming down to walk their own horses, leaving Pierre and Jacques free to walk the others. Walking the thoroughbreds helped to heal up their bruises from the storm. Jacques was determined they should be in good shape when they reached Montreal to be delivered to their new owners.

With all the shouting above, Jacques laid aside the harness and started up the ramp. Harry climbed out of the goats' stall and ran to catch up with him. When they reached the main deck, most of the passengers were now on deck. As they went forward, Jacques could barely see the dark shapes in the distance. What he also saw to the north and the west were small white shapes, shining in the sun. *Icebergs!*

"Well, how does it feel to be almost home?" The cheerful question came from Roger, coming up behind him. Andrew was following him, but when he saw Harry, the two boys started running around the two men in their glee to be together.

"I'll be glad whenever I can stand on solid ground," replied Jacques. But look over there—isn't that ice?"

"You're right. I wonder how close we'll get to it."

Captain Palmer approached in time to hear that comment. "We'll be going around the south side of Newfoundland this trip. Hopefully, we won't encounter much ice. Later in the season we go through the Straits of Belle Isle, but it's too dangerous this early in the year. We have another week or so of travel up the Saint Lawrence."

As the land forms loomed larger they began to see other vessels, mostly fishing boats, but also other large ships coming into or leaving the Canadian ports. Jacques felt more of an urgency to be prepared for their arrival so he turned back for the horse deck. The others followed him.

When Roger saw the work Jacques was doing with the harness, he said, "That's a good idea. I should be doing the same." Jacques showed him where his harness and coach were stowed, and helped him get the harness out. They were so busy cleaning harness, they were surprised when Deral arrived with the milk cans.

The boys were so happy to be together Andrew was willing to help Harry clean the goat stalls, not even thinking of it as work. When Jacques came over to start the milking, Andrew was thrilled to be able to watch. Since the storm the milk production was much reduced, even more than just the loss of the three goats which had not survived the storm. Two of the goats were completely dry. When they finished, they all carried the milk up to the galley in time for dinner.

Of course, at dinner the excitement was all about the land sighting. Everyone was thinking about their plans for the near future. Roger asked Jacques, "What are your plans when we reach Montreal?"

"I'll have to find an inn with a stable to stay while I get the information I need and make plans to leave for Canada West."

"Can you stay in Montreal long enough to see our solicitor about Harry's adoption?"

"Oh, yes!"

Harry looked at him. Jacques asked him, "Do you want to be my son for real?"

"Oh, yes!"

Jacques looked back at Roger, "Does that answer your question?"

"Oh, yes!"

After dinner Pierre and Jacques returned to the horse deck to pull out hay bales to provide plenty of seating for the people who were coming for the Bible reading. The attendance was steadily increasing since the storm. After Jacques went to get his Bible, he was surprised to find Roger, Andrea and Patricia prepared to sing some hymns and lead the others in singing. After the first song, they turned to Jacques to begin reading:

> "Then the high priest rose up, and all they that were with him, (which is the sect of the Sadducees) and were filled with indignation.
> "And laid their hands on the apostles, and put them in the common prison.
> "But the angel of the Lord by night opened the prison doors, and brought them forth and said,
> "Go; stand and speak in the temple to the people all the words of this life.
> "And when they heard that, they entered into the temple early in the morning, and taught. But the high priest came, and they that were with him, and called the council together, and all the senate of the children of Israel, and sent to the prison to have them brought.
> "But when the officers came, and found them not in the prison, they returned and told,
> "Saying, The prison truly found we shut with all safety, and the keepers standing without before the doors: but when we had opened, we found no man within.
> "Now when the high priest and the captain of the temple and the chief priests heard these things, they doubted of them whereunto they would go."
> (Acts 5:17-24, KJV)

As Jacques paused to allow Pierre's translation, he watched the expressions. "An angel opened the door? Are you kidding?" The question came from a man Jacques did not know.

He answered, "It's what I read. It's God's Word. It's the account of these men of God. If I believe God, I trust his word," Jacques explained. Then someone said, "Read more," so he continued.

"Then came one and told them, saying, Behold the men ye put in prison are standing in the temple, and teaching the people.
"Then went the captain with the officers, and brought them without violence: for they feared the people, lest they should have been stoned.
"And when they had brought them, they set them before the council: and the high priest asked them,
"Saying Did not we straitly command you that ye should not teach in this name? and, behold, ye have filled Jerusalem with your doctrine and intend to bring this man's blood upon us."

"Then Peter and the other apostles answered and said, We ought to obey God rather than men.
"The God of our fathers raised up Jesus, whom ye slew and hung on a tree.
"Him hath God exalted with his right hand to be a Prince and Savior, for to give repentance to Israel, and forgiveness for sins."

"And we are witnesses of these things, and so is also the Holy Ghost, whom God hath given to them that obey him.
"When they heard that, they were cut to the heart, and took counsel to slay them.
"Then stood up one in the council, a Pharisee, named Gamaliel, a doctor of the law, had in reputation among all the people, and commanded to put the apostles forth a little space:
"And said unto them, Ye men of Israel, take heed to yourselves what ye intend to do as touching these men.
"For before these days rose up Theudas, boasting himself to be somebody; to whom a number of men, about four hundred, joined themselves: who was slain; and all, as many as obeyed him, were scattered, and brought to naught.
"After this man rose up Judas of Galilee in the days of the tax, and drew away much people after him: he also

perished; and all, even as many as obeyed him, were dispersed.

"And now I say unto you, Refrain from these men, and let them alone: for if this counsel or this work be of men, it will come to naught:

"But if it be of God, ye cannot overthrow it; lest haply ye be found even to fight against God.

"And to him they agreed: and when they had called the apostles, and beaten them, they commanded that they should not speak the name of Jesus, and let them go."

"And they departed from the presence of the council rejoicing that they were counted worthy to suffer shame for his name.

"And daily in the temple and in every house, they ceased not to teach and preach Jesus Christ." (Acts 5:25-42, KJV)

Jacques stopped every few verses to watch the expressions of the listeners as Pierre translated. Everyone seemed to be listening with rapt attention, but offered no comments after that first reaction. When he reached the end of the chapter, he closed his Bible which gave signal to the singers, who started to sing quietly as Pierre translated the last few verses. The listeners started to join in with the singing.

As Pierre finished the translation, he gave an invitation to any who wished to come forward for prayer or to confess their belief in Jesus. The prayer and fellowship went on into the night until some of the children just lay down on the hay bales and went to sleep. The night was cold as the attendees started up the ramp. Harry and Andrew both fell asleep on hay bales, so Roger picked up Andrew and carried him on his shoulder back to their cabin. Many came to Jacques and Pierre to thank them for their part.

Jacques and Pierre were carrying the milk up to the galley before breakfast. When they arrived on deck, they were amazed at the sight. Newfoundland loomed before them. The sea to the north was dotted with the white patches of icebergs. Newfoundland had rocky rugged cliffs broken by fjords and topped with lush but windblown forests. It appeared there was a rugged island in front of the main body of Newfoundland, as barren and rugged as the main body. The *Bucephalus* was now traveling south some distance from the coast of the rugged land, but close enough to see the breaking of the white surf on the rocky coast.

Conversation at breakfast was lively, intense, first about the awesome view of the land they were circumventing; then the various plans which were soon to be followed when they all reached Montreal. They still had many days to go, but seeing land made the future seem much closer.

Over the weeks of working to learn English, of necessity, since most of the passengers and crew were English, and communicating with Harry on a daily basis, Jacques felt much more confident of his ability to speak English. He asked Roger about his plans to do business with his partner in Montreal.

"What kind of business is it?"

Roger replied, "He's an architect. His company contracts to build—stores, houses, warehouses, even bridges. He's been so busy he's had to turn down business. And he would rather just do the design work. So he wants me to take over the contracting. Would you be interested in a job?" Roger's grin was encouraging.

"Oh, no," Jacques quickly answered. I want to homestead in Canada West. I want to build a home in the country and farm—and raise horses." He laughed.

"Well, if it takes a while for you to leave for Canada West, maybe you might need to do something in the meantime." Roger sounded hopeful.

"Well, I don't know. I don't know much about building. I'm going to have to build a house—and a barn, so maybe you guys can help me with some plans." Jacques expressed his interest.

Roger replied, "Well, you could work for us this year, and learn how to put up your buildings, so you'd have that experience before you head for Canada West next spring. Your big horses would be a lot of help as well. We would pay well for that." Willis and Patricia were sitting with them, listening intently. Willis looked interested, but said nothing.

After breakfast Jacques was ready to head back to the horse deck. Harry and Andrew were seated together, laughing and talking, so Andrea reassured Jacques she would love to have Harry stay with them for the day.

Jacques was anxious to walk horses, especially the ones that would be delivered to new owners, such as the Godolphin thoroughbreds. The wounds they sustained in the storm were healing fast, to Jacques relief. He wanted to be able to present them to their new owners in sound, robust condition. He was pleased to see the substantial growth of the yearlings, and with the regular walking they were all better behaved.

Early in the afternoon, Roger, accompanied by the two boys, came down the ramp to the stable area. He was jovial, as usual, and the boys were excited to be together. Roger had a purpose for the visit.

"I need your input on a decision I need to make," he explained.

"Oh, what is that?" Jacques asked.

"I would have asked Willis about working with us, but I didn't want that to affect your decision. I really want you to stay and work with us, even if it is only until next spring. But I want to be sure how you feel about the Caldwells. Are you okay with them now? I won't ask them if it would affect your decision."

"Oh, no, I'm fine with them. I wondered that you didn't ask him. It might be a good idea for both of us. I think we're planning on heading for the same area. I think it would be helpful to learn about building before we head west." Jacques was nodding as he talked. Then he added, "It would give Harry more time to be with Andrew. They sure like each other." After a pause he went on, "I just need to be sure of a place to keep my horses. The mares will both be foaling in the next few weeks, and I'll need room also for the foals."

Roger laughed, "Don't worry, we'll take care of it. I've come to know you as a reliable person. I'm sure you'll be worth it, whatever it takes." Then he turned to his own son. "Come on, let's get our horses worked," as he headed for his horses.

It was not long before Deral appeared with the milk cans, so Jacques headed for the goats. Harry ran ahead of him, now with Andrew following. Harry wanted to show Andrew how to do it. Jacques watched them closely, making sure it was done properly. Then they all helped to carry the milk back to the galley.

After dinner, Jacques prepared for the group that was now coming regularly for the Bible reading. When they were all settled on the hay bales, Jacques began reading:

"And in those days when the number of disciples was multiplied, there arose a murmuring of the Grecians against the Hebrews, because their widows were neglected in the daily ministrations.

"Then the twelve called the multitude of the disciples unto them, and said, It is not reason that we should leave the word of God to serve tables.

"Wherefore, brethren, look ye out among you seven men of honest report, full of the Holy Ghost and wisdom, whom we may appoint over this business.

"But we will give ourselves continually to prayer, and to the ministry of the word.

"And the saying pleased the whole multitude: and they chose Stephen, a man full of faith and of the Holy Ghost, and Philip, and Prochorus, and Nicanor; and Timon, and Parmenas, and Nicholas a proselyte of Antioch:

"Whom they set before the apostles: and when they had prayed, they laid their hands on them.

"And the word of God increased: and the numbers of the disciples multiplied in Jerusalem greatly; and a great company of priests were obedient to the faith:

"And Stephen, full of faith and power, did great wonders and miracles among the people." (Acts 6:1-8, KJV)

Jacques paused, while Pierre finished his translation. The listeners were attentive, but didn't question, just urging Jacques to continue:

"Then there arose certain of the synagogue, which is called *the synagogue* of the Libertines, and Cyrenians, and Alexandrians, and of them of Cilicia and of Asia, disputing with Stephan,

"And they were not able to resist the wisdom and the spirit by which they spake.

"Then they suborned men, which said, We have heard him speak blasphemous words against Moses, and against God.

"And they stirred up the people, and the elders, and the scribes, and came upon him, and caught him, and brought him to the council,

"And set up false witnesses, which said, This man ceaseth not to speak blasphemous words against this holy place, and the law:

"For we have heard him say, that this Jesus of Nazereth, shall destroy this place, and shall change the customs which Moses delivered us.

"And all that sat in the council, looking steadfastly on him, saw his face as it had been the face of an angel." (Acts 6:9-15, KJV)

Jacques watched the faces turned toward Pierre as he finished the translation. The sun had long since receded, and the horse deck was lit only by lantern light, but Pierre's face was shining as if by a light from heaven. Jacques was startled, but as he looked around, he knew the rest saw it also. Arms were raised and people began to pray and praise God, and Jacques began to hear those strange syllables of the heavenly language. People began to gather around Pierre, many kneeling, many embracing and praying with each other, and some began to sing softly. The worship and praise went on and on. Gradually, some began to leave, but many stayed even longer. Finally, the last few participants came up to embrace and thank Jacques and Pierre for the reading, before heading up the ramp.

CHAPTER 17

Romani Mission

JEANNETTE WAS IN high spirits. Tomorrow they would be going to spend the week at the Romani camp just south of Birmingham; being Sunday, she planned to introduce to them the sacrament of communion. She had wonderful memories of the week they spent at the other camp. Jacques first professed his love for her there, and she made such wonderful friendships there.

But today she was with her brother. They hitched their horses, Katy and Dani, to the wagon, and were on their way to Bristol to shop the Saturday market for food supplies to take with them. She was happy to have the day alone with Darren. He was driving, and seemed to be in a light hearted mood.

"I'm happy we're spending this time at the camp. I've really missed Elena. Aren't you happy to spend time with Roman?"

"Oh, yes," he answered. He almost forgot about the young Romani, Fidel's son, who spent several weeks with them in Southampton. He thought more about how he would miss seeing Rachel for the week they would be gone. But he did not mention her.

"All the riding we've done lately," Jeannette started in, "—what fun! I really enjoy learning to jump. Our horses seem to take it quite well, don't they?"

Darren grinned at her. "I love it. I'm glad you're having fun, too. I hope we can still ride like that when we get to Canada."

"I hope so, too!" she agreed. "You've really made friends with Rachel Montgomery, haven't you? I hope it won't be too hard on you to leave her."

Darren did not answer right away. Then he answered carefully. "Maybe she'll come with us." ·

Jeannette's mouth dropped open as she looked at her brother. "You know better than that! You don't think her parents would allow that?"

No, I don't suppose." Darren looked down. "They want her to marry the prince!"

When Jeannette and Darren arrived back at the cottage with the supplies, Fidel and Roman were there, to escort the Newalls and the Merlots to the camp early in the morning.

After dinner, the Durans were anxious to hear from God's Word, especially since this would be their last evening together until after the visit to the Romani camp. There was great anticipation for the week to come, and the participants felt a need for prayer for the days ahead. Jeannette opened her Bible and began to read:

> "After these things the word of the Lord came unto Abram in a vision, saying, Fear not Abram, I am thy shield and thy exceeding great reward."
>
> "And Abram said, Lord God, what wilt thou give me, seeing I go childless, and the steward of my house is this Eliezer of Damascus?
> "And Abram said, Behold, to me thou hast given no seed: and lo, and one not born in my house is mine heir."
>
> "And behold, the word of the Lord came unto him, saying, This shall not be thine heir; but he that shall come forth out of thine own bowels shall be thine heir;
> "And he brought him forth abroad, and said, Look now toward heaven, and tell the stars, if thou be able to number them, and he said unto him, so shall thy seed be."
>
> "And he believed in the Lord; and he counted it to him for righteousness." (Gen. 15:1-6, KJV)

Jeannette looked up from reading, waiting for response. She looked at the faces around her, then focused on her brother. He was listening attentively, but said nothing. She finally looked at the others.

Jules offered, "That sounds like a New Testament concept—that he believed the Lord, and it counted for righteousness. So it doesn't matter what we've done, it's our belief in God."

"That's good," Jeannette affirmed. "That's the real issue." She looked back at Darren. "It's not what we've done or not done, or what we might be blaming ourselves for, it's believing in the Lord that determines our righteousness."

She waited another moment for comments, and then continued:

> "And he said unto him, I am the Lord that brought thee out of Ur of the Chaldees, to give this land to inherit it.
> "And he said, Lord God; whereby shall I know that I shall inherit it?
> "And he said to him, Take me an heifer three years old, and a ram three years old, and a turtledove and a young pidgeon.
> "And he took unto him all these, and divided them in the midst, and laid each piece one against another: but the birds divided he not.
> "And when the fowls came down on the carcasses, Abram drove them away."
>
> "And when the sun was going down, a deep sleep fell upon Abram; and lo, an horror of great darkness fell upon him.
> "And he said unto Abram, Know of a surety that thy seed shall be a stranger in a land that is not theirs, and shall serve them, and they shall afflict them four hundred years.
> "And also that nation, whom they shall serve, will I judge, and afterward they shall come out with great substance.
> "And thou shall go up to thy fathers in peace: thou shalt be buried in a good old age.
> "But in the fourth generation they shall come hither again; for the iniquity of the Amorites is not yet full.
> "And it came to pass, that, when the sun went down, and it was dark, behold a smoking furnace, and a burning lamp that passed between those pieces.
> "In the same day the Lord made a covenant with Abram, saying: Unto thy seed have I given this land, from the river of Egypt unto the great river, the river Euphrates.
> "The Kenites and the Kenessites, and the Kadmonites,
> "And the Hittites, and the Perizzites, and the Rephaims,
> "And the Amorites and the Canaanites, and the Gergashites, and the Jebusites. (Gen. 15:7-21, KJV)

When Jeannette looked up she saw several looks of surprise. Antoine spoke, "He's giving him the future of his descendants who are not yet born!"

"Yes," agreed Jeannette. "He's receiving a prophecy of the children of Israel in Egypt and of their exodus long before they even existed. God's plan was complete before it ever manifested."

Antoine added, "The coming week is a great adventure to us, but to God it is already a reality. We just need to allow his will to unfold before us."

Streaks of dawn were just appearing in the eastern sky as the party left the lane past the Montgomery's great house and headed north toward Gloucester. The Merlot's wagon was in the lead with Fidel and Roman riding ahead. Darren was amazed the Merlot's stocky chestnuts could move so fast. Katy and Dani were doing a fast extended trot to keep up. They had a long way to go, to reach the camp by early afternoon.

Darren still felt somewhat embarrassed following the colorful wagon ahead of him, even though he was getting quite accustomed to being around the Romani. He was surprised he no longer felt the animosity he once felt toward Fidel and Antoine, but it was still embarrassing to be associated with that strange, colorful wagon on the road.

The sun was high when they slowed to a walk going through Gloucester, giving the horses a break. As they left Gloucester behind, they resumed their extended trot, and before long Fidel and Roman galloped ahead and disappeared from sight. After a good hour of driving at this pace, they slowed to a walk again, and before long, a party of riders appeared far up the road. As they came nearer, Darren recognized Roman with several other Romani riders. They were laughing and yelling back and forth, greeting the Merlots, joking with them in Romani. Darren felt irritated he could not understand anything they were saying.

Soon they were on the road that went off the main road to Birmingham. The riders paused at the turn, waved to the others and were off at a gallop toward the camp. Darren saw the camp was much smaller than the camp near Andover, but otherwise looked similar. There were a lot of outside campfires started and many of the fancy painted wagons similar to the Merlots' wagon. Many horses grazed around the circle of wagons. A small group of men were walking up the road toward them.

Fidel was walking with a man in a dark suit and a worn looking top hat, who stopped and greeted Antoine and Ellienne. Then they proceeded to the Newalls' wagon, and Fidel made the introductions. Stavros Arnapoulis was the chief of this camp, and he welcomed the party and pointed out a space for them to park their wagon.

Jeannette was thrilled to see Elena walking toward them with two other women. One of those was about Ellienne's age and quite plump, the other was a young woman who was obviously pregnant. As they came near, Elena introduced her friend Paloma Gala and Paloma's daughter Grace. Paloma reached out to Jeannette with both hands.

"Elena told me. It was your young man who brought God to us, and brought our family back together. We will never forget him!"

Jeannette beamed with pride to hear these things about Jacques. Her mother added, "He's such a good boy!"

Darren rolled his eyes. Then Roman rode up to them, swung off his horse, went over to embrace and kiss Grace. Darren's jaw dropped. Roman grinned at him, "Grace has promised to marry me!"

Darren was still speechless. He was looking at Grace's belly, then at Roman, and still said nothing.

`Roman laughed, "I'm a lucky man. I get two for one. She came to me already started."

Jeannette and her mother were also waiting for an explanation. Paloma began to explain, "My daughter was married to an English boy, but he was killed. Thanks to your Jacques, she came back to us with our grandchild on the way. Now she has found love again, and Roman is such a good boy!"

Elena was also looking proudly at her son. Darren was still speechless. But in his mind, his thoughts went back to Rachel. The question kept coming back. *How could he make it work?*

Jeannette and her mother would be staying with Elena and Ellienne in the Merlots' wagon, while the men, Antoine and Darren would be staying with Fidel and Roman in the Balansay's wagon.

The women headed for the wagon with Elena to start preparations for dinner. Fidel and Antoine waved to the younger men to go with them to start a campfire and tend to the wood. Roman reluctantly left

Grace and waved to Darren to go with him. Darren followed, anxious to get answers to his questions.

"What's going on here? You're not the same guy."

"That's right," grinned Roman, "I'm not."

"But it's only been a few weeks." Darren looked incredulous. "What do you know about her?"

"Oh, we've known each other since we were kids, but I haven't seen her for the last coupla' years because her parents moved up here. I was glad to see her as soon as we saw each other. Then she told me about her marriage and then getting back with her parents. She told me it was that Jacques who Jeannette's promised to who got them back together.

"Really. How so?" Darren was disbelieving.

"She was staying at the Montgomerys—working there as a maid—when Jacques was there. She was visiting the Durans when Jacques was reading the Bible with them, and she believed what he was reading about Jesus. She was afraid to go home, but they convinced her to consider it. Then when Jacques was here, he prayed with her parents and told them she wanted to come home.

"You mean she knows Rachel Montgomery?"

"I think so—why?"

"Why?" Darren laughed nervously.

"What's going on?" Roman looked suspicious.

"Well—I thought you didn't believe all that stuff." Darren quickly changed the subject.

"I guess I finally saw how my mother changed. And Father really is different, too. He's really happy about my mother's healing. Now Grace has shown me what a difference it's made for her." Roman was smiling. "But what about the Montgomery girl, Rachel? What's going on?"

The young men had been moving slowly, so Antoine and Fidel had moved beyond hearing, but Darren still kept his voice down. "I love that girl, and I think she loves me too. I never met anyone so beautiful. And she's really smart about horses, too."

"So what's the problem?" Roman asked.

"Her father is Lord Montgomery. Her mother wants her to marry a prince, which, obviously, I am not." Darren looked discouraged.

"How old is she?" Roman queried.

"Eighteen years, same as me," Darren answered.

"You're both of age—it should be your decision."

Darren was quiet. *How could it be his decision? Everyone else seemed to be in authority.* His mother, Jeannette, and even Antoine seemed to hold authority over him. *And Lord Montgomery—what would he do?* He could not imagine Lord Montgomery welcoming him as a son-in-law.

"Well, don't you think so?" Roman was still waiting for a response.

"I don't know—I don't know if I could pull it off." Darren looked down.

"Hey, you boys! Come and give us a hand!" Fidel was calling back to them. Antoine had his hands on his hips, looking exasperated. Darren turned to move toward the older men. Roman followed, but replied, "Hey, friend, you can't leave it at that. It's your life and hers. If you don't do something, her parents will make her marry some old man she can't stand!"

This made Darren feel even worse. *What could he do?"*

After a sumptuous dinner shared by many families, Jeannette, her mother, Elena and Ellienne got up and began to sing, getting everyone's attention. Darren felt pride for his family, despite his feelings about the Gypsies. He was even starting to like Roman's family. Seeing Roman and Grace together gave him encouragement about Rachel. He thought about going to Lord Montgomery, declaring his intention and asking for Rachel's hand in marriage. The thought was fleeting as he imagined what the response would be. *What did he have to offer someone like Rachel?*

After several songs Darren realized many had joined the singing with a variety of instruments. Many hands were raised in worship. He looked over to see Roman with one arm around Grace's shoulder, and saw both had a free arm raised in worship. Darren looked around the rest of the group, feeling no one shared his unbelief.

The singing ended, and after a few moments of prayer and continued worship, Jeannette opened her Bible and began to speak: "I'm so glad to be with all of you this week. I want to talk to you about the Christian sacrament of the Lord's Supper. This is something we do as Christians to show our belief in Jesus as our sacrifice for sin and also our connection with each other as children of our heavenly Father. We also refer to it as communion. It was begun by Jesus with his disciples just before his crucifixion, and he requested that we continue to celebrate it whenever we come together. I will begin with the account from the Book of Luke:

> "And when the hour was come, he sat down, and the twelve apostles with him,
> "And he said unto them, With desire I have desired to eat this Passover with you before I suffer:
> "For I say unto you, I will not anymore eat thereof until it be fulfilled in the kingdom of God.
> "And he took the cup and gave thanks and said, Take this and divide it amongst yourselves.
> "For I say unto you, I will not drink of the fruit of the vine, until the kingdom of God shall come.
> "And he took bread, and gave thanks, and brake it saying, This is my body which is given for you: This do in remembrance of me.
> "Likewise also the cup after supper, saying, This cup is the New Testament in my blood, which is shed for you. (Luke 22:14-20, KJV)

Jeannette began to explain, "Jesus is telling his disciples of the sacrifice he is about to make, using the example of the bread and wine as representing his body and blood. He is also instituting this as a sacrament to be followed regularly as a sign of our acceptance of his sacrifice.

"Now I'd like to read a little of Paul's first letter to the Corinthians to show how he taught about this practice." Jeannette turned pages and read:

> "When ye come together therefore into one place, this is not to eat the Lord's Supper.
> "For in eating everyone taketh before other his own supper: and one is hungry and another is drunken.
> "What? Have ye not houses to eat and drink in? or despise ye the Church of God, and shame them that have not? What shall I say to you? Shall I praise you for this, I praise you not."

"For I have received of the Lord, that which also I delivered unto you, That the Lord Jesus the same night in which he was betrayed and took bread:

"And when he had given thanks, he brake it, and said, Take eat, this is my body, which is broken for you: do this in remembrance of me.

"After the same manner also, he took the cup, when he had supped saying, This cup is the new testament of my blood: this do you as oft as ye drink it, in remembrance of me.

"For as often as ye eat this bread and drink this cup, ye do show the Lord's death till he come.

"Wherefore whoever shall eat this bread, and drink this cup of the Lord, unworthily, shall be guilty of the body and blood of the Lord.

"But let a man examine himself, and so let him eat of that bread, and drink of that cup.

"For he that eateth and drinketh unworthily, eateth and drinketh damnation to himself, not discerning the Lord's body.

"For this cause many are weak and sickly among you, and many sleep.

For if we judge ourselves we shall not be judged.

But when we are judged we are chastened of the Lord, that we should not be condemned with the world.

"Wherefore my brethren, when ye come together to eat, tarry one for another.

"And if any man hunger, let him eat at home; that ye not come together under condemnation. And the rest I will set in order when I come."

(1 Cor. 11:20-34, KJV)

Jeannette paused a little with each verse for Antoine to translate from English to Romani. She waited for comments, for the attention was rapt in listening but no comments were forthcoming. Then at the end there was some talking among the people. Finally, someone said, "It sounds like they weren't taking seriously the meaning of the sacrament." The comment was so well spoken it surprised Jeannette.

"Yes, that's good. When Jesus first presented it to his disciples, it was very serious. He was about to die as our sacrifice for our sin. But it sounds like some of the early Christians were growing apathetic in their partaking of it. That's what Paul is warning against.

When we take communion we should seriously judge ourselves and consider the meaning of the sacrament. We are celebrating that Jesus sacrificed himself for our sake, and that we can live free from sin because of his sacrifice."

"In John 3:16 it says, "For God so loved the world that he gave his only begotten Son that whosoever believeth on him should not perish, but have everlasting life." She continued on, "For God sent not his son into the world; but that the world through him might be saved. He that believeth on him is not condemned, but he that believeth not is condemned already because he hath not believed in the name of the only begotten Son of God." (John 3:17, 18, KJV)

"So," Jeannette explained, "belief in Jesus' sacrifice is the key. But the alternative has the opposite affect, so that is the warning.

"Now we are going to partake in the Lord's Supper for all who wish to. We will pass a loaf; each of you will break off a small piece and we will partake together. Then we will pass the cup of wine, and each take a small sip. This not only signifies our belief in Jesus sacrifice, but our kinship with one another as part of the family of God."

The elements were passed and soon the women began to sing together in worship as many joined in.

Darren listened to all that his sister read and explained. It was true, the feelings he held against God still seemed to cling to his spirit, but not as strongly as before. Roman told him about how badly crippled and mean his mother was previously. Now she seemed quite normal, or perhaps abnormally happy. Roman was no longer disbelieving. But what about Rachel? He didn't think she had changed her belief, or rather her unbelief. It seemed to be an important part of what they should agree on.

Rachel spent the day in her room. She was awake early this morning and saw the horses and wagons going down the lane past the house toward the road to Bristol. She saw Darren driving the two bay mares, with his sister and mother on either side of him, following the Gypsy wagon. She felt despair in her heart, as if she was seeing him exit her life forever. Yes, she heard the talk about their imminent visit to the Gypsy camp, with the understanding they would be back in a week, but somehow it seemed to her he was leaving forever. She felt depressed, could not think of anything positive about her life. Her mother was flitting about for weeks, absorbed in her plans for the upcoming event. Rachel's attraction to Darren was a break from her despair in contemplating her mother's plans. *Now he's gone.*

The maid knocked on her door early this morning to bring her breakfast. She wasn't hungry, so the food sat on her dresser uneaten. Her sister came in finally, inquiring why she was not at breakfast. Rachel was not in a mood to talk.

Peggy tried to be cheerful, tried to instigate conversation, but gave up when she got so little response. Now, it was mid afternoon, and Peggy was back. First she came in and sat on the bed and tried conversation. "Rachel, wouldn't it be fun to go visit the Duran girls while all those other people are gone?"

Rachel gave her sister an incredulous look, gave a great sigh and flopped over on her bed. Her sister as silent for a moment, then lay down on the bed next to Rachel, put her arm around her sister, leaning her head on Rachel's shoulder. The sisters lay together like that for a few moments, then Rachel turned back to embrace Peggy, beginning to sob.

"What's all this about, Sis?" Peggy asked. "You've so much ahead of you to be excited about. We've been having such a great time riding lately, and you have your big party coming up. Aren't you excited about it?"

Rachel sat up so quickly, she almost pushed her sister off the bed. "I hate the thought of Mother throwing a big party to try to get me married off to some old man! Then there won't be anymore riding!"

Peggy was speechless. Then she finally spoke. "Well, what do you want to do?"

"I'm in love with Darren. I don't want to marry anyone else. I'm afraid he's leaving forever!"

Now Peggy was again speechless for a moment. "Oh, dear, Rachel, what are you going to do?"

Rachel laughed bitterly, "Well, why don't you pray to your Jesus for me?"

Peggy looked chagrinned. "I would if I thought you were serious. I think you should pray for yourself. I don't think God wants you so unhappy. We could pray about it."

Peggy waited for her sister to reply, but Rachel was silent. Rachel was thinking there were moments lately she thought the Bible reading made more sense, but now she thought of how she agreed with Darren's unbelief and this was a big thing they shared. She knew she laughed at her sister's faith, so now it was even harder to agree with her.

When Rachel continued her silence, Peggy began to pray, "Oh, Father, I pray for my sister because I hate to see her so unhappy. I pray for her joy. I pray for her to be happy in love and happy in believing in your Son Jesus."

When Peggy looked at her sister, Rachel's cheeks were wet with tears, but her jaw was set. Peggy embraced her sister again, then left the room.

HELENA POORTVLIET

CHAPTER 18

Saint Lawrence

THE HULK OF Newfoundland was due north of them and passing on their right as they began to line up with the entrance of the Laurentian Channel into the Gulf of Saint Lawrence. All around were small islands, looking forlorn and wild in the sea. Many of the passengers were on deck to see the unfolding of this new land. Harry was holding onto Jacques' hand, so excited he could not stand still.

"Where's our new home? Can we see it yet?"

Jacques refrained from laughing. "No, it will be quite a while before we see it. Be patient, son. We'll get there." He turned to head back to the horse deck, well aware there was work to be done before their arrival in Montreal in a few more days.

Captain Palmer asked him for confirmation he was not interested in continuing his position as stableman for the return voyage to England. Of course, he knew Jacques' plans to make his home in Canada, but he wanted to make sure the job was his to continue if he wished. Jacques reassured him his plans had not changed. Next, he went to Pierre with the same offer, and Pierre accepted. He agreed to stay with the ship for future voyages. Pierre told Jacques that he felt his place was here on the ship, not only to care for the horses, but to share God's Word with passengers and crew. Captain Palmer gave his approval and promised to consider him not only stableman, but also ship's chaplain.

Since Jacques' agreement to work at least for the winter with Roger and his partner, Roger began to tell him about the building boom in Montreal. Construction in and around Montreal had bloomed at an amazing pace for the past decade, but in the past few years it increased exponentially. Roger's partner, Edward Findlay, involved in the design of larger and larger projects, was having difficulty managing the huge projects, so he begged his friend Roger to join him. There was plenty of manpower in the city, but Edward's skill was in designing projects, not in managing the building crews. Roger was to take on that task, so he was happy to get both Jacques and Willis to commit to working for him at least this year. Roger was able to reassure them both of housing for both their families and their horses.

As they headed down the ramp to the horse deck, Harry ran ahead to the goats' stalls. As Jacques watched the boy, he marveled at how robust Harry had become. As he climbed the rails into the goats' stall, Jacques realized he had grown inches in the last few weeks. The britches he purchased for Harry in Birmingham were gapping above his ankles. Jacques thought to himself, *we'll have to go shopping again as soon as we get to Montreal.* The boy had grown otherwise as well, taking over most of the responsibility of caring for the goats. He proudly showed Jacques his learning projects, results of Andrea's teaching, quickly catching up with Andrew in both writing and numbers. Hearing footsteps, he turned to see Roger and Andrew, accompanied by Willis, coming down the ramp.

"We came to walk horses," was the cheerful explanation. Andrew ran to join Harry with the goats, happy to help clean stalls.

Jacques had worked all of the thoroughbreds yesterday, so he was happy to spend time with his own horses, beginning with Tounerre. As he led the stallion out of his stall the others stopped to watch in admiration. Tounerre pranced in place with his neck arched, full of spirit, but easily under Jacques' control. The others marveled at the power displayed. Over the winter his coat thickened to withstand the cold, but he never looked shaggy. On the contrary, it fairly shone over the rippling muscles.

Roger and Willis each led out one of their horses to follow Jacques in laps around the horse deck. After several laps Jacques returned Tounerre to his stall and then led out Joni. She was much more placid than the stallion and growing extremely round, great with her coming foal. After several laps he switched her for Pari who was nearly as round as her teammate.

Roger could see the mares' conditions made it extremely critical for Jacques to have a place for them almost immediately. He knew Edward assured him of accommodations for his family and horses, but now he realized if he was to retain these men, he needed to provide the same for them. As.he led out his third horse Willis came to him.

"Since I've only two horses, I can walk your last horse if you wish, sir." Willis was headed for the stall of the last of the bay geldings. Roger smiled and nodded.

"This was a good idea," Roger commented. "The time goes faster if we keep busy. I guess we can't make the ship go faster, but keeping busy helps. We're so close to our new lives it's hard to wait out these last few days." Willis agreed.

As they were carrying the cans of milk up the ramp, the fog was moving in all around them, blurring the images on the main deck. The land forms all around them were fading.

At dinner some of the sailors brought up the story of the *Hannah,* which, three years ago in April, bringing immigrants from Ireland, crashed on the ice in the Gulf of Saint Lawrence. Three other vessels helped to rescue the survivors, but many were lost. Captain Palmer came by their table to catch part of the conversation with one eyebrow raised.

One of the passengers asked him about the possibility of hitting ice. "I haven't hit ice in over thirty years of sailing," he smiled slightly, looking disapprovingly at the sailors telling the story. Then he added, "It wouldn't hurt for you folks to be praying for God's guidance and protection through the Gulf."

A great many of the passengers as well as sailors who were off duty were coming to the Bible reading after dinner. So when all were settled on the hay bales, Jacques began reading:

> "Then said the high priest, Are these things so?
> "And he said, Men, brethren and fathers, hearken; The God of glory appeared unto our father Abraham, when he was in Mesopotamia before he dwelt in Charran,
> "And said unto him, Get thee out of thy country, and from thy kindred, and come into the land which I shall show thee.
> "Then he came out of the land of the Chaldeans, and dwelt in Charan: and from thence, when his father was dead, he removed him into this land, wherein ye now dwell.
> "And he gave him none inheritance in it, no, not so much as to set his foot on: yet he promised that he would give it

to him for a possession, and to his seed after him, when as yet he had no child.

"And God spake on this wise, That his seed should sojourn in a strange land; and that they should bring them in bondage, and entreat them evil for four hundred years.

"And the nation to whom they shall be in bondage will I judge, said God: and after that shall they come forth, and serve me in this place.

"And he gave him the covenant of circumcision: and so Abraham begat Isaac, and circumcised him on the eighth day, and Isaac begat Jacob; and Jacob begat the twelve patriarchs." (Acts 7:1-8, KJV)

Jacques paused again while Pierre was translating, noticing that all were in rapt attention. When Pierre finished the last verses and looked up, someone urged, "…read more!" So he went on:

"And the patriarchs, moved with envy, sold Joseph into Egypt: but God was with him.

"And delivered him out of all his afflictions, and gave him favor and wisdom in the sight of Pharaoh king of Egypt; and he made him governor over Egypt and all his house.

"Now there came a dearth over all the land of Egypt and Canaan, and great affliction: and our fathers found no sustenance.

"But when Jacob heard there was corn in Egypt, he sent out our fathers first.

"And at the second time Joseph was made known to his brethren; and Joseph's kindred was made known unto Pharaoh.

"Then sent Joseph and called his father Jacob to him, and all his kindred, threescore and fifteen souls.

"So Jacob went down into Egypt, and died, he, and our fathers,

"And were carried over into Sychem, and laid in the sepulcher that Abraham bought for a sum of money of the sons of Emmor the father of Sychem.

"But when the time of the promise drew nigh, which God had sworn to Abraham, the people grew and multiplied in Egypt,

"Till another king arose, which knew not Joseph." (Acts 7:9-18, KJV)

Again, as Pierre was translating, Jacques watched the reaction of the listeners. Their faces showed rapt attention. Someone commented, "It sounds like a compact history of the Jews." There were nods and noises of agreement, and urges to "read more," so Jacques continued:

> "The same dealt subtly with our kindred, and evil entreated our fathers, so that they cast out their young children, to the end they might not live.
> "In which time Moses was born, and was exceedingly fair, and nourished up in his father's house three months:
> "And when he was cast out, Pharaoh's daughter took him up, and nourished him for her own son.
> "And Moses was learned in all the wisdom of the Egyptians, and was mighty in words and in deeds.
> "And when he was full forty years old, it came into his heart to visit his brethren the children of Israel.
> "And seeing one of them suffer wrong, he defended him, and avenged him that was oppressed and smote the Egyptian:
> "For he supposed his brethren would have understood how that God by his hand would deliver them: but they understood not.
> "And the next day he shewed himself unto them as they strove, and would have set them at one again, saying, Sirs, ye are brethren; why do ye wrong one to another?
> "But he that did his neighbor wrong thrust him away, saying, Who made thee a ruler and a judge over us?
> "Wilt thou kill me as thou did the Egyptian yesterday?
> "Then fled Moses at this saying, and was a stranger in the land of the Midian, where he begat two sons." (Acts 7:19-29, KJV)

Jacques watched the expressions during the translation and waited for comments. Roger spoke up, "Moses had a crisis in his life and changed his environment. The old one was no longer an advantage, so he moved. I wonder how often that happens in our lives. We are all on the move. Could we have continued in our previous situation? Should we look more closely at why we are moving to a new land?"

Roger looked around the group. Jacques was observing the reactions of the listeners. Many were quiet, looking at each other, or just looking down. Then Pierre spoke, "Maybe this is a good time to stop and pray. We need to pray for our safety and guidance through the next few hours of navigation through this weather. Some of you may have personal issues or decisions to make. I invite you to come forward for prayer."

Many came forward and many prayed for each other. Roger stepped up and began to pray. As he prayed the dense fog that was enveloping the ship from above was even rolling down into the horse deck until the group huddled together could only see clearly those closest to them.

"Our Father, you are our guide and our protector. We are in your hands. While many of us decided to embark on this voyage by our own decisions apart from you, we now recognize you hold our futures in your hands. May the relationships we form in this new land be for your purpose and glory. We acknowledge faith in your Son Jesus as the basis of our belief in your guidance and protection."

As Roger paused, there were heard "amen" from every part of the group, which extended out into the fog. Then singing began. People moved in closer as the singing continued. The sea was calm, but the fog remained dense and the mystery held the group together and time seemed to stand still.

When Jacques awoke he had the feeling it was later than usual. Harry and Pierre were still asleep, so he got up quietly and slipped out of the cabin. The horse deck was damp and quiet with the fog, which still lingered. The horses were unusually quiet. He started for Tounerre's stall, and as he drew near, the stallion nickered a welcome, nodding his head in anticipation, so Jacques began the feeding. Soon the other horses were making the same type of noises.

The ship was making very little movement or sound, other than minimal creaking. Jacques was halfway through the feeding when Harry and Pierre emerged from the cabin, still looking sleepy. Pierre started on the cleaning of the stalls, while Harry headed for the goats. They were all quiet, going about their work. The foggy atmosphere was very eerie, which seemed to inhibit talking. It did not take long to finish the work with all three busy, and Deral had not yet arrived with the milk cans so the three headed up the ramp for the main deck. The fog was even thicker outside and the sails were furled to minimize movement. They went to the rail but could see nothing for

HELENA POORTVLIET

the thickness of the fog. It was difficult even to see the water below, which could be heard faintly lapping at the hull of the ship.

"Wonder how long this will last," said Pierre.

"I hope not for long. We're not going anywhere in this." Jacques was shaking his head. Harry moved closer to hang onto his hand. The air was chilly, the dampness penetrating. Everything around them was eerily quiet. Even the sailors on duty were uncommonly inactive, waiting out the weather.

The silence was broken only by the clanking of the milk cans as Deral came out of the galley and headed for the ramp to the horse deck. It seemed that was the signal for activity to begin. More sailors came on the deck, and some of the passengers began to appear. Still, the ship was motionless.

Breakfast was a time of excitement for their imminent arrival at their destination, tempered by their apprehension at the gloom of the stifling fog which was inhibiting their progress. Roger broke the hush, directing his conversation to both Jacques and Willis. "Edward, my partner has written to me of his involvement in the development of the 'Square Mile,' or the 'Golden Square Mile,' as some are calling it."

"What's that?" asked Willis.

"It's an area on the west edge of Montreal where some of the biggest businessmen are building huge homes. Edward has been involved in the design of some of the best new buildings in Montreal, and now he is getting requests to design of some of these great estates.

"Because of the cold weather in the winter, they try to accomplish the major building in the summer, but there is so much interior craftsmanship required on these buildings, they stay pretty busy through the winter. It should be a good opportunity for both of you to learn." Roger's tone was encouraging to the others.

Willis was enthusiastic, glancing at Jacques as he suggested, "We can get some experience and practice and ideas on how we're going to build when we get to Canada West. Do you know where you're going there?" he asked Jacques.

"Not really," was the answer. "That's something I'll have to check into when we get to Montreal. At least now, I can take a little longer to make that decision. But I can't put it off for long. I can't picture raising horses in the city." He laughed a bit, and the others laughed with him.

After breakfast Jacques and Pierre kept busy walking horses. The fog lifted from the horse deck, but the air was damp and chilly. It felt good to be busy and conditions were good for walking the horses since the ship was so still.

Ramon Claudel came down to work his horses beginning with the filly. At only a few weeks old, she was well-behaved and seemed to love the attention of being handled.

Toward the afternoon the fog finally began to lift. The sun was bright, glistening on the water, as the clouds gradually dissipated. The sails were unfurled and the anchor weighed and the *Bucephalus* began to move. Jacques, Pierre and Harry climbed the ramp to get a look, now that it was possible to see. From the rail they could see the shore of Prince Edward Island, materializing out of the haze. There were clean worked fields of farms just beyond the rocky coast. Jacques could barely see men on the backs of heavy horses harnessed together pulling something in the surf that he could not recognize.

The *Bucephalus* was now moving due north, slowly toward Anticosti Island, barely visible in the distance. The island became more visible, along with white dots in the distance: floating ice. Avoiding these as they moved into the Saint Lawrence Waterway was essential to their safety. Once into the current of the river, that danger would diminish. The view was engaging, and only the sound of the clanking metal of the milk cans a Deral approached from the galley reminded them of the milking to be done before dinner.

At dinner the demeanor of the passengers was more relaxed, like prisoners released from bonds. Being able to see into the distance and the renewed progress of the ship seemed to give everyone a new sense of expectancy. The conversation was livelier than at breakfast. Several came to Jacques and Pierre to say they were looking forward to the reading this evening. So after dinner they headed back to the horse deck to continue reading from where they stopped the night before:

> "And when forty years were expired, there appeared to him in the wilderness of mount Sina an angel of the Lord in a flame of fire in a bush.
> "When Moses saw it, he wondered at the sight: and as he drew near to behold it, the voice of the Lord came to him,

"Saying, I am the God of thy fathers, the God of Abraham, the God of Isaac, and the God of Jacob. Then Moses trembled, and durst not behold.

"Then the Lord said to him, Put off thy shoes from thy feet: for the place where thou standeth is holy ground.

"I have seen the afflictions of my people which is in Egypt, and I have heard their groaning, and am come down to deliver them. And now come, I will send thee into Egypt.

"This Moses whom they refused, saying, Who made thee a ruler and a judge? The same did God send to be a ruler and a deliverer by the hand of the angel which appeared to him in the bush." (Acts 7:30-35, KJV)

When Jacques paused, he saw some jaws drop, especially from some of the newer attendees. While listening to the translation, he saw looks of disbelief and knew the questions were coming.

"God spoke out loud? Are we supposed to believe that?"

Jacques answered, "I believe it because I made the choice to believe God's Word. Does anyone else have an answer to this question?"

Andrea offered, "I understand the story in Exodus is attributed to Moses, so he would have been an eyewitness."

Someone else asked, "How should we believe that? It's his story."

Andrea answered, "I think we need to hear more to answer that." So Jacques continued.

"He brought them out, after that he showed wonders and signs in the land of Egypt, and in the Red Sea, and in the wilderness forty years.

"This is that Moses, which said unto the children of Israel, A prophet shall the Lord your God raise up unto you of your brethren like unto me, him shall ye hear.

"This is he, that was in the church in the wilderness with the angel which spake to him in the mount Sina, and with our fathers: who received the lively oracles to give unto us.

"To whom our fathers would not obey, but thrust him from them, and in their hearts turned back again unto Egypt."

"Saying unto Aaron, Make us gods to go before us: for as for this Moses, which brought us out of the land of Egypt, we wot not what has become of him."
(Acts 7:36-40, KJV)

Jacques listened as Pierre translated, watching expressions of disbelief and confusion. Finally, he looked at Andrea for help. "Do you understand what's going on here?"

Andrea smiled, "You see then, disbelief is not new. You see, Moses gained followers when he performed miracles to get them out of Egypt. But when he was out of their sight for a few weeks when he went up on Mount Sinai to receive the Ten Commandments, the people began to lose faith."

Jacques was amazed, relieved Andrea seemed to know the Bible as well as Jeannette. He was thankful now to see expressions of understanding from the listeners. He began to relax as he resumed reading:

> "And they made a calf in those days, and offered sacrifice unto the idol, and rejoiced in the works of their own hands.
> "Then God turned, and gave them up to worship the host of heaven; as it is written in the book of the prophets, O ye of Israel, have ye offered to me slain beasts and sacrifices by the space of forty years in the wilderness.
> "Yea, ye took up the tabernacle of Moloch, and the star of your god Remphan, figures which ye made to worship them; and I will carry you away to Babylon.
> "Our fathers had the tabernacle of witness in the wilderness, as he had appointed, speaking unto Moses, that he should make it according to the fashion that he had seen.
> "Which also our fathers that came after brought in with Jesus into the possession of the Gentiles, whom God drave out before the face of our fathers, unto the days of David;
> "Who found favor before God, and desired to find a tabernacle for the God of Jacob.
> "But Solomon built him a house.
> "Howbeit the most High dwelleth not in temples made with hands; as saith the prophet.
> "Heaven is my throne, and earth is my footstool: What house will ye build me? Saith the Lord: or what is the place of my rest?
> "Hath not my hand made all these things?" (Acts 7:41-50, KJV)

HELENA POORTVLIET

Jacques now felt more confident as he waited for Pierre's translation to end. He was ready for the looks of confusion and disbelief, as he looked to Andrea for explanation.

Smiling, she began to explain. "He's referred to some of the prophecy concerning the Children of Israel's disobedience and their worship of false gods, Moloch and Rempham. Then he refers to the tabernacle in the wilderness, which was a tent of worship, like a church, but eventually confirms that even though we worship God in a tabernacle or temple, he really inhabits the universe, both heaven and earth." This brought looks of understanding.

Pierre added his comment, "It's comforting to know God inhabits both heaven and earth, so we are not alone to survive the whims of nature on our own. I will trust him to get us to Montreal without threat of disaster during the rest of the trip."

This brought cheers and "amens" as the people worshiped in a much more positive humor. The worship continued as some began to sing. It was late, the reading was long, but everyone sensed the lesson was not yet complete, but they were content to return for more later.

The chores done, Jacques headed up the ramp, Harry and Pierre close behind. From the rail they could see the ship was anchored overnight just west of the Gaspe Penninsula. To the south they could still see Prince Edward Island. Across the channel to the north was the rocky coast of Anticosti Island. Today, they would begin the journey up the Saint Lawrence Waterway. To the north Jacques could see the mainland beyond Anticosti Island lined with ice and snow, with many chunks of ice floating out into the waterway.

"Only a few days now, we'll see Montreal," Jacques grinned at the others. Harry was jumping up and down in excitement. Alerted by the clanking, turning to see Deral heading toward the ramp with the milk cans, they all headed back for the horse deck.

The milking went quickly, and they headed for the galley to deliver the milk. They could feel the movement of the ship as the anchors were weighed, knowing they were underway up the Saint Lawrence. So, before going to breakfast they went back to the rail. The tide was low, exposing the muddy shoreline which was dotted with chunks of ice on the north side of the river. But the tide was changing, carrying the ship with a tremendous surge. The sails were filling with wind, pushing the ship even faster upstream. Jacques felt a thrill of excitement, knowing they were quickly moving toward their destination. As they turned to head toward the dining room, several others stood behind them, looking up the river, which was so wide it was like an endless bay.

After breakfast Jacques intended to return to the horse deck to walk the shires, since they had not been walked in a few days. He shared his intent with Pierre, hoping for help with the task. Andrea asked that Harry might stay with her and Andrew for the day, but he was surprised when he got up to leave and Roger and Willis got up to follow him. Roger grinned and said, "Let's go walk horses."

Roger and Willis walked their own horses first, then helped with the rest of the shires, so the job went fairly fast, walking nineteen horses between four men by mid-afternoon. About the time they were getting the last of the shires settled, the motion of the ship was becoming more uneven, with quite a bit of rocking.

They all headed up the ramp to look from the rail. The ship moved far upstream on the incoming tide which was now high, enlarging the breadth of the river even more. The sails now furled, the anchor was being dropped. Jacques suddenly realized just how they were traveling upstream. They would remain anchored until the low tide tomorrow morning. Jacques was amazed how far they moved in just a few hours.

After dinner Jacques adjusted the arrangement of hay bales in preparation for the Bible reading. He expected a lot more of the sailors would be attending, since they would be at anchor overnight. It was not long before the group arrived, ready to listen, so Jacques began:

> "Ye stiffnecked and uncircumcised in heart and ears, ye do always resist the Holy Ghost: as your fathers did, so do ye.
> "Which of the prophets have not your fathers persecuted? and they have slain them which shewed before the coming of the Just One; of whom ye have been not the betrayers and murderers:
> "Who have received the law by the disposition of angels, and have not kept it." (Acts 7:51-53, KJV)

When Pierre finished the translation of these verses, Jacques reminded them this was still Stephen speaking to the council of the priests.

"Wow, he's really let them have it," commented Pierre. "What's next?"

Jacques continued:

> "When they heard these things they were cut to the heart, and they gnashed on him with their teeth.
> "But he, being full of the Holy Ghost, looked up steadfastly into the heaven, and saw the glory of God, and Jesus standing on the right hand of God.
> "And said, Behold, I see the heavens opened, and the Son of man standing on the right hand of God.
> "Then they cried out with a loud voice, and stopped their ears, and ran upon him with one accord.
> "And cast him out of the city, and stoned him: and the witnesses laid down their clothes at a young man's feet, whose name was Saul.
> "And they stoned Stephen, calling upon God, and saying, Lord Jesus, receive my spirit.
> "And he kneeled down, and cried with a loud voice, Lord, lay not this sin to their charge. And when he said this, he fell asleep." (Acts 7:54-60, KJV)

Now Jacques watched the expressions of the listeners as Pierre translated. He saw looks of amazement at Stephen's vision, then shock and anger when they realized Stephen was being stoned to death.

There were some folks weeping and others raised their hands in prayer. Pierre sounded very emotional as he commented on Stephen's bravery and dedication to preach God's Word. "I hope I can be that strong if I ever have to face persecution for God's sake." He looked around at the group and then invited anyone in need of prayer to come forward.

CHAPTER 19

Plans

D ARREN LAY IN the bunk wide-awake with thoughts racing through his mind. He was sharing space in this strange little wagon, built like a small cabin on wheels, with these three Romani men. A few weeks ago, he tried to get them out of his mother's home, making terrible accusations against them. Now he was in their home, grudgingly accepting their hospitality. It was true, his animosity softened somewhat, but still he felt as if he was in enemy territory.

He thought about things his sister said in her Bible reading. It seemed she was directing her words at him. It scared him to think her words were beginning to make sense. Rachel was always on his mind. He was afraid she would be disappointed if he accepted the Bible teaching. He searched his mind for an answer to keep them together. He wanted to stand up to her parents, but the thought filled him with fear. He knew he wanted to marry Rachel, but he was terrified of the thought of telling anyone else. *How could he make it work?* Darren finally fell asleep, dreaming of Rachel. Then he seemed to be confronted by her father, awaking in panic. No one seemed to understand how he felt about her.

Streaks of dawn were beginning to lighten the interior of the wagon. Darren slipped out before the others were awake, and went to his horse. Dani and Katy greeted him with expectant nickers, so he pulled some hay and feed out of the back of the wagon for the mares. The horses were a great comfort to him, but his mind went to another horse—*the dapple-gray ridden by the most beautiful girl.* Again he thought, *how could he make it work?* He dug into the wagon to find a brush and began to brush Dani. She nudged him appreciatively with her head, then resumed munching her hay. He continued brushing, deep in thought, until the other mare, Katy, paused in her munching to shake her head toward him, so he turned to brush her. Time slipped by and the sun was burning off the early morning haze. He turned back to his own horse and resumed brushing her.

Then on impulse, he turned to the wagon to pull out his saddle. Dani was still munching hay as he cinched on the saddle. He pulled her away from the hay to put on her bridle before mounting her, turning toward the road out of the camp. He walked her quietly until they were out of the circle of wagons, then kicked her into a canter. In a few moments he was on the highway which led back toward Gloucester. The cool morning air was exhilarating and he let her have her head to run. He leaned forward and gripped with his heals letting her run until the wind brought tears to his eyes. As he relaxed his heels and leaned back, she slowed her pace to a canter.

Darren thought about the road ahead that led through Gloucester, then Bristol and back to the Montgomery estate. *It would be so easy to continue back to where he really wanted to be. But what could he do that would make a difference?*

However, that short gallop made him feel freer than he thought he could. The idea was growing. *What could stop him from making his own decisions, being free to go his own way? How could he take control of his own life? He had his portion of the sale of the property, but that was only for the safety of the family. The money was for fare, and establishing a new family business in Montreal. But, money was not the issue. The real issue was breaking the authority of the family—his mother and his sister. He was the one who had encouraged them to move. How could he break that tie?*

Finally, he pulled up the mare and turned her back toward the camp and his family. As he approached, he could see a rider coming toward him at a gallop. Soon he recognized Roman's horse. The other man was laughing as he pulled up his horse along side Darren's.

"If you go for a ride this early in the morning you may miss breakfast. Or maybe what's on your mind has more pull than breakfast!" Roman's expression was as knowing as it was questioning. "It's a long ride back to the Montgomery's. Do you have a plan?"

Darren met Roman's question with acknowledgement of his suspicions. "I don't have a plan yet, but I'm working on it. Any idea?"

"Does she know how you feel?"

"I think she does."

"Does she feel the same?"

"I think—I hope so."

"Well, would she go with you if you asked her?"

"I—I don't know," Darren felt unsure. *Would Rachel really leave her family for him?*

"Well, man, you've got to find out!" Roman was adamant.

"But what could we do? Her father would probably come after us." Darren was shaking his head, feeling defeated.

"Get her away from them and get handfast as fast as you can, preferably with witnesses. Then consummate it." Roman was smiling.

"What do you mean—handfast?" Darren looked doubtful.

"You hold hands or tie your hands together, and vow your intent to each other. We do that in front of our chief and witnesses. Romani don't get married by priests. We're not part of all that. But the English accept it as marriage, especially if it's consummated." Roman was grinning. "What can they do?"

Darren was open-mouthed. "Really?"

"Really!"

They were now walking their horses down the road into the camp. There were campfires started all around the area and the smell of food cooking was tantalizing.

Roman turned back to Darren. "Do it when your family and the Merlots are not here. Grace and I can be your witnesses and we can get Stavros to listen to your vows and make it official."

Darren began to feel a glimmer of hope. He rode up to the wagon and unsaddled Dani, giving her an extra portion of feed before approaching the Merlots campfire.

Jeannette watched the two riding in and greeted her brother with a smile. "You are enjoying spending time with Roman, aren't you?"

"Oh, yes," he answered.

Jeannette and her mother had been practicing singing with Ellienne and Elena, and now they were sharing their music with the others who came to breakfast. Before long, others joined in with instruments and they were teaching the songs to the rest of the people. After several songs which were joined by all, hands were raised in worship. After a bit, there were those who were asking for Jeannette to read, so she happily consented, opening her Bible again to Genesis:

"Now Sarai Abram's wife bare him no children: and she had a handmaid, an Egyptian, whose name was Hagar.

"And Sarai said to Abram, Behold now, the Lord has restrained me from bearing: I pray thee, go in unto my maid; it may be that I may obtain children by her. And Abram hearkened to the voice of Sarai.

"And Sarai, Abram's wife took Hagar her maid the Egyptian, after Abram had dwelt ten years in the land of Canaan, and gave her to her husband Abram to be his wife." (Gen. 16:1-3, KJV)

Even before Antoine finished his translation, Jeannette could feel the reaction of shock and disapproval of the people. This was a new concept for them and Jeannette quickly began to explain the different cultural practices of that time.

"It was very important for a married woman to have children, and Abram and Sarai were married for many years without children. Men often took concubines to have children, and this was a way for a wife to claim children for herself according to their tradition. Sarai thought she could help out God." Jeannette had a sly smile as she continued reading:

"And he went in unto Hagar, and she conceived: and when she saw that she had conceived, her mistress was despised in her eyes.

"And Sarai said unto Abram, My wrong be upon thee: I have given my maid unto thy bosom, and when she saw that she had conceived, I was despised in her eyes: the Lord judge between me and thee.

"But Abram said to Sarai, Behold, thy maid is in thy hand; do to her as it pleaseth thee. And when Sarai dealt hardly with her; she fled from her face."
(Gen. 16:4-6, KJV)

Jeannette saw the indignant expressions.

"It serves her right; it was her own fault." Said one man.

A woman replied, "Well, Abram didn't turn down the offer." This brought some laughs.

Someone else said, "Well, Hagar took the opportunity to play superior to her mistress."

There was much more talk among the people, until Jeannette began again:

> "And the angel of the Lord found her by a fountain of water in the wilderness, by the fountain on the way to Shur.
> "And he said, Hagar, Sarai's maid, Whence camest thou? And whither wilt thou go? And she said, I flee from the face of my mistress Sarai.
> "And the angel of the Lord said to her, Return to thy mistress, and submit thyself under her hands.
> "And the angel of the Lord said unto her, I will multiply thy seed exceedingly, and it shall not be numbered for the multitude." (Gen. 16:7-10, KJV)

Jeannette waited a bit, but several people said, "Read more, read more," so she continued:

> "And the angel of the Lord said unto her, Behold, thou art with child, and shall bare a son, and shall call his name Ishmael: because the Lord hath heard thy affliction.
> "And he will be a wild man; his hand will be against everyman, and every man's hand against him; and he shall dwell in the presence of all his brethren.
> "And she called the name of the Lord that spake unto her, Thou God seeist me; for she said, Have I also here looked after him that seeist me:
> "Wherefore the well was called Beer la hai roe, behold it between Kadesh and Bered.
> "And Hagar bear Abram a son: and Abram called his son's name, which Hagar bare, Ishmael.
> "And Abram was four score and six years old when Hagar bare Ishmael to Abram." (Gen. 16:11-16, KJV)

Jeannette waited for the translation, then added, "Even when we do crazy things and it seems like they don't turn out so well, God still cares about us." She was looking at her brother who was looking down.

"What was it like?" Rachel asked.
"What was what like?" her sister countered.

HELENA POORTVLIET

"The Gypsy camp—you went there with the Durans when they took Grace back. What was it like?"

Peggy smiled, remembering. "Oh, they were nice. Grace's mother was so happy to see her."

"Do they really live in those funny wagons?"

"Yes, they do. They're really cute—everything in its place. They even have little flower gardens in the windows. They're just like tiny cottages, only on wheels. I miss Grace though. I hope she's happy with her family."

"I can't imagine Darren and his family staying there all week." Rachel was gazing out the window. "Where do they sleep, I wonder?"

"Oh, they share their wagons with the visitors. We could have stayed there, but Jules thought he should get me home."

Rachel was quiet, thinking about what Peggy told her. After a while she spoke again. "Do you want to ride this afternoon? Maybe the Duran girls would ride also."

Now Peggy looked surprised. Yesterday she could not get her sister to consider riding. "Sure, that would be fun. I'll go tell Morton."

The next morning, Darren awoke early and again slipped out of the wagon while the others were sleeping to go to his horse. After feeding both mares, he spent the time grooming Dani while she ate, before buckling on the saddle. In a while he was riding up the hill to the main road, feeling light-hearted with the possibility he might have a plan. He felt good yesterday riding before breakfast. It seemed a good thing to do, not out of frustration, but because he enjoyed the time with his horse.

As he neared the highway, he heard hoofbeats behind him, and looked back to see Roman on his horse, galloping up the hill after him. He reined up Dani and waited for his friend to catch up.

"You have a good idea, to ride early in the morning!" Roman was laughing breathlessly, as he pulled up his horse next to Darren, as he acknowledged the other's comment by an affirmative grin.

As they let the horses walk, Roman commented, "Your sister is quite a teacher. I like the way she used the Bible stories to get people talking about life issues. Pretty smart!"

Darren was surprised at the comment, then thinking about how Jeannette seemed to focus on him the night before, answered, "I think she's trying to talk to me, but I never know what to say."

"What do you think she's trying to say to you?"

"I don't know, but I'm sure she wants me to accept all this God stuff."

"Maybe if you tried praying to God, it would be easier to figure out all your big questions."

Darren looked back at his friend. "You mean about Rachel?"

"Well, that's sure one of them, isn't it?"

"What about that handfasting thing? Is that really true?"

"Of course!" Roman looked offended. "Would I lie to you?"

"Would you?" Darren asked, serious.

"Of course not! Seriously! Are you thinking about it?"

"Well, I'll talk to Rachel when I get back there. You think Grace and Stavros will really go along with it?"

"I already told Grace and she's thrilled. She'd really love to be Rachel's bridesmaid. And Stavros will just see it as part of his job."

Darren thought it seemed too easy.

CHAPTER 20

Isle Aux Coudres

THEY DELIVERED THE milk to the galley, but before going to breakfast, the three headed for the rail. The *Bucephalus* was still at anchor, and thick fog which enveloped them overnight, was now beginning to lift. Low tide exposed the muddy banks, and in places, the remains of wreckages from ships of the past which had not been so lucky.

"Can we see our new home yet?" Harry was holding onto Jacques arm, looking up hopefully.

"Not yet, son," Jacques answered patiently.

Sailors were now unfurling sails, and weighing anchor anticipating the imminent incoming tide. The ship, like the waking of a sleeping giant, began to creak and shudder as it began to move on the tide.

"We're moving!"

"All right!"

All of them laughing, they turned toward the dining room, looking forward to the time with their friends. The Breakfields and the Caldwells were entering the dining room just as Jacques, Harry and Pierre approached. As usual, the boys were overjoyed to see each other.

The conversation at breakfast focused on the near future and the construction business in Montreal. Both Willis and Jacques had questions, many of which Roger could not answer yet, since he himself would not know until their arrival and his assessment of the situation first hand.

"One thing I will say, though," he offered, "I am relieved to start the job with three good workers I know and trust."

Willis and Jacques looked at each other with the same question, "Three?" just as they were joined by Ramon Claudel.

"Ah, it is a good day—for we are so close to our new home!" Jovial as usual, but looking more excited than usual, he greeted the group.

"You're working with us, too?" Willis was the first to respond.

"I hope that is good news to all of you," Ramon added, still grinning.

The others all nodded, making comments in agreement.

Roger was smiling, looking very satisfied. "I have good knowledge of how all of you work well together. It's good to know I can start this new job, with at least part of my crew already known to me."

The insecurity of the days ahead softened for all with the knowledge they would have each other's companionship in the next chapter of their lives.

After dinner, Jacques and Pierre readied the area with enough hay bales for seating for a large group. The ship again would be anchored overnight, so most of the sailors as well as the passengers would be coming. When the group was assembled, Jacques began to read:

> "And Saul was consenting unto his death. At that time there was a great persecution against the church which was at Jerusalem; and they were all scattered throughout the regions of Judaea and Samaria, except the apostles.
> "And devout men carried Stephen to his burial, and made great lamentation over him.
> "As for Saul, he made havoc of the church, entering into every house, and haling men and women and committed them to prison."

> "Therefore they that were scattered abroad went everywhere preaching the word. (Acts 8:1-4, KJV)

> "Then Philip went down to the city of Samaria, and preached Christ unto them.
> "And the people with one accord gave heed unto those things which Philip spake, hearing and seeing the miracles which he did.
> "For unclean spirits, crying with a loud voice, came out of many that were possessed of them; and many were taken with palsies, and that were lame, were healed.
> "And there was great joy in that city." (Acts 8:5-8, KJV)

Jacques listened to Pierre's translation while watching the listeners.

Some looked perplexed, and one spoke up, a sailor there for the first time.

"Who is Saul? who is Stephen?"

Pierre explained to him about Stephen's death and Saul's involvement. Then another man asked about the events in Samaria.

"What about those unclean spirits—you mean there is such a thing?

Pierre again explained, "We are finding a lot of this throughout the Bible. Jesus, while he was on earth, showed us we can have power over them, and now the apostles are showing us a good example that it really is possible."

Jacques heard several "amens" from those who had been coming regularly. Then he heard several say, "Read more!" so he continued.

> "But there was a certain man called Simon, which beforetime in the same city used sorcery and bewitched the people of Samaria, giving out that himself was some great one.
>
> "To whom they all gave great heed, from the least to the greatest, saying, This man is the great power of God.
>
> "And to him they had regard, because of that long time he had bewitched them with sorceries.
>
> "But when they believed Philip preaching of the things concerning the kingdom of God, and the name of Jesus Christ, they were baptized, both men and women.
>
> "Then Simon himself believed also: and when he was baptized, he continued with Philip, and wondered beholding the miracles and signs which were done.
>
> "Now the apostles which were at Jerusalem heard that Samaria had receive the word of God, they sent unto them Peter and John:
>
> "Who when they were come down, prayed for them, that they might receive the Holy Ghost.
>
> "(For as yet He was fallen upon none of them; only they were baptized in the name of the Lord Jesus.)
>
> "They laid their hands on them, and they received the Holy Ghost.

"And when Simon saw that through laying on of the apostle's hands the Holy Ghost was given, he offered money,

"Saying, give me also this power, that whosoever I lay hands, he may receive the Holy Ghost.

"But Peter said unto him, Thy money perish with thee, because thou has thought that the gift of God may be purchased for money.

"Thou hast neither part nor lot in this matter, for thy heart is not right in the sight of God.

"Repent therefore of this wickedness, and pray God, if perhaps the thought of thy heart may be forgiven thee,

"For I perceive that thou art in the gall of bitterness, and in the bond of iniquity.

"Then answered Simon, and said, Pray ye to the Lord for me, that none of these things which ye have spoken come upon me.

"And they, when they had testified and preached the word of the Lord, returned to Jerusalem, and preached the gospel in many villages of the Samaritans."

(Acts 8:9-25, KJV)

Jacques paused every few verses to allow Pierre to translate, so now he observed the listerners were very serious, listening attentively to the story.

As Pierre finished translating, he commented on the story. "I think this story about Simon tells us it is not good to mess with God's gifts in any way that is self-serving. Are there any comments?

"I agree," said Roger. "The things of God are not to be taken lightly."

Everyone remained quiet, pondering the lesson. Pierre gave an invitation for anyone who wanted to come forward to profess belief in Jesus as Saviour, and several of the sailors responded. Soon the group was all praying together.

As light slowly seeped through the rain from the east, the *Bucephalus* was still at anchor awaiting that lowest ebb of the tide before it began to reverse. Sailors were already unfurling the sails, anticipating the weighing of the anchor their faces wet with the sideways rain and sleet, coming on the wind as they worked. That wind catching, grabbing at the sails as they opened, while sailors held on tightly to prevent ropes from being snatched from their hands.

The water was so low in the broad waterway that skeletons of ancient treasures were exposed for a brief glimpse before they were hidden again. A river cormorant swooped from skeletal trees to take advantage of the visual evidence of its river food source. In one motion it dipped, then rose with its prey, swooping back to the border of trees.

As the three were climbing the ramp with the milk, they were met with freezing rain and biting wind. On the north side of the river snow still covered the bank and the melt seeped toward the water, dripping from icicles where the bank was undercut by the current. They hurried to the galley to escape the cold, delivered the milk and hurried to the welcoming warmth of the dining room.

Harry ran ahead happily to greet Andrew, as Jacques and Pierre followed to join the Breakfields at their table. As they sat down, they could feel the shuddering and rocking of the ship as it began to lift and move on the incoming tide. The current was rougher than usual in the wind and sleet.

"Just a sample of our future weather of Canada," Roger commented. "But then the sun does not always shine on the British Isles either!"

"Can't be any worse than being at sea in a storm. At least we'll have solid earth under our feet," Willis responded, then looked apologetically at Pierre, since they all now knew he would be staying with the ship.

Pierre grinned and shrugged. "It's what I chose. I believe it's where God wants me. He will take care of me. It will be smooth sailing, even in the storm!"

Ramon joined them. "You are a fortunate man to know where God wants you to be. Many people never know!"

After breakfast, Jacques and Pierre hurried back to the horse deck. They had no desire to shiver in the cold wet weather where they could see very little anyway. It was enough to know the tide was moving them quickly toward their destination.

Darkness closed in, it seemed, earlier than usual in the cold, wet weather, the steady rain and sleet continuing all day. The tide reached its peak, the anchor dropped and the sails furled for the night.

After working on the chilly horse deck all day it was a welcome break to head for the warmth of the dining room, which was crowded with sailors, now idle for the night. Pierre left the group to talk to several of the sailors. Jacques noted that after talking to a few young sailors, Pierre continued around the room to talk to several others before returning to their table.

"I think we'll have a crowd tonight," he told Jacques as he sat down. "Most of the guys who haven't come yet, have heard about it from the others."

Jacques was amazed to see the fruits of Pierre's promotional efforts, as many sailors and passengers headed down the ramp. He hoped there were a few left on the job to look after the ship, as he began:

> "And the angel of the Lord spake unto Philip saying, Arise, and go toward the south unto the way that goeth down from Jerusalem unto Gaza which is desert.
> "And he arose and went: and, behold, a man of Ethiopia, an eunich of great authority under Candace queen of the Ethiopians, who had the charge of all her treasure, and had come to Jerusalem to worship,
> "Was returning, and sitting in his chariot reading Esaias the prophet.
> "Then the Spirit said unto Philip, Go near, and join thyself to this chariot.
> "And Philip ran thither to him, and heard him read the prophet Esaias, and said, Understandeth what thou readest?"
> "And he said, How can I, except some man should guide me? And he desired Philip that he should come up and sit with him.
> "The place of the scripture which he read was this, He was led as a sheep to slaughter and like a dumb lamb before his shearer, so opened he not his mouth:
> "In his humiliation his judgement was taken away: and who shall declare his generation? for his life was taken from the earth.
> "And the eunich answered Philip, and said, I pray thee, of whom speaketh the prophet this? of himself, or of some other man?" (Acts 8:26-34, KJV)

When Jacques paused to allow Pierre to translate, he watched the rapt expressions of the listeners, expecting questions. However, after a moment, several urged him, "read on!"

> "Then Philip opened his mouth and began at the same scripture, and preached unto him Jesus.
> "And as they went on their way, they came unto a certain water: and the eunich said, See, here is water, what doth hinder me to be baptized?
> "And Philip said, if thou believeth with all thine heart, thou mayest. And he answered and said, I believe that Jesus Christ is the Son of God.
> "And he commandeth the chariot to stand still: and they went down both into the water, both Philip and the eunich; and he baptized him.
> "And when they were come up out of the water, the Spirit of the Lord caught away Philip, that the eunuch saw him no more: and he went his way, rejoicing.
> "But Philip was found at Azotus: and passing through he preached in all the cities, till he came to Caesareas. (Acts 8:35-40, KJV)

As Jacques again paused, this time he expected questions, and he was not disappointed. "What do you mean—Philip was caught away?"

This seemed to get a lot of attention. "I'm not sure exactly," Jacques began, looking first at Pierre, then toward Andrea.

"I think it's pretty exciting," Andrea began, "that Philip was so close to God that God could deal with him that way. There are several examples in the Bible of out-of-body experiences, and cases like this, where a person is instantly transported, but I don't think it would be possible unless the person was very closely in God's will."

Andrea paused and looked around, almost apprehensively before continuing. "As we continue tò read and study in the Book of Acts, we will find a lot of things which previously may have seemed to be unbelievable. But this is the Book of Acts: it's the story of the apostles of the early church, who are filled with the power of the Holy Spirit. It's meant to show us how we can live if we really allow God to have our way in our lives."

Jacques was thankful for Andrea's words. He realized even more it was not about him, but all of them had a part in the activity of the Holy Spirit.

Pierre then gave the invitation: "Any of you who would pray to receive Jesus as Savior, or for the infilling of the Holy Spirit, I invite you to come forward so we can pray for you." Many came forward and praying continued, despite the chilly night and sleet blowing down into the horse deck.

When Jacques opened the door of cabin to the noisy greeting of hungry horses, thick snow flakes were drifting from above into the horse deck. As he looked up the ramp, the sky above was gray and dotted with white. It was biting cold, so he reached for a warmer coat.

"It's cold," was the first comment from Harry, so Jacques paused long enough to make sure he also had on his warm coat before coming out. The deck was slick with the thin layer of snow around the bottom of the ramp. Now Pierre was awake and caught on quickly the state of the weather, seeing the warm coats.

The discomfort of the cold was incentive to work quickly to take care of the animals, just in time to greet Deral as he arrived with the milk cans. They hurried through that task to take advantage of the welcome warmth of the dining room. Even colder on the main deck, the wind was adding to the chill, and visibility was limited to what was close to them.

The chill of the weather made the warmth of companionship even more welcome. Friendships deepened over the voyage made everyone comfortable with each other anxious as they were to reach their destinations. Most lingered longer than usual, unwilling to leave the warmth of friendship as much as the warmth of the room.

Later each morning, the wait for the incoming tide controlled the weighing of the anchor. When the three finally left the dining room the ship was yet still, but the snow ended, allowing much more visibility. They were in the channel between the south shore and an island that looked to Jacques to be little more than five or six miles long close to the north side of the channel. The three stopped to look.

At low tide there was a wide tide flat all the way around it. There were some ridges at the top which were nearly mountains. Jacques could see what looked like windmills and church structures, and many smaller cabins and cottages. Everything was topped with snow, including what looked like snow covered fields. Sean Macrae stopped near them to answer the unspoken question, "It's Ile Aux Coudres. We'll reach Quebec City this afternoon."

CHAPTER 21

Conversion

"And when Abram was ninety years old and nine, the Lord appeared to Abram, and said unto him, I am the Almighty God; walk before me, and be thou perfect.
"And I will make my covenant between me and thee, and will multiply thee exceedingly.
"And Abram fell on his face: and God talked with him saying,
"As for me, behold, my covenant is with thee, and thou shalt be a father of many nations" (Gen. 17:1-4, KJV)

DARREN FELT STARTLED not only by the words his sister read, but by the way she read it. She seemed to raise her voice to a volume and pitch much higher than usual. The words seemed to carry much more forcefully. As he looked up, her face seemed to shine like an angel, and for a moment, the wind picked up, and even made a rushing sound. As he quickly looked around, others seemed to hear it also. Then as Antoine began to translate, Darren realized the same thing was happening again. Antoine's voice became much more forceful and it seemed a though a light shone on his face. Darren shuddered, tried to look away, but he could see the people were rapt in the spiritual light that seemed to envelope all of them. Darren looked at his sister and she was looking directly at him, smiling. He realized he was shivering.

Jeannette began to read again:

"Neither shall thy name any more be called Abram, but thy name shall be Abraham; for a father of many nations have I made thee.
"And I will make thee exceedingly fruitful, and I will make nations of thee, and kings shall come out of thee.

"And I will establish my covenant between me and thee and thy seed after thee in their generations for a lasting covenant, to be a God unto thee, and to thy seed after thee. "And I will give unto thee and to thy seed after thee, the land wherein thou art a stranger, all the land of Canaan, for an everlasting possession; and I will be their God." (Gen. 17:5-8, KJV)

Darren felt shaken, realizing even his teeth were chattering. When no longer able to sit still, he got up and left the group, feeling unable to listen anymore, walking away into the dark.

Jeannette continued reading:

"And God said unto Abraham, Thou shalt keep my covenant therefore, thou and thy seed after thee in their generations.
"This is thy covenant, which ye shall keep, between me and you and thy seed after thee; every man child among you shall be circumcised.
"And ye shall circumcise the flesh of your foreskin: and it shall be a token of the covenant betwixt me and you.
"And he that is eight days old shall be circumcised among you, every man child in your generations, he that is born in the house, or bought with money of any stranger, which is not of thy seed.
"He that is born in thy house, and he that is bought with thy money, must needs be circumcised: and my covenant shall be in thy flesh for an everlasting covenant.
"And the uncircumcised man child whose flesh of the foreskin is not circumcised, that soul shall be cut off from his people, he hath broken my covenant."
(Gen. 17:9-14, KJV)

Jeannette calmly watched the expressions of the people as Antoine translated. She was not surprised when the reaction came, and also not surprised when the questions were directed at Antoine, mostly from men, plainly avoiding looking at her.

Antoine rolled his eyes, opening his hands in an expression of forfeit, shrugging his shoulders as he looked back at Jeannette, somewhat embarrassed. Jeannette was turning pages, calmly, while even her mother was looking embarrassed and apprehensive. She began to explain.

"Genesis with the story of Abraham is of the Old Covenant. Jesus is of the New Covenant. Circumcision was required of the Jews of the Old Covenant as an outward sign in their bodies they agreed with the covenant. Belief in Jesus as our Savior is our New Covenant."

"In Galations 5:5-6," she said as she found the page, "It says, 'For we through the Spirit wait for the hope of rightiousness by faith, for in Jesus Christ, neither circumcision availeth anything; nor uncircumcision; but faith worketh by love.'"

She continued to turn pages, saying, "In Philippians, Chapter 3:3 it says, 'For we are the circumcision which worship God in the Spirit and rejoice in Jesus Christ, and have no confidence in the flesh.'"

"In verse 5 Paul speaks of his own circumcision as a Jew on the eighth day, but in verse 7 he says, 'But what things were gain to me, those I counted loss for Christ.'"

"In Colossians 2:8-14 it says, 'Beware lest any man spoil you through philosophy and vain deceit, after the traditions of men, after the rudiments of the world, and not after Christ:

'For in him dwelleth all the fullness of the Godhead bodily.

'And ye are complete in him, which is the head of all principality and power:

'In whom also ye are circumcised with the circumcision made without hands, in putting off the body of sins of the flesh by the circumcision of Christ:

'Buried with him in baptism, wherein also ye are risen with him through the faith of the operation of God, who hath raised him from the dead.

'And you, being dead in the sins and the uncircumcision of your flesh, hath he quickened together with him, having forgiven you all trespasses:

'Blotting out the handwriting of ordinances that was against us, which is contrary to us, and took it out of the way, nailing it to the cross.'"

"So you see, it is not what we do in works or what we do in our flesh, but what we do in our spirit which joins us to the Spirit of God in Christ," Jeannette explained, as she nodded toward Antoine.

HELENA POORTVLIET

Understanding came as the people listened to Antoine's translation, and responded with their hands raised in worship as the singing began. Many began to pray together as Antoine and Ellienne moved into the group to pray with them. Jeannette saw her mother praying with some of the women, so she quietly moved away from the group in the direction she thought she had seen her brother headed, finding him at their wagon, with his horse, Dani. He was leaning against her with his arms around her neck, his face buried in her mane. The mare's head was twisted toward him in reciprocation of affection. Jeannette went right to him to embrace him. Finally she spoke, "You have so much on your mind, you've got to talk about it. If you can't talk to me, then talk to God. He can solve it."

Darren felt that old familier stab of pain, making it hard to speak. Jeannette waited. Finally, he blurted out, "Why would I want to talk to him when he took our father? That wasn't fair. We needed him. How can you let that go?"

Jeannette stepped back as if struck. Then she recovered and reached out to embrace him. Now he was sobbing.

"Sweetie, God did not take our father. It was evil men who took him. It was not God's will for him to die early. And it was not your fault, either. You could not do anything to stop it. But it is God who gives me, and you too, strength to live every day, even though our father is with Him. And we can know through God's promises we will see our father again. Our father loved God, and I am confident he is with Him now, looking down on us."

Darren looked at his sister for a moment, before he spoke. "But all those people at the funeral said 'God took him; it was his time!' That's not fair; we needed him!" His expression clearly bore witness to his pain.

Jeannette still had her Bible in her hand, so now she opened it again as she said, "Paul tells us in 1 Thessalonians 4:13, 'But I would not have you to be ignorant, brethren, concerning them which are asleep, that ye sorrow not, even as others which have no hope.

'For if we believe that Jesus died and rose again, even so them also which sleep in Jesus will God bring with him.

'For this we say unto you by the word of the Lord, that we which are alive and remain unto the coming of the Lord shall not prevent them which are asleep.

'For the Lord himself will descend from heaven with a shout, with the voice of the archangel and with the trump of God; and the dead in Christ shall rise first.

'Then we which are alive and remain shall be caught up together with them in the clouds, to meet the Lord in the air; and so shall we ever be with the Lord.

'Wherefore comfort one another with these words.'"

Darren listened quietly while his sister read. It was still hard to speak with the stabbing pain in his chest, and even up to his throat. But somehow the words she read were comforting.

"Our father is with Christ. Our time on earth is very short compared to eternity in heaven. We believe according to God's Word, He is coming for us in the resurrection. At that time we will be reunited with our father. But while we are still here in this life, we can find strength in God to rebuild our lives and live well."

Darren was still silent, but began to relax. Jeannette seemed to understand his inability to speak, so she just embraced him again. Finally he spoke, "Thanks, Sis." They turned together to walk back to the group.

As the earliest streaks of dawn appeared in the eastern sky, Darren was on Dani, cantering toward the highway, when hoofbeats behind him let him know that Roman was about to join him.

"You had a good talk with your sister last night. Is she in on your plans now?"

Darren answered, "Oh, no, I really don't have a plan yet. She just wanted to talk about our father." Darren suddenly realized he mentioned his father without feeling that stabbing pain. He even felt relatively warm-hearted toward God.

"What about your father?"

"Well, he died last summer," Darren answered carefully, almost expecting the pain.

Roman looked startled. "Oh, I'm sorry! Are you okay?"

"Well, I think I'm getting better now, but it was pretty bad for a long time."

HELENA POORTVLIET

After breakfast the people were again anxious for Jeannette to read from the Bible, so she went back to Genesis again:

> "And God said to Abraham, as for Sarai your wife, thou shalt not call her name Sarai, but Sarah shall her name be.
> "And I will bless her, and give thee a son also of her, and she shall be a mother of nations, kings of people shall be of her." (Gen. 17:15-16, KJV)

> "Then Abraham fell upon his face, and laughed, and said in his heart, Shall a child be born unto him that is an hundred years old? and shall Sarah, that is ninety years old, bear?
> "And Abraham said unto God, O that Ishmael might live before thee!
> "And God said Sarah thy wife shall bear thee a son, indeed; and thou shalt call his name Isaac; and I will establish my covenant with him for an everlasting covenant, and with his seed after him.
> "And as for Ishmael, I have heard thee: Behold, I have blessed him, and will make him fruitful and will multiply him exceedingly; twelve princes shall he beget; and I will make him a great nation.
> "But my covenant will I establish with Isaac, which Sarah shall bear unto thee at this set time next year.
> "And he left off talking with him, and God went up from Abraham."
> (Gen. 17:17-22, KJV)

The response of the people was very excited with this reading, some almost unbelieving, but most with an attitude of worship. Jeannette felt it was important to finish the chapter, so she went on:

> "And Abraham took Ishmael his son, and all that were born in his house, and all that were bought with his money, every male among the men of Abraham's house; and circumcised the flesh of their foreskins in the self-same day, as God had said unto him.
> "And Abraham was ninety years old and nine, when he was circumcised in the flesh of his foreskin.

"And Ishmael his son was thirteen years old, when he was circumcised in the flesh of his foreskin.

"In the selfsame day was Abraham circumcised, and Ishmael his son.

"And all the men of his house, born in his house and bought with money of the stranger, were circumcised with him." (Gen. 17:23-27, KJV)

"And that," Jeannette explained, "was the Abrahamic covenant, but we have a better covenant in Jesus Christ."

Darren was sitting close to Roman and Grace. Roman sat with his arm around Grace and both had a free arm raised in worship. Their eyes were closed and both were praying as many of the people worshipped God. Some were singing in worship, and others were praying with each other. As Darren watched Roman and Grace worshiping together, he felt envious. He could see they not only loved each other, but they shared their love of God. He thought of Rachel and wondered if they could ever be like that.

Rachel and Peggy spent the afternoon riding with the Durans. After a short workout in the arena, they all begged Jules to take them for a ride outside, since the sun was enticingly warm for mid-April.

When Morton came by earlier to tell Jules the young ladies wanted to ride, Teresa immediately invited them both to have dinner and stay over. Their other guests were not expected back for a few more days, so this was a good opportunity for the four young ladies to spend time together.

Peggy was in high spirits to see the other girls and the excitement was even rubbing off on Rachel, who loved riding her horse more than anything, so it was hard for her to stay depressed.

Jules held the gate open as all the young people rode into the meadow, then remounted and cantered to the lead. When they came to the fence where one bar was still in place, his bay gelding hopped over it, followed easily by the rest.

After cantering across the next field, they all slowed to a walk as they entered the trail through the trees approaching a thicker forest area. Out of the sun, the forest was a much cooler ride. The trail was narrow, so they all rode single-file behind Jules.

Simon Duran found himself riding behind Peggy Montgomery. He marveled that her long auburn hair was so close to the same color as her horse's chestnut tail. He knew Peggy all his life, as far as he could remember, but suddenly felt as if he saw her for the first time. As they progressed down the trail, shafts of sunlight came through the branches periodically to touch Peggy's hair and her horse's tail, causing them both to sparkle like embers of a fire. After a while, the group came out of the heavy forest into the next meadow area, where the sunlight suddenly seemed blinding. Simon kicked his horse, moving up alongside Peggy, and exclaimed, "What a day—it's so beautiful!"

Peggy was startled, feeling her skin turning pink under a myriad of golden freckles, but regained her composure quickly enough to agree with him, "Oh, yes, it is!" Then everyone was cantering toward the next fence, which, one after another, they all sailed over.

Marielle was thrilled to have her friend visiting, especially since they seemed to have the feeling of companionship, which had been absent for some time. Marielle remembered when Rachel was so unhappy when they all accepted Jesus, and Rachel would not, complaining they all were so "religious." Then she came back, but because of Darren, so Marielle still felt left out. At least Jeannette was nice to her. But now Rachel would be staying over with her. Marielle hoped they were still friends.

After dinner, the Durans were ready to read the Bible together. Rachel rolled her eyes at her sister, remembering seeing Darren doing the same. Now she felt herself missing him again. *Would he ever be back?*

While the others were gone the Durans chose to continue reading in Genesis, the story of Abram, so Jules began:

> "And when Abram was ninety years old and nine, the Lord appeared to Abram and said unto him, I am the Almighty God; walk before me, and be thou perfect.
> "And I will make my covenant between me and thee, and will multiply thee accordingly.

"And Abram fell on his face: and God talked with him, saying,
"As for me, behold, my covenant is with thee; and thou shalt be a father of many nations." (Gen. 17:1-4, KJV)

All who were there looked at Jules, amazed, as he read those verses. His voice rose and became very forceful, as if God himself spoke. He looked as if in a trance and his face shone. After a moment, it seemed as though he came back to the present, as he handed the Bible to Simon and pointed out the verse. Simon began to read:

"Neither shall thy name anymore be called Abram, but thy name shall be Abraham; for a father of many nations I have made thee.
"And I will make thee exceedingly fruitful, and I will make nations of thee, and kings shall come out of thee.
"And I will establish my covenant between me and thee and thy seed after thee in their generations for an everlasting covenant, to be a God unto thee, and to thy seed after thee.
"And I will give unto thee and to thy seed after thee, the land wherein thou art a stranger, all the land of Canaan, for an everlasting possession; and I will be their God."
(Gen. 17:5-8, KJV)

Again, it was as though the light source which seemed to hover on Jules as he read, now seemed to hover over Simon. He did not appear to realize how loud he was reading. Everyone looked at him in surprise. He handed the Bible to Peggy, pointing out the verse, where she began to read. Her voice, normally gentle and soft, became strong with authority.

"And God said unto Abraham, Thou shalt keep my covenant therefore, thou, and thy seed after thee in their generations.
"This is my covenant, which ye shall keep, between me and you and my seed after thee; every man child among you shall be circumcised.
"And ye shall circumcise the flesh of your foreskin; and it shall be a token of the covenant betwixt me and you.
"And he that is eight days old shall be circumcised among you, every man child in generations, he that is born in thy

house, or bought with money of any stranger, which is not of thy seed.

"He that is born in thy house, and he that is bought with thy money, must needs be circumcised: and my covenant shall be in thy flesh for an everlasting covenant.

"And the uncircumcised man child whose flesh of his foreskin is not circumcised, that soul should be cut off from his people; he hath broken my covenant." (Gen. 17:9-14, KJV)

It was late in the evening so normally the parlor would have only the light of lanterns, but there seemed to be a heavenly light brighter than the midday sun. As Peggy read, she understood nothing more than the words of the promise of God's covenant. It seemed to her that she was hearing the heavenly language. The verses which referred to things which no proper Victorian lady would utter sounded only like the voices of angels praising God. Everyone was amazed. Peggy handed the Bible to Marielle, pointing out the next verse. As Rachel's friend next to her began to read, Rachel began to tremble.

"And God said unto Abraham, as for Sarai your wife, thou shalt not call her Sarai, but Sarah shall her name be.
"And I will bless her, and give thee a son also of her: yea I will bless her, and she shall be the mother of nations: kings of people shall be of her.
(Gen.17:15-16, KJV)

Rachel was shaking, fearful, thinking she heard what sounded like the rushing sound of a windstorm, she looked down, hiding her face, but could still see the glow that seemed to emanate from Marielle as she read. Marielle started to hand the Bible to her, but Rachel's hands were shaking so she could not hold it. She began to weep, not knowing why.

Both Teresa and Peggy came over to her. Teresa took hold of her hands. "What is it, Honey?"

"I'm afraid…"

"There's nothing to be afraid of. God is here and He loves you."

"How can he l-love m-me? I've hated h-him!"

"Because he loves you first!"

The others in the room were all praying in the heavenly language. Rachel was still weeping. Teresa was holding one of her hands and Peggy the other. Teresa said, "You can ask God for forgiveness. I know now you believe He exists. You can ask Jesus to come into your heart."

The words came pouring out, "Oh, Jesus, forgive me, and come into my heart!" Her face was tear-streaked, but she was smiling through the tears. He sister squeezed onto the settee beside her, hugging her as she nearly sat on her. Others were praising God, some still praying in the heavenly language.

HELENA POORTVLIET

CHAPTER 22

Quebec City

T HE TIDE WAS still rising as they sailed into the channel which narrowed considerably between the south shore and the island in the center of the waterway. Much larger than the Ile Aux Coudres, which they left this morning, one of the sailors told them it was Ile d' Orleans, and Quebec City was just beyond the southwest end of it. It took careful navigation to safely make their way. Continuous adjustment of sails along with expert use of the wheel and rudder moved the *Bucephalus* around the angle of the channel, then it was almost a straight shot into the Quebec City Harbor. There was a reserved moorage where the *Bucephalus* tied up every trip. Quebec City was quite a sight from the waterway. Built on a series of cliffs overlooking the river, a fortress designed to protect the city from invasion, an imposing sight with grand buildings of old world architecture covering the ridge above the water.

There was certain cargo to be delivered here, but none of the horses, all bound for Montreal. They would be overnight in the Quebec Harbor, so they could have gone ashore, but looking up at the city on the ridge, Jacques did not feel inclined. He did not feel comfortable leaving his horses, and he would not know where to go. There were, however, certain sailors who had seniority and would have shore leave, and would be happy to take advantage of it. Those were high with excitement for an excursion off the ship.

Snow was on the ground everywhere, and though it was not snowing now, it was bitterly cold. Jacques was happy to go to dinner, for the warmth of the dining room. Most of their friends were at dinner, indicating the city was not much of a temptation. Several people asked them if the Bible reading was still on, so they assured everyone that it was.

So, when the time came, Jacques began to read:

"And Saul, yet breathing out threatenings and slaughter against the disciples of the Lord, went unto the high priest. "And desired of him letters to Damascus to the Synagogues, that if he found any of this way, whether they were men or women, he might bring them bound into Jerusalem. "And as he journeyed, he came near Damascus: and suddenly there shone round about him a light from heaven; "And he fell to the earth, and heard a voice saying unto him, Saul, Saul, why persecutest thou me? "And he said, Who art thou Lord? And the Lord said, I am Jesus whom thou persecutest: it is hard for thee to kick against the pricks. "And he trembling and astonished said, Lord what wilt thou have me to do? And the Lord said unto him, Arise and go into the city, and it shall be told thee what thou must do. "And the men which journeyed with him stood speechless, hearing voices, but seeing no man. "And Saul arose from the earth; and when his eyes were opened, he saw no man: but they led him by the hand, and brought him into Damascus. "And he was three days without sight, and neither did eat nor drink." (Acts 9:1, 9, KJV)

As Jacques paused in his reading, he felt overwhelmed by what he just read. It was so awesome to him that Jesus actually appeared to this man on the road. He spoke with authority, but kindness. As soon as Saul yielded to Him, Jesus gave him the answer that he needed. Jacques was so lost in his own thoughts as Pierre translated, he was startled when the questions started.

"Do you really believe Jesus spoke out loud to someone?" It was one of the sailors who only recently started attending.

"I believe it," Pierre answered, "because I'm learning to believe what the Bible says." He looked toward Jacques.

Jacques looked toward Roger and Andrea. Roger spoke, "We've read this story many times, and are thrilled to learn from the legacy of Paul's teaching. Something astounding had to happen to change this young man's life as it did. If we keep reading, we'll understand more."

At this word several others spoke up, "Read more, read more!" So Jacques continued reading:

> "And there was a certain disciple at Damascus named Ananias: and to him said the Lord in a vision, Ananias. And he said, Behold, I am here, Lord.
> "And the Lord said to him, arise and go into the street which is called Straight, and inquire at the house of one Judas for one called Saul of Tarsus; for behold, he prayeth.
> "And hath seen in a vision a man called Ananias coming in and putting his hand on him, that he may receive his sight.
> "Then Ananias answered, Lord I have heard by many of this man, how much evil he hath done to thy saints in Jerusalem:
> "And here he hath authority from the chief priests to bind all that call on thy name.
> "But the Lord said unto him, Go thy way, for he is a chosen vessel unto me, to bear my name unto the Gentiles, and kings, and the children of Israel:
> "For I will show him how great things he must suffer for my names sake."
> (Act 9:10-16, KJV)

Jacques thought to himself, *here is another example of Jesus speaking to someone, and telling him outright what to do, inspite of what he would have been inclined to do. But it was to carry out God's will.*

As Pierre finished his translation the questions came. So again, Jacques looked toward Roger and Andrea.

"Ananias was a disciple who trusted in Jesus." This explanation came from Andrea. "He probably wasn't considered an important man, but he was willing to do the Lord's will, in spite of human warnings, so God used him. And through it, his faith grew, and he became a stronger person in the faith community."

Roger added, "Jesus also prophecies here of Paul's future—about his sufferings."

Someone again urged, "Read more," so Jacques continued.

> "And Ananias went his way, and entered into the house; and putting his hands on him, said, Brother Saul, the Lord,

even Jesus, that appeared unto thee in the way as thou camest, hath sent me, that thou mightest receive thy sight, and be filled with the Holy Ghost.

"And immediately there fell from his eyes as if it had been scales: and he received sight forthwith, and arose and was baptized." (Acts 9:17-18, KJV)

This time as Jacques waited for the translation, it was followed simply by more, "read more," so he continued.

"And when he had received meat, he was strengthened. Then was Saul certain days with the disciples which were at Damascus.

"And straightway he preached Christ in the synagogues, that he is the Son of God.

"But all that heard him were amazed, and said, Is not this he that destroyed them which called on this name in Jerusalem, and came hither for that intent that he might bring them bound unto the chiefs?

"But Saul increased more and more in strength and confounded the Jews which dwelt at Damascus, proving that this is the very Christ." (Act 9:19-22, KJV)

Jacques felt thankful for the word of God while listening to Pierre finish the translation considering how it changed his life. He was not surprised when Pierre continued after his translation to talk about his own story.

"I love this story, because it reminds me of how God chose me. I may not have been persecuting Christians, but I was a bad person. I was a bum, a vagrant. I was mean and hateful. I thought people should respect me, and I hated them when they did not. But I wasn't doing anything respectable. Then Jacques came and shared Jesus with me—just like Ananias did with Saul. It changed my life. Now for the first time I have respect for myself, and especially for what Christ has done for me."

Now there was applause and praise to God. Many began to worship and some were even singing. "If any one would like to profess Jesus as Savior, please come forward so we can pray with you," Pierre invited.

HELENA POORTVLIET

Deral McDonald and Dirk Mallory came forward with concerned expressions. Jacques felt strongly that something out of the ordinary was on their minds.

"Several of the sailors went ashore today, and we both feel concerned, just a feeling something is wrong. Three of them are still out. One of those has a wife and family here in Quebec, so he probably won't be back until tomorrow. But we both feel uncomfortable, that something is wrong." Deral was talking but Dirk was continually nodding his head.

Pierre joined them to hear most of the story. "Who are they?"

"Well, Louie Macharenze went to see his wife, so we know he won't be back till tomorrow..." Dirk began.

Deral laughed, "...if he's back at all!" Then he went on, "but Nate and Denis were supposed to be back before we secured the ship. It's not so odd that someone don't make it back, but we both got a bad feelin' 'bout this."

Pierre declared, "Well, we should pray for them. Have they been to any of our meetings?"

Dirk and Deral both shook their heads. "They laugh at us, like all this is silly."

"Well, let's pray—Father, we know you love our brothers even if they don't fear you. But even more, they need your protection. Be with them now, and protect them, and we pray your Holy Spirit would draw them to you, from whatever danger may threaten them. We ask in Jesus name. Amen."

There were several others who joined in the "amens." Shortly after, the meeting ended and the participants went up the ramp.

When they were headed for breakfast, the three noticed the fog was still enveloping the ship, and they were still tied up securely, since the tide was still going out and would not be turning back until mid-morning.

The ramp was down, and several passengers and sailors planned short shore excursions, so the man returning to the pier was seen by many, causing much shock, for his appearance. His clothes were bloody and torn; he had a look of panic, was walking awkwardly, limping and staggering. Jacques recognize Nate—that is, Lucas Natereno, whom he knew by name only, not really acquainted.

Several of the sailors ran to meet him, appalled by his appearance. He was hysterical, barely able to talk.

"Denis is dead; I'm sure of it!"

By now Captain Palmer appeared. The injured sailor was taken to sick bay to be seen by the ship's surgeon. Everyone watched them go with looks of shock and questions. At breakfast, talk was minimal and nobody had much appetite. After a while, Captain Palmer came into the dining room with a brief explanation. "It looks like these boys met with some foul play, but we need more answers, so we'll be here for another day or so. If anyone feels like going into the city, don't go alone and be back before dark."

Pierre and Jacques still had a few stalls to clean and Harry headed for the goats' stalls for the same. He cleaned them joyfully, because he loved these animals. He did his best to keep them happy and comfortable. As they finished the stall cleaning, Roger and Willis came down the ramp with a story to tell.

"Something pretty strange has happened," Roger began.

"Yeah," Willis added, "That sailor had quite a story to tell!"

"Oh?" Jacques asked, "What happened?"

"He says," Roger replied, "that he and Denis were in a bar drinking beer, talking to the bargirl. They stayed until she was getting off work. Both young men were pretty intoxicated, but they offered to see the girl home. As they were on their way Denis went into an alley to relieve himself. Nate and the girl walked slowly to allow Denis to catch up, when they heard Denis screaming. Nate ran for the alley, but as he got there a huge man came out at him. Nate tried to move aside, but the man was able to grab him. In the struggle, he was stabbed several times. Nate says he was sure he was dead, but apparently he didn't receive any deadly wounds."

Pierre asked, "How did he get away?"

Willis continued the account which they heard from Nate, "At one point the man hit him so hard, he fell against the side of the building. Then the man took off."

Roger picked up the story. "Nate thinks he passed out for a while. When he came to, he said it was just getting light. He saw Denis' body in a heap, very bloody; he thought Denis was dead and he was still so scared, he just got back to the ship as fast as he could, considering his condition."

"What about the girl?" Jacques inquired.

"He doesn't know. She disappeared; he thinks she probably ran away."

Everyone felt shocked, shaken. Jacques was glad Harry was still with the goats, so he missed most of the story.

"Anyway," Roger began again, "Andrea and Patricia would like to go shopping, but they're really scared. We thought if several of us went together, we'd be safe, as long as we get back here before dark."

Willis added, "I guess we'd all like to see the city, especially if we have to stay here a few days, but I think we all agree there's safety in numbers."

Jacques looked at Pierre. "I'd really like to get Harry some new clothes. He seems to be outgrowing everything I got him in Birmingham."

Pierre agreed, "He's really grown a lot!" He was thoughtful a moment. "Maybe I can get part of my pay. I could use some new things myself."

They all agreed to meet in a while to go ashore. Before they parted, they prayed together, both for their safety and for Nate's healing.

Not only Jacques, Harry, and Pierre, but Ramon, the Breakfields, the Caldwells, the Tennisons and all their families were up for the excursion. As the group left the ship, they straggled out along the streets of lower Quebec. Snow was everywhere, making walking difficult, so they moved slowly. When they came to a clothing shop, Jacques wanted to find new clothes for Harry. Some went in with them, while others explored other shops on the block, always keeping an eye out for one another. Andrea also wanted to shop for her children, suddenly aware of how they had grown. Then they all met together at a café for dinner.

Jacques felt a stab of longing as they approached the café, it reminded him so much of *La Petit Fleur*. The narrow streets of lower Quebec were lined with brick and stone buildings several stories high with shops and cafes at ground level. As they entered the café, Jacques noticed the front windows, almost floor to ceiling. There were French looking paintings on the wall. The tables were covered with sparkling white linens, and all had wooden chairs painted bright red. The picture immediately took him back to the first day he walked into *La Petit Fleur*. He could picture Jeannette walking into the dining room to greet them.

Harry smiled shyly as the others complimented his new clothing. Andrew also had some new things, so they were happily complimenting each other. The women were all so laden with packages they commandeered their husbands to help carry their treasures.

Having dinner all together in the café was a special time for all. The choices were many, appreciated even more since the menu on the ship was so limited of late. The little café offered French cuisine which Jacques missed so much since those days in Southampton. It was delightful to order from all the special delicacies offered, and sharing with friends made it even more special. As they saw the sun sinking to the west, causing pink streaks in the foggy atmosphere, they all headed back for the *Bucephalus*.

The Captain of the Lower Quebec Precinct and the Port Security Commissioner paid a visit to the *Bucephalus*. Denis indeed died at the hands of the brute, who was still at large. Unfortunately, the girl from the bar whom the sailors were escorting home, also died a few blocks away. "Le Brute" was well-known to the police, the newspapers and the people of Quebec. So far, he eluded pursuers, and caused much fear in the city. What he did to the girl was even more hideous than what he had done to Denis. As real as he was to the police, he was becoming somewhat of a legend to the people of Quebec. Descriptions of him were so shocking many could not accept that such a person could exist. But still the fear of him kept many at home, especially at night, which still came early this time of year.

Some said the brute had no face, his features mostly destroyed by burns, leaving him with but one eye still working. What remained of his face was black and leathery. He was a great hulk of a man, seemingly rendered a raging psychotic from some traumatic accident. Since his horrific appearance was so frightening, he must avoid contact with others, as his mere sight caused so much fear, making him a virtual fugitive.

When the group arrived back at the *Bucephalus*, it was late afternoon and not only dusk but a freezing fog enveloped the ship. As Jacques and Harry were descending the ramp, they were met by

HELENA POORTVLIET

the bleating of the goats, anxious for milking. Harry ran to them anxious to relieve their distress. Deral already delivered the milk cans, leaving them nearby. Jacques left the boy to do the job as he made the rounds of the horses, making sure they still had plenty of feed. Even though most had partaken of early dinner at the café, they still all met in the dining room for additional snacking before getting together for their evening Bible meeting. It seemed as though the horrible incident on shore last night increased the need to gather and worship. So when they all gathered, Jacques began:

> "And after that many days were fulfilled, the Jews took counsel to kill him:
> "But their laying await was known to Saul. And they watched the gates day and night to kill him.
> "Then the disciples took him by night, and let him down by the wall in a basket.
> "And when Saul was come to Jerusalem, he assayed to join himself to the disciples: but they were afraid of him, and believed not that he was a disciple.
> "But Barnabas took him and brought him to the apostles; and declared unto them how he had seen the Lord in the way, and that he had spoken to him, and how he had preached boldly at Damascus in the name of Jesus.
> "And he was with them coming in and going out at Jerusalem.
> "And he spake boldly in the name of the Lord Jesus, and disputed against the Grecians: but they went about to slay him.
> "Which when the brethren knew, they brought him down to Caesarea, and sent him forth to Tarsus.
> "Then had the churches rest throughout all Judaea and Galilee and Samaria, and were edified; and walking in the comfort of the Holy Ghost, were multiplied." (Acts 9:23-31, KJV)

After Pierre translated, Jacques continued to wait as he commented: "I can so relate to this Saul, considering what the Lord has done for me. When I was without Jesus, I was so bad to people. I could not expect them to believe I have changed. I will spend the rest of my life serving Him to show the world I am a new creature in

Christ!" As he talked, his smile was wide, his countenance shining. Many clapped at his testimony.

Jacques continued to read:

> "And it came to pass, as Peter passed throughout all quarters, he came down also to the saints at Lydda.
> "And there he found a certain man named Aeneas, which had kept his bed eight years, and was sick of the palsy.
> "And Peter said unto him, Aeneas, Jesus Christ maketh thee whole: arise and make thy bed. And he arose immediately.
> "And all that dwelt at Lydda and Saron saw him and turned to the Lord." (Acts 9:32-35, KJV)

Several sailors came for the first time, good friends of Nate and Denis, and were greatly distressed by the attack on their friends. As Pierre translated, they all stood up and came to stand before of Jacques and Pierre.

"If this Peter," began one of them, "can heal this man, so he can get up out of bed, can he heal Nate, or is healing only for people back then?"

Pierre answered, "I believe what the word of God says is just as much for today as it was then. We should pray for Nate, and for anyone else who needs prayer." He paused as he looked around, then added, "If anyone here needs prayer for anything, please come forward."

Many responded, coming forward to pray for each other and praise God.

The passengers returned to their cabins, sailors to their quarters or to their assigned stations for the night. Jacques, Harry and Pierre retired to the little cabin on the horse deck. The ship was secured for the night.

A huge hulk of a man moved in the shadows toward the ship, grasping one of the lines holding the stern to the pier, swung out over the freezing water to wrap his leg around the line, surprisingly agile for his size, climbed hand over hand up the line to the deck, climbing through the cables under the rail. Looking around cautiously, he slipped carefully up to the outer cabin wall, slid along the wall to the galley which was closed and dark. As he looked around in the

HELENA POORTVLIET

dim, almost non-existent light he sniffed. He could smell food. His hunger gripped him desperately. He found his way to the pantry. He first found the remains of a pitcher of milk and quickly gulped it down. Then he found in the cold storage a stock of several hams. Grunting with a non-verbal animal-like sound, he grabbed one of them and turned to the door. Furtively looking both ways, he slid along the side of the cabin to where he saw the ramp down to the horse deck. Holding the ham like a club, he crept carefully down the ramp, then behind the ramp he found the hatch to the cargo hold and slipped into the darkest dark of the hold and found a corner behind cargo containers, where he squeezed into a space to devour his stolen prize. He rubbed the one sightless eye socket, and moaned slightly at the discomfort to the scarred tissue. Visions of rage occupied his distorted mind, but fear would keep him in his hiding place.

CHAPTER 23

The Ring

"And the Lord appeared unto him in the plains of Mamre: and he sat in the tent door in the heat of the day:

"And he lift up his eyes and looked, and, lo, three men stood by him: and when he saw them from the tent door, and bowed himself to the ground,

"And said, My Lord, if now I have found favor in thy sight, pass not away, I pray thee, from thy servant:

"Let a little water I pray you to be fetched and wash your feet, and rest yourselves under the tree:

"And I will fetch a morsel of bread, and comfort ye in your hearts; after that ye shall pass on: for therefore are ye come to your servant. And they said, So do, as thou hast said.

"And Abraham hastened into the tent unto Sarah and said, Make ready quickly three measures of fine meal, knead it, and make fine cakes upon the hearth.

"And Abraham ran to the herd, and fetch a calf tender and good, and gave it unto a young man, and he hasted to dress it.

"And he took butter, and milk, and the calf which he had dressed, and set it before them; and he stood by them under the tree, and they did eat." (Gen. 18:1-8, KJV)

AS SHE WAITED for Antoine's translation, Jeannette could see the questions coming. It was clear these visitors were very special. Jeannette began to explain, "There was something about these men that made it clear to Abraham it was a divine visitation. It's exciting to me if this could happen to Abraham, I wouldn't rule it out happening to any of us!"

Someone spoke up, disbelieving, "What do you mean—'the Lord appeared to him?'" There were many questions all at once.

Jeannette began to explain, pointing out what she read at the beginning. "Yes, it says, 'The Lord appeared to him at Mamre,' and later, 'three men stood by him.' Many believe one of these was the precarnate son of God, and the other two were angels, but he would bow down to the Lord, and call him Lord as he did. And there must have been something about them different from normal men, because Abraham recognized them right away."

Many still looked astounded and perplexed, but many raised their hands in worship, and a few others were saying, "Read more!" so she continued:

> "And they said unto him, Where is Sarah thy wife? And he said, Behold, in the tent.
> "And he said, I will certainly return unto thee according to the time of life: and, lo, Sarah thy wife shall have a son. And Sarah heard it in the tent door, which was behind him.
> "Now Abraham and Sarah were old and well stricken in age; and it ceased to be with Sarah after the manner of women.
> "Therefore Sarah laughed within herself, saying, After I am waxed old shall I have pleasure, my lord being old also?
> "And the Lord said unto Abraham, Wherefore did Sarah laugh, saying, shall I of a surety bear a child which am old?
> "Is anything too hard for the Lord? At the time appointed I will return unto thee, according to the time of life, and Sarah shall have a son.
> "Then Sarah denied, saying, I laughed not; for she was afraid. And he said, nay, but thou didst laugh." (Gen. 18:9-15, KJV)

As Jeannette waited for the translation, she looked around for her brother, and saw him sitting with Roman and Grace. He listened intently while she was reading the English, but now was talking to Roman and Grace. As Antoine completed the translation, many were now singing and worshiping. She watched her mother and Ellienne praying with various people. The worship continued for some time.

After a while, as many began to leave the group, others came forward to bring gifts to the visitors, thanking them for the week of sharing God's Word. In turn Jeannette handed out many of the

Gospel of John booklets she brought with her. They would soon be leaving to return to the Durans.

Darren found he enjoyed the reading, feeling as though he was closer to believing the things he was hearing, but he still resisted making a decision that might affect his relationship with Rachel. Lost in thought, he was surprised when Grace turned to him. She held a small package in her hand.

"I want you to give this to Rachel," she said, as she handed it to him. "It's the wedding ring my husband gave me. Now that he's gone and I'm going to marry Roman, I won't wear it again. So I want Rachel to have it when you marry."

For a moment Darren was speechless. Finally, he said, "So you think it's really going to happen?"

"Yes, you've got to follow your heart, and don't give up!" She was adamant, nodding her head as she put the package in his hand, using both her hands to close his fingers around it. Roman was grinning, approvingly.

Before long the family was in the wagon heading back to the Montgomery estate. Darren was driving the mares, Dani and Katy, and Antoine and Ellienne were following in their wagon. The plan was to arrive back at the Duran's before dusk.

Rachel was more relaxed and cheerful than she had been for months. She and her sister spent most of their time together, finally, best friends again. They prayed together daily and studied their Bibles together. Rachel still dreaded the upcoming event her mother was planning, but she was praying for God's will to be done and a good outcome of the event. But one thing had her worried.

"I hope Darren isn't upset because I decided to accept Jesus."

Peggy raised her eyebrows. "Why should that make a difference?"

"Well, it was one thing we agreed on."

"Well, if he doesn't like it, are you going back on your commitment?"

"No. I meant it, and I'm glad I did it. I know it was right."

Peggy looked relieved. "Good for you! Praise God! And she clapped her hands happily.

"But I'm praying he'll change his mind and accept Jesus, also." Rachel looked hopeful.

Her sister moved closer to take her hands and pray with her. While they were praying they heard horses and wagons in the lane, and turned to the window.

"They're back!" Rachel turned to run for the door.

"Heh, wait!" Peggy said. "Are you just going to go running out there after him?"

Rachel stopped, blushing brightly. "Oh, I guess not. I guess that's not a good idea. We can see each other tomorrow when we go riding." But she hugged her sister as they danced around.

Darren pulled up his horses in front of the cottage, just as the door burst open, and most of the Duran family rushed out. Teresa rushed from one to another to hug and ask questions.

"You're home! Wonderful! Did you have a good week?"

Jules looked at Darren, then at Antoine, laughing as he watched his wife's behavior. "She's been talking about nothing else all week."

The women all went inside while the men took care of the horses and wagons. Among the women, the chatter was continuous, catching up.

Teresa turned to the others, "The best news, you've got to hear— the Montgomery girls were here last evening, and the most wonderful thing we've all been praying for."

"What, what?" The other three women faced her, awaiting the rest.

"Rachel accepted Jesus as her Savior!"

Jeannette looked amazed. "That is good news!"

"Oh yes, the Holy Ghost was certainly here. It was like the day of Pentacost. It was amazing. This morning she was a different girl. And her sister is just thrilled.

Later, the men returned as they were getting dinner on the table. It was an enthusiastic reunion, reliving the week at the Romani camp, visits with their friends, and the teaching times.

Then Jeannette asked, "Did you know a girl name Grace who worked as a maid for the Montgomerys?"

"Oh yes," answered Teresa. "Such a sweet girl," she continued, remembering. "She came here with Peggy Montgomery, to listen to your Jacques read from the Bible. "She happily responded to God's call, then sent Morton the next day to do the same." Teresa shook her head in remembering, then continued, "Such a sweet girl, but a sad story." Jules took her back to her parents after we realized she was pregnant. Her husband was killed, poor thing. But it was a good thing for her to go home. Peggy and Marielle went with them, and said her parents were so happy to see her." Teresa sighed, then asked, "Did you see her? How is she doing?"

Jeannette smiled, "Well, she is going to marry Roman Balansay."

Teresa's face brightened. "That's wonderful! So she is doing well. I'm so glad. I've prayed for that girl!"

"Darren spent a lot of time with them. They seem to be making friends. Darren and Roman went riding together every morning. I think they were having a good time." Jeannette looked at her brother. He was looking a bit uncomfortable, the subject of their conversation.

Jeannette grinned at him, "Well, didn't you enjoy being with Roman and Grace?"

He rolled his eyes, then smiled at her. "Sure, Sis. They're good folks." He could feel the small package in his pocket which contained the ring.

As Teresa got up and started clearing the food, Jules spoke up, "Well, we always read from the Bible after dinner, but we missed you reading with us." He looked at Jeannette. "How do you feel about reading for us tonight?"

Jeannette agreed, happily. They all headed for the parlor, while she got her Bible, and soon began:

> "And the men rose up from thence, and looked toward Sodom: and Abraham went with them to bring them on the way.
> "And the Lord said, Shall I hide from Abraham that thing which I do;
> "Seeing that Abraham shall surely become a great and mighty nation, and all the nations of the earth shall be blessed in him?
> "For I know him, that he will command his children and his household after him, and they shall keep the way of the Lord, to do justice and judgement; that the Lord may bring upon Abraham that which he hath spoken of him.
> "And the Lord said, Because the cry of Sodom and Gomorrah is great, and because their sin is very grievous;
> "I will go down now, and see whether they have done altogether according to the cry of it, which is come upon me; and if not I will know.
> "And the men turned their faces from thence and went toward Sodom: but Abraham stood yet before the Lord."
> (Gen. 18:16-22, KJV)

HELENA POORTVLIET

Jeannette looked up to say, "Isn't it wonderful God came down with two of His angels to speak directly to Abraham? I think it's a good example to show us it's possible it could actually at some time happen to any of us. But it also shows me what a special man Abraham was, that he received the divine visitors so whole-heartedly."

The others were nodding in agreement. But Antoine pointed out, "But there's an issue with Sodom and Gomorrah. It sounds like a warning. Isn't that where Lot went?"

"Yes," replied Jeannette, "That's why Abraham was confronting them."

"Well, let's find out—read more!"

> "And Abraham drew near and said, Wilt thou also destroy the righteous with the wicked?
> "Peradventure there be fifty righteous within the city: Wilt thou also destroy and not spare the place for the fifty righteous that are therein?
> "That be far for thee to do after this manner, to slay the righteous with the wicked: and that the righteous should be as the wicked, that be far from thee: Shall not the judge of the earth do right?
> "And the Lord said, If I find in Sodom fifty righteous within the city, then I will spare all the place for their sakes.
> "And Abraham answered and said, Behold now, I have taken upon me to speak unto the Lord, which am but dust and ashes,
> "Peradventure there shall lack five of the fifty righteous, wilt thou destroy all the city for lack of five? And he said, If I find forty and five, I will not destroy it.
> "And he spake unto him yet again, and said, Peradventure there shall be forty found there. And he said, I will not do it for forty's sake.
> "And he said unto him, Oh let not the Lord be angry, and I will speak. Peradventure there shall be thirty found there. And he said, I will not do it, if I find thirty there.
> "And he said, Behold now, I have taken upon me to speak unto the Lord: Peradventure there shall be twenty found there. And he said, I will not destroy it for twenty's sake.

"And he said, Behold now, I have taken upon me to speak unto the Lord: Peradventure ten shall be found there. And he said, I will not destroy it for ten's sake.

"And the Lord went his way as soon as he had left communing with Abraham; and Abraham returned unto his place. (Gen. 18:23-33, KJV)

"Whoa—he argued with God!" This was Simon's response.

Darren almost laughed hearing this. "And God listened to him?" It sounded like a question.

Jeannette smiled, happy to hear her brother's participation. "Well, as they say, 'Abraham was a friend of God!' But again, I think it's an example of how we can talk with God, especially if the issue is that critical."

Darren felt much more relaxed about the Bible reading. It was beginning to even be interesting to him. But he worried if Rachel might not think that was a good thing.

As they were gathered for breakfast there was a knock on the door. When Jules answered it, Morton came in, red-faced and out of breath, to announce the young ladies would like to ride their horses this afternoon.

Teresa walked over with a cup of tea for him, steaming in the chilly air. "Oh, come in and warm up and catch your breath."

Morton sat only for a moment to drink the tea, then breathing a bit easier, he stood up again. "Got to get back," he said as he headed for the door. Then he turned back to say, "That young lady, Rachel, is a different person. What a blessing! Those young ladies are thick as thieves now. What a change! Good to see!" Then he was out the door.

Darren looked up sharply, blinking his eyes. Marielle was asking Jeannette if she and Darren would be riding with them today. No one said any more about Rachel. Marielle continued talking to Jeannette about her horse.

"I didn't ride much," she replied, "while we were at the camp, I was so busy." But Darren went riding every day with Roman."

After lunch, they all headed for the huge barn, excited about the prospect of riding. Jeannette hung onto her brother's arm. "I'm so glad to get to ride with you," Jeannette said. "I'm glad you enjoyed going riding with Roman, but, you know, I was quite envious. So now it's my turn."

Darren grinned and put his arm around his sister. "I'm glad we're back, too." He thought to himself, *for a different reason.*

Jeannette and Darren went directly to the two stalls where their mares, Dani and Katy, were waiting for them. Jeannette led Katy out of the stall and began to brush her. After a few moments, Antoine came over to help her saddle Katy. It was easy for her to put the bridle on herself, since Katy lowered her head obligingly. After Antoine gave her a boost, she turned Katy around to urge her brother to come with her, but he was still brushing Dani.

"Jeannette, come on with us," came the call from Marielle, urging her to join them, as she and Nicole were headed for the arena. Jeannette could see her brother was taking his time with his horse, so she turned to go after the other girls.

Darren continued brushing Dani, but kept looking around to the door. Finally, he saw Rachel and her sister walking toward them with Morton. The tall man entered the barn with them, waved to Jules, who was saddling Peggy's horse. Darren felt a heat rising from the center of his being, thrilled at the sight of Rachel. He left Dani, and went to the stall of the dapple-gray horse, Misty, to lead him out.

As Peggy headed for her horse, Rachel went directly to Darren. Without thought they simply embraced.

"I missed you," she said, her voice breaking.

He meant to say the same thing, but when the words came out it was, "I love you."

As she looked up to him, a tear escaped as she answered, "I love you, too."

As Antoine neared the stall of Rachel's dapple-gray, he paused to pick up the saddle off the rack in front of the stall. As he straightened up, he found himself looking at Rachel and Darren, who were both frozen, looking directly at him. They both started to back away, then stopped.

"I…uh," began Darren.

"We…uh," stammered Rachel

"Oh, don't try to explain," Antoine responded with a sly smile. "Do you think we're all blind?" He entered the stall and led Misty out to tie him outside, before throwing on the saddle.

"You kids want to be careful. Jules sees you as a daughter, so he might be more protective." He took the bridle from Darren to put on the horse. "Jules feels responsible for you," he said to Rachel.

"Attraction is perfectly natural at your age, but your parents may not approve of your choice." He grinned at Rachel.

She had not spoken to interrupt him, but now agreed with him. "They want me to marry some rich old man. I love Darren; I don't know what to do."

"Do you realize if you make this an issue, your father may blame the Durans? He could lose his job, and this family would lose their home."

"Oh no," Rachel looked panicked. "That can't happen! They haven't done anything wrong!"

Darren moved out of the stall and started to saddle his own horse.

Antoine boosted Rachel on her horse and said, "You better get out there with the others. I need to talk to Darren." She moved her horse off toward the arena.

Antoine turned back to Darren. "There's nothing wrong with being in love. The important thing is to be responsible. What are your plans, young man?"

Darren felt uncomfortable about this man he tried so hard to keep away from his family, but he realized Antoine really was a friend. He did not answer right away. He was putting the bridle on his mare.

Antoine spoke again. "Your family has become like my family. It was the same way I talked to Jacques when I could see he was in love with your sister. It was important to me they were responsible about their love. If you really love that girl, you'll do the right thing."

Darren felt desperate. "So what would that be—the right thing?"

"Go talk to her father. Have you asked her to marry you?"

"Not yet, but I want to," was the reply. Then, on an impulse, he pulled the package out of his pocket, and unwrapped the ring.

"What's this?"

"Grace Gala gave it to me. She wanted me to give it to Rachel when we marry. It was from her first marriage. She really likes Rachel."

"So you really are serious!"

"I am; I hope she is."

"You better make sure she knows how you feel, and that she wants the same thing." He paused in thought for a moment, then continued. "Would you stay here or go to Canada with your family?"

HELENA POORTVLIET

"I want her to go to Canada with me, but I'm afraid her parents won't want me for a son-in-law. They want her to marry a prince, which, obviously, I am not."

"Well, don't put yourself down. Your family are good people. They've operated a good business for generations." Then Antoine gave a sly smile and a wink. "At least you're not a Gypsy!"

This caught Darren by surprise and he laughed in spite of trying to keep his composure.

"Well, get yourself out there with your horse before someone misses you. Just be careful!" As Darren swung up on his horse, Antoine gave her a pat on the rump, sending them toward the arena. By the time Darren reached the arena, all the others were taking the jumps. Most of them were taking the lower jumps in the center, but Rachel was taking the higher jumps around the perimeter. Darren began to canter Dani in the lane between the jumps until he was alongside Rachel.

"I hope we're going to be riding outdoors. I need to talk to you," he said as calmly as he could from his cantering mare.

"Same here," she replied, as she turned to concentrate on the next jump.

Darren looked around to see his sister on Katy going over the lower jumps in the center so he turned Dani to go after her. Dani easily took the jumps, giving Darren a thrill competing with what he felt at the sight of that black-haired girl.

After a few more laps, Jules walked out to the center with his arms raised to get everyone's attention. When they all stopped, he raised every other jump in the center up to about two feet. Then he waved at his own children to go first and the others to follow. After a few more laps, he waved toward the end of the arena where the door opened to the outside. Antoine was waiting on his stocky chestnut mare, holding Jules' bay gelding as all the riders filed out.

Darren was at the end of the group with Rachel riding beside him. Jules mounted his bay and cantered to the head of the group. Antoine brought up the rear, leaving space between them. Darren and Rachel were far enough ahead of him to talk quietly between them. Darren asked her, "Do you love me?"

She nodded, smiling silently.

"Will you marry me? I love you. I want to marry you."

She smiled and nodded, speechless.

"I'm going to talk to your father. Is that okay with you?"

She nodded again, blinking, not able to talk.

The other riders began to canter toward the fence, which still had the bar lowered. Antoine pulled his horse around them and cantered off after the others.

Darren again looked at Rachel, "Then we're together on this." He moved his horse closer and reached for her hand, which was extended to him.

"I've got a plan, but now it's only if your father threatens to kill me or worse." He laughed a little. "I want to do this right, if that's possible.

"I'm glad for that," she replied. "But what if it doesn't work?"

"We handfast," he answered.

Her eyebrows went up. "I've heard about that in history, but I didn't know anyone does it anymore. Is it legal?"

"It is if you say your vows in front of an official and have witnesses—and consummate it." The last part was barely whispered, but Rachel still reddened when she heard it.

"It's the way the Gypsies marry, and it's considered legal. We say our vows in front of their chief. Roman Balansay and Grace Gala want to be our witnesses."

"Grace Gala? She used to work here!" Rachel exclaimed in surprise.

"I know. Grace and Roman are getting married. She really likes you. She wants to be your bridesmaid."

Rachel was looking as if it was all too much to contemplate. Darren continued, "I want to marry you and take you to Canada with me. Will you come with me?"

"Yes, I will," she answered. "But I have something else to tell you. While you were gone, I believed in Jesus as my Savior."

Darren's mouth dropped. For a moment he was speechless. He was shaking his head.

Now Rachel looked unsure. "Does that change everything for you? Because I'm not going back—I meant it." She pulled her hand away from him.

He looked hurt for a moment. "I love you; I want to marry you. I'm not there yet, but at the camp, I was feeling closer. I wasn't sure how you felt, but Jeannette and I talked about some big issues in our

HELENA POORTVLIET

family, and I don't feel against it as much as I did, but I'm not sure yet. But I know I want to marry you!"

The rest of the group was disappearing down the trail into the forest. So Darren and Rachel kicked their horses into a canter to catch up with them.

The Montgomery girls were staying for dinner after the ride, and Morton would be coming later to escort them back to the big house. Dinner was a festive affair, now that all were back together again. There was much talk about the horses, especially how Dani and Katy were jumping.

Jeannette turned to Jules, "We really appreciate you helping us learn to jump our horses." When she looked at Darren, he agreed. "Yes, thanks for your help. We really enjoy the jumping." Rachel grinned.

Jules answered, "I'm glad to see you doing so well." Then he looked at Jeannette. "So can we impose on you again to read with us?"

"Of course, I look forward to it." She got up to get her Bible, as Teresa began clearing the table. So, in a few moments they were all crowded into the parlor, and Jeannette began to read:

> "And there came two angels to Sodom at even, and Lot sat in the gate at Sodom; and Lot seeing them there rose up to meet them; and he bowed himself with his face to the ground.
> "And he said, Behold now, my lords, turn in, I pray you, unto your servants house, and tarry all night, and wash your feet, and ye shall rise up early and go on your ways. And they said Nay, but we will abide in the street all night.
> "And he pressed upon them greatly; and they turned unto his house; and he made them a feast, and did bake unleavened bread, and they did eat."
> (Gen. 19:1-3, KJV)

Darren surprised the others by his questions, since he usually was quiet. "You mean these were actual angels coming down among men? Did Lot know they were angels?"

"The Bible tells us a lot about angelic visits throughout history. Godly people seem to have no problem recognizing them and responded to them very reverently." Jeannette happily answered her brother, thrilled he was taking part in the interaction. "It's exciting to me, because if it was normal then, it should be normal now; we should be alert for these visitations."

Rachel sat next to Darren, smiling, happy also for his participation. She urged, "Read more," so Jeannette continued:

> "But before they lay down, the men of the city, even the men of Sodom, compassed the house around, both old and young, all the people from every quarter:
> "And they called unto Lot, and said unto them, Where are the men which came in unto thee this night? Bring them out unto us that we may know them.
> "And Lot went out at the door unto them, and shut the door after him,
> "And said, I pray you, brethren, do not so wickedly.
> "Behold now, I have two daughters which have not known man; let me, I pray you, bring them out unto you and do to them as is good in your eyes: only unto these men do nothing; for therefore came they under the shadow of my roof.
> "And they said, Stand back. And they said again, This one fellow came in to sojourn, and he will needs be a judge: now we will deal worse with thee, than with them. And they pressed sore upon the man, even Lot, and came near to break the door.
> "But the men put forth their hand, and pulled Lot into the house to them, and shut the door.
> "And they smote the men that were at the door with blindness, both small and great: so that they wearied themselves to find the door." (Gen. 9:4-11, KJV)

Jeannette barely finished reading when she was aware of the shock and anger all around her. The biggest issue was the two daughters whom Lot offered to the mob, as well as shock over the mobs behavior.

"How can people be that way, like vicious wolves?" This question came from Darren, bringing looks of surprise from everyone, since up to now, he had spoken very little.

Rachel was angry over the treatment of the two daughters, whom their father should have protected. Others were in shock over the brutality of the mob, but Andre was delighted over the angels, who zapped the mob members with blindness. Some of the details of the story went over his head, but he was quick to recognize the heroes.

Jeannette began to explain. "In those times, the householder, that is, Lot, was bound by honor to protect the guest. In this case, he would have seen honor in protection of the divine visitors as the utmost importance. But this story does show how little value women held in that culture.

"But something here to think about, the scriptures say when we are filled with the Holy Ghost, even we have more power than the angels. So when we see here the power demonstrated by the angels, consider how much power we have in the Holy Ghost."

At this point others were urging her to continue:

> "And the men said unto Lot, Hast thou here any besides? Sons-in-law and thy sons, and thy daughters, and whatsoever thou hast in the city, bring them out of this place.
> "For we will destroy this place, because the cry of them is waxen great before the face of the Lord; and the Lord hath sent us to destroy it.
> "And Lot went out, and spake unto his sons-in-law; which married his daughters, and said, Up, get you out of this place; for the Lord will destroy this city. But he seemed as one who mocked unto his sons-in-law." (Gen. 19:12-14, KJV)

Jeannette explained, "You see, Lot recognized the angels, so he believed what they told him, but he allowed his daughters to marry unbelievers, so they had no respect for his word."

The others nodded in agreement and urged her on:

> "And when the morning arose, then the angels hastened Lot, saying, Arise, take thy wife, and thy two daughters, which are here; lest thou be consumed in the iniquity of the city.
> "And while he lingered, the men laid hold upon his hand, and upon the hand of his wife, and upon the hands of his two daughters; the Lord being merciful to him; and they brought him forth, and set him outside the city." (Gen.19:15, 6, KJV)

Jeannette paused again to comment, "so you see God in his mercy can rescue us out of the most dangerous predicaments, if we put ourselves in his hands." Then she continued:

> "And it came to pass, when they had brought them forth abroad, that he said, Escape for thy life; look not behind thee, neither stay thou in all the plain; escape to the mountain, lest thou be consumed.
> "And Lot said to them, Oh, not so my Lord:
> "Behold now, thy servant hath found favor in thy sight, and thou hast magnified thy mercy, which thou has showed unto me in saving my life; but I cannot escape to the mountain, lest some evil take me and I die:
> "Behold now, this city is near to flee unto; and it is a little one. Oh, let me escape thither, (is it not a little one?) and my soul shall live.
> "And he said unto him, See, I have accepted thee concerning this thing also, that I will not overthrow this city, for the which thou hast spoken.
> "Haste thee, escape thither, for I cannot do anything till thou be come thither. Therefore the name of the city was called Zoar." (Gen. 19:15-22, KJV)

Several of the listeners sighed, as if out of breath. Jeannette remarked at the patience of God in dealing with Lot. Several agreed Lot definitely did not have the boldness and courage of his uncle. She felt it important to read just a bit more:

> "The sun was risen upon the earth when Lot entered into Zoar:
> "Then the Lord rained upon Sodom and Gomorrah brimstone and fire from the Lord out of heaven.
> "And he overthrew those cities, and all the plain, and all the inhabitants of the cities, and that which grew upon the ground.
>
> "But his wife looked back from behind him, and she became a pillar of salt." (Gen. 19:23-26, KJV)

The listeners were quiet, in shock at the conclusion, of God's wrath. Rachel was the first to speak. She first addressed the group, then turned to Darren. "I can see that once we start on the road God has set us on, we dare not look back. He is merciful in his patience, but we must not look back. Darren, I want to marry you, but I can't see a future with you without God. I have to know we're together on this. I'm not looking back. Are you ready to believe?"

Surprised looks appeared all around them, followed by "Praise God!" from Jeannette and then from her mother.

Darren was shaking, almost speechless, but managed a "Yes!"

Jeannette jumped up to go to him and embraced both her brother and Rachel. She began to pray with him, and Darren prayed his acceptance and promise to God.

Antoine and Ellienne raised their clasped hands in the air and shouted in unison, "Allelujia!"

Darren was still shaking and could not hold back the tears. "I have a lot to be forgiven—from God and from all of you. All of you tried to help me and I have been bad." He looked at his sister, "I did a bad thing to your Jacques and he repaid with good." He looked at Antoine and Ellienne. "I know you've been good to my family, but I've treated you like the enemy. Can you forgive me?"

Now all of them were crowding around him. Antoine took his hand, slapping him on the back. "My brother, it's past! Forget it!"

Rachel sat there wide-eyed. Peggy came close to embrace her sister. "I'm so proud of you!"

Darren turned back to Rachel, "You didn't know much about my past, but I expect the future to be better than the past. Is it okay with you if I come over tomorrow and speak to your father about our future."

Rachel let out a squeal of joy and threw her arms around his neck.

CHAPTER 24

Le Brute

THE *BUCEPHALUS* STAYED in port at Quebec City one more day. Nate was still in sick bay under the watchful eye of the ship's surgeon. Weak from loss of blood, he moved in and out of consciousness. If he showed signs of infection, he would be transported to the Quebec City Hospital.

Some of the passengers braved the snow to indulge in more shopping, but Jacques chose to stay on board, spending time walking horses and cleaning stalls, with the help of his two companions. He checked the condition of his carriage and harness, which he already cleaned thoroughly. Everything was ready.

Le Brute cowered in his hiding place in the darkness of the hold. He filled his belly with a large portion of his stolen ham, and slept for hours, feeling somewhat secure in the dark space behind the cargo container. He felt irritated and nervous earlier when that young man was in the hold snooping around that carriage, but now it was quiet. He knew it was just a matter of waiting for the ship to move again. It was no longer safe for him to remain in Quebec City. There were too many looking for him now—the police would not stop harassing him. It was not possible for him to safely find food. *Stupid people!*

Jacques heard laughing and conversation as many footsteps sounded above, coming up the ramp from the pier. The shoppers were back from town. When Roger and Andrew made an appearance on the ramp coming down to the horse deck, Harry climbed out of the goats stall, thrilled to greet his friend.

"I hear our cook went shopping in town, also," announced Roger. "He's planning a great dinner, to celebrate having something to serve besides ham and biscuits."

"All right! Ham is getting pretty tiresome—especially after the potatoes are gone," Jacques laughed. Then in a more sober tone he asked, "Any word on whoever or whatever did in Denis and that girl?"

"No," answered Roger. "Not a sign. It seems like it—whatever it was—has left the city. Pretty quiet out there. But the police say everyone's pretty scared. Most folks are too scared to leave home, especially after dark."

"Well, I'll be glad to get to Montreal."

They were interrupted by the sound of clanking metal, as Deral appeared on the ramp with the milk cans, so both Harry and Andrew ran for the goats' stall. With three of them doing the milking the job went quickly, so they soon were all on the way up the ramp.

Leon Mackay was happy to prepare a sumptuous meal to redeem himself for weeks of boring meals since so many of the perishable ingredients ran out. He now had fresh vegetables, and even the earliest hothouse greens to prepare. Best of all, he had fresh savory roast beef for those who were so tired of smoked ham. He hinted the meal would be special, hoping to tempt many on their forays into town to be back in time for dinner.

It was almost a holiday spirit at the dinner table. Many had been shopping in town and all were excited about the prospect of arriving soon in Montreal. And much of the tension and fear generated from the attack were beginning to subside. It seemed Le Brute had disappeared from Quebec City, so therefore he was gone from their world.

Many came by their table to confirm there would be a meeting to read from the Bible, so directly after dinner the three went down to prepare. Soon Jacques began reading with:

> "Now there was at Joppa a certain disciple named Tabitha, which by interpretation is called Dorcas: this woman was full of good works and almsdeeds which she did.
> "And it came to pass in those days, that she was sick, and died: whom when they had washed, they laid her in an upper chamber.
> "And foreasmuch as Lydda was nigh to Joppa and the disciples and heard that Peter was there, they sent unto him two men, desiring him that he would not delay to come to them.

"Then Peter arose and went with them. When he had come, they brought him into the upper chamber: and all the widows stood by him weeping and shewing the coats and garments which Dorcas made, while she was with them.

"But Peter put them all forth, and kneeled down, and prayed, and turning him to the body said, Tabitha, arise. And when she saw Peter, she sat up.

"And he gave her his hand, and lifted her up, and when he had called the saints and widows, presented her alive.

"And it was known throughout all Joppa, and many believed in the Lord.

"And it came to pass, that he tarried many days in Joppa with one Simon the tanner." (Acts 9:36-43, KJV)

Watching Pierre as he translated, Jacques recognized how much joy his friend expressed as he spoke. He marveled at how much Pierre took on the Spirit of Christ in his expression to others concerning the things of God. He also saw the other sailors perceived him as a leader. As he finished the translation of the Word, he launched naturally into commentary and argument towards the listeners yielding to the will of God. Jacques could see his friend had chosen the right path for himself.

Pierre gave the invitation for prayer, and many came forward. Several of Nate's friends came forward and asked for prayer for his recovery. First Pierre prayed, then he stopped and asked the sailors about Nate's condition. He was unconscious most of the last two days, but this evening he was running quite a fever, and they were told if infection was becoming an issue, he would be moved to the City Hospital. His friends were afraid if that was the case, they would never see him again.

Pierre held up his arms and began to pray for Nate's healing, protection and recovery. After a while his prayer changed to the heavenly language. Jacques soon heard the other young men also praying in the heavenly language. The rest of the group joined with them. After a while Jacques could hear singing as others still prayed. It went on for quite a while, until he began to hear "Hallelujia" and "Praise God," then everyone was hugging everyone. Jacques thought it reminded him of the times he remembered at the Romani camp. Then Jacques saw Harry standing with his hands raised, a beautiful smile as he silently mouthed prayer.

The third morning at Quebec City, they again woke up to thick fog enveloping the ship. After delivering the milk, they met the Breakfields in the dining room, thankful for the heat of the central fireplace. Cook presented them with scrambled eggs with diced ham, in contrast to the usual choice of oat porridge or cornmeal mush, making them all feel like royalty.

Pierre went to talk to some of the sailors who were there. When he came back, he asked Jacques to accompany him to look in on Nate after breakfast, so he agreed. They entered the infirmary to find Nate sitting up, smiling. Pierre introduced Jacques to him and Jacques reached his hand out to him, and asked, "Are you feeling better?"

Nate responded, "I woke up this morning feeling great, like any morning, only some mornings I don't always feel so great."

Jacques could see Nate had many bandages. "You don't have a fever now?"

"I don't think so. I feel pretty normal, except I'm afraid I feel a bit weak, and I can still feel a few bruises." Then Nate's expression took on a look of sadness. "I guess we lost Denis. That's pretty bad, poor guy! Does anyone know who that big guy was?"

Pierre answered, "The police know about him but no one can find him now. Pretty mysterious!" Then Pierre changed his tone. "Nate, we were told you were in bad condition, You had a bad fever yesterday; you've been unconscious for several days. You came close to dying. But we all prayed for you last night. Have you ever thought about your relationship with God?"

Nate laughed, a little nervously. "Not much. I never thought God cared much for me, even if he does exist."

"Well, he does exist and he loves you, and I think he protected you from a close call. I think it's a miracle of God you're awake and well this morning."

Nate now looked a little more uncomfortable. Pierre asked him if he could pray for him. Nate now looked embarrassed. "I don't know about that."

Pierre backed off, "Well, several of us get together after dinner each evening to read from the Bible and pray together. I'd like to invite you to join us."

Nate answered, "Well, I'll see how I feel. I don't know—maybe," sounding doubtful. Pierre turned to go; Jacques smiled at Nate, and turned to follow Pierre. They went back to the horse deck.

Around noon, the tide began to turn and the fog lifted. The *Bucephalus* shuddered as it slipped from the pier and began to move to the southwest. High tide would come around dusk, and they hoped for progress toward Montreal as the waterway moved into the narrower channel. The combination of the river current and the incoming tide was now giving them a fairly rough ride. The sails were unfurled, filling with the easterly wind, pushing them toward their destination.

They reached high tide about dusk and began to slow in the churning water. The anchor was dropped, securing the ship for the night, just as the fog began to roll in again, quickly enveloping the ship in murky darkness.

After dinner, the group again gathered on the horse deck, anxious to hear the word of God, so Jacques began:

> "There was a certain man in Caesarea called Cornelius, a centurian of the band called the Italian band.
> "A devout man, and one that feared God with all his house, which gave alms to the people and prayed to God always.
> "He saw in vision evidently about the ninth hour of the day and angel of God coming into him, and saying unto him, Cornelius.
> "And when he looked on him, he was afraid, and said, What is it Lord? And he said unto him, thy prayers and thine alms are come up for a memorial before God.
> "And now send men to Joppa and ask for one Simon whose surname is Peter.
> "He lodgeth with one Simon a tanner, whose house is by the seaside: he shall tell thee what thou oughtest to do.
> "And when the angel which spake unto Cornelius was departed, he called two of his household servants and a devout soldier of them that waited on him continually;
> "And when he had declared all things unto them, he sent them to Joppa."
> (Acts 10:1-8, KJV)

HELENA POORTVLIET

As Pierre translated, the listeners, especially some of the sailors who were new participants, seemed startled at this talk, especially about the angels.

"Is this for real? This angel stuff?"

"Some people talk about angels, but are they for real?" This speaker sounded doubtful.

Pierre looked around at the others. "What have any of you known about angels?"

Andrea spoke up, "Angels appeared throughout the scriptures. Now and then we hear about someone in history or in present times who claims to have seen or heard from angels. But it seems most people are disbelieving. Because it's in the Bible I believe they do appear, and it should be true now, but most people are so disbelieving about the supernatural it's harder for most of us to accept."

Others nodded in agreement, then someone said, "Read more," so Jacques continued:

> "On the morrow, as they went on their journey, and drew nigh unto the city, Peter went up upon the housetop to pray about the sixth hour:
>
> "And he became very hungry, and would have eaten: but while they made ready, he fell into a trance.
>
> "And saw heaven opened, and a certain vessel descending unto him, as it had been a great sheet knit at the four corners, and let down to the earth:
>
> "Whereas were all manner of four footed beasts of the earth, and wild beasts, and creeping things, and fowls of the air.
>
> "And there came a voice to him, Rise, Peter, kill and eat.
>
> "But Peter said, Not so, Lord, for I have never eaten anything that is common or unclean.
>
> "And the voice said to him the second time, What God hath cleansed, that call not thou unclean.
>
> "This was done thrice; and the vessel was received again up into heaven.
>
> "Now while Peter doubted in himself what this vision should mean, behold, the men which were sent from Cornelius had made inquiry for Simon's house, and stood before the gate,
>
> "And called, and asked whether Simon, which was surnamed Peter, were lodged there." (Acts 10:9-18, KJV)

Jacques observed looks of disbelief and perplexity as Pierre translated, even thinking himself this was really strange. Then Andrea spoke again. We have to go back to the Jewish laws about food. Peter was a devout Jew and followed those laws all his life. He would never eat what was considered an unclean animal. His first thought about this vision was about food, but as we'll see if we read more it was not about food, it was about people. Unfortunately, down through time, many others have taken this story out of context and have been mixed up about what they should eat."

At this, again someone said, "Read more!" So Jacques continued:

> "While Peter thought on the vision, the Spirit said unto him, Behold, three men seek thee.
> "Arise therefore, and get thee down, and go with them, doubting nothing: for I have sent them.
> "Then Peter went down to the men which were sent unto him from Cornelius; and said, Behold, I am he whom ye seek; what is the cause wherefore ye are come?
> "And they said, Cornelius the centurion, a just man, and one that feareth God, and of good report among all the nation of the Jews, was warned from God, by a holy angel to send for thee into his house, and to hear words of thee."
> (Acts 10:19-22, KJV)

No one of the group listening to the reading noticed the hatch of the cargo hold opened slightly. Jean Louis Devonneaux, "Le Brute," stood quietly just inside the hatch. He could see dimly the large group of passengers and sailors listening to the Bible reading. He was restless from two days of confinement in his hiding place. Two days of eating nothing but ham made him thirsty. He knew the ship began to move today, so he estimated they should be in Montreal by tomorrow evening. He hoped no one would be hunting him in Montreal.

The scar tissue on his jaw was itching and peeling, irritating to the point of rubbing carefully to find relief. The peeling tissues were flaking off in spots, leaving red, raw patches on the leathery surface. He imagined how horrible he looked. After the fire which flared up in his face, he went through painful weeks of recovery. He remembered the day his wife saw him the first time without bandages. He shuddered at the memory of her response, turning away, not wanting a second

HELENA POORTVLIET

look. She tried to act normal but became distant. Finally, when he tried to approach her, she backed away, looking sick. The love that formerly shone in her eyes was replaced with disgust. He barely remembered the rage he felt as he choked the life out of her. That was the beginning of his flight, as well as the progressive derangement of his mind. His basic needs now immediate: avoidance of other humans, concealment, food, and drink. His days were a constant ordeal to stay hidden, his nights a struggle to find food and avoid people. But at times the rage came on him in such intense fury, he even looked for victims, stalking them, making them pay for his miserable life.

The group of listeners had many questions about the reading and Jacques looked to Roger and Andrea for more insight.

"God has a way of bringing people together, usually in ways that seem natural, such as in our situation here on this ship. We've all been a comfort and help to each other, beyond just the benefit of friendship. But sometimes God is more direct, when His purpose is to get people together for his purpose. Ordinarily, Peter would not have crossed paths with Cornelius. In this case he had to be more direct.

There were voices of agreement, as Jacques closed his Bible. It was a long reading; he knew the rest of the story would take another day. Pierre seemed to agree as he called for prayer. Several came forward, and soon the heavenly language was heard as prayer continued into worship.

Jean Louis was still watching from the narrow opening of the hatch. His focus settled on three women who were standing close to their husbands. The sight made him furious. He thought to himself, *Would they be hanging onto those men if the men looked like me?* Then something else happened, when he began to hear that strange language. It was as if the voices were arguing and babbling in his head. There was a Spirit in that strange language which was a great threat to the voices he kept hearing. He wanted to tear into that crowd and silence them all. But also there was the fear that filled him. The fear of that strange language was more intense than anything he felt when faced with a threatening mob. He carefully, quietly pulled the hatch closed and crept back to his hiding place where he crouched, shaking, his hunger forgotten.

As the songs and worship quieted down, the group of friends seemed to bask in the glow of spiritual blessing. They stayed together, as many of the sailors left, talking about how fortunate they were to be blessed in their fellowship. Finally, the group began to break up as couples and others made their way up the ramp. The three companions retired to the little cabin. Jacques was thinking, *I should be writing to Jeannette and Papa tomorrow.* He wanted the letters to be ready to give to Pierre to post in Liverpool on his return trip. With that he fell asleep.

Jean Louis stayed hidden in his corner for hours, reluctant to move. He heard many footsteps going up the ramp, then the ship became very quiet. Now he heard only the occasional creaking as the ship strained against the anchor in the outgoing tide and current. He even dosed a bit, mentally and emotionally exhausted. But eventually he began to feel the pang of hunger and the irritation of his dry mouth. He finally got up and moved to the hatch, which he carefully opened just a crack.

The horse deck was quiet and dark. The only sound came from a horse moving around or pawing in its straw here or there. The door to the little cabin was closed and no sound came from that direction. He crept carefully, quietly to the ramp, looking up above to the main deck before he began up the ramp. As he moved along the edge of the cabin to the galley, he saw one sailor standing near the rail some distance away, his back to him. As he entered the galley, he again found a pitcher of milk on the counter. Almost overcome by thirst, he gulped it down. He found the cold storage of the pantry. There was an empty flour sack, which he grabbed. Delighted to find leftover roast beef, hot house tomatoes and leaf lettuce, and even part of a custard pie, he eagerly dumped them into the bag. When he saw the pile of hams, he growled a low "Ugh!" as he slipped out the door. Back on deck he looked around carefully. The sailor seen by the rail was gone. He headed back for the ramp, but heard voices. Looking around, he saw two sailors looking off the rail toward the shore. He crept quietly down the ramp and through the hatch back to his hiding place. He made his way clear back to the space behind the cargo container before he stopped to enjoy his stolen treasures. His heart gradually slowed its desperate beating as he began to eat.

HELENA POORTVLIET

Andrea and Roger, with their children made their way back to their cabin. The family shared good words about the Bible reading before Andrea directed the children to their beds. It was late and she needed to get them settled. When she and Roger were finally alone, she said to him, "I couldn't help but feel while we were worshipping that there was something evil close to us. I began to feel it even more when we were praying in tongues."

He looked at her in surprise, almost relieved, "I felt it too. But I thought it was just me. Maybe it was among some of those sailors who were new. We should pray before we go to sleep." They prayed a few minutes before going to bed.

Jacques awakened early, as usual, before his companions. He went to his stallion, feeding him first, before going to the others. He worked quickly to quiet the hungry horses before going back to spend some time with Tounerre. After a while he felt someone else was in the area. Looking across, he saw Ramon was in the stall brushing and talking to his own stallion, so he walked over.

The other man greeted him with his usual cheerful greeting. "It is good to be up early. I miss spending time with my horses. Traveling alone can be lonely. Horses are good companions. You are up early, too."

"I usually wake up early. I think it is so many years of taking care of animals," Jacques responded.

"But you slept well?"

"Sure. I was tired. Why do you ask?"

"I did not sleep well. Something bothered me. When we were worshiping God last night, I had a distinct feeling evil was close to us." Ramon's eyes had a look of inquiry.

Jacques answered, "Really. What do you mean?"

"When several of us were praying in the Spirit, it seemed as though there was an evil spirit nearby, as if fighting the Holy Spirit. Then it seemed like it left, but some of it stayed."

The conversation ended as Pierre and Harry emerged from the cabin. Harry ran to Jacques for a hug, a quick smile at Ramon, then ran for the goats' stall. Pierre looked at the other two men sensing something. "What's going on?"

Ramon repeated some of what he told Jacques. Pierre gave a quick look of remembrance. "Oh, yes—there was something like that, just an uneasy feeling. It seemed strange, but then I forgot about it. I was tired when we turned in."

The conversation was again interrupted by the clanking metal sound of the milk cans as Deral came down the ramp. As they began the milking, they could feel the ship shudder as the anchor was weighed, releasing the pressure of the ship against the tide which had already turned in the early morning darkness. They could feel they were again underway as the sails were again unfurled to catch the wind pushing them upstream. When they carried the milk up to the galley, Captain Palmer was in the galley talking to Leon Mackay, so they set down the milk cans and headed for the dining room.

Leon Mackay explained to Captain Palmer this was the second time the milk disappeared. Each evening he left a pitcher of milk on the counter overnight to curdle, for use in making the rolls the following morning. Not only this morning, but the morning before last, when he came into the galley the milk was gone. Only the empty pitcher was left. He did not think that was such a big thing, but now he discovered a pie was gone and the remainder of the roast beef from yesterday. Then he started looking around, and counted the remaining hams. One of them was missing.

After Leon finished telling Captain Palmer about the disappearing food, the Captain left the galley and went to the dining room. He walked around and said a few words of greeting to all who were there. He noted to himself all the passengers were present for breakfast. They all seemed normally excited about their coming arrival in Montreal. There was no one he felt suspicious about.

He announced to all, "We probably won't have enough tide to take us all the way to Montreal, but we should make it early tomorrow. We will anchor early in the afternoon, and the next low tide won't be till early in the morning. There should be enough to get us the rest of the way before noon."

A cheer went up and many clapped at the news. Then they looked around at each other in realization. This would be their last day on the ship together. It would be a celebration.

Jacques reminded himself to write the letters he would leave with Pierre to post for him. He kept that thought in mind as he returned

HELENA POORTVLIET

to the horse deck. There was work to be done. While Harry got busy cleaning goat stalls and Pierre was cleaning horse stalls, Jacques began walking the thoroughbreds, beginning with Sun Flair. He wanted to be sure they were well-behaved when their new owner took delivery. Sun Flair was now calm and well-behaved, a big difference from when he first came on board. The yearlings all had grown and filled out a great deal. The colt was much different now, very friendly and well-behaved.

Ramon's filly had also grown a lot since her birth. Today, he was walking the mare around the deck, with the filly following close beside her, a short line on her halter attached to a ring on the girth strap Ramon fastened on the mare. He would need to lead them this way when off the ship.

Jacques just finished his letters when Deral arrived with the milk cans. When they reached the dining room, they were confronted with colorful decorations which Andrea and Patricia put together with supplies on hand, streamers and bows came from Andrea's children's outgrown clothing, cut in strips. They unpacked some of their own table cloths and decorated the tables with flowers cut from paper.

Leon outdid himself to produce a feast, with roast beef, biscuits, and winter squash he procured in Quebec City. Dessert was custard pie. Spirits were high with expectation. Jacques remembered the Christmas celebration at *La Petit Fleur,* which gave him a pang of longing for Jeannette.

After dinner passengers and sailors met together on the horse deck to listen to the Bible reading. The ship was at anchor and for most of the meeting Captain Palmer remained at the top of the ramp observing the singing, reading, and worship, which began as Jacques read:

> "Then he called them in, and lodged them. And on the morrow Peter went away with them, and certain brethren from Joppa accompanied him.
> "And on the morrow after they entered into Caesarea. And Cornelius waited for them, and had called together his kinsmen and near friends.
> "And as Peter was coming in, Cornelius met him, and fell down at his feet, and worshipped him.

"But Peter took him up saying, Standup; I myself also am a man.

"And as he talked with him, he went in, and found many that were come together.

"And he said unto them, Ye know how that it is unlawful for a man that is a Jew to keep company, or to come into one of another nation; but God hath shewed me that I should not call any man common or unclean.

"Therefore I came unto you without gainsaying, as soon as I was sent for: I ask therefore what intent ye have sent for me?

"And Cornelius said, Four days ago I was fasting until this hour; and at the ninth hour I prayed in my house, and, behold, a man stood before me in bright clothing.

"And it said Cornelius, thy prayer is heard, and thine alms are held in remembrance in the sight of God.

"Send therefore to Joppa, and call hither Simon, whose surname is Peter, he is lodged in the house of one Simon the tanner by the seaside: who, when he cometh, shall speak to thee.

"Immediately therefore, I sent to thee, and thou has well done that thou art come. Now therefore are we all here present before God, to hear all things that are commanded thee of God." (Acts 10:23-33, KJV)

When Pierre finished his translation he alluded to what was said about not calling any man common or unclean, as it related to what they read yesterday about Peter's vision about food. Now there were nods of understanding. Then someone was saying, "Read more," so Jacques continued:

"Then Peter opened his mouth and said, of a truth I perceive that God is no respecter of persons.

"But in every nation he that feareth him, and worketh righteousness, is accepted to him.

"The word which God sent unto the children of Israel; preaching peace by Jesus Christ: (he is Lord of all)

"That word, I say ye know, which was published throughout all Judaea, and began from Galilee, after the baptism which John preached;

"How God anointed Jesus of Nazareth with the Holy
Ghost and with all power: who went about doing good,
and healing all that were oppressed of the devil; for God
was with them.

"And we are witnesses of all things which he did in the
land of the Jews, and in Jerusalem, whom they slew and
hanged on a tree:

"Him God raised up on the third day, and shewed him openly.

"Not to all the people, but unto witnesses chosen before
of God, even to us, who did eat and drink with him after
he rose from the dead.

"And he commanded us to preach unto the people, and to
testify that it is he which was ordained of God to be the
judge of the quick and the dead.

"To him give all the prophets witness, that through his
name whosoever believeth in him shall receive remission
of sins." (Acts 10:34-43, KJV)

When Pierre finished his translation, he pointed out two concepts
which stood out in this portion. "In the first two verses, Peter points
out that with God, differences of races or nations mean nothing. If
we fear God, we are all acceptable to him. And in the last verse, he
points out that whoever believes on him shall receive remission of sins.
I'm so thankful for that, because I had many," he laughed and others
laughed with him.

Someone again said, "Read more," so Jacques continued:

"While Peter yet spake these words, the Holy Ghost fell
on all them which heard the word.

"And they of the circumcision which believed were
astonished, as many as came with Peter, because that on the
Gentiles also was poured out the gift of the Holy Ghost.

"For they heard them speak with tongues, and magnify
God. Then answered Peter:

"Can any man forbid water, that these should not be
baptized, which have received the Holy Ghost as well as
we?" (Acts 10:44-47, KJV)

"And he commanded them to be baptized in the name of
the Lord. Then prayed they him to tarry certain days."
(Acts 10:48, KJV)

As Pierre finished the translation, there were already those who were worshipping and praising God, their hands raised toward heaven.

Jean Louis opened the hatch just enough to hear what the men were saying. When he heard the words of Peter speaking of remission of sins, he felt anguish for memories of his marriage and grief at the loss of it, and even more for the loss of his own life, for a truth, it was surely lost. As that young man read of the baptism of the Holy Ghost, the voices began shouting in his head. He pulled the hatch closed quietly and stumbled back to his hiding place, beating his fists into his head, trying to stop the voices.

CHAPTER 25

Negotiations

D ARREN SLEPT LITTLE all night. He was already awake when he heard the metal sounds of the stove door opening in the kitchen. It was still dark in the small window, but he knew from the sounds someone was already up, so he pulled on his trousers, and ran fingers through his hair. As he opened the door into the hallway, he was stuffing shirttails in as he headed toward the kitchen. Antoine was just getting the fire started. When he looked up, he smiled and said, "Good morning, my brother," as he pushed the empty wood basket toward Darren. "You know where to fill that?"

Darren smiled and took the basket, saying "sure" as he headed to the door, just as Jules was coming down the hall toward him. He knew where the woodshed was, so he hurried to fill the basket from the already cut wood.

As he got back to the cottage, Jules was coming out the door. "Good to see you up early," he said, with a good-natured tap on the shoulder.

Darren took the basket of wood into the kitchen, just as Antoine stood up and closed the stove door. "That's enough to keep it going, but we need to get a coupla' armloads."

"Sure, there's still plenty cut."

"Good."

They went out together to the woodshed, each picking up a good size armload of wood. Darren noticed Jules had gone directly to the barn. He mentioned that to Antoine, then added, "I've been so lazy about helping you guys. I apologize. I need to relearn. I used to always help my father. I don't know how I got so lazy."

"Well, it's not too late to start over!" advised Antoine with a grin.

They dropped the wood in the wood box in the kitchen, then went back out to head for the barn.

By the time they all returned to the cottage, the women were up and busy in the kitchen. Teresa and Ellienne were cooking, and Marielle and Jeannette were setting the table. Darren's mother was busy pressing his white shirt. She had already pressed his good slacks and jacket.

"Mother, what are you doing?"

"Sweetie, you're going to call on Lord Montgomery today. You want to look your best. Make that girl proud of you!"

Darren felt touched at his mother's attention. He went over and kissed her cheek. "Thanks, Mother."

"You cut a pretty picture, brother," said Jeannette, admiring her brother. Get out those nice boots you got for Christmas."

"Oh, yeah, good idea," he smiled at her. "You like Rachel, don't you?"

"She's a beautiful woman, and I think your love has made you both better people."

Soon he was out the door and walking toward the big house. It seemed like a hundred steps up to the big front door. When he arrived at the door he lifted the huge brass knocker and tapped it on the brass plate. He was almost afraid someone might hear it. Then he reminded himself, *this is where Rachel lives—Rachel, the love of my life!*

He almost jumped back when he heard someone start to open the door. Then he looked up at Morton, looking stern and serious. "Ye-es?" The word was drawn out into two long syllables and ended like a question. The tall man gave little sign of recognition.

"I'm here to speak to Lord Montgomery."

Morton opened the door wider and nodded for Darren to come in. He walked into the foyer that was separate from the great room.

"Your name?" Morton asked.

"Darren Newall"

"Wait here." And he turned away.

He was back in a few moments, "Come with me."

Darren followed him down the hall to a door, which Morton opened, motioning him through. He entered, finding himself facing a man behind a desk. Morton's voice behind him announced, "Master Darren Newall."

The man stood up and reached out his hand. "Arthur Montgomery, Mr. Newall?"

HELENA POORTVLIET

"Darren," Darren corrected, as he reached for the man's hand. "Lord Montgomery."

"Please, sit down. Would you like anything to drink?"

"No thanks, but thank you." Darren was thinking fast, *I better not sound stupid.* He tried to take in the appearance of the man whom he hoped would be his father-in-law: *The man looked a bit older than he though he remembered his father looked—taller, and heavier. His hair was shades betweem black and silver.*

"What can I do for you, young man?" The question sounded gruff. Darren thought he could feel his stomach vibrating. He gulped.

"I'd like your permission to marry your daughter, Rachel. We love each other and want to marry."

The other man was silent for several moments. Darren felt like running, but he held his ground. Finally the older man spoke, "Do you think you are the only man who wants to marry Rachel?"

It was not what Darren expected. He thought for a moment. "That's not surprising. She's a beautiful woman. But she loves me."

"How long has this been going on?" He still sounded gruff.

"We became acquainted riding with the Durans." Then he added. "But we've never been alone together. We've always been with the rest of the family. Her sister or the Durans have always been with us."

"Well, young man, you tell me more about yourself. Where are you from. Who are your family." He was looking directly at Darren.

"I've lived my whole life till now in Southampton," he began.

"Isn't that where the Durans came from?"

"Well, partly, after they came from France. My family owned an inn in Southampton all my life, and the Durans lived with us when I was little. Teresa Duran helped my mother and Jules worked for my father."

"Edmund Newall—your father is Edmund Newall. Is he here?"

"You knew him? No, he passed away last year."

"Oh, sorry to hear that. He recommended the Durans to me." The tone was a bit softer, then he continued. "And why are you here? Are you returning to Southampton?"

"No, sir," replied Darren. "We sold *La Petit Fleur,* and are moving to Montreal. We plan to open a new business in Montreal. I want Rachel to go with me."

"You what? You want to take Rachel to Montreal?"

"Yes, sir."

Lord Montgomery was on his feet pacing around.

Darren felt like he was cringing in his chair. When he realized it, he consciously straightened up, squared his shoulders and raised his chin.

"My wife spent weeks planning an event to introduce Rachel to society. There are many noblemen and even princes invited. Do you know the purpose of this event?" he asked.

"Yes, sir," Darren answered. "Rachel tells me you want to find a rich husband for her."

Montgomery practically whirled toward Darren. "Do you have a problem with rich?"

"No, sir," Darren answered. "But Rachel is not happy about it. She wants to marry me. We love each other. And I'm not poor. I can give her a good life. We have a lot in common."

"Oh, really. What do you have in common?"

"We both love God, and we like horses. We have enjoyed riding together. She loves to ride and I want her to be able to do what she loves."

"What about babies? Sometime she has to grow up and raise babies. She can't always ride horses."

"That's okay, in good time," Darren replied. "My mother and sister like her, too."

Lord Montgomery walked to the door. "I've got to give this some thought, and talk to my wife. You'll hear from me." He was holding the door.

Darren knew it was time to leave.

The lane from the big house to the Durans' cottage was the longest quarter mile in the world to Darren. He felt he was been honest and direct with Lord Montgomery, but seemed to have met up with a stone wall. While walking, he prayed desperately, "Lord, I'm trying to do it your way. But I can't see the way. What can I do?" When he reached the cottage, many faces were asking the same question. He had no answer. He went to the room he shared with the Duran boys to shed the white shirt his mother so carefully pressed for him, and changed into his riding clothes. When he came out of the bedroom, the women were in the kitchen, so he slipped out the front door.

When Jeannette heard the front door close, she went to the window to see her brother walking toward the barn. She went to her room and quickly changed into the riding skirt Marielle had given her. A moment later, she was also headed for the barn, where she found her brother brushing his mare. She went to him to embrace him.

"What happened?" she asked.

"Nothing—uh—nothing." He looked away from his sister.

"Come on, brother, talk to me!" she prodded.

"He didn't say yes; he didn't say no. He just left me hanging. He holds all the cards."

"We should pray."

"Sure, if you like. I already did."

"Well, let's pray together—okay?" she asked, reaching for his hand. She began to pray, while he just looked down and waited for her to finish.

"I'm going for a ride," he said as he turned around for his saddle.

"All right if I come with you?"

He looked surprised. "Sure, if you want.'

She turned to lead Katy out of the stall. She began to brush her while her brother went for her saddle. In a few moments they were trotting down the lane. Before they were past the big house Darren nudged Dani into a canter and Jeannette gave Katy her head, allowing her to follow.

Arthur Montgomery was standing in the great room watching out the front window as the two bay mares with their riders cantered down the lane.

Morton was beside him as he watched the pair. "They're a nice looking pair, sir."

Montgomery looked sharply at his butler. "You mean horses or riders?"

"Both, sir."

"Who is that young lady?"

"Master Newall's sister, sir."

"They're both very good riders."

"Yes, sir."

"What else do you know about them?"

"Their family is long term friends of the Durans. Madam Newall's parents immigrated from France. She married Edmund Newall, who is the second son of Squire Geoffrey Newall of Southampton. Edmund Newall was formerly Captain Edmund Newall of the Royal Dragoons. With his family connections and his military service, he could have attained the title of Lord had he not left the service when he married."

"What about the woman Edmund married?"

"She is Louisa Amorette. She came to Southampton with her parents as a child. Her father built the inn in Southampton, *La Petit Fleur*. She married Edmund Newall and continued to operate *La Petit Fleur* after her father died. Edmund Newall died last year in the summer.

"They sold *La Petit Fleur* in February this year, with the purpose of immigrating to Canada. Young Newall's sister is engaged to that young Frenchman who was visiting the Durans a few weeks ago with those big black horses. He is already in Canada. They plan to marry when she gets there. The family is planning to purchase another business when they get to Montreal."

Darren and Jeannette cantered the length of the lane to the highway. When Jeannette pulled Katy to a walk she was laughing with excitement and joy. Her brother smiled to see his sister so happy. As they turned for home she began to inquire about his morning interview with Lord Montgomery.

"It was pretty short. I don't think I impressed him much. I didn't know what to say. I know Rachel and I love each other, but he doesn't seem much impressed by that."

"I'm sorry, brother. I don't know what to say." She felt sad for her brother. "But let's continue to pray about it. You love each other, and you both love God. Expect God's favor on your lives. Was there anything he said that gave you an idea of how he was feeling?"

"Well, he asked me if we were going back to Southampton. I told him no, we were going to Montreal and I wanted to take Rachel with me. That seemed to get him upset. He brought up the event they are planning to get her married off to the prince. Then he made it clear it was time for me to leave."

"Well, what if he agreed to let her marry you if you agreed to stay here?"

"But we planned to go to Montreal together. You're going to marry Jacques and then Mother would be alone."

"Well, brother, she knows we're all going to marry eventually. That doesn't mean we'd leave her alone."

"But anyway, I don't know even if that will happen. Besides, remember, I'm still not the prince," Darren lamented.

"Darren, stop that! Besides, you are a prince—remember, you are a child of the King—so you are a prince!"

Darren smiled at his sister. "Thanks, Sis."

They were coming into the barn entrance, so Darren rode in ahead of her and dismounted at Dani's stall. He looked over at Misty's stall. The dapple-gray was in his stall as before. It looked as though the others were not coming to ride today; he wondered if his visit to the big house caused that.

When brother and sister entered the cottage, Teresa greeted them, "I'm sorry you missed lunch, but sit down. I'll have a snack for you in no time." Before long she had sumptuous sandwiches and treats in front of them which surely rivaled whatever was served for lunch.

"Since we have a little break from riding," suggested Jules, "maybe we could use the time to read from God's Word." He looked at Jeannette. "Are you too tired from your ride?"

Jeannette agreed. "I think that's a good idea. What about you, brother?"

Darren agreed. Antoine and Ellienne were smiling, so they gathered in the parlor, waiting for Jeannette to begin:

> "And Abraham got up early in the morning to the place where he stood before the Lord.
> "And he looked toward Sodom and Gomorrah and toward the land of the plain, and beheld, and, lo, the smoke of the country went up as the smoke of a furnace." (Gen. 19:27, 28, KJV)

> "And it came to pass when God destroyed the cities of the plain, that God remembered Abraham, and sent Lot out of the midst of the overthrow, when he overthrew the cities in the which Lot dwelt." (Gen. 19:29, KJV)

"This shows how God responds to our intercession for our loved ones." Jeannette began to explain. "Lot wasn't really living in God's will, but Abraham was a friend to God, and he loved his nephew Lot, so he desperately interceded for him and God listened.

"Lot tried in the best way he knew how to protect the angels, but the rest of the family were pretty much unwilling to go along with him. But God still rescued him. We should see this as an example of getting involved with an ungodly society. Lot really put himself and his family in a bad place when he moved to Sodom."

The others agreed with her, then urged her to continue:

> "And Lot went up out of Zoar, and dwelt in the mountain, and his two daughters with him, for he feared to dwell in Zoar, and he dwelt in a cave, he and his two daughters.
> "And the firstborn said to the younger, our father is old, and there is not a man in the earth to come in unto us after the manner of all the earth:
> "Come, let us make our father drink wine, and we will lie with him, that we may preserve the seed of our father.
> "And they made their father drink wine that night: and the firstborn went in and lay with her father; and he perceived not when she lay down, nor when she arose.
> "And it came to pass on the morrow, that the firstborn said unto the younger, Behold, I lay yesternight with my father: let us make him drink wine this night also; and go thou in, and lie with him, that we may preserve seed of our father.
> "And they made their father drink wine that night also; and the younger one arose; and lay with him, and he perceived not when she lay down nor when she arose.
> "Thus were both the daughters of Lot with child by their father."
> (Gen. 19:30-36, KJV)

Jeannette waited, while they all just stared at her looking uncomfortable. "This is a difficult part of the Bible. In our culture we don't like to look at this sort of thing. But I believe it's important to read all the Bible, and not ignore the parts we don't like. There's a message in all of it."

Her mother looked at her. "Okay, darling, what's the message in this part?" Her mother sounded a little sarcastic and a lot disapproving.

"This part also illustrated how important it was in that culture to have children and to perpetuate their lineage. However, sin leads to

HELENA POORTVLIET

sin. These women did not trust God to take care of their needs. They chose to devise their own solution. Remember Sarah when she tried to help God by giving her maid Hagar to her husband? You see how well that worked out for her. Ishmael's descendants have often been a threat to Isaac's descendants. Let me read you the rest now."

> "And the first born bare a son, and called his name Moab: the same is the father of the Moabites to this day.
> "And the younger, she also bare a son, and called his name Ben-ammi: the same is the father of the children of Ammon unto this day."
> (Gen. 19:37-38, KJV)

"So you will see as we read on, the Moabites and the Ammonites were idol worshipers, and were often a problem to the Hebrews."

Just then there was a knock on the door. Jules went to answer it, to find Morton, red-faced and out of breath as usual. Teresa rushed over to invite him to come in and sit down and catch his breath. Once he was able to breathe easier he announced the reason for his visit.

"The Montgomerys would like to extend an invitation to the Newalls to dinner tomorrow at seven in the evening. Shall I tell them the three of you will be there?" He looked around at the three of them, then looked at Madam Newall with his eyebrows raised, waiting for her answer.

She looked surprised, but answered graciously, "Yes, I will be there with my children at seven. And please tell them thank you."

Then Morton's professional demeanor softened, "This has to do with young Master Newall's visit this morning. The family has been discussing the issue. Rachel is adamant in her determination and her sister is supporting her, for what that is worth. Lady Montgomery is quite distraught, and Himself feels he needs to acquaint himself with all of you to make that decision."

The big man was again out of breath, so he paused before continuing. "Rachel made a wonderful decision for God, and is a brave, strong girl. She and her sister are back to back on this, and thrilled Master Darren made a decision for God. But Lady Montgomery has her own plans for her daughter and her husband has his purposes, also. This could easily go one way or another. I believe it is a matter for prayer. That is my advice, if you will permit me to voice my opinion." Again, out of breath, Morton waited a moment before he stood up. Before he turned to the door he said, "I will be praying for you also." Then he was out the door and gone.

Madam Newall looked at her son, "Son, I understand you want to marry Rachel, but tell me what your plans are."

"Mother, I want to marry Rachel, and I want her to come to Montreal with us."

"What if her father wants the two of you to stay here."

"Mother, I told you I thought we should move to Montreal. You sold the place on my word, and Jeannette's. I don't want to let you down. I want to marry Rachel more than anything, but what about you?" Darren sounded torn.

Madam Newall was dressed in the gown Jeannette helped Jacques pick out for her mother for Christmas. Jeannette was equally adorned in the dress her mother picked out for her. Darren was also dressed in his best. For the first time he felt grateful for his mother's insistence of wanting him to dress well all his life. When they opened the door to leave, they were surprised to see Dani and Katy hitched to a fine carriage, and in the driver's seat was Antoine, dressed in his best. Jules was waiting by the door of the carriage, ready to help the ladies climb in.

With his eyes twinkling, he explained, "You can't be hiking two furlongs in the mud and dirt in your best shoes!" as he helped them in. Darren climbed in after them. He thought he'd seen this fine carriage in the barn.

When they arrived at the big house, Antoine jumped down to help the ladies out. Darren offered his arm to his mother to walk up the steps, and his other arm to his sister. As nervous as he was, he felt proud of his family, and thought they presented a good picture together.

He had not yet lifted the brass knocker when the door opened, and they were met by Morton, in his dignified professional demeanor once more. Morton led them to the dining room and took their wraps just as Lord and Lady Montgomery entered the room to greet them. Lady Montgomery had a kiss for each of the ladies and Lord Montgomery reached for Darren's hand, as Morton announced each of them by name, and then left the room. Soon he returned leading the way with

Rachel and Peggy following. As he stepped aside, he announced each of them by name.

Darren almost dropped his jaw when he saw Rachel. She was wearing a gorgeous silver-blue gown, designed to accentuate her tiny waist. Her black hair was arranged high on her head, with long strands hanging down her back. Morton offered his elbow to Madam Newall and escorted her to the table. Jeannette followed her mother. Rachel walked over to Darren and gave him a dazzling smile, and reached for his arm. He caught on fast, offering his arm, and escorted her to the table. Peggy followed her sister. Lord Montgomery escorted Lady Montgomery to one end of the table and motioned to Darren to take the seat next to his sister, before he sat at the opposite end of the table. Darren was thrilled to find himself directly across the table from Rachel.

As soon as they sat down there was a flurry of activity with the servants bringing food and placing serving dishes on the table. Lord Montgomery started eating immediately, signaling the others to do the same. The eating was interspersed with pleasant comments from both the host and the hostess, setting the guests at ease, despite the circumstances.

Lord Montgomery first focused his attention on Jeannette. "That's a lovely horse you have and you sit her very well."

Jeannette answered with, "Yes, she makes it easy for me to ride well. Both of our mares are good for both riding and driving. My father bought them a couple of years ago." She smiled. "We really enjoy them."

"I've also heard they're good hunters," he added, before taking another bite.

Jeannette and Darren both looked at Rachel and Peggy who were both smiling.

Before long, servants were coming in to collect empty plates and deliver more courses. Lord Montgomery then spoke to Madam Newall. "Your husband was Edmund Newall, a good man, from a good family. Tell me, how did you meet?"

"Yes, he was a good man, and a good father. He is greatly missed. But he was a good example to his son." She looked directly at him as she spoke.

"But tell me," Montgomery repeated, "how did you meet him?"

"He first came to our dining room when I was quite young. My father built *La Petit Fleur* in Southampton, when I was very small. Edmund came in often, when he was in the military, sometimes with his friends, sometimes alone. One day he asked my father permission to court me."

"Didn't he have a commission in the army?"

"Yes, but he didn't want to stay in the army."

"Wasn't his father Squire Newall?"

"Yes," Madam Newall looked puzzled.

"Are you still in contact with his family?"

"No," she looked down, then looked back at him. "We never had much to do with his family. They were not happy about our marriage." She paused, looked at Lady Montgomery, than looked back at him. "His older brother was their favorite son. Edmund was more comfortable with our family. He loved his children and he loved me. He also loved my father."

"Father!" Rachel exclaimed. "You're making Darren's mother uncomfortable."

Peggy was looking apprehensive.

"Rachel, my dear," he answered her, "this young man has asked me to allow him to marry you. That means he would be part of our family and an heir to our estate. Does not that entitle me to determine what kind of person he is and who his family are?"

"But I don't want your estate," Darren protested. "We want to build our own home and our own lives in the new land."

"Young man, a man in my position raises his family in order to pass on the heritage of what we represent to our heirs. Our daughters will marry men who are qualified to continue to run this estate, and to carry on what I have built, and what my father built. The men they marry must have the means to contribute to the future success of this estate, not just take from it."

"Father, are we to be prisoners of this place?"

"Rachel!" Lady Montgomery spoke for the first time. "You know that we are giving you every benefit to enable you to succeed as a member of our society. You cannot throw that away. You know how hard I have worked to organize your presentation to society. All the best, most eligible men will be there. I've even received word Prince Edward and Lord Russell will be here."

HELENA POORTVLIET

"Mother, why don't you use that great event to announce our engagement." She glanced quickly at Darren. "We love each other, and I won't marry anyone else!" She looked at her father. "Darren did the right thing to come and talk to you first, and ask your permission to marry me. Why did you invite him over here to insult his family?"

Jeannette was seated in the middle, between her mother and Darren. She reached out her hand to take her mother's hand on one side, and her other hand to take her brother's on the other. The three of them sat there with linked hands looking at Lord Montgomery.

"I can see," he began, "that you are a strong principled family and I would consider a period of getting acquainted, but the event will take place."

"Father, I will not take part unless Darren is there!" Rachel was firm.

Madam Newall asked, "When is your event?"

"Next weekend," answered Lady Montgomery, a chill in her voice.

"Darren," Lord Montgomery addressed him, "will you indulge me to share an after dinner drink in my study?" He turned to smile indulgently at his wife. "These ladies would like to talk about— whatever ladies like to talk about." With that he stood up and motioned toward his study. Darren got up to follow him.

As soon as they reached the study, Morton appeared behind them with a tray of drinks. When they were seated, Lord Montgomery began with, "Frankly, Darren, I like you. I think you're a good son of your father. I think you would be good at taking on some of the responsibility of this estate. It's clear you and Rachel care for each other. I would consider that the two of you could become engaged, if you were willing to stay here and learn to run this estate. I know enough about your father's family to know that you could, under the right circumstances, attain a title, possibly as high as mine."

"But what about my family?"

"Your sister is engaged to that Frenchman. Isn't your mother planning on going to Montreal with her?"

"I agreed to go with them."

"It's up to you, son. I know your mother would not force you to go with her. I can ensure they will have safe passage to Montreal."

When the Newalls left the Montgomery house, they found Antoine waiting with Dani and Katy and the carriage. The mares were blanketed and had nosebags of grain on. Antoine was bundled up, standing with the mares. When the front door opened, he looked up, then pulled off the blankets, and stashed them under the driver's seat before they reached the carriage. He helped the ladies into the carriage, then climbed up on the driver's seat as Darren got in. He turned the mares back up the lane toward the cottage.

Darren's mother and sister were waiting for him to report to them what went on in Lord Montgomery's study. When he told them, both his mother and sister told him to feel free to accept.

"Don't worry about us son," his mother said. "We'll be safe. Antoine and Ellienne will be with us. You must stay with Rachel. It's the best thing for you. You can regain the position your father gave up, and you'll be with the woman you love."

"But, Mother, I talked you into selling *La Petit Fleur.* I can't let you down."

"You won't let me down. You'll be doing what children do when they grow up. I'm very proud of you. I'll be fine if I know you're happy."

"She'll be with us, brother," Jeannette reached out her hand to take his.

CHAPTER 26

Montreal

JACQUES SLEPT LITTLE as his anticipation was high. Tomorrow would be a big day. When he found himself wide-awake, knowing sleep was no longer possible, he got up. His two companions were sound asleep. As he slipped out the door, freezing fog still enveloped the ship, even floating down into the horse deck.

He got busy feeding horses, then began grooming them. Many of them would be leaving this afternoon, and he wanted them looking good, some for their new owners, and the others would be taking passengers to their new destinations.

Everything was still dark on the main deck, dense with fog. Jacques could hear much activity, but he could still feel the ship straining against the anchor. The tide had already turned, but they would not weigh anchor until the fog lifted.

Jacques was brushing one the the Breakfield's geldings when he realized Harry was next to him. He turned to hug the boy.

"Today's the day, son!" He smiled at the child.

"Are we going home today?"

"We'll be in Montreal today, but we might not get off the ship until tomorrow. Then we have to find a place to live."

Harry yawned, still sleepy, but smiled at the prospect.

He led the gelding back into its stall then led out another. He noticed Harry was beginning to fidget, so he suggested, "Why not clean goats' stalls now, so you'll have it done before time to milk." Harry smiled happily and ran to the goats' stalls.

It wasn't long before Pierre appeared looking sleepy and bewildered. "What's everyone up so early for?"

"Early? The morning's half gone! There's work to do!" Jacques was laughing. Pierre was shaking his head. He went to get the cart and fork to start cleaning stalls.

Jacques was brushing the last of the bay geldings when he heard the clanking of the milk cans. He realized the fog was lifting and daylight was lightening the sky. He could feel the vibration of the cables turning as the anchor was weighed. The ship was moving toward Montreal.

After delivering the milk, they headed for the dining room to meet with the Breakfields and the Caldwells.

"Good morning," was Roger's cheerful greeting. Andrea was next to him, grinning expectantly. Willis and Patricia were also cheerfully grinning. "Today may be the day," Willis said.

"Yes," Jacques agreed, "I'm getting your vehicles out of the hold. You probably want to disembark as soon as we get there. I've got your bay horses brushed down. They're looking good," he said to Roger.

Turning to Willis, he said, "I'm starting on yours next."

"Maybe we should come down and help." Willis suggested. Roger was nodding in agreement.

"That would be great," Jacques answered, then he turned to Roger, "Will you know by tomorrow where we should be going when we get off here, or should I just find an inn for now?"

"If we can get off the ship by this afternoon, I'll come back tomorrow and tell you where you should go."

Jean Louis was awake and aware the anchor was weighed and the ship was moving with the tide. He heard the steps of many going up the ramp, and then quiet. He crept carefully to the small hatch, opened it just a crack to look out. All was quiet, but he was nervous, anxious of the imminent activity as they neared Montreal. He noticed the passengers' vehicles stored in the hold and assumed these would be taken out soon. He went back into his hiding place behind the cargo container. He still had food remaining in the flour sack, so he crept far into the corner and dug into the bag to satisfy his hunger. After a while the large cargo door was opened, allowing an abundance of light to flood in. He squeezed further into the dark space, and stayed still and quiet, barely breathing.

By the time the *Bucephalus* was guided carefully into the moorage in the eastern end of the port, the four men pulled three vehicles out of the hold, with the help of a husky cable and winch. They lined up the two coaches and the Caldwell's farm wagon at the bottom of the ramp.

HELENA POORTVLIET

The first to go was the Breakfields' coach with their four bay geldings. Then they hitched the Suffolks to the Caldwells' wagon, for they would be going with the Breakfields to, hopefully find lodging.

In those last moments, intense feelings surfaced. Andrew and Harry clung to each other, until the adults were able to convince them it would be a short separation. They would see each other again in Montreal. It was expected they would be going to school together.

They carefully led the horses down the ramp onto the pier before the families boarded, sure that the horses were well under control. Andrea and Julia climbed inside, but Andrew happily climbed up into the driver's seat with his father so he could wave back at Harry as they drove up the pier toward the city. Next the Caldwells followed, waving back at them. Ramon followed the two vehicles on his stallion, leading his mare and filly.

By the time Jacques got back to the horse deck, the Tennisons were ready to go and Pierre already had their team harnessed and ready to hitch to their coach. Jacques sized up their two lightweight coach horses and harnessed Tounerre and hooked his singletree to the tongue of the coach and backed the stallion in place in front of the team.

He smiled at Richard Tennison. "I don't want to put a strain on your horses and make them lame, when they haven't had any hard work in all these weeks." Richard looked relieved, as he took hold of his team to lead them up the ramp. When they reached the top of the ramp, Jacques unhitched his stallion and waved to Richard as he led Tounerre back down the ramp.

They were all gone, some of the best friends Jacques had known. Even though he knew he would be working with these men for the next year, the ship seemed strangely quiet. Almost half the horses were gone, and most of his best friends were gone. But there were still many horses to care for, maybe for several days, depending on when the new owners came for them.

The sun was sinking fast and a chilly fog was beginning to envelop the ship, bringing darkness with it. Jacques noticed as all the vehicles were leaving, the heavy snow they saw in Quebec City was not the case in Montreal. The ground showed patches of melting snow and ice, but it was mostly just wet.

As the three climbed the ramp with the milk for dinner, they got a limited view of the city of Montreal, very faintly through the fog. The lights which twinkled on the waterfront quickly faded in the distance as the fog thickened. They would have to wait for another day to see more of Montreal.

Jacques, Harry and Pierre had a table to themselves. It seemed strange, with the others gone. Captain Palmer came into the dining room, filled up a plate of food and came over to sit with them for the first time since they left Liverpool.

"It's been a good voyage, thanks to the three of you," he began. "I appreciate your hard work. He handed them all envelopes, including Harry. "These are your pay vouchers. You can cash them at the port office."

Harry excitedly opened his envelope to find a voucher for pay for "Care of Milk Goats." It was not as large as the others' pay but it was unexpected. Jacques looked surprised and began to speak up, but was interrupted by Palmer.

"Oh, he was worth it. It's good to see a young man so willing to work. And I have another offer for him if it's okay with you." After a pause waiting for response from Jacques, he went on. "You have nine goats that survived the storm. Two of them are dry, so they're worth nothing. The others may give milk for a while, but won't be good for another trip. If you've room for them, they're yours—or Harry's, if he's not tired of goats."

Harry's eyes grew big and his smile wide. He began to jump up and down on the seat. He looked a Jacques. "Oh, can we take them?"

"I'll have to see what kind of place we get. I've got to find space for my horses, anyway. And my mares are foaling in the next two months. I can let you know in a day or so."

There were several sailors in the dining room. When Captain Palmer left the table, some of the sailors came over, including Deral, who asked, "With all your friends gone, are you still going to read from the Bible tonight?"

Jacques nodded, "Sure."

So, a short time later, Deral arrived on the horse deck with several of his friends, so as they gathered around, Jacques began to read:

"And the apostles and the brethren that were in Judaea
heard that the Gentiles had received the word of God.

HELENA POORTVLIET

"And when Peter was come up to Jerusalem, they that were of the circumcision contended with him.

"Saying, Thou wentest into men uncircumcised, and didst eat with them.

"But Peter rehearsed the matter from the beginning, and expounded it by order unto them, saying,

"I was in the city of Joppa praying: and in a trance I saw a vision, A certain vessel descended, as it had been a great sheet, let down from heaven by four corners; and it came even to me.

"Upon the which when I had fastened mine eyes, I considered and saw four footed beasts of the earth, and wild beasts, and creeping things, and fowls of the air.

"And I heard a voice saying, Arise, Peter, slay and eat.

"But I said, Not so Lord: for nothing so common or unclean hath at any time hath entered my mouth.

"But the voice answered me again from heaven, What God hath cleansed, that call not thou common.

"And this was done three times: and all were drawn up again into heaven.

"And, behold, immediately there were three men already come unto the house where I was, sent from Caesarea unto me.

"And the Spirit made me go with them, nothing doubting. Moreover, these six brethren accompanied me, and we entered in the man's house.

"And he showed us how he had seen an angel in his house, which stood and said unto him, Send men unto Joppa, and call for Simon, whose surname is Peter.

"Who shall tell these words, whereby thou and all thy house shall be saved.

"And as I began to speak, the Holy Ghost fell on them, as on us at the beginning.

"Then I remembered the word of the Lord, how that he said, John indeed baptized with water, but ye shall be baptized with the Holy Ghost.

"Forasmuch, then as God gave them the like gift as he did to us, who believed on the Lord Jesus Christ; what was I that I could withstand God?

"When they heard these things, they held their peace, and glorified God, saying, then hath God also, to the Gentiles granted repentance unto life." (Acts 11:1-18, KJV)

Jacques stopped several times to wait for Pierre to translate. The sailors listened with interest but just urged him to continue. Now he waited for questions, but as Pierre finished the translation he began his own explanation.

"The Jews were very prejudiced against anyone who was not a Jew, so this was new to them. Their prejudice was based on Jewish law, which they grew up with. Now God is telling them their prejudice is no longer valid. They're seeing righteousness is based only on one's relationship with Christ. We're all the same in God's eyes.

The sailors looked at each other in surprise. Many were from various countries. Old rivalries are invalid. Whether Scot, Irish or English, it made no difference. These two Frenchmen were showing them through the Scriptures, it did not matter. Someone urged, "Read more!" So he went on:

> "Now they which were scattered abroad upon the persecution that arose about Stephen traveled as far as Phenice and Cypress, and Antioch, preaching the word to none but unto the Jews only.
> "And some of them were men of Cypress and Cyrene, which when they were come to Antioch, spake unto the Grecians, preaching the Lord Jesus.
> "And the hand of God was with them: and a great number believed, and turned unto the Lord." (Acts 11:19-21, KJV)

As Pierre translated he commented here they were showing less prejudice and many were responding to the teaching. Then someone again said, "Read more," so Jacques continued:

> "Then tidings of these things came unto the ears of the church which was in Jerusalem: and they sent forth Barnabas, that he should go as far as Antioch.
> "Who when he came, and had seen the grace of God, was glad, and exhorted them all, that with purpose of heart, they would cleave unto the Lord.
> "For he was a good man, and full of the Holy Ghost and faith: and much people were added unto the Lord.
> "Then departed Barnabas to Tarsas, to seek Paul:
> "And when he had found him, he brought him unto Antioch. And it came to pass, that a whole year they

assembled themselves with the church, and taught much people. And the disciples were called Christians first in Antioch. (Acts 11:22-26, KJV)

As soon as Pierre finished the translation, Jacques heard again, "Read more!" He could tell the sailors were enjoying the stories, so he continued:

"And in these days came prophets from Jerusalem unto Antioch.
"And there stood up one of them named Agabus, and signified by the Spirit that there would be great dearth throughout all the world: which came to pass in the days of Claudius Caesar.
"Then the disciples, every man according to his ability, determined to send relief unto the brethren which dwelt in Judaea,
"Which also they did and sent it to the elders by the hands of Barnabas and Saul." (Acts 11:27-30, KJV)

Jacques closed his Bible, feeling exhausted. Pierre invited the sailors to come together for prayer. Someone voiced concern for Nate, who was still in the infirmary. After praying for him, several talked about visiting him.

Jean Louis held the small hatch open just a tiny crack. He noticed the three women and their husbands were no longer part of the group. He reasoned those were the families who left the ship earlier. They must be in Montreal now. He quietly closed the hatch, making a noise between a growl and a moan. He heard that man again speak of the Holy Ghost. It was as if every time he heard that name, the voices in his head would fight and scream at each other. He knew he needed to get off this ship tonight. He crawled back into his hiding place, and dug into the flour sack to find the last bits of roast beef from his stolen cache. It wasn't much, but it temporarily eased the hunger pangs. He settled back to wait for the activity of the ship to settle down.

The sailors thanked Jacques and Pierre for the meeting as they headed up the ramp. The three companions retired to the little cabin, exhausted.

The fog thickly enveloped the ship, even floating down to the horse deck. The hatch of the cargo hold opened just a crack, as one eye peered out into the foggy night. All was quiet; dark had closed in. The little cabin was quiet. Jean Louis crept out of the hatch and waited a moment behind the ramp. He held his breath, waiting to discern any sounds from above. Hearing nothing he crept up the ramp. He retraced his footsteps from the first night around the side of the main cabin to where the stern of the ship was tied to the pier. It was only a few feet to the pier, but he knew the water below was freezing. He slipped over the rail and crouched next to the cleat wrapped with the thick rope. He slipped over the edge, hanging onto the rope, swinging his legs up to wrap around the line, sliding hand over hand down to the pier. Rising to his feet, he stayed close to the shadow of the hull of the ship, as he hurried off the pier toward the city, disappearing into the night.

Waking early, Jacques was too restless to remain in the bunk, knowing there was much to do. As usual, Harry and Pierre were still asleep. He quickly got busy feeding the horses still in his care, the Godolphin thoroughbreds, and the Shires, besides his own horses. As he began the stall cleaning, Harry and Pierre emerged from the cabin. Jacques laughed, "You're just in time for the good stuff!"

Pierre replied sleepily, "Where have I heard that before?"

Harry headed for the goats.

Jacques went into Sun Flair's stall and began brushing the stallion, who was content to continue eating while being groomed. He went to the yearling colt next, but this one showed an expectant nervousness, moving around in his stall instead of standing still for the brushing and enjoying his food. After a little bit of this behavior, Jacques put a lead on the colt and led him out of the stall. After several laps around the horse deck, he settled down and was quite happy to get back to his stall and eat. Jacques spent time grooming each of the thoroughbreds until Deral arrived with the milk cans.

At breakfast Captain Palmer came over to speak to them. "We just have horse cargo to be picked up by owners or owners' reps, right?"

Jacques agreed with him. "The Godolphin thoroughbreds and all those Shires. Do you have any idea who is first to go?"

Palmer shook his head. "We've just got to wait for them to show up. But they should be here today. The report is out that we're in port. Are they all in good shape?"

"Great shape!" Jacques reported proudly. The thoroughbreds are in better shape. I've done a little training with them. Their behavior has improved a lot."

"And the Shires?"

"Oh, they're in great shape. They're all pretty docile, even the stallion. They're nice horses."

"Well, you've done a great job. Let me know if you ever need a recommendation!" With that Palmer got up and left the table.

After breakfast the three companions returned to the horse deck to groom the rest of the horses, eleven Shires. While Pierre and Jacques were grooming Shires, Harry was earnestly brushing goats. It wasn't long before Captain Palmer appeared on the ramp with several men, one of which was the new owner of the thoroughbreds. The others were the grooms who would be handling the horses.

"I hear that stud's a real handful," said one of the grooms. Jacques smiled as he led Sun Flair out of his stall. The stallion pranced a bit and arched his neck, but his head was tucked down close to Jacques elbow.

"Take good care of this boy," Jacques grinned. "He's a good boy," he added as he handed over the lead.

Pierre brought out the yearling colt, which was now reasonably calm, handing him almost reluctantly over to one of the grooms. They went back for the two fillies, which were friendly and docile. Jacques perceived that Pierre looked sad to see the thoroughbreds leaving. Pierre quickly turned back to the stalls as if to clean them.

The grooms were leading the thoroughbreds up the ramp and then they were gone. Jacques went to lead out one of the shire mares and began to groom her. After all the time he spent working with the thoroughbreds, the horse deck seemed very empty without them. Grooming the mares was good therapy to help resolve his feelings. He looked over at Pierre brushing another mare. He hoped it helped his friend also.

It was not long before the new owners arrived to collect the six shire mares. And shortly after, a farmer from west of Ottawa arrived to pick up the last five shires, the stallion and four mares. As he watched them as they were led up the pier, he saw two familiar horses at the head of the pier. One was the piebald stallion and the other was the bay gelding he knew well. As they came closer, he recognized Ramon and Roger.

"Are you ready to go?"

"I will be as soon as I get my horses hitched."

His two friends rode onto the ship and led their horses down the ramp to the horse deck. After pulling his carriage out of the hold, he cleaned his and Harry's belongings out of the little cabin and packed them into his carriage. Then he looked over to see Harry in the goats' stall with his arms around one of the goats, looking at him, then he remembered. He looked at Roger, feeling a little awkward.

"What can you tell me about accommodations? Do I need to find an inn?"

Both men grinned at him happily. "We've got a great place for you," Roger began. "The company owns a property with two nice homes and a barn and paddocks between them. Our friend Willis and his wife are settling into one of those homes. When we left, he already had his horses settled in one side of the barn. There's plenty of room for your horses on the other side."

"The house is plenty big for your wife, too, when she gets here. But in the meantime, do you mind sharing the house?"

Jacques looked at the two men and asked, "Who?" Then he was caught by the grin on Ramon's face.

"Do you mind? For a while?" Then he said, "If not, I can find something else, but my horses sure like that nice barn."

Jacques laughed, relieved. "Oh sure, that's fine." Then he remembered, "One more thing." He looked back at Harry, still hugging the goat. "Captain Palmer offered the goats to Harry. Do we have room for goats?" He felt a little foolish.

Roger laughed, "Oh sure." Then he added, "I think Andrew will be happy to hear that!"

When Jacques led his mares out to harness them, the others even remarked about how round they had become. He even had to let out some buckles on their harness. It did not take long to get them all hitched, with Tounerre in the lead in the unicorn position.

Captain Palmer appeared just as they were ready to leave. Jacques told him, "I'll be back tomorrow to pick up the goats."

He led his horses up the ramp and off the ship before getting on the driver's seat with Harry. Pierre followed him to the pier, facing him with his hand out, "Thanks, my brother, for all you've done. My life is completely different than it was two months ago, thanks to you and Jesus."

"Well, you've been a good friend, brother, and a good preacher, too. You're life is different because of the choices you've made." They shook hands, then embraced, before Jacques climbed into the driver's seat. Ramon and Roger were already riding up the pier toward the road.

It was several miles to their new home, located less than two miles from the "Golden Square Mile," which was situated at the foot of Mount Royale. The fog lifted and the day was clear, though still cold. Jacques saw the sun now far to the west, soon to set. Driving through the city, through heavy traffic, seeing many children alone on the street, he remembered Birmingham, where he found Harry. He put his arm around the boy, pulling him close.

On the northwest side of the city, the buildings were smaller and the streets far less congested. Finally, they reached the property. When they pulled up, Willis came out to greet them. Jacques pulled his bags out of the carriage and followed Roger to the house. Willis and Ramon led his horses off toward the barn. The house was sparsely furnished, but it did have beds in three of the bedrooms and a table with chairs in the kitchen. Roger showed him the master bedroom and Jacques was relieved to see the bed appeared to be clean.

They went to the barn to find his friends had unharnessed his horses and put them in clean, roomy box stalls. On the other side he saw Willis' two Suffolks and the piebald mare and filly. Amazed how things seemed to be working out, he looked up and said, "Thank you, God!"

Willis then said, "Patricia is fixing dinner, so you guys come over and share our table."

Later, when Jacques slipped into bed, he felt as though he was more tired than he had ever been in his life. He was glad Harry seemed pleased with his own space. Jacques was just slipping off to sleep when he was aware of the squeak of his door opening. He turned over quickly to find Harry, shivering next to his bed.

"Can I come in with you—I'm cold."

After several weeks in that tiny cabin, waking up in the huge master bedroom was a startling surprise. Something awakened Jacques; his feet were on the floor before he realized it was a knock on the front door. Sun was shining in the window, beginning to warm the chilly room. By the time he got to the front room, Ramon already opened the door to Roger.

Roger backed away from the front door and nodded toward the front yard. Jacques looked out to see Roger's bay gelding hitched to a small wagon with a cargo area closed in with a wood and wire frame. "Look what I found in the equipment yard; just the thing for you to pick up your goats."

The bay had a saddle on his back, and Roger unhooked the traces from the wagon and buckled them together behind his saddle. Then he mounted and waved, "Got to go; see you later."

Jacques shook his head, amazed. It seem as though his prayers were answered even before he prayed. Ramon laughed, "God is good!"

Now Harry was tugging on his arm, "Can we get the goats, now?"

Just then Willis appeared in the yard, "Patricia sent me to get you guys for breakfast."

Jacques looked at Ramon, grinning, and they both said in unison, "God is good!"

At breakfast, Willis told them he would be taking his team and wagon to get hay. Roger directed him to a farmer who would invoice the company for payment. Yesterday, a delivery of groceries and supplies arrived. While they were eating breakfast, a team pulled up in front with a load of cut firewood. They all looked at each other, just shaking their heads. Willis spoke up again, saying, "It seems as though whenever one of us mentions something we need, it just shows up here!"

After breakfast, Jacques hitched Tounerre to the wagon Roger had delivered. They headed back through the streets to the waterfront. Jacques saw a sign with these words:

Libraire
Bookseller
Bibliobole

He pulled Tounerre over to the first open hitching post. Ramon looked around at him with eyebrows raised. Jacques said to Harry, "Come on, we need books," smiling at Harry. As they went through the door, bells tied to the door alerted the clerk.

"Can I help you?" (In French)

Jacques smiled hearing the French. "Do you have Bibles?"

The man showed him a large selection in both French and English. Jacques picked out two in English and one in French. He looked around for Harry, who had wandered off. He found him looking through a volume entitled, *Comprehensive History of Montreal.*

"Would you like to take that home?" Jacques asked.

Harry's eyes widened, his smile huge.

Jacques picked up the book and handed it to the clerk, along with the Bibles.

When they got to the ship, they were welcomed by Pierre who helped them load the goats. "This is my last job for two days until we load up again."

"Well, come home with us. There's plenty of room. We'll get you back to the ship on time.

All right!"

When they got in to the wagon, Jacques reached for the package of books. He pulled out one of the English Bibles and the French Bible and gave them to Pierre. "If you're going to be a preacher, you need a Bible."

Pierre accepted with his eyes shining, blinking back tears. "Thanks, brother. God is good!"

There was a roomy shelter and pen behind the barn that looked as if it had been built just for goats, with a gate opening to the larger pasture. As they unloaded the goats, Jacques saw the hay was delivered and loaded into the hayloft; his mares and the others were fed.

By the time they were done, as he was showing Pierre the house, Willis and Patricia arrived to invite them to dinner. They were thrilled to see Pierre, both of them hugging him, all the earlier animosity forgotten.

After dinner, Willis suggested it would be nice to hear Jacques read from the Bible, especially since Pierre was there with them for the last time. It took only a few moments for Jacques to get his Bible and begin:

> "Now about that time Herod the king stretched forth his hands to vex certain of the church.
> "And he killed James the brother of John with the sword."
> (Acts 12:1, 2, KJV)

There was a collective "Ah!" As Jacques looked around, there were no more comments, only sad looks. When no one spoke up, he continued reading:

> "And because he saw it pleased the Jews, he proceeded further to take Peter also. (Then were the days of unleavened bread.)
> "And when he had apprehended him, he put him in prison, and delivered him to four quaternions of soldiers to keep him; intending after Easter to bring him forth to the people.
> "Peter therefore was kept in prison: but prayer was made without ceasing of the church unto God for him." (Acts 12:3-5, KJV)

Jacques paused as Pierre translated into English. There was a hush, as if those listening were in prayer for Peter. Jacques continued:

> "And when Herod would have brought him forth, the same night Peter was sleeping between two soldiers, bound with two chains: and the keepers before the door kept the prison.
> "And, behold, the angel of the Lord came upon him, and a light shined in the prison: and he smote Peter on the side, and raised him up saying, Arise up quickly. And his chains fell off his hands.

HELENA POORTVLIET

"And the angel said to him, Gird thyself and bind on thy sandals. And so he did. And he saith unto him, Cast thy garment about thee and follow me.

"And he went out, and followed him, and wist not that it was true which was done by the angel; but thought he saw a vision.

"When they were past the first and second wards, they came unto the iron gate that leadeth unto the city; which opened to them of his own accord; and they went out, and passed on through one street; and forwith the angel departed from him." (Acts 12:7-10, KJV)

"Wow!" Jacques heard the exclamation from Ramon, just as Pierre began the translation. Then came a collective "Wow! from the rest. No more comments, just heads shaking in amazement. Then someone said, "Read more!" so he continued:

"And when Peter came to himself, he said, now I know of a surety, that the Lord has sent his angel, and hath delivered me out of the hand of Herod, and from all the expectation of the people of the Jews.

"And when he had considered the thing, he came to the house of Mary the mother of John, whose surname was Mark, where many were gathered together, praying.

"And as Peter knocked at the door of the gate, a damsel came to hearken, named Rhoda.

"And when she knew Peter's voice, she opened not the gate for gladness, but ran in, and told how Peter stood before the gate.

"And they said unto her, Thou art mad. But she constantly affirmed that it was so. Then they said, It is his angel.

"But Peter continued knocking: and when they had opened the door, and saw him, they were astonished.

"But he beckoning unto them with the hand to hold their peace declared unto them how the Lord had brought him out of prison. And he said, Go show these things unto James, and to the brethren. And he departed, and went into another place." (Acts 12:11-17, KJV)

As Jacques listened to Pierre's translation, he observed the relief on the faces of the listeners.

"Praise God!" came from Ramon.

Jacques looked at Harry to see his eyes closed, a smile on his face and his hands flat on his chest. He looked around at the rest of the group.

"That story gives us reason for confidence in God's ability to deliver us from any situation that threatens us," was Willis comment.

Jacques closed the Bible and stood up. He was suddenly very tired, and wanted to retire to his own house with Harry.

'After two days of fellowship, Jacques drove Pierre back to the ship, accompanied by Harry. He reflected on how much transpired in the two months since they made that trip in this carriage from Birmingham to Liverpool. When they got to the ship, Jacques pulled out the two letters, which he handed to Pierre. "My brother, if you will, do me a favor and post these from Liverpool when you get there. One is for Jeannette and the other is for my father. By now they both probably think I've fallen off the end of the earth!"

"Yes, of course—be glad to!" He seemed almost unwilling to get out of the carriage. Then they saw Captain Palmer waving to them. They parted company and Jacques turned the carriage for home.

CHAPTER 27

Handfast

T HE LANE IN front of the big house was filling up with
carriages, dazzling with the opulence of high society and
even royalty. The well-bred horses were tended by servants, while
their masters made their way, with their elegant ladies toward the
huge double doors. Lights sparkled from every window and from
the lampposts lining the walk and stairway. Music from an orchestra
floated in the air.

Peggy was in Rachel's room with her sister as both young ladies
were finishing their preparation, while many servants were coming
and going. Their mother again entered the room, frantic that her
daughters were becoming presentable. Lady Montgomery moved
in close enough to Rachel to grasp her by the shoulders, smiling
proudly. "Oh my, you look just beautiful!"

Peggy stood by, grinning excitedly at her sister, "Oh yes! You
really do!"

Rachel's gown was a deep teal blue, cut in to emphasize her tiny
waist, with the neckline cut deeply in front, edged with fine lace
almost the same colors as her shimmering gown. She could see her
image in the mirror, feeling anxious that Darren would be captivated
by her appearance.

Madam Newall and Teresa Duran spent the last few days making
sure Darren was attired as elegantly as the prince he may be competing
with. Darren's mother and sister were attired as beautifully as any
other lady who might be attending.

When they were ready, there appeared in front of the cottage an
elegant carriage pulled by the two bay mares, driven by Antoine. As
the carriage moved down the lane, Darren felt as though in a trance

facing some horrible destiny in front of him. But he would have walked past hungry lions to get to this beautiful woman he loved.

As the three walked through the great doors, Morton announced them each by name. Other guests looked around curiously to see who they were, then continued their conversations, until in the next moment, all eyes turned to the door as two men entered and were introduced. One was little more than a boy, but confident and regal in his bearing. The other was a middle-aged man, though barely as tall as the boy, wearing the regalia of high office.

"His royal highness, Crown Prince Edward, son of Victoria, Queen of England, and Lord John Russell, Prime Minister of England. Darren suddenly felt small, knowing this was the prince, realizing the young man was barely more than a boy, he could not help smiling. He wondered whether either the prince or the prime minister were looking for a wife.

Lord Montgomery appeared to greet the prince and the prime minister, not noticing Darren or his family. Following behind Lord Montgomery was another man about the same age, but very thin, with somewhat aquiline features. He may have been as tall as Lord Montgomery, but he had a distinct hunch with rounded shoulders. He wore fashionable attire as fine as the royal visitors. Darren stood back as Lord Montgomery introduced the man, Squire Marshall Tanaghaven to the prince and Lord Russell. Darren heard Squire Tanaghaven saying to Montgomery and the others, grinning through crooked and missing teeth, "This is a great day to celebrate the joining of two great families!"

Darren looked at his mother and sister, seeing they both heard what the man said. Then the room became very quiet as all eyes turned toward the stairway. Peggy was descending the stairs, her red hair piled high on her head, with a great length of it cascading down one shoulder, wearing a gorgeous emerald gown. The crowd was speechless, in awe, as Morton appeared to announce her.

"The Lady Miss Margaret Montgomery," was followed by applause, only to be cut short when Rachel appeared at the top of the stairs. After a collective "Awe!" Morton announced, "The Lady Miss Rachel Montgomery."

The applause recognized Rachel was what this event was all about. Darren started forward, his heart overflowing with pride for this woman he loved, but stopped as Squire Tanaghaven brushed past him and started up the stairway, offering his arm to Rachel.

"How wonderful to see you, my dear!"

"Oh, Uncle Marshall, how nice of you to come," Rachel answered, smiling at him. Then she looked around, until her searching eyes met Darrens'.

Darren started forward. Squire Tanaghaven, still holding Rachel's hand on his arm, brushed past Darren. "Come, my dear, you must meet Prince Edward and Lord Russell. Rachel looked frantically back toward Darren, who found himself next to Peggy as Rachel disappeared into the crowd attached to the arm of the squire.

"This can't be happening!" Peggy was shaking her head in disbelief. "All her preparation was for you. She came out for you!" She sounded apologetic as she looked at Darren. "I'm so sorry!" She looked past Darren at Jeannette and Madam Newall.

Jeannette felt her anger rising as she saw the hurt in her brother's eyes. Then with her jaw set firmly, she looked after the couple who were now out of sight. She turned quickly to follow, leaving Peggy and Darren, still in shock. As she caught up with them she gushed, "Oh, Rachel, you look so wonderful!" Then she clumsily bumped into the squire, impulsively embracing Rachel, breaking the squire's grip on her arm.

"Let's go see the beautiful table your mother created. Mother and I are just famished!" She continued to say anything which came to mind as she steered Rachel toward the refreshment table, leaving the squire with his mouth open. Darren and Peggy recovered enough to follow in time to see the two women heading for the table arm in arm. The squire stood fuming, outraged.

"Rachel," Darren began. She turned and reached for him. Peggy and Jeannette closed in around them.

The squire pushed into their midst to take Rachel's arm. She tried to back away. "Rachel, my dear," he began, "You must come with me! Your father is about to announce our engagement."

She looked at the squire in shock. "I'm not engaged with you, Uncle Marshall. You're as old as my father! We've never been that way! You're my uncle!" Her face was a picture of anger and disbelief.

"Oh, no, my dear," he continued, "You've always been my intended. Ever since my dear Maddie died, you've been promised to me!"

Much of the crowd had turned to look at them, as Lord Montgomery approached. "Father, tell Uncle Marshall he's mistaken. I'm going to marry Darren." She was pleading.

"Rachel, my dear, the squire and I have spoken of this matter, and we have come to see it is for the best for all." Her father's voice was firm, showing little emotion.

Rachel turned, face red, eyes flashing in anger. "I'd rather die!" she shouted as she turned, starting for the stairs.

Then the squire was again in front of her, putting his hands on her shoulders. "Much as I love your spirit, I will not allow you to embarrass me so, in front of company especially!" He was smiling, with superior acknowledgement of his power. "You'll be my wife for many years, and this will not happen again!" He slipped his arm around her waist, turning her back toward her father.

Darren felt his world crashing down around him. Then his mother and sister were next to him. "Let's go," his mother urged, as she took his arm. Jeannette, angry and feeling humiliated for her brother, put her arm around him. "Yes, we've been here too long already!"

Antoine was dozing on the driver's seat, with a blanket wrapped around him, when he realized the family was coming down the walk. He quickly threw the blanket aside and started toward them. The three were clinging to each other for support. He helped them into the carriage without a word, climbing back up to turn the mares back down the lane. He did not have to ask. It was clear things had gone wrong.

Darren changed from the finery of the evening into his riding clothes and headed for the barn. Antoine was just backing the carriage into place, the mares were still standing in harness as Darren entered. Antoine began to unharnessed Katy as Darren took Dani.

"Do you want to tell me what happened?" Antoine asked.

Darren was shaking with desperation and anger, so much so he felt the stabbing pain in his chest returning. "She's marrying some old guy!" He was shaking his head, still in disbelief. "Some friend of her father's!"

Antoine grasped Darren's arms. "Let's pray right now," he said firmly. Darren looked around him, shaking his head. "It's done! Her father's announcing their engagement!"

HELENA POORTVLIET

Antoine broke in, "It's not done in God's eyes! Let's pray!" He was still firm, holding onto Darren as he began, "Dear Lord, give us peace as we try to understand your will. We need to know your will in this matter. These two young people love each other and they love you. I believe they belong together. I pray for your peace as we understand what we should be doing in obedience to your will. I pray for peace, in Jesus name."

Darren turned to remove the harness from Dani, before reaching for his saddle.

"What are you going to do?" Antoine asked.

"I'm going for a ride," Darren replied, as he swung up on the mare.

Rachel slipped to the floor, out of the squire's arms, seemingly in a faint. Her sister dropped to her side, looking up at the squire. "Now look what you've done," she exclaimed defiantly at the squire. "This is all too much for my sister. I'll see her upstairs. She needs time to calm down." Peggy was embracing her sister. By then, their mother was with them, helping Rachel to her feet. She waved the squire away.

In Rachel's room her mother held her as she wept. "I'm so sorry, my dear. Your father should have told you he was talking to Marshall. It was something they talked about when Aunt Maddie died, but we thought he forgot about it." Her mother sighed. But Marshall is very rich; and he is to be a lord now he has inherited his brother's property. You will have the most elegant home." Then she smiled. "It won't be so bad. And I didn't realize the prince was so young." She sighed. "Oh, well."

Rachel looked at her mother in dismay. "Mother, please leave me now. Leave Peggy with me. We'll come down in a little while, please," she pleaded.

"Oh, all right," Lady Montgomery replied. "I must get back to our guests." She started for the door.

Peggy turned to her sister. "What now? You're not giving up just like that. What are you going to do?

Rachel answered, "You go back down. Tell Uncle Marshall I have a headache. I just need rest. I'll talk to him tomorrow."

"Really?"

"Sure. Go on and talk to the prince. At least you can have a good time." Rachel urged her sister toward the door, closing it behind her.

Once Peggy was gone, Rachel quickly slipped out of the teal gown and into her riding skirt, hurriedly stuffed a few things into a bag and left her room, hurried up to the servants' floor and down the stairs to the kitchen, where she slipped out the door.

Rachel knew well the path from the big house around the back of the cottage to the path around the back of the woodshed to the side door of the huge barn. Entering, she saw the main door standing open and lantern light in the main aisle, at the same time hearing voices. She moved past the carriage row in time to see Darren swing up on Dani.

"Darren!"

Darren turned in his saddle at hearing her voice. At seeing her, he leaped from his horse to run to her.

As Antoine saw the two embrace, he turned to the stall of the dapple-gray, reaching for Rachel's saddle on the way. As he led the horse out he saw the bags she was carrying, and strapped on saddle bags behind her saddle.

Darren met Rachel with an embrace before he pulled back to face her, reaching in his pocket for the small box with the ring. "Rachel, I love you and want to marry you. I pledge my life and my love and all I have to you. I pledge to be your husband for life for good or bad forever before God!" He took the ring from the box and reached for her hand. "If you take this ring, I trust you'll agree to the same, and we'll go before the Romani chief to witness these same vows while handfast.

With tears in her eyes, Rachel reached out her hand as he slipped the ring on her finger. "I do agree and I will go with you."

Then Antoine led the dapple-gray horse to them grinning. "I heard your words and I witness your vows. Now go to Stavros and make it official." He took her bags and packed them into the saddlebags on her horse as Darren helped her mount.

"Take the meadow trail to the highway and bypass the house," warned Antoine. Darren was already on his horse and they were out the door.

Peggy again descended the stairway, met by Squire Tanaghaven, who was looking impatiently expectant. "Rachel has a headache and needs to rest. She said to tell you she'll talk to you at breakfast."

The squire looked satisfied with that, even though he still looked irritated. He turned back to join the others in the crowd, joined by Lord Russell. The young prince, Edward, was standing there looking at Peggy, waiting for her attention. When she turned to him, he held out his arms and said, "Will you dance with me, milady?"

Startled, Peggy answered, "Certainly, your highness," and they walked together toward the orchestra. Prince Edward was a few inches shorter than Peggy but he walked with such aplomb, that Peggy felt only strength and maturity far beyond his years. He swept her into the music with such ease the tension of recent events began to fade. The music was wonderful. Her mother certainly achieved success there. There were many around them taking advantage of it.

As the music began to change, the prince led Peggy to the huge table laid out with all the delicacies available with such opulence manifested here. They were both laughing with exertion and enjoyment, as they picked out some choices. Then the prince led her to one of the settees placed around the perimeter of the great room, stood while she sat down, then sat next to her.

"Milady, as pleasurable as it is to dance with you, I perceive that earlier events of this evening are still troublesome to you."

Peggy was touched by the sincerity of this young man's concern for her feelings. "My sister is in love with Darren Newall and they want to marry. We thought my father gave them permission with some conditions, but now it seems he made a deal with Squire Tanaghaven to marry her. He's an old friend of our father. We always thought of him as our uncle, but he's not really related to us. Rachell is heartbroken."

The prince was thoughtful. "Who is Darren Newall?"

"His parents operated an inn in Southampton, but I think his grandfather was a squire. But his father gave up his inheritance to marry Darren's mother, who came from France."

"How did Darren and your sister meet?"

"His family is visiting our stable manager. We all go riding together."

The conversation continued, drifting to other subjects. They danced again, until Lord Russell approached to remind the prince of their imminent departure.

"I'd like to see you again, milady," the prince said to Peggy. "If you will allow it, I hope we would become friends. Is that all right with you?"

"Oh, yes," Peggy replied.

Darren and Rachel trotted their horses through the meadow trail and the woods in the moonlight, staying far from the house. Where the trail came out on the highway to Gloucester, they cantered in the moonlight, only slowing down to a walk as they approached the town, allowing their horses to regain their breathing. On leaving town, they again broke into a canter, eating up the miles. The moon was full and high as they reached the turn off the highway down the trail into the Romani camp. As soon as they started down the trail, several riders appeared out of the darkness.

"Who goes there?" was asked in English, while others spoke in Romani.

Darren answered, "Darren Newall and my wife. We're looking for Roman Balansay and Grace Gala."

Now a rider came forward and took hold of Dani's bridle; another reached for the dapple-gray. "Why do you want them?"

"We're friends of theirs. We've just handfast in marriage and we want them to witness our vows."

One of the riders turned and galloped away in the direction of the camp. The others turned to follow, still holding the horses' bridles. Soon two riders came racing back up the hill. When they got close Darren recognized his friend Roman. As they reached the camp, Grace and both her parents came out to greet them. As Darren dismounted the Galas already assisted Rachel off her horse, and someone led the gray away. Grace and her mother led Rachel to their wagon.

By now someone roused Stavros Arnopoulos, who was the Romani chief of this camp, so he was already headed in their direction, even as Roman and Darren turned to go to him. Dying campfires all around the camp were now coming back to life, as the Romani were now coming out of their wagons. It was not long before Rachel and Grace reappeared with Grace's mother. Rachel was wearing an elaborate white gown, as elegant as she could have found in the most expensive collection her mother would have shopped, with row after row of ruffles and ribbons.

HELENA POORTVLIET

They all moved toward a now large central campfire. Stavros was carrying an English Bible, and Darren recognized it as one his sister was giving away. As their right hands were tied together with a white ribbon, they placed them on the Bible Stavros held before them, and again repeated their vows, with Roman and Grace standing with them and many others crowding close. The ceremony ended with a long kiss with the Romani cheering and clapping. It was amazing to see how fast food and wine appeared as the Romani celebrated with them.

The biggest surprise came when they were shown an empty wagon, the one Roman and his father built for Roman and Grace, soon to be married. Soon they were alone, free to love each other in the way they only dreamed of until now.

CHAPTER 28

New Connections

J EAN LOUIS FELT pangs of hunger, but was relieved the climate of Montreal was not quite so bitter cold as Quebec City. It was no longer freezing at night here as it was in the more northern city. It was not difficult to find a doorstep in an alley to avoid the wind and drizzle, but he had not eaten since that last stolen meal on the *Bucephalus.*

As he left his doorstep, making his way through the alley, he stopped in his tracks at the voices ahead of him. In another doorway, a roughly dressed vagrant was accepting a package from someone in the recessed doorway. When the door closed, the vagrant turned around and sat on the step to open the package. He barely began to eat when he looked up at "Le Brute." In terror, he dropped the package on the step and scrambled to his feet and quickly vacated the alley. Jean Louis sat with a satisfied grunt and picked up the abandoned package, the still-hot food warming his cold hands.

Up early in the crisp, cool Montreal morning, caring for his horses, Jacques revisited the familiar memories of his family home in France. It was a relief to be on solid ground finally, taking note his horses would agree. They were all contentedly eating, oblivious to the past few weeks of sea motion. As he went down the row distributing hay to each of his horses, without thinking he crossed over and fed the Caldwell's Suffolks, and was just getting to Ramon's piebalds when he heard voices at the door. Willis and Ramon arrived at the same time, laughing.

"We're not still on the ship, now. You don't really have to take care of everyone's horses," Willis exclaimed.

"Well, it doesn't hurt me, though," he answered. "One of you might have to look after mine sometime."

The sound of the metal pail outside let him know Harry was milking goats. The boy took seriously the responsibility of their care, but the milk was happily shared by all.

This was the beginning of their second week in Montreal, and all the men were on the job, but with different tasks at different locations. Willis took his team and wagon with him, being well paid for their use on the job, hauling building materials from suppliers to building sites. Jacques took Tounerre with his carriage, first to take Harry to the Breakfields' house where he spent the day with Andrea and her children. Andrea was still giving Harry lessons, working hard to bring him up to his expected grade level by the time the children started school in a few weeks. Hopefully, the boys would be able to be in the same class.

After leaving Harry with Andrea, Jacques accompanied Roger to whatever worksite they needed to go to, getting a good overview of the business. Roger always seemed to have plenty for him to do, but Jacques hoped at sometime to actually do work at one of the building projects. Some of these projects involved major buildings in the growing business district of Montreal. But the projects Jacques was most interested in were the new homes on Mount Royale on the west side of Montreal, especially those in the "Golden Square Mile," where many of the cities most successful bankers and merchants were building their fine estates. He often envisioned the house he would build in the wilderness of Canada West. Along with that dream, was his yearning for Jeannette, seeing hopefully into their future together, but seeing that a major step toward that dream was acquiring the skills necessary to build that home. He believed that was the reason he was still in Montreal: to acquire those skills.

Patricia Caldwell might have been lonely at home by herself once all the men left for work, if there was not so much to do. A good share of the goats' milk came to her to process into butter, cheese and other food products. She also kept an eye out for the animals left on the property with all the men gone.

The Caldwells' house was as sparsely furnished as Jacques' house, so she had many ideas to improve on that. She was only hampered by the impossibility of shopping once her husband left with the wagon and team for the day at work.

Churning butter was hard work, but seeing the creamy result of her work gave her a pleasing feeling of satisfaction. Not only did her husband enjoy it, but also the other men. She smiled, admiring her work, as she cleaned the last of the fragrant butter out of the churn and packed it into several low, round pots to store in the cooler in the cellar.

This was their first home, away from her parents' home. She did not mind spending the first two years of her marriage on her parents' farm, but she was always her mother's daughter there, never in charge of anything. Now she was finally beginning to feel like somebody— like an adult.

Lost in her thoughts, she did not hear the approaching horse, but heard the knocking on the door. Wiping the rim of the last pot of butter, she went to the window first. She could see a single horse tied off the porch and could barely see a woman at the door. She warily opened the door, not sure what to expect.

"Well, come on—don't leave me out here in the chill. I'm just yer neighbor; I don't aim to hurt ye. Just want to be neighborly!"

Patricia felt a little foolish, but still a bit fearful as she opened the door. The woman came through the door like a gust of chill wind, slapping her own arms, as if to warm herself. "Spring comes late in these parts; it's still weather for stayin' close to the fire! But time enough to see a new neighbor!" She pulled a package from inside her cloak, offering it to Patricia, who was still speechless.

"Go on—take it. Some nice fresh bread—just baked this morning. Boys are all gone, but I still bake like the menfolk are still around."

When Patricia took the package, she could tell it was still warm.

"Oh, I'm sorry. Come in. Come into the kitchen where it's warmer. I'm Patricia Caldwell." She looked at the other woman, waiting for a name.

"Oh, I'm the widow McIntyre," she laughed. "Some of the kids think I'm a witch, but not really, I'm just old." She laughed again.

Patricia felt a shiver, turning to the woman as they entered the kitchen. She did not know how to respond to that comment. She pulled a chair out and gestured toward it as she set the bread on the table.

"I just finished making some fresh butter, so let's try your bread with some tea," she offered, as she filled the teakettle and moved it to

HELENA POORTVLIET

the hot surface of the stove, then opened the front of the stove to add some more wood. She turned to the other woman, "Mrs. McIntyre…"

"Oh, it's Maude. Call me Maude." The older woman laughed again.

Patricia could not help but laugh, even though something about this woman still made her nervous. She got out two china cups and saucers and a teapot her mother had given her, and readied the tea just as the teakettle on the stove began to boil. Maude McIntyre accepted the tea offered with a grateful smile, and Patricia realized the woman really appreciated the warm offering. Patricia proudly presented one of the little round bowls of butter, and put out two plates for the bread.

Maude looked around the sparsely finished house before asking, "What do you need to fix up this house the way you want to?"

Patricia returned a look of surprise.

Maude continued, "I know you don't want to continue like this. We women need to fix things up. I know—men don't care, as long as they're fed."

"Well, it's mostly just to be able to shop. Willis is gone everyday with the other men, and he takes the team, so I'm pretty stuck here. I keep pretty busy, though—there's plenty to do and I keep an eye on the animals."

"Animals?"

"Yes, the two men who live in the other house have several horses—and the goats."

"Goats?"

"Yes, goats. They belong to the boy."

"What boy?"

"Harry—he's with Jacques—he's adopting him."

"Interesting."

Patricia paused, suddenly feeling unsure of herself. She wondered if she should be telling so much about their group to this woman she hardly knew. The silence grew strange as she waited, unsure to continue.

"Oh, honey," Maude broke the silence. "I'm just askin' too many nosy questions, and you just barely know me. I do apologize. Look, I can guess one thing would help your house. I have a brand new wool rug I just finished braiding. I've made dozens of these rugs. Can't seem to help myself. I sure don't need them, so I usually just give'm away, but if you want to trade, I'd love to have a bit of your sweet goat butter. I'll harness my old mare to the wagon tomorrow and bring it over. If you don't like it, I'll just take it back, no harm done."

Patricia took a deep breath. She thought to herself, *I don't know why I am hesitant, but she seems nice, even if a little strange.* She smiled at Maude as she let out her breath.

"Okay," she answered, "I'll have a pot of butter ready for you. I'm glad you like it."

"All right," Maude answered. "I'll just be on my way. Shore don' wanna wear out my welcome," she added as she stood, turning to the door.

When Maude was gone, Patricia felt the emptiness of the house even more. Stubbornly seeking to dispel that feeling, she reached for the broom and began vigorously sweeping the worn wood floor.

When Jacques arrived at the Breakfields' house to drop off Harry for the day, he was waved in by Andrea. Roger was right behind her. "We want you to come for dinner tomorrow when you come for Harry. So come dressed for dinner; we'll have other guests. Don't worry about work clothes. Roger will have inside work for you, so dress like a gentleman." Roger was smiling and broke into laughter at his wife's last instruction.

"Don't worry; just dress nice; you won't have to work like a horse tomorrow. I want a day with you in the office."

"Yes, sir."

Jacques wondered about the activities of the next day, but today he was busy all day with errands for Roger that kept himself and Tounerre moving until the sun went down. By the time he arrived back at the Breakfields' house to pick up Harry, he almost forgot about the change of routine for the next day, until Andrea reminded him.

"Remember, dress for the office tomorrow, and don't forget dinner tomorrow evening. And maybe Harry could wear one of those nice outfits you just got for him in Quebec City."

At this Jacques felt a little more anticipation about the coming event. But all he got from the Breakfields was Andrea's infectious smile.

Jean Louis found an ideal neighborhood for his needs. The townhouses were homes to the families of many executives on their way up, not yet looking toward Mount Royale. Vagrants traveled the alleyways and patiently waited at backdoors. Servants were happy to hand off leftovers from family meals. Jean Louis knew better than to knock on doors himself. He would stay in the shadows until another procured a warm meal. No one ever argued with him over a meal. It was less terrifying to just knock on another back door.

On this morning, Jean Louis turned down an alley, cautiously taking in what was ahead of him before proceeding: three children in rags, two very small girls and an older boy. The boy procured a package for the girls, but as he began to open it, two men appeared to take it from him. The men were laughing as they moved toward "LeBrute," still in the shadows. As they came near, he stepped out of the shadows, snarling like an animal. The two men stopped abruptly, dropping the package as they looked up at the faceless monster. In less than a moment, they turned to run past the children. Jean Louis picked up the still warm bundle, enjoying the warmth to his cold hands. The children seemed frozen, staring at him. For a moment he was torn, enjoying the warmth of the package he held. Then he reached out, offering the package to the boy, looking down, aware of his frightful appearance in the eyes of the little girls. Turning back up the alley the way he had come, he found a recessed doorway to sit down out of the wind, watching as the children moved down the alley, watching for anyone else who might threaten them.

Jean Louis sat on the step with his head in his hands, wary of the voices which might return at any moment. Still hungry, that brief moment holding the warm package was surprisingly comforting, knowing someone else would be along to provide him a meal. After a moment, he was aware he was not alone. He opened his one eye to see the feet of the young boy. As he raised his head, the boy was holding out a package to him—not the rescued package, but another. As Jean Louis took the package, the boy turned to run.

In the days following, it was like an unspoken agreement. The children were able to procure food from the backdoors of townhouses, sharing their rewards with Jean Louis, and no one else threatened them. As frightening as his appearance was to others, somehow, the children were not afraid.

As Jacques helped Harry dress in his new clothes, he took satisfaction in the boy's appearance. Harry's excitement over the day's activities was hard to contain. Jacques got dressed, and took the occasion to unpack the topcoat Jeannette and her mother gave him for Christmas. He laughed at himself, getting Harry's attention.

"I guess a farm boy can be a gentleman."

Harry giggled.

Just as he was about to head for the barn, he heard noises in the front yard. He looked out to see Tounerre already hitched to his carriage, Ramon at his head. When he reached the Breakfield's house, Harry happily ran to the door, excited to show Andrew his new clothes. As he entered, Roger came out. Andrea stood behind him waving to Jacques. Roger walked to Jacques carriage, smiling

"I'll impose on you today, and ride with you, if you don't mind. I'll be working at the office all day, so I won't need my horse.

"Sure," was the reply from Jacques.

There was a stable next to the office building, and when they arrived at the office a groom appeared to take Tounerre to the stable. Jacques looked up at the large sign above the front door and two large windows which read: *Edward Finlay, Architect & Contractor.* As they walked in the door, Jacques immediately noticed the fine finished wood of the front counter and desks. Roger motioned for Jacques to follow him.

"This is my office," Roger said as they entered the commodious room, which contained not only a spacious desk, but an even larger work table and a long wall of files and shelves and cabinets, all in beautifully finished wood. Jacques was impressed.

One large window wall looked out over the Montreal harbor. On the opposite wall were framed illustrations of some of the major projects the firm was involved with. One was a bridge over the La Chine Canal. Another was the office building they now occupied. And there were several of the fine homes of the growing community on Mount Royale.

Roger left the room for a few moments, but soon returned with another man. "Jacques, this is Edward Findlay, this cities best architect." And turning to the other, he said, "Ed, this is Jacques Boudreau, whom I've spoken of. He's followed through with every task I've given him, and I feel good about recommending him as someone you can depend on."

Jacques felt himself reddening, even as he reached out for Edward Findlay's proffered hand.

"Hello, Jacques," Findlay began, "I'm glad to finally meet you after all I've heard. How do you like Montreal now you've had a couple of weeks here. Or better, how do you like it from your view of our operation here?"

Jacques was thinking fast. He hoped his response did not sound like a complaint. "I like it fine, sir. I really like the house and the space for my horses. And the job has been pretty easy. It almost doesn't seem like work. But—not to complain—it's just that I'd like to actually work on the houses—but only if that's what you need." He quickly added that last comment.

"Well, that's going to happen real soon. I'm going to put you with one of my foremen to learn basic framing and structure. Then, if that works out for you, I'll give you a crew to build houses the rest of the summer." Findlay paused a moment, looking back at Roger.

"Roger tells me you have another issue," he said, "about a young man."

Jacques looked bewildered for a moment. Then he caught on, "You mean Harry."

"The boy you want to adopt."

"Yes."

Findlay moved to the door, to open it, as another man entered. "This is Toby Graham, our solicitor."

"Tell me about the boy you want to adopt. How do you know him?"

Jacques did not realize right away both Roger and Findlay left the room shortly after Toby Graham entered, as he became absorbed in telling Graham the story of finding Harry.

Graham continued, "I understand we'll all be meeting for dinner at the Breakfields', so I'll have the opportunity to meet the boy. Do you mind?"

Jacques nodded, "No, that's fine."

Graham responded, "Good. It will be helpful to see the two of you together. I understand there will be one other guest."

"Who would that be?"

"Judge Niles Harris—the final decision will be his." Now Graham reached out to shake hands again.

"All right. Good to meet you. I look forward to meeting your son."

As he turned to leave, the other two men re-entered the office.

True to her word, Maude McIntyre was back, driving the same horse she was riding yesterday. In the back of her wagon was the promised rug. Patricia heard the wagon approaching. In spite of herself, she anticipated the visit, now happy at the prospect of company. As soon as Willis left with the others, she cleaned the kitchen, brought in wood to keep the fire going, and swept the whole house. She brought up one of the pots of butter from the cooler, wrapped it in a small piece of fabric and tied it with a string. It was sitting on the table waiting when Maude arrived.

As Maude climbed down from the wagon, she saw Patricia waiting in the open door. "Well, come on," she called. "Two of us can carry it easier than one." She waved at Patricia, who took the cue to go to the wagon. The two women each took an end of the rolled up rug to carry it in the house.

When they brought it in the door, they dropped it on the parlor floor. Maude pulled a small knife from her pocket and popped the strings she had tied around the rug to keep it rolled up, releasing it to open before Patricia.

"Whoa!" exclaimed Patricia, amazed at the sight. The rug was braided from strips of woven wool in harmonizing shades of yellow, purple, and gold. It was embroidered all around the edges in flowers of new wool in shades of green and rose. A few more embroidered flowers were scattered over the area of the rug.

Patricia stood gazing at the rug. "Oh, my, it's beautiful!"

"Does that mean you like it?" Maude was smiling.

"I love it!"

"Well, I'm glad, 'cause I'm shore lookin' forward to that sweet goat butter!" Maude was now laughing, with many lines crinkling the corners of her eyes.

Patricia laughed with her as she led the way to the kitchen. "Well, I have a pot of butter ready for you. So let's have a cup of tea and share some cinnamon rolls I made."

Maude smiled approvingly.

The rest of the day, Roger went over floor plans and construction orders with Jacques. "This is the kind of paperwork you'll be working with," Roger explained. "Some of the construction orders are pretty complicated, because we try to get all the details squared away in the original bid. Sometimes that's not possible, so we try to leave room in the contract for later decisions on details."

Jacques nodded as he looked down the first page of the contract. He thought the numbers looked unbelievably huge, but he said nothing, waiting for Roger to continue. Roger unrolled the first page of the floor plan in front of Jacques, covering the contract they were looking at.

"This is the general plan, just the basic construction plan. You can see it shows very little detail, just the basic plan. A big part of your job will be learning to read these plans accurately and turning them into finished projects. Details are drawn up on the detail drawings. The general drawing will have a number here, showing how many detail drawings are required. You have to make sure you have all of them, or know the reason why not. Every step of the way we continually go back to the client for approval of every detail. There is nothing standard about anything we do. It's all custom order."

Jacques felt overwhelmed, taking it all in. He had no idea how complicated the business could be. Roger seemed to read his mind. "I'm confident you can do it. It's just a learning process," he said, smiling.

Jacques did not feel so confident, but he appreciated his friend's encouragement.

Roger spoke up again. "We know what your real expertise is: Anything to do with horses. But, at the same time, I know you're a smart man, and you're motivated to learn this business, so you can build your own home. So I know you'll do whatever it takes to get there.

"However, I talked to Ed about your area of expertise and we would like to talk to you about the future in that area. As our business expands here, we have more and more need of good horses and good teamsters. When you get to your destination, you may be just the person we want to deal with. So we're anxious that you get what you need here to enable you to put together your business there. What do you think?"

Now Jacques felt overwhelmed again, but in a different way. He felt grateful for his friend's confidence in him, even though he was not quite so confident in himself.

Maude was clearly enjoying the cinnamon rolls and tea. Today, Patricia felt less hesitant in talking to the older woman. Thrilled with the rug, now she was thinking about what else would make her house look like the home she wanted. It was as if Maude read her mind.

"Now, what do you need next for your house?" Maude asked, a twinkle in her eye.

"Well, maybe some parlor furniture, and some curtains. But with Willis gone every day, I don't know how I can go shopping. And he might want to shop with me."

"We can take my wagon into town and shop for your house, if he doesn't mind."

"Oh, that would be wonderful. I'll ask him."

Maude continued, "Most men don't want to shop anyway. They just expect us to take care of it. But you ask him, honey. I'll come by tomorrow and see what you find out." Maude then got up to leave.

CHAPTER 29

Deceptions

A S THE ROYAL carriage moved down the lane, beginning their trip back to London, Prince Edward began to question Lord Russell.

"What do you know about the squire Marshall Tanaghaven?"

Russell began to laugh, "You mean our competition?"

Prince Edward laughed back, "Sure, as if we were suitors for the lovely Rachel!" His voice cracked and modulated as is common with young men, changing from the older child to the young man.

"Why ask about the squire?"

"Why would he be a suitor? Just because she's pretty and rich?"

"Why are you so interested, your highness?"

"Her sister says she's in love with that young man, Darren Newall, and they thought her father gave them permission to marry. What does Squire Tanaghaven have?"

"Squire Tanaghaven is the oldest son of his father. When he first married Madeline Winslow, they were given the Winslow estate. Her father just died, so Madeline and her mother lived there alone. Madeline died a couple of years ago in an accident. I think it was a fall."

"Really."

"Your highness, where is this going?"

"Well, what about the Tanaghaven family? You say he is the oldest son?"

"Yes, his younger brother inherited the family estate when their father passed. Strangely, the younger brother died in a hunting accident last year. So the squire has now inherited that property. Because of the increase in property, he may attain the title of lord."

"He may? Why is there a question?"

"His younger brother was a member of the House of Lords and very popular. It's a shame to lose him. I'm not terribly impressed with the squire, but I'm afraid I really don't know him well."

"I wonder if we can find out more about Darren Newall. How could we find out about his family? I understand his grandfather was a squire near Southampton."

"We could do a little research, if you really want to know."

"I really want to know."

Melinda Newall paced around Newlandia's Grand House like an automaton, seemingly unaware of her surroundings, lost in the past. Servants kept their distance, while still keeping aware of her movements. The house was quiet, except for the ghosts of the past. She revisited the time when she first came here as Wilfred Newall's bride. It was enchanting. She felt like a princess, in love with her prince, the young squire. She often heard stories about Wil's young brother Edmund, who was such a promising officer in the Royal Dragoons, until he fell for that foreign woman. Her husband Wil was a good son of his parents, loyal to the family heritage, and continued to run Newlandia after his parents passed on. Their reward for their loyalty was their inheritance.

But now Wil was gone. The cancer overtook him quickly, in just a few weeks. Hard to accept, Melinda often thought he was still in the house, perhaps in a different room. She waited for him to join her.

Darren gradually awakened as the early morning sun began to warm the wagon. At first he thought he was still visiting the Gypsies with his family. Then as the world became clearer, he realized he was not alone. Then it all came back to him—the ball, their flight on horseback, the wedding, his beautiful wife next to him, still asleep. He wanted to reach his arm around her, but could not bear to chance awakening her.

He remembered that conversation with Roman about the details of "handfasting" their marriage and his reaction when Roman mentioned the importance of "consummating" their marriage. Hiding his embarrassment over the word, he now smiled as he thought of it. Their marriage was certainly consummated. He felt so wedded to Rachel, he now saw how their relationship overshadowed every other in his life. He felt consumed by the need to do his best to be the best husband in the world to her. Rachel sighed, rolled over to face him and opened her eyes. She smiled as she reached for him. But as he returned the gesture, they began to hear giggles outside the wagon.

"Oh, no," he sighed. "They would do that."

Rachel held her breath, listening. There were whispers and more giggles. She sat up and reached for her dressing gown, then turned to smile at Darren.

"I feel married," she said to him, as she leaned over to kiss him on the mouth.

"Well, you are," he laughed.

The giggles and whispers became a little louder. Rachel stood and picked up Darrens trousers to hand him. "I don't think we'll get any more privacy here." She began brushing her hair, hearing more giggles outside, and voices talking no longer in whispers. In a few moments, they were dressed and opened the door of the wagon to cheers and clapping. Roman and Grace were outside smiling, and with them were Elena Balansay and Paloma Gala, along with a bevy of children, all giggling.

Grace was the first one to run to Rachel and hug her. "Oh, I'm so glad you're here and married now. We've been praying for you." Elena and Paloma stood smiling. There were shouts from the central campfire area. The women motioned for them to come to breakfast.

Rachel never experienced anything like this in her life. She remembered Grace from when the Romani girl worked as a maid at the Montgomery house. She, of course, knew her husband. But the rest of these people were strangers, but they treated her as warmly as if she was one of them. She was inclined to eat sparsely, but several people offered her more, encouraging her to enjoy. Few of these people spoke English, but that did not stop the conversation and laughter.

When they could eat no more, someone brought two horses into the circle. They were both dark brown, almost black, but someone put Darren's and Rachel's saddles on them, and Rachel recognized her bags on the gelding. When they got close, both horses showed their recognition of their owners.

"What happened to my horse?" Rachel exclaimed in dismay.

"That grey can be seen into the next county. You don't think anyone is looking for you?" Roman asked, smiling. "Don't worry, the dye will wear off in a few days."

Dani was the same dull brown black as Misty, but she had no trouble recognizing Darren, begging his attention.

Grace brought Rachel a colorful Gypsy cloak and scarf, and someone gave Darren a slouchy hat, which looked nothing like anything he had ever worn. Roman and Fidel Balansay arrived with their horses, prepared for travel. "We'll escort the two of you to Liverpool and make sure you get on a ship. Do you have fare?"

They both nodded.

Prince Edward received a message there was a man to see him, soon meeting in Prince Albert's office. The man had several sheets of paper in a thick envelope which, he briefly explained to Edward, contained the history of Newlandia, the estate of the Newall family northwest of Southampton. Important news was of Wilfred Newall's recent passing. There was communication from the family's solicitor Harold Breadon indicating his frustration in attempting to deal with Wil's widow, Melinda Newall, who was clearly was not rational. It seemed the servants were running the estate, if indeed, any one was. Breadon knew Wil had a brother, but did not know where to find him. Prince Edward quickly wrote a note to be given to Breadon about a Newall family staying with the Duran family on the Montgomery estate.

Lord John Russell considered the sudden death of Davis Tanaghaven last year, a shock to many, even more unbelievable since he was known to be an excellent horseman. He finally called his own solicitor to discuss his concern. It was agreed he would put an investigator on the case, to look into the circumstances surrounding the accident. Once others were working on the issue, Russell felt much freer to deal with his own job's demands. *It just seemed strange that this man's wife and brother both died fortuitously.* He smiled thinking about Prince Edward's concern. *That boy was already more man than many men he knew.*

Peggy was so thrilled about her time with Prince Edward it was difficult to sleep, late as it was when she finally went to her room. She looked into Rachel's room before going to her own room, seeing what looked like Rachel asleep under the covers. When she spoke there was no answer, so she quietly closed the door and went to her own room.

Peggy could not remember when she finally fell asleep, but it was late in the morning when she finally awoke. Dressing quickly, she went to her sister's room. It appeared as though Rachel was still asleep. Since it was so late already, Peggy went to her sister, concerned for her. That was when she discovered several pillows under Rachel's blankets, so it looked like she was sleeping. Rachel was gone!

Oh, my. What do I do now? Peggy thought to herself, moving around the room, looking for possible clues. The teal gown Rachel wore last night was in the wardrobe, but Peggy could see at least two of her sister's riding skirts, and at least one of her warmer coats was gone, along with two small traveling bags.

Peggy went back to her own room for a few minutes, freshening up for breakfast, while she pondered what to say to the others, namely Uncle Marshall. She wished she could run to the barn to see if Misty and Dani were gone. If that were the case, Peggy wanted to give her sister the benefit of all the time possible. Finally, she started downstairs.

In the dining room were her parents, Marshall Tanaghaven, and a few other guests who stayed overnight. As she entered, both her father and Tanaghaven arose. "Do you know if we can expect your sister soon," her father asked, sternly.

"I looked in on her and she was still sleeping. I did not want to disturb her because she had such a headache last night, so she probably had a terrible night. I think she needs her sleep now." Peggy's voice was full of concern for her sister, and her expression showed more than a little irritation for both men.

"Oh, I should go to her," was the worried response from her mother. "No, Mother, let her sleep," she said as firmly as she could.

Lady Montgomery stopped, focusing on her younger daughter. "All right, sit down," she motioned as she called a servant to bring Peggy some breakfast.

One of the ladies at the table now asked, "We saw you dancing with the prince. We did not realize he was so young. What is he like? Is he not a bit young to be a suitor?"

Peggy felt relieved the attention was now on her, rather than her sister. "Oh, I didn't think he's so young. I thought he was quite mature. And oh! He dances wonderfully!"

The other women were laughing at her response and Peggy's mother beamed proudly. "Oh, you think you made a good impression on the prince?" It now was clear to Peggy if her mother could not get her oldest daughter married to a prince, perhaps now she would focus on her younger daughter.

"Yes, Mother," Peggy answered. "In fact, the prince asked me if we might become friends. I expect to hear from him."

At this all the women were giggling and whispering to one another.

Squire Tanaghaven gave a long sigh and an irritated expression toward Peggy's father. Arthur Montgomery got up, nodded to Morton and gestured the squire to follow him. When the men were gone from the room, the women all began to talk at once.

"Oh, I'm glad they finally left," said one woman. "They're both in such a foul mood."

"Well, are you surprised? The squire so wanted Arthur to announce his engagement to Rachel."

Peggy felt her anger rising, especially at the next comment.

"Well, Rachel certainly did a wonderful faint. She's learned to get her way somewhere." This woman smiled knowingly at Lady Montgomery.

Peggy stood up to face the woman. "How can you say such a thing about my sister? She would never marry Uncle Marshall. She loves Darren Newall and Father promised her to him! This thing with Uncle Marshall is all a big mistake! He's wrong! Father would never do such a thing!"

Lady Montgomery was momentarily speechless, as were the other women. "Margaret," she began. Peggy knew her mother was horrified at her behavior to use her given name.

She interrupted her mother, "That event was supposed to be special for Rachel—in her honor. You just used her, with no thought of her feelings. Don't you care about your own daughter? She was miserable! How would you like to be forced to marry Uncle Marshall? Especially when you love our father!"

Lady Montgomery was again speechless.

HELENA POORTVLIET

Antoine held the gate to the meadow open and watched as the two galloped down the trail, disappearing into the dark. He prayed as he walked back to the barn. "Oh Lord, protect them wherever you lead them, for you love them even more than they love each other. In Jesus name, Oh Lord, hear my prayer. Amen."

As he walked back to the barn, he saw Katy, still cross-tied with her harness on. He unharnessed the mare, spent some time brushing her, before putting her in the stall, repeating, "Oh Lord, what have I done? I pray I haven't hurt all the wrong people."

When he arrived back at the cottage, he found the remnant of an unhappy family, and the other family, full of concern.

"Did he tell you?"

"Yes, he was very unhappy; we prayed together."

"Well, where is he?"

"He went for a ride on his horse. You know, he's got to work off some steam."

Jules said, "I think we need to pray together. Maybe read a little.

Others were in agreement.

After praying, he looked at Jeannette. "I know you feel terrible. Is it too much to ask you to read?"

Jeannette wiped tears away, looking at her mother. "I know I feel terrible, and so angry! But maybe reading from God's Word is a good thing right now." She turned to get her Bible while the others headed for the parlor. Soon she began:

"And Abraham journeyed from there toward the south country, and dwelled between Kadesh and Shier, and sojourned in Gerar." (Gen. 20:1, KJV)

"And Abraham said of Sarah his wife, she is my sister: and Abimelech king of Gerar sent and took Sarah." (Gen. 20:2, KJV)

"But God came to Abimelech in a dream by night, and said to him, Behold thou art but a dead man, for the woman which thou hast taken; for she is a man's wife.
"But Abimelech had not come near her; and he said, Lord, wilt thou slay also a righteous nation.

"Said he not unto me, She is my sister? And she, even she herself said, He is my brother: in the integrity of my heart and the innocency of my hands I have done this.

"And God said to him in a dream, Yea, I know that thou didst this in the integrity of thy heart, for I also withheld thee from sinning against me; therefore suffered I thee not to touch her."(Gen. 20:3-6, KJV)

As Jeannette paused to look around at the others, Simon was the first to speak, "Doesn't he ever learn?"

Some of the others laughed, others were angry. They were learning about the ancient customs, but still thought this behavior was terrible.

Jeannette began, "Well he is in many ways typical. The Bible tells us Abraham was a friend of God. But he's still a man. And those were fearful times.

There were nods of understanding. Jules spoke, "Read more," so she went on:

"Now therefore, restore the man his wife; for he is a prophet, and he shall pray for thee, and thou shalt live: and if thou restore her not, know thou that thou shalt surely die, thou, and all that are thine.

"Therefore, Abimelech rose early in the morning, and called all his servants, and told all these things in their ears: and the men were sore afraid.

"Then Abimelech called Abraham, and said unto him, What hast thou done unto us? And what have I offended thee, that thou hast brought on me and my kingdom a great sin? Thou has done deeds unto me that ought not be done.

"And Abimelech said unto Abraham, What sayest thou, that thou hast done this thing?" (Gen.20:7-10, KJV)

Jeannette looked up from her reading. Simon was again first to speak. "Abimelech sounds pretty self-righteous, as if it was all Abraham's fault. Did he ask permission to take Sarah, or just use his position to take what he wanted?"

"Good point, son," his father commented, then looked back at Jeannette.

"This is an example of how people in power often just take what they want, regardless of anyone else. Sometimes they are only stopped by God's intervention"

Jules said again, "Read more," so she continued:

> "And Abraham said, because I thought Surely the fear of God is not in this place; and they will slay me for my wife's sake.
> "And yes indeed she is my sister; she is the daughter of my father; but not the daughter of my mother; and she became my wife.
> "And it came to pass, when God caused me to wander from my father's house, that I said unto her, This is thy kindness that thou shall show unto me; at every place whither we shall come; say of me, He is my brother."
> (Gen.20:11-13, KJV)

Jeannette commented on this last: "This is an example of human nature. It's often about survival rather than honor. Often women were the victims, with little to say. But it also shows us, that if we have God in our life, he looks out for us, even if we are at fault."

Now Marielle spoke, "I'm thinking of Rachel. I think she really loves Darren. But it seems like her father is not giving her any choices. That's pretty terrible. They're so rich, but she really doesn't have any rights. What about us, Father? Do we have any choices in our future?" She quickly looked around at her sisters.

Teresa's jaw dropped, "Marielle!"

Jules looked at Teresa. "It's okay, my love. I think it's a fair question." He turned to his daughter. "Sweetheart, I hope when the time comes, that my decisions come with godly wisdom and care for your feelings. But if we are all in God's will, the decisions should be easier." He looked back at Jeannette, so she continued:

> "And Abimelech took sheep, and oxen, and menservants, and womenservants, and gave them to Abraham, and restored him Sarah his wife.
> "And Abimelech said, Behold, my land is before thee: dwell where it please thee.
> "And unto Sarah, he said, Behold, I have given thy brother a thousand pieces of silver: behold, he is to thee a covering

of the eyes, unto all that are with thee, and with all others: thus she was reproved." (Gen.20:14-16, KJV)

"So Abraham prayed unto God: and God healed Abimelech and his wife, and his maidservants; and they bare children. "For the Lord had fast closed up all the wombs of the house of Abimelech, because of Sarah, Abraham's wife." (Gen. 20:17, 18, KJV)

This time when Jeannette stopped, she closed her Bible, and all present moved in close to pray together. Afterward, Madam Newall expressed her worry that Darren was not back yet.

Antoine replied, "I wouldn't worry. He's probably with his horse. He seems to get a lot of comfort being with her."

That seemed to comfort Darren's mother.

When Antoine and Ellienne were finally alone she asked him, "Okay, tell me the truth."

"Certainly, my darling," Antoine began. "You know I'll never lie to you, but sometimes it is necessary to protect others."

His wife looked at him, waiting.

"I witnessed their handfast vows in the barn. I saddled her horse for her. I sent them to Stavros to make their marriage official. I am responsible. I prayed with them and felt it was the right thing to do. But if I tell the others, then they will also be responsible. If the blame comes to Jules, he will lose his job, and his family will lose their home."

"Oh, my darling," whispered Ellienne, "we should pray." She took his hands and they prayed, continuing with the heavenly language.

CHAPTER 30

Shopping

JEAN LOUIS SAT in his doorway shivering in the chill of the advancing evening, pulling his coat tightly around him. The three children were just one doorway away for him, clinging to each other for warmth.

"I'm cold, Sean," said the littlest girl, in the middle of the three. Sean pulled the girl closer, appreciating the warmth of her body. His other sister moved closer as well, shivering. It seemed as though it was getting colder, even though he knew spring was advancing in Montreal. But it was still rainy and windy. For several days they were close to the big man who seemed not to have a face. Others no longer bullied them for food or for a doorstep. Some called the big man "monster," others, "Le Brute," but somehow the three children were not afraid of him.

Jean Louis was aware of their presence before he looked up. The boy simply said, "We're cold." Jean Louis moved over as the little girls sat down next to him, and their brother sat on the other side of them, the four of them sharing the warmth, multiplying it.

Arriving at the Breakfield house with Roger, Jacques was amazed to see Andrea in a beautiful gown. He was introduced to Judge Harris and his wife. Andrew and Harry were quiet, on their best behavior, already coached by Andrea. But when Jacques came in the door, Harry ran to him.

As dinner progressed, Toby Graham began to repeat some of the story which Jacques shared with him about finding Harry. He looked at both Jacques and Harry for comfirmation.

The judge looked toward Harry, "What was it like in Birmingham before you met Jacques?"

"It was cold," Harry replied.

"How did you eat? What did you eat?" the judge asked.

"Mama knocked on doors, and people sometimes gave us food. Sometimes they yelled at us." Harry looked down. The words came hesitantly.

Graham asked, "What happened to your mama?"

"She fell asleep." Harry was still looking down. He moved a little closer to Jacques.

The judge now asked, "What do you mean, 'she fell asleep?'"

"She fell over." Harry's answer was barely audible, still looking down. Then he began to cry. "She didn't wake up." Now Harry was shaking, as he barely said, "I was hungry." Jacques put his arm around the boy, as he moved closer, looking at the judge, hoping he would stop the questioning.

The judge looked at Jacques. "Tell me about finding Harry."

Jacques thought back, picturing that cold afternoon in Birmingham. "When I stopped my team, he was there with his hand out. It was hard to believe a little boy was on the street alone without his parents. I offered him a coin to watch my horses, when I went to look for Pierre. When I came back, I could see he was so cold he was shivering. So I put him up on the driver's seat with a blanket to wrap up in. When I came back he was asleep."

What did you do then?"

"Well, I was worried because he was so thin and his clothes were just rags, no winter coat. He was so sleepy, he just kept falling asleep. My friend Pierre was with me and we were going to find a café to eat, so we just took him along. I was not speaking English so well then, so Pierre asked him about his parents. He said he didn't know his father and his mother went to sleep on a step in the alley and never woke up. Jacques felt anquish remembering how he found Harry. Since then, as their relationship grew, it was even more difficult remembering those days.

"I thought we should try to find some relatives but Pierre said, 'what kind of family would leave him and his mother to live on the street.' so we just took him with us. I gave him a bath and washed his clothes, and felt awful because he was covered with bruises and sores. The next day, after breakfast, I bought him some new clothes and shoes and a good winter coat. It was snowing so heavily, that we stayed at that inn for several days, and Harry went to eat with us.

HELENA POORTVLIET

He always ate plenty, and I saw his bruises and sores began to heal. I was really torn about what to do with him. I knew he needed help, but I was on my way to Canada."

"So what did you do?" the judge asked.

Jacques thought back to those last days in Birmingham, and remembered reading the last chapter of *The Gospel According to Saint John*. A hard lump formed in his throat. In a very quiet voice he answered, "I prayed."

The judge and Toby Graham both responded with a jaw dropping gasp of surprise. The judge regained his composure and asked, "Well, did you get an answer?"

"Yes," Jacques answered, still in a quiet voice. "He said, 'Feed my sheep.'"

"What do you mean by that?"

"I took it to mean I was to take both Pierre and Harry with me, and not abandon either of them."

"So you have a witness in this Pierre?"

"Yes, he was with me when we found Harry."

"I'll have to talk with him then—is that possible?

"Well, he stayed on the ship. He's on his way back to England. It will be three or four months before he's back here again."

The judge sighed deeply. "Well, his word as a witness is important. I don't think I can make a final decision until I hear his testimony. But what I will do is suggest Mr. Graham write a motion for temporary custody for Harry to stay with you until your friend Pierre is back. Now the other thing, are you a single man?"

"Yes, but I'm engaged to be married as soon as my fiancée arrives here from England."

"When will that be?"

"I hope on the next ship with Pierre, but I couldn't say. It could be longer. I hope to hear from her by then."

The judge shook his head. "A lot of maybes, but few real answers. It would look a lot better if you were married, or had some solid answers."

He turned to Graham. "You put in that motion and we'll at least get things started." Then he turned back to Jacques. "What about schooling? Do you have him in school?"

Jacques looked at Andrea, feeling very tired.

Andrea explained, "He's been coming here to spend the day when Jacques goes to work. I've been giving him lessons. We started while we were on the ship. He's a very bright boy. We plan to send him to the Academy with Andrew when the next session starts."

The judge nodded approvingly. "The whole idea of the courts involvement in adoption is to encourage conditions in favor of the child's concerns." The judge turned his attention to the food in front of him.

When Willis came home from work with the team, he was surprised to see the new rug. Patricia explained to him about Maude McIntyre and the offer to trade the rug for the little pot of butter, and her offer to take Patricia shopping. Patricia held her breath, waiting for Willis' response. He drew a deep breath, not in a hurry. For a few moments he just stared at the rug. Then he spoke as he reached into his pocket.

"Here is a requisition for Lanier's Furnishings from the Findlay Company. I wanted to take you myself, but I don't know when. So why don't you ladies go have a good time shopping." Willis laughed a bit, "She's probably a better decorator than me, anyway."

Patricia took the form and stared at it. "You mean we can just get what we want with this?"

"Whatever you want. You don't have to get it all at once. Take your time. Maybe I can go with you next time."

Patricia could hardly contain her feelings. She threw her arms around her husband. "Oh, thank you!"

As the daylight began to extend into the alleyways of Montreal, vagrants began moving about, seeking the most likely route to a handout. Jean Louis was conscious early in the morning just how deficient the little girls' clothing was as they shivered next to him. Voices in his head began to chant, "They're going to die; they're going to die—die—die!" In desperation he looked toward the sky. At second floor windows there were clotheslines strung across the alley between townhouses, on pulleys, so they could be pulled back and forth for loading and unloading. There he saw two little princess style coats, one slightly larger than the other. Normally, they would be out of reach to most. But Jean Louis was quite tall, and a growing boy on his shoulders could reach the coats.

HELENA POORTVLIET

When the judge and his wife left, Toby Graham went with them, leaving Jacques and Harry alone with the Breakfields. Andrea spoke up quickly. "I think we should read God's Word and pray together."

Her husband agreed. Jacques looked at Harry, who was looking embattled, hanging onto his hand. Looking back at Andrea and Roger he said, "I think that's a good idea, but I don't have my Bible with me."

"That's okay; we do." Andrea turned to pick up her Bible. "Last night we were reading about Peter's release from prison by the angel," she began to explain.

Jacques recalled reading that part the last night Pierre was with them. He had not read the Bible since then, he admitted to the Breakfields.

"Okay," she answered, "I'll just start there."

> "Now as soon as it was day there was no small stir among the soldiers, What was become of Peter?
> "And when Herod had sought for him, and found him not, he examined the keepers, and commanded that they should be put to death. And he went down from Judaea to Caesarea, and there abode." (Acts 12:18, 19, KJV)

> "And Herod was highly displeased with them of Tyre and Sidon: but they came of one accord to him, and having made Blastus, the king's chamberlain their friend, desired peace; because their country was nourished by the kings country.
> "And upon a set day Herod, arrayed in Royal apparel, sat upon his throne, and made an oration unto them.
> "And the people gave a shout, saying, it is the voice of a god, and not a man.
> "And immediately, the angel of the Lord smote him, because he gave not God the glory: and he was eaten of worms, and gave up the ghost. (Acts 12:20-23, KJV)

As Andrea looked up from her reading, Roger laughed, and clapped his hands, saying, "I guess that means, don't touch God's people! I think we've read of that before." Soon they were all praying in the heavenly language. Jacques looked at Harry to see him praying, his hands raised and tears flowing. He moved closer to hug the boy, whispering, "Don't worry, no matter how long it takes, you're already my son."

Before Maude McIntyre arrived, Patricia swept and dusted the whole house. She made cinnamon rolls again, and had tea ready. When Maude walked in she sniffed the air and smiled, saying, "nice."

As soon as Patricia poured the tea she showed Maude the requisition for Lanier's. Maude replied with "Hallelujah! That man must think a lot of your husband." She laughed uproariously.

"Well, Willis was hired by the partner we got acquainted with on the ship. "His wife was awfully good to me."

"Well, that's a lucky break!"

"I don't think Willis wants me to use it all at once. I think he still wants to go shopping with me. I'm thinking for now, maybe a settee for the parlor and some fabric for curtains."

Patricia climbed into the wagon with Maude, thinking *this woman is really independent, driving her own horse.* Maude spoke cheerfully, encouraging the mare, whose ears turned back listening to her. It took only a short time to reach the shopping district of Montreal, quickly finding Lanier's Furnishings.

Patricia was amazed at all the furniture on the floor. She had an idea, but could not see just what she was thinking of. There were many settees of the type she was familiar with in England, but not just the right color. Then she saw two armchairs of a similar style, in a brocade stripe, incorporating rose, green, gold, and lavender, with trim of English oak.

"That's it. I wish they had a settee like that." As soon as she said it, a man appeared at her elbow.

"Madam, we can have that made for you in two weeks."

Startled, Patricia answered, "Really?"

"Yes, we can make a settee in that fabric and style and deliver it in two weeks."

Patricia decided to take the two chairs today, glad the settee would be delivered. Then she looked for curtain fabric. After finding ivory lace for kitchen café curtains, and another softer, thicker style of ivory lace for long curtains in the parlor, they headed for the door, with two employees following to load her treasures in the wagon. Once the chairs were loaded, the two women turned to climb in. There, before them, were two little girls, with very disheveled blonde

HELENA POORTVLIET

hair, wearing matching pink princess style coats, standing before them with their hands out, saying, "We're hungry."

Maude started to say, "Scat!" but Patricia was touched with pity. At first she was repulsed by the little girls' filthy condition, which did not match the pretty coats. Then she remembered her conversations on the *Bucephalus* with Captain Palmer and Andrea Breakfield.

"Where is your mother, sweetheart?" she asked the bigger girl.

"She died on the ship," was the reply. The smaller girl added, "Papa, too," very softly.

Patricia could see their ragged, too small shoes and thin dresses under their coats. "Where did you get those pretty coats," she asked.

"The big man got them."

"And who is this big man?"

They just shrugged. Patricia looked around, seeing no one, but other shoppers. She looked back at the girls, asking the oldest, "What is your name?"

"I'm Kat; she's Lizzie."

"Where do you stay?"

Again, all she got were shrugs. Patricia turned to Maude, who was looking exasperated. "I'm taking them home," she said.

Maude's mouth dropped open, speechless.

"I'm taking them home, and first I'm going to feed them, and then give them a bath, and then, if they want to stay, I'll make some clothes for them."

Maude, still speechless, climbed up on the wagon.

Patricia turned to the girls, "Will you come home with me, and have lunch with me?"

The littlest girl just shrugged, but her sister nodded.

Patricia picked up each of the girls, lifting them up into the rear seat of the wagon, marveling at how light they were. When she climbed up into the driver's seat with Maude, the other woman turned to her. "Are you crazy? What do you think you're going to do with those street urchins? How do you know they haven't got someone following us? What's your Willis going to say?"

"I'll cross that path when he gets home! I know these girls are hungry and I'm going to feed them!"

The young boy and the big man stayed in the shadows of the alley as they watched the wagon move away with the boy's sisters in the back seat. The boy felt frantic, wanting to follow them, but the big man shook his head, waving his hands in a reassuring motion. Jean Louis recognized the young woman from the *Bucephalus*. He saw a momentary vision of the group, singing and praying on the horse deck, remembering the woman holding on to her husband's arm as they prayed together. He knew the little girls were safe with her. But still, he shuddered, expecting the voices to return.

As promised, Roger took Jacques to one of the building sites on Mount Royale. It was a huge building, so large it was hard to believe this was to be a private residence. Most of the structure was already in place, largely built of stone. The work that remained was outside trim, porches, decks, balconies, doorways, windows, etc.

Roger introduced him to the foreman, Russell Thornton. "This is Jacques Boudreau. I want you to train him to reproduce yourself. Don't worry, you're not training your replacement. It's just that I need two of you. He'll be with you through this project and the next. Then I hope to have you on separate projects."

Jacques was glad Roger gave Thornton instructions in front of both of them so there was no misunderstanding. The work throughout the day kept his mind occupied, except for those moments when he relived the previous evening at the Breakfields' home. He felt guilty going the last two weeks without opening his Bible. He felt threatened by the judge over Harry's custody. At moments like this he would shake his head and refocus on the task at hand. If only Jeannette were here. She always seemed to know what to do. The day went quickly and he was glad when it was time to pick up Harry.

When the two women reached the Caldwell home, after being quiet for most of the trip, Maude spoke up, "You take your little girls in and get them some lunch ready, and I'll unload your chairs."

"Oh, I can help with them," Patricia protested.

"No, you take care of your girls first." Maude was adamant.

Patricia got down from the wagon and turned to lift the girls down. Then she turned to smile at the other woman. "Thanks, Maude."

Her morning fire in the kitchen stove had long since expired, but compared to the chilly Montreal day outside, it was still quite warm inside as she led the two little girls into the house. The remaining cinnamon rolls she baked this morning were still on the table, so she directed the girls to two chairs at the table, and setting a plate in front of each, she put a roll on each plate. Then she hurried to the cellar cooler for a pitcher of milk. When she returned the girls had not moved from the chairs, except Lizzie was standing on the chair in order to eat her roll. Patricia poured a cup of milk for each of the girls, then looked to the parlor to see Maude angling the first chair in the door.

Patricia went to help her before going to get the other chair. The chairs were quite heavy, but not too much for the two women to handle together. By the time they had the second chair in place, Maude was laughing, her good-natured self again, which got Patricia laughing also.

"Oh, come in the kitchen and have a cup of tea before you go," Patricia invited.

"Don't mind if I do," laughed Maude.

After starting up the fire again, Patricial filled several pots of water to heat on the stove. Then she brought her laundry tub into the kitchen and began to fill it with water, which she heated with some of the pots on the stove.

The kitchen was beginning to warm up, so now the little girls were shedding their coats. When Patricia saw their thin dresses and ragged outgrown sweaters, she was even more in shock, wondering how they could have survived. She went quickly to her bedroom and found two of her own blouses for the girls to wear as dresses, until she was able to make them new clothes. Now in the warm kitchen, she started with the youngest, stripping her down and putting her in the tub first. She was amazed both girls submitted to her ministrations.

Maude sat, drinking her tea and watching the activities, shaking her head. "You were right, my friend. You are their hero. They needed you and I think you needed them." She then stood up, saying again, "You were right, it was the right thing to do. I'm going home now, but I'll be back tomorrow to help you make new clothes for the girls. Furthermore, I don't think you'll have any trouble with Willis."

It was after dark when Willis finally drove the Suffolks into the yard. As usual, he took them directly to the barn, unhitched them and put them into their stalls. After feeding them, he headed for the house, anxious to see his wife, curious to see the result of her shopping trip with that neighbor woman.

When he opened the door he experienced the pleasant smells of dinner cooking, and he was barely inside when Patricia greeted him with an embrace.

"I have a surprise for you," she said smiling, as she led him to the kitchen. There at the table, on chairs propped up with cushions, were two little girls with shining blonde hair, faces scrubbed clean, dressed in Patricia's blouses which fit them like dresses. She led him to the oldest, saying, "This is Kathleen," but was interrupted as the girl corrected her with "Kat." Then she introduced him to the younger, "This is Elisabeth," and again, the oldest corrected her, "Lizzie."

Willis regained his composure somewhat. "I thought you were shopping for furniture."

"Oh, I did—I'm sorry—you walked right by our new chairs in the parlor. Let's go look." She took him by the arm to direct him back to the parlor. The two chairs were pleasingly situated on either end of the new rug.

Willis nodded approvingly. "Is that all you got today?" Then he laughed, "Except two small girls?"

"I ordered a settee to match the chairs. It will be ready in two weeks." Her voice hinted her excitement. "And I got lace yardage to make curtains," she added proudly, but anxiously waited for his reaction.

He nodded, "Very nice." But then he turned back to her. "But the girls—what, wh-what are your plans?"

"They need us. I will take care of them—unless someone comes along to prove they're related to them."

CHAPTER 31

Vanished

"**S**HE'S GONE!"

All eyes turned to the top of the stairway where Lady Montgomery was shrieking hysterically.

"She's gone—vanished!" she continued, shouting and crying as she stumbled down the stairs, grabbing at the railing to catch herself.

Lord Montgomery came running from his study, with Marshall Tanaghaven close on his heels. Peggy stood up, turning to the stairway. The women at the table sat frozen with their mouths open.

As Lord Montgomery started up the stairs, his wife turned and started back up, still crying while talking. "She's gone! She left pillows under her covers! She took her traveling bags! Her riding skirts are gone!" She kept on, repeating over and over the same words, "She's gone!"

Marshall Tanaghaven started up the stairs, his face burning red with anger. Lord Montgomery turned back to him, "That's as far as you go!"

"What? How dare you!"

"That's enough!"

The squire stopped, and backed down the stairs. When he turned to see the ladies in the dining room staring at him, his face became even redder. He turned to the front door.

Lord Montgomery turned to Morton, "Go to Jules and tell him to saddle my horse. And find out what horses are missing from the barn—including the Duran's guests' horses."

"Yes, sir." Morton started for the door, coughing and wheezing a little more than usual. As he started down the steps, the galloping horse caught his attention. It was Marshall Tanaghaven racing down the lane toward the highway, at breakneck speed.

When Jules reached the barn, he was feeling irritated Darren was not up early enough to help the others with the chores. *Oh, well,* he thought, *the activities last night were late* and he was still concerned and sympathetic for the young man. Then he realized Dani and Misty were gone from their stalls. *Oh, no,* he thought, *This is not good.* Then he began to pray as he worked, feeding the rest of the horses. It took a while since there were still several extra horses in the barn, and even longer with the stall cleaning, before he headed back to the cottage.

"Ma Cherie," he began as Teresa met him at the door, "Is Darren up yet?"

Madam Newall looked over at him as Teresa answered. "We thought he was in the barn with you. He's not with the boys, nor anywhere in the house."

"Well, he's gone then, along with his horse, and Rachel's horse."

"Oh, no," responded Teresa, echoed by Madam Newall. Now Jeannette came to the kitchen to join them.

"I'm not surprised," she said. "We should pray." Now Antoine and Ellienne joined them. The praying lasted only a few moments, as the rest of the family joined them for breakfast, which was already on the table.

Jules and Teresa both felt the gravity of the situation, as did the others. Likely they would be blamed for their guest's behavior. It was only a matter of time. Ellienne reached for her husband's hand. Even the children were quiet at the table. Wordlessly, as they finished breakfast, they all headed for the parlor. Jeannette picked up her Bible on the way. But the Bible lay on the table before them as they all stood praying. They prayed for wisdom to know God's will, and for the safety of the young couple. Then they gathered around Jules and Teresa and prayed for their future. It was no secret what was at stake.

As they stood praying, there came a knock at the door. Teresa started for the door, but Jules caught up with her, to open the door to Morton, very red-faced, almost overcome with coughing and wheezing. Teresa, concerned at his appearance, invited him in, insisting he sit down. It took a moment before he could speak.

"Lord Montgomery asks that you saddle his horse and take it to their front step. He also wants to know which horses are missing from the barn, including your guests' horses."

Quickly, glances passed between Jules and Teresa and their guests. Jules faced Morton, answering, "Both Darren's and Rachel's horses are gone. Darren is not here. He was with his horse last night and did not come in."

Morton let out a long breath. "This is not good. Between us, I believe those two should be allowed to marry. I am aware her father had other objectives, related to business with the squire. This is a matter which requires resolution in prayer."

The group, including Morton came together in prayer. Then Jules went out the door with Morton, heading for the barn. Jules went straight to the stall of Lord Montgmery's horse. He noticed the squires horse was gone, the stall door still open. He pointed that out to Morton.

The big man answered, "Yes, I saw him leaving in a great hurry."

Harold Breadon was surprised to receive a note from Prince Edward by way of a special messenger. He opened it, not knowing what he should expect; even more surprised it contained information regarding a Newall family which was staying with the Durans on the Montgomery estate.

He first went back and attempted to question Melinda Newall about whether these were relatives of her husband. She repeatedly told him to ask Wil. "Wil would know who they are." He finally gave up, determining to go to the Montgomery estate and see what he could find out there.

It appeared as though four Gypsies, three men and one woman were traveling together. At times they traveled the highway; at other times they traveled off road, when they found trails cutting through the countryside. They tried to stay away from farmhouses and villages. The trail they were following turned to the northeast from just south of Birmingham. They continued at a fast pace most of that first day, moving through the country east of Birmingham. As they rode through the more remote area north of Birmingham, the terrain became rolling and rough; even the small farms were farther apart. Fidel and Roman finally slowed, reaching a clearing near a small stream where they stopped their horses and dismounted.

"We'll go a ways north of Nottingham, then take a pass through the Pennines and come out just south of Manchester. Might be a good idea to stay away from cities, at least for a bit." Fidel pointed to the saddlebags on Darren's horse. "I think the women packed you some food—take a look. I'm surprised they didn't come along to cook it for you," he laughed.

Darren got off his horse and checked the saddlebags strapped on behind his saddle, finding some fresh bread, meat and cheese and a soft flask of wine. Before taking the food out, he turned to help his wife off her horse. Rachel, out of breath, had little to say. She looked pale, worried. Darren embraced her, feeling her cling to him. He led her to a flat stone and helped her sit down. Fidel came over and sat down, facing them, addressing Rachel, "You're serious about going to Canada with your husband?"

Rachel faced him, not smiling. "I can't go back. This was my choice. But I guess I didn't think much about how we'd get there."

Darren was now feeling the gravity of what they had done. He looked at his friends. "I would have gone directly to Liverpool. Won't it take us days to go this way?"

"We'll find you an inn to stay tonight north of Nottingham, then we'll go through the Pennines tomorrow. We know where you can stay just south of Manchester tomorrow, and my son and I will go into Liverpool and find a ship that's ready to embark. We can look out for the gendarmes," he added with a grin. Then he looked at Rachel, who as yet, had eaten none of the food she was holding. "Better eat up, girl. You'll need to keep up your strength."

In a short while, they were on the trail again, staying close to the Pennines well west of Nottingham, fording a fast moving creek coming out of the hills, winding toward the city. They found an inn on a remote road north of that city.

Arthur Montgomery galloped his horse most of the way to Bristol, slowing to a walk only to cool his horse the last mile to the constable's office. When he went in the door there were quite a few people with problems standing in line, blocking him from the officer at the front desk. He tried to get through to the desk, but those already waiting protested. He hesitated a few moments, then pushed his way to the desk, trying to look authoritative. "See here, I'm Arthur Montgomery. I need to report a kidnapping. I need to speak to the constable."

A rough looking man faced him, speaking in a growl, "I don't care who you are, you kin wait your turn like everyone."

HELENA POORTVLIET

Lord Montgomery answered, "See here, man, this is an emergency!"

"Yeah, everyone's got an emergency!"

Some of the others were facing him with fists clenched. Knowing he would not be able to get past this gang, he moved back, feeling frustrated. Meanwhile, he thought about Rachel, *away from home, with whom, and what was happening? I didn't really dislike Darren Newall. He was really a likable young man, but Marshall really got pushy. It was embarrassing to remember the old promise, trying to comfort his friend. But now the squire was really irritating. What a fool to think Rachel wouldn't mind. It was a beautiful home. But how angry she became! I should have known.*

"Arthur Montgomery! Is that really you?" It was the constable, pushing past the others to reach him.

Marshall Tanaghaven raced straight for Gloucester, where his first stop was the constable's office. He had better luck than Montgomery—there was no one in line. He put in the report his wife—that is, his intended was kidnapped, and he feared, raped.

"She's not your wife yet?" the constable asked him.

The look was dramatically frantic. "We were to be married soon. Our engagement has just been announced," he lied.

"Who do you think kidnapped her?" he was then asked.

"Riffraff! A young man visiting the stable help. He stole two of Lord Montgomery's horses, as well."

"Why did you not report this at Bristol?"

"I believe Arthur Montgomery is reporting it there, but I believe that young ruffian is headed to Liverpool with her."

When Marshall left the Gloucester constabulary, he headed for Birmingham, having little pity for the exhausted horse. A little south of Birmingham, he slowed his horse, seeing several riders up ahead. As he came closer, two of them moved in front of him.

"Oh, man, are you trying to kill that horse?" asked a man with an accent. The other man rode up close enough to take hold of his bridle. "Such abuse to a good horse! You must let him rest!" The second man was laughing.

"Take your hands off my horse. Do you know who I am?"

"You're a man with a tired horse on a highway alone, are ye not?" Again, the man was laughing.

"But you don't understand; my wife has been kidnapped by a young riffraff!"

"Your wife? Really?"

Lord John Russell met with his solicitor again, to learn an investigator was appointed to the case of Davis Tanaghaven's hunting accident. What now came to light was the death of a long-term employee of Davis Tanaghaven, his head groom, found in the barn with his throat slashed. The assumption was he may have surprised a trespasser, who was never found. After a short conversation, the two men agreed there were questions enough to continue the investigation.

After his conversation with the constable at Bristol, Arthur Montgomery headed for home. Feeling tormented with worry for Rachel, trying to ignore his guilt over the forgotten offers made to Darren Newall and his family, his irritation toward his old friend Marshall continued to grow. Also disturbing was his wife's continuing hysteria since she discovered Rachel's disappearance.

The inn north of Nottingham was, at best, very primitive compared to the Montgomery house. The only consolation to Rachel was her husband's comforting body next to hers. However, her aching body did not enjoy his attentions as much as on her wedding night. Then the trek through the Pennines was nothing like the Saturday hunts she loved for so many years. She felt as though every part of her body ached, some parts more than others. She thought the mountain trail would never end. Even worse was the descent on the west slope. Finally, Fidel and Roman led them to a rough-looking cottage, alone in the wilderness. The proprietors were a Romani couple farming on the mountainside. Greeted with a hearty meal in a primitive kitchen, to Rachel's relief, they were shown a small bedroom with a comfortable bed. She quickly fell asleep, oblivious to her husband next to her.

Darren awoke with the delicious warmth of his wife's body next to his. For those first few moments, he felt as though he were in heaven. Then he felt the weight of the responsibility, and also his helplessness. What could he do? He was completely dependant on these two Gypsy men who were assisting their flight. His desperate thoughts were interrupted as his wife rolled over to face him, reaching for him.

HELENA POORTVLIET

Their desperation was temporarily forgotten in the comfort of each other's embrace.

When the young couple emerged from their room, they felt the warmth of the wood stove in the kitchen. The Romani couple sat at the kitchen table with their hands clasped together, praying. There was an ornate wooden cross hanging on the wall above the table. As the younger couple entered the room, they let go of each others' hands, as they turned to face them. The older couple spoke English but with a french accent. As they rose to greet them, the woman offered Rachel a cup of tea, inviting her to sit down, while the man waved to Darren to follow him.

"Your friend and his father have ridden on to Liverpool to secure passage for you," the man told Darren, as they walked to the barn. The horses were already fed, but the man pointed to a cart for Darren, as he reached for two hay forks. They cleaned the stalls, which not only held Dani and Misty, but two large work horses, and several other animals, including two cows, several goats and a couple of sows.

"They should be back here by tomorrow afternoon."

When the men returned from the cottage, the kitchen was fragrant with the smells of breakfast. Darren was temporarily overcome with waves of homesickness when the woman placed a plate of food in front of him. There was a steaming omelet containing sautéed onions, and covered with a tantalizing creamy cheese sauce, and a croissant, similar to the food he was accustomed to having cooked by his mother and sister. The anticipation of the delicate flavors almost rivaled his anticipation of his wife's embrace—almost, but not quite.

Rachel was accustomed to eating sparcely, but looking around, she could see no one else was. Her husband was enthusiastically scraping the plate clean. Smiling at her he said, "Great food, my love—what a blessing!"

The others laughed. The woman nodded, gesturing at Rachel's plate, "You need your strength—yes?"

Rachel took a bite, realizing it really was delicious, and devoured the food in spite of herself.

When Lord Montgomery arrived at home he was met by his younger daughter, Peggy. "Oh, Father, Mother is just impossible. She hasn't stopped pacing around crying out that Rachel is gone. The servants are even frightened of her."

Montgomery's heart sank. He blamed himself that his whole family was in turmoil. But it was hard to admit openly he'd been wrong. "I don't know what to do about your mother, but I will have people working on finding your sister."

"Father, don't you realize, she's with Darren and they're probably married by now. They thought you gave them permission. All this about Uncle Marshall is what caused this!"

Peggy's father stopped to look at his younger daughter. "Peggy...," he began, anger rising in his voice.

Peggy was silent, feeling ashamed for her lack of respect in speaking to her father. She felt on the verge of tears, unable to speak.

Seeing her stricken expression, his voice softened. "I will go speak with Marshall. I must let him know the engagement may not be possible."

Peggy's look of relief was his reward. She ran to embrace her father. "Oh, Father, I have been praying for Rachel and Darren, for their safety. They're out there alone, without their families. Oh, don't you see?"

Arthur Montgomery looked at his daughter. She had grown up so quickly. Where had he been? He turned to the door again.

It did not take long to reach the adjoining Tanaghaven property. He looked at it differently now. He had been hopeful his oldest daughter would make her home here, close to him, joining the two properties. Now it seemed like a foreign land. He turned his horse up the lane toward the house where Davis Tanaghaven lived with his family for so many years. Now they were all gone, since Marshall had taken over the estate.

When the door opened and Montgomery asked for Marshall, the servant told him, "He's gone to Gloucester to see the constable." Montgomery thought, *Oh, no. I should have known Marshall would not be sitting still for this.* He turned back to his horse.

The constable at Gloucester assigned two officers to go to Birmingham to report the disappearance of Lord Montgomery's daughter, and perpetuate the investigation. About halfway to Birmingham they encountered the altercation on the highway—that is, the three men arguing over the exhausted horse.

Relief was plain on Marshall's face when he saw the two officers. At the sight, the man holding the exhausted horse's bridle let go and backed away. Tanaghaven turned to the officers, "These men have detained me and are attempting to steal my horse. I insist you arrest them."

The officers turned to the Romani, "What's going on here?"

One of the Romani, very politely answered, "Sir, we were merely trying to convince this man not to continue to abuse his exhausted horse.

The officers looked at the animal in question, who was still breathing hard, his sides heaving, drenched in sweat. Turning to Tanaghaven, they asked, "Who are you and where are you going in such a hurry?"

"I'm on my way to Birmingham to report the kidnap of my wife, and hope to rescue her, before she meets with a worse fate," said the squire in his most desperate voice.

"Is this the same Rachel Montgomery we have been sent to investigate?" one of the officers asked the other.

"Yes, she is my wife! We must find her!"

The officer now looked skeptical. "She is your wife?"

"I mean my intended—we are engaged."

The Romani men sat on their horses, quietly listening to the conversation, now seemingly forgotten by the others.

"Well, we'll just accompany you to Birmingham, but there's no need to abuse your horse. We don't have to gallop all the way."

As the three turned to head north, the Romani turned back down the trail into their camp.

Arthur Montgomery reached the constabulary in Gloucester to find that Marshall Tanaghaven was there much earlier, and two officers were already sent to Birmingham to investigate. His anger at Tanaghaven increased as he realized the extent of the squire's initiative to search for Rachel on his own. The constable asked Montgomery if the squire and Rachel were married or engaged.

"Neither," he answered. "The squire wanted me to agree to announce their engagement. That never happened, because my daughter became very angry, and then she disappeared."

"Why was she angry?" asked the constable.

"She refused to marry the squire. She claims to be in love with the young man, Darren Newall. Then she disappeared."

"What about the young man?"

"He is gone also."

Rachel and Darren spent a somewhat relaxing day hiking around the area of the small hillside farm. In the afternoon, the fog lifted a bit, only to turn to rain, so they went back to the cottage, welcomed by the warmth of the woodstove. When they sat down for dinner, the older couple reached out and invited them to pray with them, so they gladly joined hands. The man prayed for their safety and their blessed life together. Rachel felt deeply touched. The meal was hearty and now Rachel did not hesitate to enjoy it, as did also her husband.

After dinner the woman gestured toward the bedroom. "Go ahead, relax and get a good nights rest, while you can. You'll need to be rested when your friends get back."

This time they were happy to take leave of the others, to have time to themselves, while not so exhausted. It was wonderful to enjoy each others embrace, without the exhaustion and desperation of the night before.

The following afternoon, Fidel and Roman finally appeared, coming up the trail from the west, through the thick fog, so they literally appeared out of the fog a short distance from the cottage.

Roman was excited to tell them, "We found the *Eclipse* in port. It will be embarking in two days, so you have just enough time to get down there and board. It's a sailing ship, with alternative steam power. It's one of the newer ships, and it has great accommodations for horses, as well as cabins."

"Did you see anyone we know around town?" asked Darren.

"No, and we looked around for anyone hanging around port who might be looking for anyone," Roman reassured them, adding, "We made reservations for you, so when we get to town, we'll go directly to the ship."

"We'll board with you, so it will look like we're all together," Fidel said, then laughing, "All four of us together will look more like a bunch of Gypsies."

Rachel took a deep breath, and let it out slowly. The men all looked at her with concern. Darren put his arm around her, saying, "I'll feel a lot better when we're on that ship."

HELENA POORTVLIET

The older woman had a sumptuous meal prepared for the whole group, delicious for its freshness of ingredients produced on the farm, including stewed chicken, with the fluffiest of dumplings, and a variety of vegetables. Everyone enjoyed the meal, the woman proudly sharing what she loved doing. They all were anticipating their imminant separation forever, bringing them even closer in these last days.

When morning came, the men readied the horses directly after breakfast. When they were all ready to go, the older couple came out and prayed with them all before they mounted. The older woman hugged Rachel, then handed her a small package.

"This is for you. Open it after you get on that sailing ship." Then she shook her finger at Darren, saying, "You take care of this precious lady. Always know what a treasure you have in your wife!"

Her husband was nodding his agreement.

Then they mounted and moved down the mountain trail to the west. The morning sun was on their backs for a short time before they moved into the fog.

Arthur Montgomery left the Gloucester constabulary feeling angry, frustrated and torn. He felt a need to be with his wife and younger daughter, but angry that Marshall was involved in looking for Rachel, concerned what the squire might do if he found her. Agonizing that Darren and Rachel might make it to Liverpool and get on a ship to Canada, he was nearly overcome with fear he might never see his older daughter again. In spite of his concerns at home he turned his horse north.

Reaching Birmingham well after dark, knowing there was little he could do before morning, he secured a room at an inn. As he tried to relax alone in the room, his mind raced with anxiety for his daughter's safety, anger at his old friend's behavior, and guilt over his own recent choices. He thought about things his younger daughter said of her ideas about God in the last few weeks. He noticed Rachel was agreeing with her recently, and he even saw them reading the Bible together. He wondered how much this had to do with recent events. He seldom thought much about God in his life. Sometimes his wife got him to go to church with her, but it did not make much sense to him. He assumed his wife would have been planning for Rachel's wedding in the church—tradition! But this Bible reading and God-talk between his daughters was not the same. It was much more than tradition. *Oh, God,* he thought—more to himself really—not a prayer.

Exhausted as he should have been, he was not so inclined to go to bed. He continued with his thoughts, sitting in the chair in the light of the lamp on the table. *What about this God thing? Morton even seemed to hint about it.* He now remembered when, months ago, that Frenchman with the big black horses, was visiting the Durans, Morton and that Gypsy maid both spent time there, both coming back with a noticeably different attitude. The maid was very quiet, even sad. After her visit with the Durans she seemed much happier. The same thing was true of his daughter Peggy. For a while, Peggy and the maid, Grace, spent most of their time together, often reading the Bible together. Morton was also different now. He was always serious, dignified and professional about his job, but now he seemed more relaxed, caring toward the family and other servants, and especially toward Arthur.

He thought about his wife, so preoccupied lately with preparations for her event, she seemed oblivious to everything else. He nearly laughed out loud, thinking about her inviting the prince and Lord Russell. No one told her the prince was only eleven years old, and the prime minister was no taller than the prince. And again, no one told her the prime minister finally married, after many years of bachelorhood. But at least the royal visitors provided some diversion to an otherwise disastrous event.

Oh my God (not praying), he thought, feeling sorry for his wife. *She must be devastated, the party a disaster, and now Rachel gone. Oh, God* (not quite praying). Now he felt even more depressed. He looked around the still empty room. Near despair, he thought, *Oh my God,* and realized he was praying. *Oh my God, be with those young people. Protect my daughter. If I never see her again, I pray she is safe and happy.*

The four rode out of the hills a few miles south of Manchester. They still traveled old trails, avoiding the highway. As they approached Liverpool from the north, Fidel and Roman led them straight to the *Eclipse.* It was late afternoon as all four boarded the *Eclipse* together, taking the horses to the lower deck where the stable area was located.

HELENA POORTVLIET

The young couple was shown their cabin, then they walked back with Fidel and Roman to retrieve their horses.

Roman shook hands with Darren, "Goodby, my brother. I pray your future is all it should be—with you and your beautiful wife. Turning to Rachel, he hugged her, to her surprise, saying, "This is from Grace. You know she loves you and wishes you the best. Go with God!"

The Romani were gone and they were alone in the cabin. They reached for each other. "We did it! We're on our way to Canada!" Darren exclaimed. "I love you!"

Rachel felt so relieved, she felt tears coming. As the ship began to move, she felt the package in her cloak the woman on the mountain gave her. As she unwrapped the well-worn leather-bound book, she read aloud the words on the cover, *"God's Promises to Young Wives."*

CHAPTER 32

All the Little Horses

"But the word of God grew and multiplied.
"And Barnabas and Saul returned from Jerusalem, when
they had fulfilled their ministry, and took with them John,
whose surname was Mark."
(Acts 12:24, 25, KJV)

AFTER THE DINNER at the Breakfields, Jacques made a
practice of reading from the Bible each evening. But he found
Harry became restless if he read to himself or read aloud from the
French Bible, so he began to read a passage from the French Bible, then
repeated the same passage from the English Bible for Harry's benefit.
At first he found it difficult to pronounce but Harry often corrected
him. It was not, at first, easy for him to understand the English in print,
but in reading the two together, he began to see the benefit. He was not
only learning to speak English better, but finding it easier to read. He
soon realized this was benefiting him on the job as well.

The first two weeks on the job, Russell Thornton showed him step
by step how to fabricate the structures they built. He could see how
they looked on the drawings, but the written instructions were almost
impossible for him to understand. Since that first Friday of working
in the office, Roger made it a practice for him to come to the office
on Fridays to work and learn to deal with contracts and drawings.
Laborious at first because of his difficulty with written English, now
he began to realize the solution to the problem was the nightly session
of reading from the Bible in both the French and the English. The first
benefit, though, was Harry was also learning from the Bible.

"Now there were at the church that was at Antioch certain
prophets and teachers; as Barnabas and Simeon that was

called Niger; and Lucious of Cyrene, and Manaen, which
had been brought up with Herod the Tetrarch, and Saul.

"As they ministered to the Lord and fasted, the Holy
Ghost said, Separate me Barnabas and Saul, for the work
wereunto I have called them.

"And when they had fasted and prayed, and laid their
hands on them, they sent them away. (Acts 13:1-3, KJV)

Now when he read the passage from the English, Harry asked
him to explain certain points such as, "What is 'fasted' mean?"

"It means 'not eating,'" Jacques replied. "Many Christians, and
even Jews before them felt that fasting before or during prayer caused
their prayers to more likely be answered—or at least it seemed to
enhance the sincerity of their prayer."

It was becoming an important time for Jacques and Harry to
interact. Sometimes, they did not read very much as the questions
and conversations took more time. They always finished with prayer.

At other times they covered more:

"So they, being sent forth by the Holy Ghost, departed
unto Seleucia; and from thence they sailed to Cyprus.

"And when they were at Salamis, they preached the word
of God in the synagogue of the Jews: and they had also
John to their minister.

"And when they had gone through the isle unto Paphos,
they found a certain sorcerer, a false prophet, a Jew, whose
name was Barjesus:

"Which was with deputy of the country, Sergius Paulus,
a prudent man: who called for Barnabas and Saul, and
desired to hear the word of God.

"But Elymos the sorcerer, (for so is his name by
interpretation) withstood them, seeking to turn away the
deputy from the faith.

"Then Saul (who is also called Paul) filled with the Holy
Ghost, set his eyes on him,

"And said, O full of all subtilty and mischief, thou child
of the devil, thou enemy of all righteousness, wilt thou not
cease to pervert the right ways of the Lord?

"And now behold, the hand of the Lord is upon thee, and
thou shalt be blind, not seeing the sun for a season. And

immediately there fell upon his a mist and a darkness; and he went about seeking someone to lead him by the hand.

"Then the deputy, when he saw what was done believed, being astonished at the doctrine of the Lord.

"Now when Paul and his company loosed from Paphos, they came to Perga in Pamphyllus; and John, departing from them returned to Jerusalem."

(Acts 13:4-13, KJV)

Harry was delighted when Paul called an affliction of blindness on the sorcerer. Jacques affirmed to him our power in the Holy Ghost is much stronger than the evil power of the sorcerer.

The next evening they were joined by Ramon as he came in from work, just as the two were beginning to read:

"But when they departed from Perga, they came to Antioch in Pisidia, and went into the synagogue on the Sabbath Day, and sat down.

"And after the reading of the law and the prophets the rulers of the synagogue sent unto them, saying, Ye men and brethren, if ye have any word of exhortation for the people, say on.

"Then Paul stood up, and beckoning with his hand said, Men of Israel, and ye that fear God, give audience.

"The God of this people of Israel chose our fathers, and exalted the people when they dwelt as strangers in the land of Egypt, and with a high arm brought he out of it.

"And about the time of forty years suffered he their manners in the wilderness.

"And when he destroyed seven nations in the land of Chanaan, he divided their land to them by lot.

"And after that he gave unto them judges about the space of four hundred and fifty years, until Samuel the prophet.

"And afterwards they desired a king: and God gave unto them Saul the son of Cis, a man of the tribe of Benjamin, by the space of forty years.

"And when he had removed him, he raised up unto them David to be their king; a man after mine own heart, which shall fulfill all my will." (Acts 13:14-22, KJV)

At this point, Jacques stopped and read back the English version to which Harry listened with rapt attention. Then Jacques stopped, as he remembered the first mention of David in Acts which caused both him and Pierre to ponder who this was. Now he said, "Aw, that's who David was." He looked at both Harry and Ramon. "So if we just keep reading, we usually get our questions answered."

Ramon nodded, "So David was the first king of Israel—except for Saul, that is."

Harry grinned, saying, "Read more."

But Jacques shook his head, saying, "another night, Son, time for bed."

The settee was delivered and Patricia was pleased. It matched the chairs nicely and looked wonderful with the rug. Maude not only helped her with the sewing of new clothes for the girls, but brought over armloads of books for her to read to the girls, books well-used by her own children, now grown.

By the beginning of April, it seemed as though the two little girls had always been part of their family. Growing and happy, cleanliness and good food made a world of difference for them. Patricia was so busy, it seemed as though she fell in bed each night, exhausted but happy.

One evening, Willis drove his team into the yard, and went to the door instead of going directly to the barn. "Come out and see what I found for you," he called to Patricia.

When she came to the door, he went to the back of his wagon, and untied a small black mare, bigger than a pony, but not quite a horse. She was hitched to a two-wheeled cart, the kind sometimes seen in the English countryside. Some would call it a "dog cart," with a driver's seat in front and a short box with two leather seats, one on each side, facing each other. "Oh, Willis, she's beautiful!" she exclaimed. "But why?"

"Well, you can't be stuck here all the time with the girls. What if there's an emergency? Now you have your own transportation. I know you know how to drive if you have to."

Patricia turned to hug her husband. "Oh, thank you!"

While they were still standing there, admiring the little mare, Jacques and Harry arrived in the carriage with Tounerre. Seeing the new rig, they stopped and got out of the carriage. Harry ran up to pet the new mare.

"You worked your horses so hard you had to get extra help?" Jacques asked.

"Sure thing," Willis shot back. "You'd be surprised how strong she is!"

Patricia smiled happily at Jacques. "This is my new horse. Don't pick on her! You can see, even Harry likes her."

Willis turned to Patricia to ask, "Do we have enough cooking for dinner to invite these two to share with us?"

"Of course! Ask Ramon too, if he comes home in time."

The men turned their horses toward the barn, as Patricia went back toward the porch. Kat and Lizzie were standing in the doorway, curious about the men and horses, but still too timid to come any closer.

When the men reached the barn they all took part in admiring and analyzing the qualities of the new mare. They guessed she might have Welsh or Connemara blood, judging from her sturdy build, while still around thirteen hands. Harry was especially interested in the little horse. He would pet her and grin at Jacques, who just shook his head (reading the boys thoughts) as he unhitched Tounerre. He brushed the stallion before putting him in his stall and turning to fill the hay cart to feed all three of his horses. His mares were both out in their shared pasture, but ambled toward their stalls as soon as the men and horses arrived. They were both huge with their foals, but Joni looked especially ungainly and awkward. Her nose went into the feedbox, blowing and snorting, but not eating. Then she turned her head toward Jacques, begging attention, while her teammate Pari, enthusiastically engaged in devouring her feed.

"Oh, boy," said Jacques, looking around. Willis was still busy with his horses, and Harry was now milking goats.

The stall was quite roomy. Jacques got busy with the fork, cleaning out soiled straw, and replacing it. Joni was circling, turning around, at times swinging her head toward her round sides. He left her for a while to clean the other stalls quickly, checking back on her every few moments. He finished the stall cleaning, gathered towels and rags which he kept ready.

Willis finished with his horses, came and looked in on them. "She's getting close?"

Jacques nodded, "Yes—looks like it."

Joni circled the stall several times, then began to drop down on her bent forelegs. Her huge body followed with a "whump!" Jacques could see movement within her bulging belly. He moved to her rear end.

HELENA POORTVLIET

"What do you want me to do?" Willis asked.

"Come in and stay by her head; talk to her," was the answer from Jacques as he bent closer to her hindquarters, carefully avoiding the movement of her hind feet. Using twine from hay bales, he began to wrap and tie the long hairs of her tail, watching the opening of the birth canal. It was only a moment before a small hoof began to appear.

"Oh, no," he said, seeing only one. Then, with relief, he began to see the other. As soon as the second hoof emerged, he grasped it, pulling the leg straight, as the foals nose began to emerge, covered with a slimy coating. As the small black head began to emerge, he used a soft rag to clean the slimy membrane from the foal's nose. Now Joni's contractions were coming fast and hard, and Jacques could see the swelling of the shoulders. With great effort into the next thrust, the baby slipped out, into Jacques waiting arms. He pulled the foal away from its mother, away from her moving hind hoofs.

"What's happening?" asked Willis, from her head.

"We've got a new little stallion! Looks like all the parts are there," Jacques laughed, thrilled at the sight. Now Joni was struggling to her feet, turning around in the stall to seek her new baby. Jacques backed up, allowing the mare to begin licking the foal, cleaning up the remainder of the slimy membrane.

"If you don't need me anymore," began Willis, "I think I better let Patricia know you'll be late for dinner."

Jacques laughed again, just as Harry came into the barn with a pail of milk, to fill the milk can. Willis took the pail from him, directing him to the stall to see the new foal.

"Wow," was his only word, with eyes big, full of wonder, he climbed into the stall with Jacques and the new foal. As he came close, he repeated, "Wow!"

In a short while Jacques looked up to see Willis, again, this time with Kat on his shoulder, and Patricia was right behind him with Lizzie. The two little girls, still a little shy, were fascinated at the sight of the new colt. While they were all still admiring the newcomer, Ramon arrived, even more enthusiastic about the new foal.

After dinner, eaten in a spirit of celebration by all, the question of reading came up and everyone was in agreement. This time it was Willis who began to read in English:

"When John had first preached before his coming the baptism of repentance to all the people of Israel,

"And as John fulfilled his course, he said, Whom ye think that I am? I am not he. But, behold, there cometh one after me, whose shoes I am not worthy to loose.

"Men and brethren, children of the stock of Abraham, and whosoever among you feareth God, to you is the word of this salvation sent.

"For they that dwell at Jerusalem, and their rulers, because they knew him not, nor yet the voices of the prophets which are read every Sabbath day, they have fulfilled them in condemning him.

"And though they found no cause of death in him, yet desired they Pilate that he should be slain.

"And when they had fulfilled all that was written of him, they took him down from the tree and laid him in a sepulcher.

"But God raised him from the dead." (Acts 13:24-30, KJV)

When Willis read this last line, there was a spontaneous cheer from all the adults present. The little girls looked surprised, and Harry showed a hesitant smile. Willis caught on and explained, "This is the reason for our salvation—Jesus lives!"

The others clapped and praised God. Harry smiled, repeating "Jesus lives." The little girls were watching, wide-eyed. Willis continued:

"And he was seen many days of them which came up with him from Galilee to Jerusalem, who are his witnesses unto the people.

"And we declare unto you glad tidings, how that the promise that was made unto the fathers,

"God hath fulfilled unto us their children, in that he hath raised up Jesus again; as it is written in the second psalm, Thou art my Son, this day I have begotten thee.

"And as concerning that he raised him up from the dead, now no more to return to corruption he said on this wise, I will give you the sure mercies of David."

"Wherefore he saith also in another psalm, Thou shall not suffer thine Holy One to see corruption;

"For David, after he had served his own generation by the will of God, fell on sleep, and was laid onto his fathers, and saw corruption:
"But he, who God raised again, saw no corruption." (Acts 13:31-37, KJV)

Now everyone was clapping a praising God. Even the little girls joined in, enjoying the good cheer of the group.

By the end of April, Jacques, with Russell Thornton and the rest of that crew, were working on the framing of the next home. Now, Roger also assigned Ramon to that crew with the same instructions given in regards to Jacques. And now Roger again invited Jacques to dinner after work on Friday, reassuring him, "Don't worry; no solicitors or judges this time. We just want to get all of you from the voyage together again."

Jacques was relieved the atmosphere at the Breakfields' house was more casual this time. Just before dinner, Willis arrived with his whole family. Andrea was thrilled to meet the girls. She knelt on the floor to get down to their level to greet them.

"Hi, Kat," she began, careful to use the preferred form of her name, "It's wonderful to welcome you to our home."

Both girls became very shy, very wide-eyed, not speaking.

Andrea asked, "How old are you, Kat?"

"I'm six," she answered, holding up five fingers.

"How old are you, Lizzie?"

The smallest girl looked down with a shy grin.

"She's four," Kat answered for her sister.

"Thank you, Kat," Andrea replied as she held out her arms, encouraging the girls to allow a hug. They came forward, slowly, shyly.

She asked Patricia, "Are they getting any lessons, yet?"

Patricia looked apologetic, "I'm not quite sure what to do. But I have been reading to them. My neighbor, Maude, brought us a lot of books left by her children, so we've been reading those. But I'm not sure what else to do."

"Well, I have an idea," began Andrea, "You bring the girls over every Friday, and we'll have school here, and you can learn how to teach them. I'll teach you, okay?"

"All right," agreed Patricia.

"I think that would be a good time for all of us to get together for dinner, also." She looked around at Roger and the other men, getting grins and nods of agreement from all, including Roger.

A servant came into the room to announce dinner, so they all moved into the dining room. Talk at dinner was a lot about work, but there was much admiring talk about the new Percheron colt. Someone asked if he had a name yet.

"I've thought about it a lot," Jacques replied, "and changed my mind several times already. I've decided on the name from our ship, *Bucephalus*. The ship was named after the favorite horse of Alexander the Great, maybe the most famous horse in ancient history. But it has more meaning to us, since we were on the ship while his mother was carrying him. If the name's too long to say, we can call him 'Buck.'"

Everyone agreed the name was a good choice. As dinner was nearing an end, someone suggested reading from the Bible, so Andrea agreed to read. A short time later she began:

> "Be it known unto you therefore, men and brethren, that through this man is preached unto you the foregiveness of sins:
> "And by him all that believed are justified from all things, from which ye could not be justified by the Law of Moses.
> "Beware therefore, lest that come upon you, which is spoken of in the prophets;
> "Behold ye despisers, and wonder, and perish; for I work a work in your days, a work which ye shall in no wise believe, though a man declare it unto you.
> "And when the Jews were gone out of the synagogue, the Gentiles besought that these words might be preached to them the next Sabbath.
> "Now when the congregation was broken up, many of the Jews and religious proselytes followed Paul and Barnabas; who, speaking to them, persuaded them to continue in the grace of God. (Act 13:38-43, KJV)

As Andrea paused there were amens and other positive comments.

Willis suggested, "It sounds like these people were hungry for the word of salvation, like we are."

Everyone agreed, looking to Andrea to continue:

"And the next Sabbath day came almost the whole city to hear the word of God.

"But when the Jews saw the multitudes, they were filled with envy, and spake against those things which were spoken by Paul, contradicting and blaspheming.

"Then Paul and Barnabas waxed bold, and said, It was necessary that the word of God should first have been spoken to you, but seeing ye put it from ye, and judge yourselves unworthy of everlasting life, lo, we turn to the Gentiles.

"For so hath the Lord commanded us, saying, I have set thee to be a light to the Gentiles, that thou shouldest be for salvation unto the ends of the earth.

"And when the Gentiles heard this, they were glad, and glorified the word of the Lord: and as many were ordained to eternal life believed.

"And the word of the Lord was published throughout the region.

"But the Jews stirred up the devout and honorable woman, and the chief men of the city, and raised persecution against Paul and Barnabas, and expelled them out of their coasts.

"But they shook the dust off their feet against them, and came into Iconium.

"And the disciples were filled with joy, and with the Holy Ghost."

(Acts 13:44-52, KJV)

As the reading ended, it was met by "amen" and other positive comments, as all came together to pray. Curiously, the three older children came around the two little girls to pray over them. Then the others moved around the group of children, to pray over them all. Before long, they were all praying in the heavenly language.

It was still dark when Jacques came into the barn. The mares and Buck were still out in their pasture, but Tounerre always seemed to know the moment Jacques came into the barn to be in his stall. By the time, the mares ambled in with Buck following, running and jumping most of the way. Jacques felt exhilaration and pride seeing the beautiful colt. It brought back some of his memories of when Tounerre was born. He went to Pari's stall, carefully checking the mare for signs. He foal was now due and Jacques tried not to worry, but Buck's birth was so easy, he was afraid he might not be so fortunate with Pari. There were so many things that could go wrong. He felt reluctant to go to work over his concern for the mare and her coming event. It was almost the middle of May, but he had no choice.

As he drove out of the yard, heading for work, he looked back to see the mares and Buck back in the pasture. The mares were busy with the spring grass, and Buck was playing, running circles around the mares.

The project Jacques was working on was taking shape, with most of the framing up. Some of the stonework had begun, and the work was progressing, an education for Jacques. There was so much to it, he wondered how he would ever learn it all. And today, he still felt distracted, thinking about Pari. *Oh, Lord,* he thought, *protect her from any problems.*

Ramon came up to him, pushing an empty cart, on his way to get more of the material they used to make mortar. "My friend, you can help me with this, if you're not lost inside your head," he laughed. "Where are you, my friend?"

"Oh, sorry," Jacques apologized. "I guess I've been worrying about Pari. She's due now, and no sign of it. I just hope she has no complications while I'm gone."

"Well, give it to God, my friend," Ramon said. "Seriously, give it to God. You can't be there, He can."

"You're right, of course. I keep trying to, and then I take it back." Jacques admitted.

"Well, relax. She'll have a beautiful, healthy foal, just like little Buck. You wait and see. That'll be your reward for saving my little Stormy on the ship!" Ramon encouraged, his voice confident. "Now let's get this job done!"

Jacques felt somewhat better and determined to focus on the job at hand, grateful for his friend's encouragement.

Sean McGillis, in eleven years, saw his parents joy, over the birth of his two little brothers, then their heartbreak over their loss from the fever just two years lator. Then came the arrival of Sean's sister, Kathleen, who soon became "Kat." The next year came Elizabeth, whom they soon called "Lizzie." These were good times, but temporary, for soon the potatoes produced nothing but blight and they were all hungry.

There was the day the landlord's men came to burn their cottage and drive them off the land, when there was nothing to pay the rent. When they arrived at the ship, which would take them to the new land, there were men who paid their fare only when Papa signed some papers. They were all thin and hungry when they boarded the ship, but once on board they discovered there was little to eat or drink, and no separate cabins for any of the families. After a few weeks at sea, first his mother sickened and died, then after a few more days, his father. The captain unceremoniously ordered sailors to throw their bodies overboard. Sean watched over his sisters, and did his best to get their share of the food that was available to them in the last weeks before they arrived in Montreal.

Sean remembered bitterly the day they arrived in Montreal. There were men waiting to collect the papers from the captain, who then told Sean to take his sisters and go with this man. They were taken to a large building where they were assigned beds in a large room with all the other children. They ate in a large room with all the other children, but the food was meager. In the morning there was oatmeal, and in the evening there was soup. But through the day, they all labored in a great hall, where all the children worked, even the little ones. They only saw each other at meals and for the few hours they were allowed to sleep. After a few days, Sean began to see certain children get sick or even faint, and saw them carried away. He usually never saw them again. Then he saw his sisters were becoming more quiet, more timid, more pale, and sickly. The adults who supervised the work made threats about letting them sleep outside if they did not produce enough.

One day he noticed a door open in the hallway on the way from breakfast to work. The sun was shining, even though there was a chilly draft coming from the open door.

When his sisters arrived at supper that night, he could see Lizzie had been crying and Kat was very angry.

"What is it?" he asked.

"They yell at her all the time," began Kat, "saying she's slow. I want to hit that lady." Then Kat began to cry also.

Sean tried to comfort his sisters, but felt even angrier. He was afraid Kat would do something to get into trouble. They all saw children slapped or beaten for even a little resistance to the cruelty.

The next morning, when all the children were herded back to the great hall to work after breakfast, Sean saw the door in the hallway almost closed but not latched. He grabbed both his sisters, leaning against the door. As it swung open, he slipped through, pulling his sisters with him. The other children were pushed along by the adults; it seemed no one noticed three of them disappear.

They were outside, free. The sun was bright, even though the air was still chilly, it did not seem cold. Sean pulled the girls along the side of the building until they were on the main street in the middle of the city. He looked around, seeing no one.

"Come on," he urged, holding each by the hand. When there was a break in the traffic, he led them quickly across the street. It did not take long before they were completely out of sight of the factory which had enslaved them for weeks.

Jacques was glad to see the days work end. He hurried to get Tounerre hitched quickly so he could go pick up Harry. All he could think of was getting home to make sure Pari was okay. It was getting dark by the time he turned onto their street. Because of the trees and buildings, he could not see their pasture until he turned into the driveway. He drove the carriage straight back to the barn. He thought he saw Joni and Buck in the pasture, so he assumed Pari was already in her stall. He unhitched Tounerre and took him to the barn to unharness. When he finished, he went to check on Pari, but instead found Joni and Buck in her stall. He turned around just as Pari came into her stall followed by her own black filly which had been born during the day out in the pasture.

"Oh, thank you, Lord!" Jacques exclaimed as he went into the stall and checked over the two of them. He found nothing amiss, and continued to give thanks out loud, bringing Harry in from the goat pen to find out who he was talking to.

"It's Pari's new baby. Isn't she beautiful?" He laughed, and Harry was squealing with delight.

"Another baby horse?"

"Yes, Son, another baby horse."

Just then, Ramon rode into the barn. He came right over to see what was happening. "What did I tell you? God is good, right?"

Soon they were joined by Willis who just arrived with his team. Seeing the activity, he came right over, also giving thanks for the safe arrival of the new filly. As soon as he got his own horses cared for and fed, he hurried to his house, soon to return with the rest of his family to see the newest arrival.

Jean Louis was trying to ignore the voices in his head. Sometimes they argued like spitting cats. At other times they just quietly suggested death. To him or to others he was not quite sure. He thought *probably because I've killed.* It was hard to admit to himself how many, but the voices assured him his time was coming.

At night Jean Louis and Sean sat on a step in the alley, close together for mutual warmth. As light filtered down into the alley, Sean would knock on doors until he received a package of food, rather than a sharp word of reproach.

Jean Louis could not speak more than a word or so in a hoarse whisper because of the burns to his vocal cords. It seemed the pain in his throat was increasing both in frequency and intensity. At those times the voices chattered incessantly, warning of doom. He accepted that he would not live much longer.

When Sean returned with a package of food, Jean Louis accepted a portion of it because of the sharp hunger pang, but ate only what little eased the pang, not only because of the pain in his throat, but the voices which kept reminding him that he would soon die.

It was now mid-May, and the market shops began to open around the edges of the city. The two drifted toward the market district, but Jean Louis managed to avoid close contact with people. He nudged Sean and pointed to the market booths down the street. He managed to say, hoarsely, "Get work," as he nodded toward the booths. Sean looked puzzled at him, but he again pointed toward the booths and muttered, "work." Sean started toward the booths, but looked back again. The big man just pointed at the booths and nodded, before he turned and walked away.

There were farmers unloading their early produce, and women setting up shelves of craftwork. One man was unloading a huge wagon of firewood. Sean walked up to him and said, "Can I help?"

At first the man looked surprised, then said, "Yes, Laddie," as he handed off an armload of wood. "Pile it right over there."

Sean did just what the man told him. They soon had it all piled neatly. The man said, "You stay here with the Missus?"

"Yes, sir."

"Good. When somebody pays her, you load his wagon. I go get more wood. Okay?"

"Yes, sir."

Jean Louis walked toward the west side of the city. He remembered seeing the two women driving this way at least twice now, the first time when they took the little girls. The second time Lizzie pointed at him, but the woman turned to her and shook her head. Her sister also shook her head. The older woman flipped the reins over the horses back, and the brown mare began to trot much faster. But Jean Louis saw the direction they went, and far down the road, he saw where the mare turned off on another road.

He kept walking, making the same turn where he had seen the mare turn. Soon he saw a large house up on a knoll with a barn and paddock nearby. There in the paddock was the brown mare. In front of the house was a small black mare hitched to a dog cart, tied to a rail by the wide front porch. Jean Louis settled down next to one of several trees a little way up the road. Across from the big house were two houses next to each other with a driveway between them, leading to a barn. Behind the barn was a large pasture with three mares, all with foals. Two were huge black mares and the third was a smaller piebald mare. It seemed as though the foals were all miniatures, the same color as their mothers.

Leaning against the tree he began to doze a bit, and lost track of time, until he was awakened by the voices. Then he was aware of other voices, bringing him back to the present. The young woman and the two little girls got into the dog cart together, and soon they were coming down the driveway. Jean Louis moved a little behind the trees, staying out of sight of the three in the dogcart, until they moved up the driveway and into the big open front door of the barn. After a while, he saw the small black mare run from the back of the barn, in a high stepping trot, to join the other mares. A short time later he moved back to the far side of the tree, staying out of sight, as the woman walked back to her house, with the two little girls, each hanging onto one of her hands.

A short time after they entered the house, he noticed smoke coming from the chimney. He could see the sun sinking in the west, so he began to walk back toward town. By the time he arrived back in the market area, most of the vendors were beginning to load their remaining wares back in their wagons. He saw Sean helping to load wood in a customer's wagon. When they finished the man turned to speak to Sean while he dug in his pocket, producing a coin which he handed to Sean. The man's wife came over to hand Sean a package, before he turned to go. Jean Louis backed into the shadow of the alley until he saw the man and his wife turn back to load their own wagon.

When Sean saw the big man he began to run toward him, so he backed into the shadow of the alley again. He motioned to the boy to slow down, becoming aware of the others looking toward them. Then they both disappeared into the shadow of the alley. After sitting on a step the boy handed the package to the man, who shook his head, pointing at the boy and whispered "no."

"But they gave me dinner earlier," the boy protested. "I'm full— you eat." So the man opened the package. There was roast meat, bread and cooked vegetables; he took some of the bread and meat, handing the package back to the boy. Then Sean reached in his pocket and produced the coin the man had given him. Jean Louis gave him a thumbs-up sign and nodded, patting the boy on the back. In a hoarse whisper he managed to say, "work—good!" nodding to the boy.

For the rest of the week the boy went back to help the wood cutter. Every day, he ate with the wood cutter and his wife. At the end of each day the man gave him a coin, and his wife gave the boy a package of food to take with him, which he shared with Jean Louis.

Hunger was no longer an issue, but Jean Louis was aware of the hard lump growing in his throat. It was becoming harder than ever to swallow food, and nearly impossible to speak. The worst part were the voices continuing to taunt him, "You're going to die—die—die!"

CHAPTER 33

Inheritance

THE *ECLIPSE* WAS moving away from the pier on the Mersey River. Darren and Rachel could feel the strange vibration of the engines as they moved out into the river. Their excitement was high, anticipating the next few weeks at sea, and even more for their future in Canada, on their own, since they were leaving Darren's family in England.

Hesitant to leave their cabin while the ship was in port for fear of being discovered, but with the ship moving down the river, they began to feel more relaxed and wanted to see the sight of leaving England, so they left the cabin, made their way to the rail where many passengers were getting their last view of England.

Then they noticed the two power boats flanking the *Eclipse*, still some distance away, but soon it was clear they were gaining on them. As they began to pass, Darren saw the port police insignia on the bow, and as the two boats began to cut closer in front of them, they saw signals between the two boats and the *Eclipse*. Then they felt a change in the rhythm of the *Eclipse's* engines and the ship began to coast, now losing speed.

Darren felt panic and saw it in Rachel's eyes. "Maybe we should go back to our cabin for now. Maybe it's nothing."

Rachel reached for his arm as they turned to go. "I should have known Father would be after us. Oh, I'm so sorry." She was shaking as they reached their cabin and locked the door. They could feel the ship turning around now and moving back up the river. As the ship returned to the pier, they clung to each other, praying.

"Whatever happens don't ever doubt I still love you," Darren told her.

"Same for me, no matter what," she responded, still holding him.

They heard all the sounds of docking and several men coming aboard. Before long there was a knock on the door, then a pounding. Then they heard the key in the lock and the door opened.

"There she is; that's my wife!" shouted Marshall Tanaghaven, red-faced with anger. "And that's the riffraff who kidnapped her and probably raped her!"

Rachel angrily retorted, "Uncle Marshall, I'm not your wife! Darren and I are married! What are you doing here?"

Marshall turned to the police officers who were now in the room. "Arrest that man," he said, pointing at Darren. "He's a kidnapper, a rapist, and a horse thief!"

Darren was in shock. He couldn't believe what he was hearing. *Was this man crazy?*

Marshall moved toward Rachel, "Come, my dear, we must go home, now. You'll be safe with me."

"No, Marshall; I'm married to Darren! Don't touch me; I've never been married to you! Where's my father? Is he with you?"

Darren started to reach for Marshall, saying, "Don't touch my wife!" But the two officers reached for him, quickly pulling him away from the squire, and then he felt shackles snapped on his wrists.

Next, he was being escorted off the ship between two officers. Looking around, he saw Marshall Tanaghaven holding onto Rachel's arm. She was trying to pull away from the squire crying and screaming. "Let go of me—let go of me." Then he saw his horse Dani along with Rachel's horse Misty being led up from the lower deck where they had been stabled. Both horses were saddled.

Tanaghaven nodded when the horses were led up. "Yes, those are the stolen horses."

Then Darren was led away to a coach which had a sign on the side which read *Birmingham Central Police District*. He tried to turn back to see Rachel, but the officers pushed him toward the coach. He could hear her crying and screaming at Tanaghaven, as the officers pushed him into the coach.

The trip to Birmingham in the police coach was a nightmare to Darren. He was terrified, angry, and frantic to think about Rachel with Tanaghaven. And they had his horse Dani, as well. *What would happen to her? What would happen to Rachel now?*

Fidel and Roman rode their horses up the hill above the Mersey River where they watched from a distance as the *Eclipse* left the pier and started down the river toward the Irish Sea. They watched as the police boats overtook the ship, turning her back to port, as they started back down the hill to the river front. They were in time to watch helplessly from a block away as Darren was led off the ship and put into the police coach from the Birmingham Central Police District. They saw the officers from the Liverpool police lead away Dani and Misty. Then a cab arrived to pick up Tanaghaven and Rachel.

"That's our job," said Fidel, as the cab turned onto the highway to Birmingham. They followed the cab.

"Now what do we do, Papa?" asked Roman.

"We stay with them until we know where they're going," Fidel replied, grinning. "We may have to do some kidnapping of our own."

Roman looked at his father in disbelief.

Fidel looked at his son. "Do you think this guy is for real? Where is Rachel's father? I think something stinks."

On the fifth day after Rachel's disappearance, Morton knocked on the door of the Duran's cottage, out of breath, as usual. This time Lady Montgomery had sent him. "I'm afraid we are all in need of prayer, my friends," he began, as Teresa urged him to come in. "I don't agree with what I have been told to tell you. You have one week to vacate this house, all of you and your guests. Your pay through one week from today will be given to you at that time. You are to fulfill your daily chores until that day. I am sorry. I think it is wrong." He looked dismayed, excused himself and left.

Peggy heard her mother telling Morton to tell the Durans they would have to leave, but he was already out the door.

"Mother, what is that all about?" Peggy was furious.

"Those people have ruined us! They cannot stay here," her mother shouted.

"Mother, they've been here all my life. They're our best friends!"

"Margaret, you have no idea what you are saying. They have ruined us. They're worse than traitors! That young man is a criminal!"

HELENA POORTVLIET

"Mother, that's not true! Rachel is in love with Darren and Father even told them they could marry! They're probably even married by now. Oh, Mother!" With their voices raised, they did not even hear the knock at the door.

Harold Breadon almost turned to leave, then turned back and lifted the brass knocker once more. Finally, the door was opened by a red-haired girl who looked very angry. He quickly asked, "I'm looking for a Newall family who are supposed to be staying with a Duran family at this address. I have news about their relatives in Southampton. Do you know where I can find them?"

"Yes, they're staying with the Durans in that cottage down the lane."

As Breadon walked back down the steps to his horse, a big man was coming back up the steps, slowly, coughing. "Are you all right, sir?"

"Yes," Morton nodded, as he paused on the step. His heart was pounding. The other man continued down the steps.

Peggy was still at the open door as Morton came in. "That man was looking for the Newalls."

Lady Montgomery was just behind Peggy. "Did you give them the message?"

"Yes, Milady."

Morton was gone only a few moments when there was another knock on the door. Teresa went to answer it, finding a strange man with a briefcase.

"I'm Harold Breadon, solicitor for Wilfred Newall's family. I'm looking for anyone who is related to Edmund Newall. I was told a Newall family was staying here."

Teresa turned to Madam Newall, who came to the door on hearing the name. "I am Louisa Newall. My late husband was Edmund Newall." Now Jeannette was next to her. "This is my daughter, Jeannette," she added.

"I regret to inform you your husband's brother Wilfred, has passed on, leaving no children. Is your daughter your only child?"

"I have a son, but he is not here."

"Where is he?"

At this question, Madam Newall felt embarrassed, without a good answer. Antoine stepped up and answered, "He has just married and is on his honeymoon," with a sly smile.

The door was still open, so it was not difficult to hear the galloping horse approaching. Jules went to the doorway, joined by Antoine, who recognized Fidel Balansay. Both went out to meet him.

"Darren is in the Birmingham Gaol! That squire had the ship stopped before they got out of the Kersey River. The squire took Rachel."

"Oh, no!"

"But Rachel is safe for now. She is with Grace and her parents."

"How's that?"

"He left her locked in a cab, while he went to secure a room. The cabby was happy to unlock the cab for her," Fidel answered, grinning.

Harold Breadon asked Madam Newall, "When do you expect to see your son and daughter-in-law?"

"Why are you asking?" she said, warily.

"It seems your son is heir to the Newall estate, which includes the family home, "Newlandia.""

"There's no one else?" She asked.

"Wil's widow, Melinda is still there, but sadly, she is very fragile, shall we say, and not able to run the affairs of the estate."

The men came back into the house now, and all the adults heard this last statement. Antoine stepped up next to Madam Newall and Jeannette. "So what does that mean, exactly, for this family?"

"As the son of Edmund Newall, your son is entitled to the estate and the title of 'squire.'" Breadon paused, then asked, "Who has he married?"

Madam Newall hesitated, but Antoine answered, "He has married Rachel Montgomery."

Breadon looked surprised, "This Montgomery family?" He gestured toward the big house.

"Yes, sir."

"Well, then, he is probably eligible for a lordship."

Madam Newall's eyes grew wide with amazement. "But he may not still be in this country."

"Then you and your daughter are certainly entitled to live there."

Antoine quickly stated, "Darren and his wife are still in England."

"Then where is he?"

"He is in Birmingham Gaol on trumped up charges."

Madam Newall's mouth dropped open. She began to tremble. Jeannette moved close to her mother, reaching her arm around her. The other women also moved in close to her.

Breadon asked, "What charges?"

Antoine looked at Fidel who answered, "Rachel told me the squire accused him of kidnap, rape, and horse thievery."

Breadon's eyebrows raised high. "How much truth is there to those accusations?"

"Absolutely none," said Antoine. "I witnessed their handfast vows, before they went to the Romani chief to make it official. They went together. Rachel agreed to go with him, even accepting his ring in front of me. Darren was riding his own horse, Dani, and Rachel was riding her own horse, Misty." Antoine turned to Fidel. "Did you see their wedding?"

Fidel nodded, "Yes; I was there when they said their vows before Stavros. The whole camp was there. My son and his fiancée stood with them as witnesses."

Breadon then asked, "Was it consummated?"

Fidel smiled, "Well, they had the wedding wagon for the night. Then they were together for three more nights before we got them to the ship."

A royal messenger was knocking on the huge front door of the Montgomery house. When Morton answered the door, the young man handed him the envelope, saying, "This is for Lady Margaret Montgomery, from Prince Edward. I am to wait while she pens her answer to him."

Morton asked the man to step in while he took the envelope to Peggy.

When Peggy realized the note was from Prince Edward, she tore into it excitedly, reading: *Milady, I would be pleased if you would allow me to visit you in a few days. I would be most gratified if you would give your answer to the messenger who brings this note to you. My most grateful regards for you indulgence, Prince Edward.*

Peggy quickly wrote her answer, *Your highness, yes, of course, I would most welcome your visit. I very much look forward to seeing you again. Miss Margaret (Peggy) Montgomery.* She quickly went downstairs to give her note to the messenger. Then she went to tell her mother the prince was coming.

Lord Russell's solicitor had an investigator who worked for him many years. This was a different assignment: to look up all available information of three deaths, all somehow related to Marshall Tanaghaven. *But how?* First was the death of Madeline Winslow Tanaghaven, two years ago. It seems she fell on the stairway and broke her neck. Then last year, Davis Tanaghaven died, after his horse fell attempting to take a fence during a hunt. Then a few days later, Tanaghaven's head groom was found, his throat slashed.

The investigator started with police reports, first at the Bristol constabulary, then at Gloucester. Taken separately, the first two seemed to be mere accidents. But with all three together, things were looking suspicious.

At Gloucester he discovered two officers were sent to Birmingham to investigate the disappearance of Rachel Montgomery, reported by Marshall Tanaghaven who claimed she was his "wife" then his "intended." From there he went to Birmingham, to the Dept. of Birmingham Central Police District.

There he found that Darren Newall was arrested and imprisoned for the kidnap and rape of Rachel Montgomery. In looking at the report, he found the accusations were made by Marshall Tanaghaven, who claimed to be married to Rachel Montgomery. He remembered the report at Gloucester, that the squire was married to her, no, she was his "intended."

It was late evening when the police coach with Darren arrived at the Birmingham Gaol. He was taken to a cell, pushed through the door, and the door closed behind him. The cell was all stone, no windows, no furniture, and bars on the door, nothing in the cell except the bucket in the corner. When the door closed behind him it was dark in the cell.

He felt his way around the cell, finding nothing other than the bucket. He closed his eyes, trying to adjust to the dark. Exhausted, he leaned against the stone wall, finally sliding down until he was sitting on the floor. He felt terror, anguish and worry for Rachel, anger at the thought of the squire's hands on her, and shame for all he had done to cause this. *Oh, God,* he thought, no, prayed. *Oh, God, protect my wife.* He opened his eyes and the room was filled with light, such light as he had never seen. As he looked around, he envisioned Rachel in the lamplight, smiling at him from across the table. Then he caught sight of her on her dapple-gray horse, flying over fences. Then he saw her face, as she reached forth her hand to accept the ring he slipped on her finger. The images faded, but not the memory. The supernatural light persisted, as a voice, no more than a thought, told him, *You are not alone; I am with you.*

Harold Breadon assured Madam Newall and Jeannette he would make arrangements for them to move into Newlandia. Madam Newall replied, "Then please make arrangements for our friends to move with us," as she gestured around at all the Durans. They will be living there with us, and they will need to move all that is in this house."

Again Breadon's eyebrows were raised high. A look of amazement was expressed by both Jules and Teresa, as the arrangements were made. Then Breadon said he was headed for Birmingham to see what he could do for Darren.

Jules said, "I would love to hear from God's Word. I think we need that fellowship now. The others agreed and Jeannette went to get her Bible, then began:

> "And the Lord visited Sarah as he had said, and the Lord did unto Sarah as he had spoken.
> "For Sarah conceived and bare Abraham a son in his old age, at the set time of which God had spoken.
> "And Abraham called the name of his son that was born unto him, whom Sarah bare to him, Isaac." (Gen. 21:1-3, KJV)

Jules laughed, "That just goes to prove God keeps his promises."

"Yes," Jeannette added, "He said he would never leave us or forsake us, and he also said he would supply all our needs according to his riches in glory."

Antoine said, "Read more," so she continued:

> "And Abraham circumcised his son Isaac being eight days old, as God commanded him.

"And Abraham was an hundred years old when his son
Isaac was born unto him. (Gen.21:4, 5, KJV)

They all looked around at each other, amazed. *A hundred years
old?* Jeannette continued.

"And Sarah said, God hath made me laugh, so that all that
hear will laugh with me.
"And she said, Who would have said unto Abraham, that
Sarah should have given children suck? For I have born
him a son in his old age.
"And the child grew and was weaned: and Abraham made
a great feast the same day that Isaac was weaned." (Gen.
21:6-8, KJV)

Teresa suggested, "I think this may be about how we see our lives
unfolding as our children mature." Jules smiled at her, nodding, as
Jeannette continued:

"And Sarah saw the son of Hagar the Egyptian, which she
had born unto Abraham, mocking,
"Wherefore she said to Abraham, Cast out this bondwoman
and her son: for the son of this bondwoman shall not be
heir with my son, even with Isaac.
"And the thing was very grievous in Abraham's sight
because of his son." (Gen. 21:9-11, KJV)

"Now we see more of the folly of their behavior unfolding, now
the son of God's choice has arrived. If they trusted God to begin with,
this would not be a problem." Jules commented, before Jeannette
continued:

"And God said unto Abraham, Let it not be grievous in thy
sight because of the lad, and because of thy bondwoman;
in all that Sarah hath said unto thee, hearken unto her
voice; for in Isaac shall thy seed be called.
"And also of the son of the bondwoman will I make a
nation, because he is thy seed.
"And Abraham rose up early in the morning, and took
bread and a bottle of water, and gave it unto Hagar, putting

it on her shoulder, and the child and sent her away: and she departed, and wandered in the wilderness of Beesheba.

"And the water was spent in the bottle, and she cast the child under one of the shrubs.

"And she went, and sat her down over him against him a good way off, as it were a bowshot: for she said, Let me not see the death of the child.

"And she sat over against him, and lift up her voice and wept."

(Gen. 21:12-16, KJV)

"Hagar sounds like the typical unbeliever who is a victim of their circumstances, because she does not believe she can change things by prayer," suggested Ellienne. "We are believers. What was the outcome? Did God leave her there?"

Jeannette read the following:

"And God heard the voice of the lad, and the angel of God called Hagar out of heaven, and said unto her, What aileth thee, Hagar? Fear not, for God hath heard the voice of the lad where he is.

"Arise, lift up the lad and hold him in thy hand; for I will make him a great nation.

"And God opened her eyes, and she saw a well of water; and she went, and filled the bottle with water, and gave the lad drink.

"And God was with the lad and he grew, and became an archer.

"And he dwelt in the wilderness of Peran: and his mother took him a wife out of the land of Egypt." (Gen. 21:17-21, KJV)

There was a collective sigh of relief from everyone. Simon now spoke, "God took care of them both, because Ishmael was Abraham's son, and the boy called out to God, even though Hagar did not believe."

Jules looked amazed, "That's good, son! Is this not a good lesson for us? And he will not forsake our children. Darren and Rachel have an inheritance waiting for them. Let's give thanks they will be safe to get there."

They all began to pray together, which soon culminated in the heavenly language.

By the time Lord Montgomery arrived at the Birmingham Central Police Station the officers already were there with Tanaghaven, and officers were sent with him to Liverpool. They would first be checking passenger lists at the port office, to see if the young couple had embarked in the last few days.

Arthur Montgomery was furious his old friend acted so aggressively in pursuing Rachel. He now had serious doubts about the squire's presence of mind. His behavior did not seem quite rational. Arthur made a statement to the police there in Birmingham that, "No, Tanaghaven was not married to Rachel, nor were they engaged."

While Montgomery was still making his report, the investigator arrived there with the information he already gathered, and finding Arthur there, asked to interview him.

"How long have you known Marshall Tanaghaven?"

"As long as I can remember," replied Arthur. "Our families have always been close. We were boys together."

"Did you ever think it strange his wife and brother both died from accidents?"

"I felt so sorry for him," Arthur replied. "He was so devastated when Maddie died, I tried to comfort him. I humorously mentioned Rachel would be of age soon, just trying to cheer him up, but I couldn't believe he took it seriously."

"But when his brother died…"

I was shocked. Davis Tanaghaven lived next to me. We didn't always get along well, but I knew he was an excellent horseman, and he was well-respected in parliament. Then when Marshall took over the estate, he started talking about marrying Rachel—that I should be happy to know she would be next door."

"You mean you agreed to it?"

"I never actually agreed to it, because by then that young man, Newall, came to me, and it was plain Rachel wanted to marry him."

"So what did you do?"

"Marshall was pressuring me, insisting I promised him. He wanted me to announce their engagement. But Rachel became very angry when Marshall started talking to her like they were already promised. That's when she disappeared."

"She disappeared?"

"Yes, along with Newall," Arthur answered. "I'm afraid they've already gotten married, and are on their way to Canada."

"So, Tanaghaven must be pretty angry."

Darren fell into a deep relaxed sleep, despite the cold, hard stone floor of the cell. He dreamed of the time spent at the mountain cabin with Rachel. He awakened to the sound of the cell door opening. An officer was at the door with another man who introduced himself as Harold Breadon, his solicitor.

Darren was confused. "I have a solicitor?"

Breadon laughed, "You inherited me. I have been your uncle's solicitor for years, and now he has passed on, you are his heir."

Darren was even more confused.

"You and your family have inherited Newlandia. Your mother and sister are now moving there. You have been cleared of all charges here, and we'll be on our way there."

"What about my wife?—and our horses?"

"Your horses are waiting outside. We'll pick up your wife on our way."

It was like a great weight rolling off. Darren let out a sigh, saying, "Oh, thank you, God!"

As they left the station, they found an officer in front holding Misty and Dani. By now the dark brown dye was wearing off, and Darren could see his mare's bright red coat beginning to show through. Silver hairs were beginning to show through the brown dye on Misty. Darren was thrilled to see his horse, and she was clearly happy to see him.

He mounted and turned to Breadon, "Where do we pick up Rachel?"

"Do you know of a Gypsy camp just south of here?"

"She's there?"

"Seems she's staying there with some friends of yours—someone named Grace."

"All right," Darren replied, smiling with relief, as they turned toward the highway

When they arrived at the trail into the camp, two riders came galloping up the hill to greet them. As soon as the Romani recognized them, they turned to gallop back down to the circle of the wagons. They were back shortly to accompany them, laughing.

Darren said, "I'm looking for my wife, Rachel. Is she with Grace Gala?"

"Oh, yes," one man said, laughing.

"Well, where is she?"

"She's with Grace." Both men were laughing.

Darren felt dumbfounded, so he asked, "Is Roman here?"

"Oh, yes," and the man waved at him to follow.

Darren looked at Harold Breadon, who just shrugged.

They were riding toward the Gala's wagon when Darren saw Roman outside the wagon with some other men. He got off his horse, and walked toward Roman, wondering what to expect. "Where's Rachel?"

Roman smiled at him. "She's in there with Grace and her mother and my mother."

Finally Darren asked, "What's going on?"

"Grace is having her baby!"

Some other men arrived and began to pass around a bottle of wine. Roman was pacing in front of the wagon. Several of the men were joking at him, but his attention was on the wagon. Finally, Grace's mother Paloma appeared in the doorway, smiling "Roman, you may come in now."

As Roman went through the door into the wagon, Paloma grinned at the men waiting outside, saying, "It's a girl!" Loud cheers were the result. Paloma looked over to see Darren and waved at him, before she disappeared back into the wagon.

Darren looked helplessly at Breadon, who grinned and said, "You better get used to it. This is how it happens!"

Finally, Darren saw Rachel appear in the doorway. As she started down the steps he ran to her, and when he got close to her, she leaped into his arms.

"Oh, my love!" she squealed.

Darren felt as though he could never let her go.

Then the door of the wagon opened again, and Roman appeared to wave at Darren, inviting him in. As Darren climbed into the wagon, Rachel followed close behind him. There was Grace, propped up in bed with several pillows, holding her tiny daughter.

Darren was amazed; he had never seen a baby so tiny and young. And there were both Roman's mother and Grace's mother right there with her, just as proud as can be! As he looked around at them all, he thought of how important is family.

Rachel and Darren came out of the wagon to find Breadon, still waiting, with their horses. Rachel saw her horse Misty and went running to him. Darren heard one of the men joking about Darren being jealous of the horse, as Rachel hugged Misty's neck. Darren felt good just to see her happiness.

Finally Rachel turned to Darren, seeing Breadon standing with him.

"Have you met Rachel?" Darren asked Breadon, who shook his head. So he introduced the two. "This is our solicitor," he laughed.

"I didn't know we had one," she responded, "but I'm glad, because he probably has something to do with the fact that you are here, and not in gaol."

After Darren introduced Breadon, the solicitor explained the details of the inheritance. Rachel was astonished, and asked, "Have you been there? Have you seen it?" Then she asked, "What about Uncle—I mean Marshall?"

Breadon answered, "He's been arrested on suspicion of murder. Darren has been cleared of all charges, and your marriage has been verified. Tanaghaven had no right to interfere with your voyage on the *Eclipse,* but if he hadn't you would be on your way to Canada without even knowing about your inheritance."

Rachel smiled, "That would have been all right with me."

"Well, if you still want to go to Canada after you see Newlandia, we can make arrangements to transfer the property to whomever you decide."

"Really," the couple grinned at each other.

They spent the night in an inn in Goucester, before traveling on toward Southampton and Newlandia. Breadon already made arrangements to let the servants know the new squire was on the way, and the property now looked in better repair than the last time he was here.

There was one Grand House and three smaller houses. Breadon let himself into the Grand House where they were met by the butler who went to notify Melinda Newall her nephew and his wife had come to stay with her. She looked surprised, but welcomed them, saying, "Wil should be down soon."

Darren and Rachel looked confused. Breadon explained, "That is your Uncle Wil. Melinda expects him soon. So she will show you your room and, we'll wait for him. You understand?"

Darren caught on. Then Breadon explained, "Your mother and sister and the Durans will be here in a few days, so you'll have a few days to get acquainted. I'll be leaving now, but I'll check back with you in a few days, to see how things are going." He turned for the door, then turned back. "Remember, you are the Squire of Newlandia. He turned to Rachel, "You are the Lady of Newlandia. You may find your own way to deal with Melinda, but you folks are in charge here; remember that."

After a few days, Jeannette and her mother arrived with their wagon, with Fidel Balansay driving, with his own horse hitched with Jeannette's horse Katy. Following behind were Antoine and Ellienne driving their wagon which looked like a colorful cabin on wheels, drawn by their two stocky chestnut mares. There was great excitement at the arrival, both from the servants and the family, when the wagons appeared on the lane approaching the Grand House. Despite Raleigh's obvious disapproval, Darren opened the door, and seeing his family's wagon approach, ran to meet them. He reached up to lift his mother out of the wagon, swinging her in a circle.

"Oh, my, Son. Control yourself," she laughed, almost hysterical. He laughed as he turned to embrace his sister. "It's so good to see you," he exclaimed happily. Then he led them proudly to the Grand House, where Rachel was waiting on the porch to welcome them into the house.

Breadon made arrangements for two drivers, using teams from the Newlandia stable to take two wagons to transport the Duran's belongings from the Montgomery estate, so in a few days the Durans arrived at Newlandia. Darren and Rachel were staying in the Grand House with Aunt Melinda, so Jeannette and her mother moved into one of the smaller homes; the Durans moved into the larger, and the Merlots took the smallest of the three.

It took only a few days for the Durans to get their house organized and liveable, when they invited the others over for dinner, recalling the days at the Montgomery estate when they all gathered at the

Durans' cottage for dinner after their riding sessions. Their new home had much more room, though, and the family members were more relaxed since the most pressing issues were solved.

Now the question came up about the proposed move to Canada. Jeannette was anxious to go and still wanted her mother to go with her. The Merlots still planned to go. Madam Newall felt it was important for her son to take advantage of his inheritance, even though Darren felt uncomfortable being called "squire." He could not imagine being "lord."

Darren appointed Jules Duran as stable manager, and arranged with Breadon that Jules should be paid a good amount over what Montgomery paid him. He reassured the family this would be their home as long as they needed it.

With these decisions made, Jules requested they read God's Word and pray together, especially realizing now that separation was again imminent. The others agreed and looked to Jeannette, so she began:

> "And it came to pass at that time, that Abimilech and Phichol the chief captain of his host spake unto Abraham, saying, God is with thee in all that thou doest:
>
> "Now therefore swear unto me here by God that thou wilt not deal falsely with me, nor with my son's son: but according to the kindness that I have done unto thee, thou shalt do unto me, and to the land wherein thou hast sojourned.
>
> "And Abraham said, I will swear;
>
> "And Abraham reproved Abimelech because of a well of water; which Abimelech's servants had violently taken away.
>
> "And Abimelech said, I wot not who hath done this thing; neither didst thou tell me neither yet I of it, but today.
>
> "And Abraham took sheep and oxen, and gave them unto Abimelech; and both of them made a covenant.
>
> "And Abraham set seven ewe lambs of the flock by themselves.
>
> "And Abimelech said to Abraham, What mean these seven ewe lambs which thou hast set by themselves?
>
> "And he said, For these seven ewe lambs shalt thou take of my hand, that they may be a witness unto me, that I have digged this well.

"Wherefore he called the place Beersheba; because there they sware both of them.
"Thus they made a covenant at Beersheba: when Abimelech rose up, and Phichol the chief captain of his host, and they returned into the land of the Philistines."
(Gen. 21:22-32, KJV)

"And Abraham planted a grove in Beersheba, and called there on the name of the Lord, the everlasting God.
"And Abraham sojourned in the Philistines land many days."
Gen. 21:33, 34, KJV)

The group sat silent for a few moments. Jeannette waited as the moment was too important to interrupt. Finally, Jules spoke, "This is our moment of covenant. We may be separating forever. But we are all connected for eternity, all of us, wherever we may go. We should pray together and agree to always uphold each other, all of us, in prayer and concern for our future well-being." Everyone stood up, moved together, and began to pray. It quickly changed to the heavenly language. Then they laid hands on Jeannette and her mother and prayed for a safe trip and the success of her marriage to Jacques. Jeannette then turned to Rachel and her brother and began to pray for the continued success of their marriage. Before long, there were prayers for everyone present.

Close to the end of April, the family was afraid the time was past for the *Bucephalus* to be in port. Fidel offered to ride to Liverpool to check what ships were in port, and which would be the best to make the trip. He was back in a few days reporting the *Bucephalus* was in port, and would be for one week.

So the decision was made: Jeannette and her mother would leave the next day. They packed quickly. Antoine and Ellienne would accompany them. There was a tall roan mare named Sassy in the Newall stable, which teamed well with Katy, so they took those two mares.

It was a hard call to make, but Madam Newall believed her son was where he belonged, so she could now leave him. The trip to Liverpool went quickly, so within a few days they found the *Bucephalus*. As they came on board with their horses and wagons,

HELENA POORTVLIET

they were not only greeted by Captain Palmer, but by his stableman, Pierre Mirande, all happily recognizing each other. Then Pierre pulled the letter from his pocket to hand to Jeannette—the letter Jacques wrote to Jeannette after reaching Montreal. At the sight of Jacques' handwriting, she tore it open.

March 5, 1852
Dearest Jeannette,

After all this time, and by the time you receive this I pray this finds you well, and still feeling the love I have for you. I have missed you so much over these weeks since I left you. I love you as much or more than ever, and pray to see you soon.

The sea voyage was so harrowing, I fear for your coming here, but I pray that day will come, and you are safe on the trip.

I hope your family is well, and also Antoine and Ellienne. Be sure to give them my greeting. I pray your brother is doing better.

I became acquainted with good friends on the ship. One is a building contractor who asked me to work with his company for one year in Montreal. Two other men from the ship are also working with us. Pierre has become such a good preacher, he is staying with the ship as chaplain, as well as stableman. Our Bible reading group bonded us all, getting us through many storms.

The boy, Harry, who joined us in Birmingham, has become a wonderful son. He's such a good boy, and an especially hard worker. He's made a good friend, Andrew, whose father I will be working with. Andrew's mother is giving Harry lessons along with her own children.

I love you Jeannette, and pray I will see you soon. If you are able to get here this year, I will be working for Findlay and Breakfield in Montreal.

All my love,
Jacques

CHAPTER 34

Firestorm

O N SUNDAY AND Monday, there was no market. On Sundays they stayed in the alleys out of sight. But Monday was different. Jean Louis pointed at Sean's now bulging pocket. The boy pulled out all the coins the woodcutter gave him. Jean Louis took one coin, and motioned for the boy to put the rest back in his pocket. Jean Louis then put the one coin in the boys hand and closed his fingers around it. Then he led him out of the alley into the street. About halfway down the street they could see the red and white striped pole in front of the barber shop. The man reached down and picked up an unruly handful of the boys too long hair. The boys face was grimy with sweat and dirt. Jean Louis pointed in the direction of the barber shop. He pointed at the fist holding the coin, and made a motion with his hand like a scissors cutting Sean's hair. Again, he pointed to the barber shop, nodding.

Sean was a bit bewildered, but caught on, still a little hesitant with shyness. Jean Louis tapped his shoulder, and again pointed to the barber shop, whispering as he barely could, "Go!" Sean went to the shop, pushed through the door. The barber was just finishing with a man, glancing at the boy as he came in. "Yeah, what can I do for ye, Sonny?"

Sean held out the coin. "I guess I need a haircut."

The man broke out laughing. "Well, I guess you do, Sonny," he answered, raising his eyebrows as he took the coin. "Just hop up in this here chair."

Sean remembered his last haircut his mother gave him. No one else ever cut his hair. He felt like running, but somehow, he wanted to do what his friend told him. The barber not only washed and cut his hair, he also scrubbed his face, his neck and his ears. And soon he was back on the street looking for his friend.

Jean Louis just motioned for him to go with him as he turned down the road, heading west. It was just a few miles to where he followed the mare when she turned down that last road. They passed the driveway between the two houses to the barn. He showed Sean the big trees which gave them plenty of room to move out of sight as they watched the house on the right. It appeared the house on the left was empty and quiet. They could see the two black mares in the pasture with their foals, along with the piebald mare, and her foal, and the smaller black mare.

Smoke was coming from the chimney of the house on the right. As Sean turned in the direction of approaching hoofbeats, Jean Louis pulled him down behind the tree, as that woman came riding her brown mare up to the house. When the front door opened, the younger woman appeared with Kat and Lizzie on either side of her, each holding on to her skirts. As Sean let out a gasp, Jean Louis clapped a hand over his mouth. Sean was wide-eyed, seeing his sisters. He could hardly breathe.

The women and the girls all went back into the house. After the door closed, Jean Louis again motioned for Sean to follow him, as he began to walk back to town. Once out of sight of the house, Sean began asking questions, one after another. The big man just continued walking, until they reached the alley near the market place which was quiet and empty today.

Tuesday, when Sean went back to work for the woodcutter, both he and his wife were startled to see how different he looked with his hair cut and his face clean. They both greeted him with smiles, and the man said, "Ready to work hard today?"

"Yes, sir!"

Two more weeks he worked for the woodcutter and his wife, loading wood for customers and eating with them. Each day when they finished the man gave Sean a coin and the man's wife gave him a package of food left over from dinner, which he shared with Jean Louis.

Jean Louis, growing weaker, knew his time was short. He ate very little, choking on what he could get down past the hard lump in his throat. He noticed lumps growing on various other areas of his body. He worried about the boy. At least Sean now knew he could work—and he knew where his sisters were. Several times he said to Sean, "Gone soon," pointing at himself, choking out the words.

The second Monday, they walked out that road to the west and sat down between the trees looking at the house. They could see smoke in the chimney, but no one came out. Jean Louis spoke to Sean, nodding toward the house, "work." Sean was confused. He knew his friend was trying to tell him something. It did not seem to make sense.

On Friday, when Jacques drove Harry to the Breakfields' house, the Caldwells all followed them in their wagon, so Patricia and the girls could spend the day with Andrea and her children. This was the second Friday of this routine, and Patricia was enthusiastic to learn from Andrea how to present lessons to the girls in both reading and arithmetic.

Roger came to the door with yesterday evening's edition of the *Montreal Tribune* to show both men. "*Le Brute,* The Monster of Quebec Thought to be in Montreal," read the headline. The article mentioned the last victims were a sailor off the *Bucephalus,* the sailing ship in port from Liverpool on it's way to Montreal, and the bar waitress he was escorting home. After that incident there were no more sightings of the monster in Quebec City. Some vagrants in Montreal described a man who scared them or threatened them, but no actual crimes were committed. They said he was in the company of some young children. Some said he was accompanied by a young boy. The description was usually the same or similar: a very large tall man, without a face, or with horrible scars. They said he did not speak; he only growled or snarled at them.

Police in Quebec City, on further investigation, discovered a case in the community of Trois-Rivieres of a man badly burned in an industrial explosion. A few weeks later, his wife was found strangled. The man Jean Louis Deveneaux, disappeared. Now the police believed this was the man probably responsible for the murders in Quebec Ciy.

Since Jacques was going to work in the office today, Roger would ride with him. As they left the house, Roger expressed to Jacques, "There was a reason I wanted you to see that article."

"Oh, what's that?"

"Well, Andrea just brought it up to me. I briefly thought about it, but dismissed it."

"What do you mean?"

"Andrea said to me on the ship, when we got back to our cabin one night, after we got the children to bed, she felt a presence of evil while we were worshiping down below."

"Oh, really?" Jacques responded. "What did you do?"

"Well, we prayed about it with each other before we went to bed. Then I guess we put it out of our mind, until we saw the paper last evening. Then we remembered that feeling of evil—it was on the trip between Quebec City and Montreal."

"I see what you mean," Jacques said, catching on. "Ramon mentioned it to me."

"Really—you mean it wasn't just us?"

"No. Ramon came down in the morning. I thought he just came down to work with his horses. But he told me he was awake all night. He said there was a feeling of evil while we were worshiping, like something evil was close by."

Roger's eyes were wide. "That's just the way we felt."

Jacques continued, "Then Pierre came out. He felt it too, just when we finished reading and we all started worshiping. Then we started speaking in the heavenly language, he said he thought it went away, but part of it stayed."

"So, it was real."

"What do you think it was?"

"Well, I thought about it. I think that guy was on the ship. I think he was hiding in the cargo hold. Maybe, when we felt it the most, he was by the hatch watching us."

"But I was in there working on my carriage and getting harness out."

"He was hiding behind cargo."

Jacques was shaking his head. "Oh, and I heard Leon talking to Captain Palmer about food missing. He may have been sneaking up there at night to get food."

"And now he's here in Montreal."

After a few moments, Roger spoke again. "Willis just gave his wife that little horse and cart, so she could get about while he's at work. Otherwise, she's home alone with the little girls."

Jacques understood what he was thinking. "Well, they're with Andrea today," he said. "But what about tomorrow?"

"They'll be with Andrea tomorrow," Roger replied, "and everyday Willis is at work. We won't leave them alone until that fellow is found."

By the end of May they were on the job at six in the morning. The daylight hours were long now and the crews needed to take advantage of the daylight and the mild weather. On Monday morning, June 7, all of the children, along with Patricia, were at the Breakfield house for the day. By the time the crews were starting to work it was already warm and strong winds were blowing from the southwest. Near the base of Mount Royale the elevation was slightly higher than downtown, so when flames suddenly lit up the sky to the west, it was not lost on them. They were working just west of Sherbrook Street; the Breakfield house was a few blocks east of Sherbrook. The fire now lit up the sky to the east, obscuring the rising sun. The Findlay office was even further to the east.

There was a stable on the property where they were working where both Jacques and Ramon left their horses. They both arrived there about the same time. Ramon saddled his stallion and mounted just as Jacques was backing Tounerre into position on the carriage.

"I'm heading for Roger's house," Ramon told him. Jacques waved him on, as he ran to the driver's seat.

Streaks of light filtered into the alley and with it flakes of soot that seemed like snow. The street was still quiet. It was Monday—no market today. Jean Louis and Sean both looked to the sky as they recognized the flakes for what they were. The sky above the alley was a red glow. Sean began to run toward the street followed by Jean Louis.

As the alley opened to the avenue, they both stopped momentarily in awe of the sight. Strong winds struck them both from the southwest.

The eastern sky was a wall of flame. Jean Louis paused only a moment, then turned to the east. Sean began to follow him. Jean Louis turned to the boy, stopping him. The words came out in a crackling whisper. "Home—sisters—your home—go—work."

Sean felt confused, in panic. He stood frozen, looking up at the faceless countenance. The words came again, in painful effort, no more than a whisper, "go—home."

Then Jean Louis turned, walking toward the towering wall of flame. The voices were chattering louder with every step, "You're going to die—die…" His fists beat against his head, but the voices only grew louder, until finally—he looked up to the sky above the wall of fire and smoke, crying out, "Oh God—Jesus!" The voices stopped. It was as if the sky was suddenly clear. He continued walking east. Many others were running past him, going west. Some of them yelled at him. But when they saw his faceless visage they turned away. He did not see the smoke swirling around him. It took only a short time for the compromised lungs to shut down, and only a few more steps before the legs gave out. As he fell to the ground, only one word was on his lips, *Jesus!*

Sean stood watching as his friend continued walking east into the firestorm. He still stood frozen as the man faded into the smoke. Now crowds of people were running to the west, past him, along with riders on horses, and horse-drawn vehicles. Someone grabbed his arm, jerking him around. "Come on—run, boy!" He began to run west.

Jacques, with Tounerre and his carriage, reached the Breakfields' house right behind Ramon on his stallion. Roger and Willis were already there. They quickly loaded the two women and all the children in Jacques carriage. Roger pointed to the west. "Take 'm to your place!" Then he motioned to Willis to follow him as he swung up on his horse.

"Hey, Boss," called out Ramon. "Wrong way! Where do you think you're going?"

"To the office," he yelled. "Too much there to lose."

Andrea protested, "No! Come with us!"

Roger became firm, "Go with Jacques! I'll be there later!" Then he was gone, Willis following him with his team.

Sean ran for a while until his feet began to hurt from the too small shoes and the blisters. Others continued to run past him. The air was thick with the swirling soot, in spite of the winds from the southwest. Sometimes there were even burning bits of material falling around him. Staggering from the blisters, he did not see the open carriage drawn by the huge black stallion.

Tounerre veered slightly to avoid the boy limping along the side of the road. Lizzie looked over, and seeing the boy, called, "Sean!" Then Kat turned to look and exclaimed, "There's Sean!" Then they both stood up, looking back, and continued calling, "Sean, Sean!" Andrea and Patricia both asked, "Who's Sean?"

Kat turned back to say, "Sean is our brother."

The women both looked back, to see the boy, far back now limping along. Andrea said, "Oh, Jacques, please stop!"

Jacques guided Tounerre to the side of the road. There were many vehicles passing them as they pulled off the road. Ramon realized they were no longer behind him and turned back.

Patricia took Lizzie by the shoulders, looking her in the face. "Do you know that boy?"

"He's our brother, Sean."

Kat repeated, "He's our brother, Sean."

There was too much traffic to turn the carriage around. Patricia looked at Ramon. "Can you get that boy back there? His name is Sean. He's Lizzie and Kat's brother."

Ramon turned his stallion, which sprang into a gallop toward the boy. Sean looked up as the man on the piebald horse came close. Ramon saw the pain in the boy's eyes and got off his stallion.

"Hey, young man, you want a ride on my nice horse so we can catch up with your sisters in that carriage up ahead?"

Sean looked past Ramon at the carriage where both of his sisters were standing up waving at him. Then he looked up at the snorting stallion. Before he could think twice, Ramon picked him up and threw him onto the saddle, then swung up behind him. In another moment they were alongside the carriage. By then his sisters were jumping up and down in their excitement.

Ramon jumped down, helped the boy down, then boosted him into the carriage. Both girls threw their arms around him, as Jacques carefully eased Tounerre back onto the road into the increasing traffic heading out of town.

Patricia immediately saw the boy's bleeding heels, and invited him to sit next to her so she could pull the worn out shoes off his feet. "Don't worry, Son, we can get you some new shoes that won't hurt your feet."

At these words both his sisters spoke up, "Look Sean, we got new shoes. Our feet don't hurt anymore."

Then Lizzie asked her brother, "Sean, where's the man?"

Sean looked apprehensive.

Patricia asked, "What man?"

Sean was silent.

Lizzie answered, "The big man that kept us warm."

"Where is he, Sean?" Kat asked.

Sean answered, "He went into the fire. He told me to go home."

Andrea and Patricia listened, not speaking, waiting for a clue. Then Patricia asked, "Is he the man who got you the nice coats?"

"Yes," said Lizzie.

It was not long before they drove into the driveway between the houses. Jacques stopped the carriage in front of the Caldwells' house. Ramon got off his horse and came over to the carriage to pick up the barefoot boy and carry him into the house.

Harry stayed in the carriage with Jacques to take Tounerre to the barn. Looking to the east, they could still see the wall of flame on the far side of the city. The sky was filled with smoke as on a cloudy day.

Roger led the way to the Findlay and Company office, which was within blocks of the fire. By now, the hot winds blowing from the southwest were sweeping the fire through homes and businesses on the waterfront and pushing it on to the north. They quickly loaded the most crucial of the files into Willis' wagon, including all the contracts and drawings of the current projects. As they loaded the last of what Roger felt was important, smoke was swirling about them and Willis' normally placid horses were nervously prancing in place as Willis talked to them, attempting to keep them under control. Finally, they turned the team to the west, and when they reached Sherbrook, they turned southwest, joining the heavy traffic of thousands leaving the city.

Andrea and Patricia first worked to provide food for all the children and make them as comfortable as possible, but they were concerned that their husbands had gone into the east side of the city to secure files from their business, so close to the fire zone. They both knew that it would take only a change in the direction of the wind to bring disaster home. When everyone had eaten, and Roger and Willis were still not there, the concern increased. Andrea suggested they all pray together. After praying, Ramon suggested some Bible reading, so Patricia produced Willis' Bible and asked Andrea to read:

> "And it came to pass in Iconium that they went both together into the synagogue of the Jews, and so spake, that a great multitude both of the Jews and also the Greeks believed.
> "But the unbelieving Jews stirred up the Gentiles and made the minds evil affected against the brethren.
> "Long time therefore abode they speaking boldly in the Lord, which gave testimony unto the word of his grace, and granted signs and wonders to be done by their hands.
> "But the multitude of the city was divided: and part held with the Jews, and part with the apostles.
> "And when there was an assault made both of the Gentiles and also of the Jews with their rulers, to use them despitefully and to stone them.
> "They were ware of it, and fled unto Lystra and Derbe, cities of Lycaona, and unto the region that lieth round about:
> "And there they preached the gospel" (Acts 14:1-7, KJV)

The children, including Sean, were all gathered around Andrea as she read, giving her rapt attention. The reading seemed to calm them all.

> "And there sat a certain man at Lystra, impotent in his feet, being a cripple from his mother's womb, who had never walked.
> "The same heard Paul speak: who steadfastly beholding him, and perceiving him that he had the faith to be healed.
> "Saith with a loud voice, Stand upright on thy feet, and he leapt and walked.
> "And when the people saw what Paul had done, they lifted up their voices, saying in the speech of Lycaonia, The gods are come down to us in the likeness of men.
> "And they called Barnabas, Jupiter, and Paul, Mercurius; because he was the chief speaker.

"Then the priest of Jupiter, which was before their city, brought oxen and garlands unto the gates, and would have done sacrifices with the people.

"Which when the apostles, Barnabas and Paul, heard of, they rent their clothes, and ran in among the people crying out.

"And saying, Sirs, why do you do these things? We also are men, of like passions with you, and preach unto you that ye should turn from these vanities unto the living God, which made heaven and earth, and the sea, and all the things therein.

"Who in times suffered all nations to walk in their own ways.

"Nevertheless, he left not himself without witness, in that he did good, and gave us rain from heaven, and fruitful seasons, filling our hearts with food and gladness.

"And with these sayings, scarcely restrained the people, that they had not done sacrifice unto them." (Acts 14:8-18, KJV)

Now Ramon remarked how the Bible gives us such confidence that God is at work and we can trust he hears us when we call on him.

Patricia was almost in tears for fear for her husband. "Then I think we need to be praying for Roger and Willis. We don't know where they are or if they are safe."

Andrea moved in close to Patricia putting her arm around her. "I agree; I'm worried about them, too." She looked around at Jacques and Ramon. "Let's pray."

The four adults came close to the children. Sean looked bewildered, but Harry and Andrew and Julia were quick to join hands with him and the girls. Ramon began praying, and others followed, praying first for Willis and Roger, then giving thanks for their safety, and especially for finding Sean. As those praying began to pray in the heavenly language, they heard horses coming into the yard.

Both women broke away from the group to go to the window, to see Willis' team, followed by Roger on his horse.

"Oh, thank God," exclaimed Patricia, as she ran for the door. Andrea was right behind her, both women running to embrace their husbands.

In Willis' wagon was a load of files, boxes of paperwork, and hidden under everything, the company safe. The men all got together to unload and move everything into the house.

All the while they were unloading the wagon, a continuous stream of traffic passed by, refugees fleeing the possibility of the fire turning back on the city. Patricia saw Maude coming down the driveway on her brown mare from her house on the knoll, but she could not cross the road because of the continuous traffic. Patricia waved to her and said to Willis, "There's Maude trying to get across the street. Can't we do something?"

The men all went out in the road, waving at drivers to stop, and at first, most just went around them. Then Ramon just went in front of a team and grabbed their bridles.

The driver yelled, "Hey, what are ye doin'?"

Roger was now next to Ramon. "Don't you see that lady trying to cross? Are you so rude you can't give her a minute?"

Other wagons and riders were pulling up behind them. Some riders just went around them. Then Willis ran across the road, grabbed the brown mare's reins and led her across the road. Maude just grabbed her saddle, hanging on with her mouth wide open, speechless.

As soon as Willis and Maude were in the yard, Ramon let go of the team and walked back to the yard, ignoring the barrage of profanity which followed him. As Willis helped Maude down from her horse, Patricia ran to giver her a hug, then introduced her to Willis.

"I saw all the smoke, and then I saw all you folks home from work earlier and I really got scared for what might have happened. And all this traffic…"

"We're all okay for now, thank God," said Patricia, "but the east side of the city is burning. We're safe here, so long as the wind doesn't change."

Patricia introduced Maude to the other men and to Andrea, and invited her in, where she introduced her to all the children, then explained how they had found Sean on the way out of the city.

"He's Kat and Lizzie's brother," Patricia explained. "The girls recognized him. His feet were bleeding from his outgrown shoes. I'll have to get him some new shoes when we can get back into town."

"Oh, well, if your menfolk can get me back across the road, I'll go get him some shoes my boys outgrew. We always had plenty, and I never threw away anything. I know we can find him something." Maude laughed.

"That's wonderful! I can see we might not get back into town for a while," replied Patricia. Then Patricia turned to Maude and then to Andrea, "In the meantime, let's get some more food ready for all these people."

The time now was much happier for all, with the relief that Roger and Willis were both safe. After eating came the suggestion from Willis that they read together and pray for the city. This time Willis did the reading:

> "And there came thither certain Jews from Antioch and Iconium, who persuaded the people, and, having stoned Paul, drew him out of the city, supposing he had been dead.
> "Howbeit, as the disciples stood round about him, he rose up, and came into the city: and the next day he departed with Barnabas to Derbe.
> "And when they had preached the gospel to that city, and had taught many, they returned again to Lystra, and to Iconium, and Antioch.
> "Confirming the souls of the disciples, and exhorting them in the faith, and that we must through much tribulation enter into the kingdom of God."
> (Acts 14:19-22, KJV)

Jacques was shocked the people stoned Paul until they thought he was dead. When he expressed this, Andrea smiled and said, "We can see God raised him up, so he could continue to preach."

"So there's much more of a miracle here than most folks realize," commented Roger.

Andrea went on, "That last verse I think we can all relate to. By praying and reading together we confirm our faith and exhort each other, which is just what we need, because we live through tribulation now, even though we as Christians see ourselves as part of the kingdom of God."

They all agreed, as Willis was urged to read on:

"And when they had ordained them elders in every church, and had prayed with fasting, they commended them to the Lord, on whom they believed.

"And after they had passed throughout Pisidia, they came to Pamphylia.'

"And when they had preached the word in Perga, they went down to Attalia.

"And thence sailed to Antioch. From whence they had been recommended to the grace of God for the work which they fulfilled.

"And when they were coming, and had gathered the church together, they rehearsed all that God had done with them, and how he had opened the door of faith unto the Gentiles.

"And there they abode long time with the disciples." (Acts 14:22-28, KJV)

As Willis closed the Bible, Andrea looked around the group. The two little girls were sitting close to their brother, one on each side. He had his arms around them both. Willis sat next to his wife, smiling at the children.

Maude was nervously looking out the window at the mass of people and vehicles on the road, heading out of town. "Don't look like traffic's slowin' down none. I'm afraid if I don't git home soon, other's 'll be movin' in on me."

Roger stood up and motioned to Ramon. "Let's get this lady home. We need to be sure no one else is looking at it!"

"Sure thing, Boss. I'll just get my horse," was Ramon's reply, as he went out the door. In a few moments the three were mounted at the road, where a steady stream of vehicles was still moving by.

The two men on their horses plunged into the melee, both reaching for lead teams' bridles to stop them, leaving a short space which the brown mare plunged through, while Maude let out a "Whoop!" As soon as Maude reached the other side, the men let go of the horses and followed her.

"Atta girl, Maude," yelled Roger, as he caught up with her. "You're all right!" Ramon was laughing with glee.

Maude's house was at the end of a two furlong drive. When they got to the house they found a wagon, with one horse hitched, and two saddle horses tied to the rail in front of her porch. Maude jumped off her horse and furiously stomped onto her porch, headed for the front door, before the men were even off their horses. As she jerked the front door open, she noticed the weather strip was broken and splintered where the locked door had been pushed in. There were three men and a woman sitting at her dining table, eating food from her cellar cooler.

Seeing the men, who looked startled at her sudden entry, she turned to the gun rack on the wall next to the door, and snatched her favorite rifle. One of the men laughed, "Sure, lady, you can join us if you know how to cook." At this, the others joined in with laughter.

'Maude swung the rifle at the speaker's head. "You swine, git out of my chair and out of my house, and git your horses off my property!"

One of the men started to get up, "Now, lady," he began, just as Roger and Ramon came through the door, both with handguns ready.

"You heard the lady," Roger said, "get out of here and don't come back to this city or I'll make sure you're prosecuted!"

Ramon stood holding the gun, smiling approval at Roger's performance, but amazed at Maude, as the intruders all stood up and left the house. Then Ramon spoke, "Lady, you scared me to death. You're one tough lady!"

Now Maude was shaking, leaning on the chair. "I was scared too, but I was madder than I was scared. Those filthy swine, messin' up my house! The nerve!" She stood for a while, catching her breath.

"I'll just get some things for that boy, if you fellas can look to that door. There's some tools in the pantry off the kitchen."

By the time Maude was ready, the men had the door repaired, not pretty, but secure. They also went around and secured other doors and windows. Maude packed several pairs of her sons' outgrown shoes, as well as trousers, shirts and underwear into saddlebags to pack on her brown mare. When they started back down the drive they could see the heavy traffic on their street was not diminished. There were already people beginning to camp in her lower pasture. She did not have the heart to chase them off. People were desperate, but she was still concerned for her home.

When they arrived at the road, the men moved right out into the traffic, as before, stopping a couple of teams, allowing Maude to slip through.

One of the pairs of shoes fit Sean perfectly, even a little big, which, with new stockings, eased the pain from his blisters. The other pairs were bigger, so he could use them later.

As evening closed in, there was talk of where to put everyone. Jacques first suggested the boys come over and share Harry's room. Andrew was excited over that prospect.

The Maude suggested Roger and Andrea and their children come over and share her home. "There's plenty of room, and it's really for my own benefit. The more people there, the less likely some of those drifters will want to break in," she smiled.

The suggestion was met with enthusiasm, but Andrew still wanted to stay with Harry. So, soon Willis had his team hitched again to take the Breakfields up to Maude's home. It was a good thing, because when they arrived there were men at both doors, trying to get past the fortification of their earlier visit. When the intruders saw two men and a woman on horses, plus the wagon with the rest of the group, they meekly left without protest.

The wall of flame moving up the east side of the city, lit up the sky for miles all night long. By morning, the flames diminished, but the smoke was so thick, it blocked the sunrise for hours. The smell of smoke lay heavy on the neighborhood, as all the families awoke. There was still heavy traffic on the road with refugees leaving town. Many who camped overnight, were pulling up stakes, continuing their flight to the west and south.

CHAPTER 35

Reunion

A RTHUR MONTGOMERY SPENT most of the night in self-reflection before falling asleep. Upon waking, his thoughts of regret covered several areas. He realized his wife had high hopes of grandeur in planning the event to present Rachel to society. It was a disaster, mainly because of his own behavior in dealing with his old friend.

He knew he dealt unfairly with Darren Newall, letting him think he could marry Rachel if he agreed to stay in England, especially when Marshall was pressuring him, and he had not made it clear to his old friend he did not want to force Rachel to marry him. He realized he had been unscrupulous with both men. Sadly, he also knew he had dealt unfairly with Rachel. He liked the idea of having her next door, but gave little thought of her happiness there.

When he arrived at the Birmingham Police Station, while giving his report, he learned the investigator from Lord Russell's office was there investigating Marshall Tanaghaven, concerning the deaths in his family. *What an eye-opener! How could I have been so blind!* He also learned Tanaghaven was there already, insisting on a police investigation into the kidnapping of Rachel Montgomery by young Newall, and officers were deployed to accompany Tanaghaven to Liverpool.

After his interview with the investigator from Russell's office, the police investigator also asked him for an interview. Feeling impatient to be on the road, he, nevertheless, agreed to stay for the interview. Finally, as more information was shared, the suspicion against Tanaghaven was growing, as was the question of his mental stability. Montgomery was finally asked to stay in Birmingham another day as the investigation proceeded.

When he returned to the police station the next day, he encountered Harold Breadon, solicitor for Wilfred Newall's family. Breadon, upon learning Montgomery was there, asked to speak with him. Upon meeting, Breadon introduced himself, "I'm Harold Breadon; I'm Darren Newall's solicitor."

Montgomery looked surprised, "I didn't know the young man had a solicitor."

"Well, he doesn't either. He just inherited me from his Uncle Wilfred, along with the rest of the Newall estate."

At this, Montgomery's eyebrows shot up. Then he asked, "What good is that if he's on his way to Canada."

"It's still his inheritance, to do with or pass on, however he wishes. But we both know, don't we he's not on his way to Canada."

Montgomery did not catch on right away. "If he's not on his way to Canada, then where is he?"

"You don't know?" Breadon asked, raising his eyebrows, surprised. "He's right here in gaol, at least for the next few minutes."

"Then where is my daughter, Rachel?"

"Well, when the police last saw her, she was with her husband, Squire Tanaghaven."

"Oh my God!" Montgomery felt sick. "I don't believe she could be married to Marshall. How could he do that?"

"Well, she isn't!" Breadon replied. "But she is married to Darren Newall, and she is in a safe place waiting for me to get him out of gaol."

Arthur Montgomery let out his breath which he did not even realize he was holding. "So, are they going to Canada?" he asked.

"Well, since she is the new Lady of Newlandia, I suppose they'll be going there first—along with Darren's family and your former stableman and his family."

Montgomery's eyebrows shot up again. "My stableman? But why?"

"Since you fired him; the Newalls hired him," replied Breadon.

"Oh, no, I didn't," Montgomery protested. "I would never fire Jules. They're like family to us."

"Well, someone fired him, so they're moving to Newlandia."

"Oh my God," Montgomery said again. He was silent for a few moments. Then he asked, "You know for a fact Rachel is safe? She's not with Marshall?"

"I have it on good word—she's in a safe place. She's not with Tanaghaven. As soon as Darren is released, they'll be going to Newlandia."

Arthur Montgomery knew there was no more he could do. He remembered he prayed for Rachel to be safe and happy. Now he knew it was time to go home and see to the rest of his family.

Peggy received another note from Prince Edward in the hands of a personal messenger, so she knew when to expect his visit. But she did not expect the grandeur of the entourage that arrived with him. Nevertheless, her mother was prepared. There were two coaches and an entourage which included chaperones and members of the Royal Guard.

As he came through the door he bowed low as he reached for her hand to kiss it, saying, "So wonderful to see you, Milady, then greeted her mother in similar fashion. He stood straight as at attention to shake hands with her father. Then as Peggy's parents turned to the parlor, the prince offered Peggy his elbow as they followed. As they sat down, Edward addressed Lord Montgomery. "I realize I am too young to ask your permission to court your daughter, but at our last meeting, at your wonderful event," he said, looking at Lady Montgomery, before continuing, "I was so bold to ask her if we might become friends, and I'm happy to say, she told me she would like that. Now, I will ask you, if I may come to visit her occasionally, so we may be friends."

Lady Montgomery smiled happily, reassuring the prince he was welcome to visit. Lord Montgomery smiled, relieved to see his wife happy, if only for the moment. The weeks since his return from Birmingham were not happy ones. She was still devastated her daughter Rachel was gone. He was angry to discover she gave the order to let Jules go, ordering the Duran family to leave.

Arthur Montgomery was chagrinned at the legal proceeding which would, in time, prove his old friend Marshall guilty of three murders, as well as wrongfully accusing Darren Newall of various crimes, interfering with a police investigation, interfering with a ship's voyage, kidnap of Rachel Montgomery, and attempted theft of two horses.

He was ashamed and depressed over the choices he made, resulting in the loss of his daughter, and the son-in-law he could have welcomed into the family. But secretly, he knew his prayer was answered: *She was safe and happy.*

Now he stood and addressed his wife, "Let us leave these two, so as friends they may be free to talk and enjoy each others' company without our interference." His wife opened her mouth to protest, but quickly closed it, and stood up with her husband to leave the room.

Once they were gone, Prince Edward turned to Peggy smiling. "It's wonderful to see you. How have you been?"

"Wonderful," she started to say.

"No, I mean really."

"Well, it's not been the best of times since you were here last. My sister got married and moved to her husband's estate near Southampton. I really miss her. I haven't seen her since that night. I'm happy she's with Darren, but I really miss her. And our friends moved, too, so it's really lonely here. I'm so glad you came!" Now Peggy was almost weeping and feeling embarrassed.

Edward moved closer and took her hand, "I'm so sorry. Would you like to see her?"

"My father went once, but she would not see him. She was really upset he tried to get her to marry Uncle Marshall—I mean Marshall Tanaghaven. It's like a miracle that Darren's uncle died and left everything to Darren—even a title," she added, laughing. I don't know how that solicitor found him, but he saved the day. But I miss my sister."

"Milady, I would love to make arrangements to take you to see your sister. And don't worry, there are always chaperones with me, wherever I go. Unfortunately, that's my misfortune for being the crown prince."

Peggy looked at him, saying a heartfelt, "Oh, that would be wonderful. But only on one condition."

He looked confused. "What condition?"

"If you stop calling me milady; and please, call me Peggy!"

The prince laughed gleefully. "All right, and you'll call me Edward."

Then they both laughed.

The fire was out by four o'clock Tuesday morning, but there were at least 10,000 people forced from their homes and thousands who fled Montreal in fear of the wind changing. Within a few days there would be tents supplied to the thousands camping in fields and vacant areas.

By Friday, *The Montreal Tribune* was able to produce its first edition that week with the headline, *Quebec Monster Found Dead in Fire Zone.* The article described how the body of the disfigured Jean Louis Devoneaux, now identified as the Quebec Monster, also known as "Le Brute," was discovered close to the burned buildings, evidently overcome by smoke.

On Wednesday morning Roger rode into the downtown area accompanied by Ramon to check on both his home and the office. His house was still standing, but had extensive smoke and water damage, as well as many broken windows. He was happy to discover that stable personnel had taken his three coach horses to the stable on company property on Sherbrook Street. Relieved his horses were safe, he was more accepting of the damage to his coach. Next, they headed to the Findlay offices, to find extensive devastation. Ed Findlay was there trying to get help from some of the men in the neighborhood, to get into the building, which had fire damage to the third and fourth floors, as well as smoke and water damage to the first two floors which housed most of the business. Findlay was quite agitated about getting in, until Roger was able to report the files he and Willis rescued, as well as the safe, which was at Willis' house, tucked away and covered up.

Police were now coming around with fire department personnel to inspect and condemn buildings with substantial fire damage, which they did with the Findlay Building. Edward Findlay already built his own home off West Sherbrook Street, a long way from the fire zone. But it was now clear they would have to relocate the business offices.

Sean had been with the Caldwells all week now, since the day of the fire. He did not talk a lot, and Patricia did not press him. But she saw that the girls talked to him, chattering happily about their new home, and often asking him questions. They often asked him about "the man." Patricia listened carefully to the children's conversation, alert for clues to who "the man" might be. She heard Sean say "the man" told him to "go home," before he "walked into the fire."

The boy was homeless, so where would home be? Where the girls were, of course!" Patricia remembered when they picked up the girls and Maude suggested someone might be following them.

By Friday, Roger found a property near West Sherbrook, which Ed Findlay helped him to secure, on which he planned to build his new home. A few blocks south they found a vacant building which was available as a temporary location for the business, which would be back in operation within a few days.

Maude happily agreed to rent her house to the Breakfields until their new home was built. She said she loved to look out to see the beautiful coach horses in her paddocks. She would stay to direct the kitchen help and the housekeeping.

A week after the fire, Jacques and Ramon were both back on the worksite with Russell Thornton, and a few of the crew members. Many had not returned to the job yet. There were new crew members pulled from other job sites, held up by the fire. Many would not return.

A messenger arrived on the site with a message from Roger that he had received notice the *Bucephalus* was in port. Roger knew Jacques would want to contact Pierre a soon as possible to get him to testify before Judge Harris concerning their finding Harry on the streets of Birmingham. The message gave Jacques permission to leave the worksite early to go to the ship.

Jacques hurried to get Tounerre harnessed and hitched, knowing it would take him longer to go around the fire zone to the pier where the *Bucephalus* was tied. On the way he was thinking about all there was to tell his friend, and questions he had. *He hoped at least to get a letter. Maybe she's changed her mind. Who was he, anyway, to think she would leave everything to come here, just for him.*

Finally he was past the detour and headed straight for the harbor. He thought back to the day he first arrived in Liverpool, looking for the *Bucephalus.* At last he saw the ship. Even in these times, it was still one of the biggest in the harbor.

He tied Tounerre at the foot of the pier and walked down to where the ramp was just being lowered. He was looking for Pierre, but thought his friend was probably below, getting horses ready. Then he saw the four of them, laughing and pointing. *Jeannette!* He ran for the ramp, just as it touched the pier. He was on the deck, holding her in his arms in barely a moment.

"Jeannette!"

"My darling!"

Nothing could ever feel so wonderful as his arms around the woman he loved. She did not hesitate to give him a long, delicious kiss, right in front of her mother and their friends. When he finally looked around to see Jeannette's mother and Antoine and Ellienne, at first it seemed perfectly natural to see them all. Then it hit him! *What?* He was speechless. Then Antoine grabbed his hand, then

HELENA POORTVLIET

slapped him on the back, then grabbed him and hugged him, both of them laughing joyfully.

He shook his head. "I can't believe you're all here!"

Ellienne was laughing. Antoine, also laughing, said, "You didn't think you could really get away from us, did you?"

Jacques looked at Madam Newall, then turned back to Jeannette, "Your mother is here with you. What about your place—and your brother?"

"Oh, we sold *La Petite Fleur,* and Darren is happily married to Rachel Montgomery!"

Jacques mouth dropped open. He did not know what to say. Then he remembered Pierre. "Where's Pierre?"

"He's probably getting our horses ready. We should probably go help him." Antoine replied, looking at the three women.

Ellienne responded, "You fellas so on. We can wait here."

So Jacques and Antoine headed for the horse deck to find Pierre just backing the Merlots' two stocky chestnuts into place on their wagon which looked like a little cabin on wheels. The Newalls' wagon was standing ready. Jacques looked around to see Katy in a stall and the horse in the next stall was a tall roan mare. He went to lead Katy out of her stall, and picked up a brush to groom her.

"Hey, brother," Pierre came over to embrace him. "You just can't help yourself if there's a horse to groom!"

"Hey, brother," Jacques returned the greeting. "This mare and I go way back. It's good to see her again—and her owner. I see you took good care of her. No rough seas?"

Pierre laughed, "Oh, we had our share, but not like the night of St. Elmo's visit!" He turned to lead the roan mare out to harness her.

Then it hit Jacques. *Darren's horse Dani is not here. They said he married Rachel Montgomery. Oh my God, I hope that's a good thing!*

He turned to Pierre, "I hope you'll have time to visit a bit before you're back to sea. Will you be here a few days?"

"Sure, I'm looking forward to a visit," Pierre responded.

"Well, I need your help while you're here."

"Sure, my brother, what is it?"

"I'm trying to adopt Harry, and I need your testimony to the judge about how we found him."

"Of course, my brother." Pierre was emphatic. "That is of most importance! When do you need me?"

"Roger will set it up with his solicitor, now he knows you're here."

"All right!"

They hitched Katy and the roan mare to the Newall's wagon. Antoine had already taken his own team and wagon off the ship. Jacques led Katy and the roan mare up the ramp off the ship to the pier. He looked at Jeannette. "Are you driving these two?"

Jeannette looked at him, laughing. "Of course I'm driving my own horses."

Jacques helped Jeannette and her mother up on the driver's seat, then said, "I have a house on the west side of the city." He looked down the waterfront at all the burned out homes and businesses. "The city had a bad fire last week, but we were lucky. It stayed on the east side. I have room for you at my house if you want to come there. You and you mother can have Harry's room and he can share mine."

Jeannette and her mother agreed to follow him, so he walked up the pier to where he left Tounerre. Antoine and Ellienne were waiting in their wagon behind Jacques' carriage. They waited for Jeannette to drive her team behind Jacques, then pulled out to follow them. The traffic on Sherbrook was still heavy, but much of it was coming back into the city. Jeannette was glad to be following Jacques' carriage, knowing that otherwise she would be completely lost in the new city. She saw the confusion and disorientation of so many of the locals who either lost their homes or knew their future was in question, and realized how blessed they were to be welcomed by family. And surely, they knew this was family, as Jeannette expressed to her mother, who agreed.

When they reached the road with the driveway which ran between the two houses, they were aghast at the many makeshift tents and shelters of so many refugees in the pastures along the way. Jeannette turned her team into the driveway following Jacques' carriage. When she stopped behind Jacques as he stopped just past the house on the right, the door opened, and several adults and many children emerged. As Jacques helped her and her mother down from their wagon, the others began to introduce themselves.

"I'm Patricia Caldwell, and this is my husband Willis," said the woman, with two little girls hanging onto her skirts. There was a young boy a little older, following close behind. Patricia then introduced the children. "This is Kat, and her sister, Lizzie and their brother, Sean."

Andrea was right behind Patricia waiting to introduce her children, with her usual infectious smile. "So you are the beautiful bride Jacques has been waiting for! We are so happy to meet you! And these are my children, Julia and Andrew, and here is Harry, who has been anxiously waiting for you to arrive."

Jeannette bent down to get on the same level as the two boys, who were clearly best friends. She thought Harry was much bigger and more robust than she expected from Jacques' first description.

"Harry, I'm so glad to meet you. Ever since Jacques wrote to me about you, I've been looking forward to meeting you. I hope we're going to be good friends." Then she turned to Andrew. "I hear you and Harry are very good friends. That is a good thing to be. I hope you'll always be good friends." On this, both boys nodded and grinned.

By now Jacques was beside them to ask Harry, "Do you mind sharing my room for a while so Jeannette and her mother can use your room?"

Harry hesitated only a moment, before grinning happily and answering, "All right!"

Jacques briefly explained, "They're going to be with us now. The real benefit is they can really cook. You'll love their cooking!"

By now the Merlot's joined the group, to be introduced to everyone. Then everyone helped to unload the Newall's belongings from the wagon, before taking Tounerre and the Newall's team to the barn, followed by Antoine. Madam Newall and Ellienne were invited to have tea with Patricia and Andrea, but Jeannette was anxious to go along with Jacques to see the new Percheron foals. On the way, she explained about "Sassy," the tall roan mare which her brother gave them as a wedding gift. The mare was part of his inheritance at Newlandia. "I think he's really hoping you'll like her as a saddle horse, because he's really sorry and wanted to apologize to you for what he did to you, and he really appreciates that you found Dani and brought her back to him."

Jacques was curious about Darren's marriage to Rachel Montgomery and asked about them.

"Oh, it's a real miracle," Jeannette replied, then continued, "In fact, it's several miracles."

Jacques agreed. "When I was there, Rachel was pretty rebellious. What a pair!"

"Well, that's true," Jeannette went on. "But God is good. He really did a work in both of them. First, they were really attracted to each other, maybe because they were both so rebellious. But then, they each came to God separately. Then Rachel's father tried to get her to marry his awful old friend. Then our Uncle Wilfred died and left Darren his estate and title. And there were many friends who helped them, to be able to get married. But I think God was in control of it all. I think they've both grown up through it all."

Jacques was shaking his head. "That's amazing; praise God!"

Jeannette added, "Can you believe, Darren even made friends with the Romani? He and Roman Balansay made friends, and remember Grace Gala?"

Jacques thought back, "She was the Romani girl who was working for the Montgomerys. I prayed for her to go back to her parents. Did you see her?"

"Oh, yes. She and Roman are getting married. She had her baby, a little girl. Rachel was there with her when the baby was born. She and Roman stood with Darren and Rachel when they said their marriage vows before the Romani chief, Stavros."

Now Jacques was laughing.

As they turned Katy and Sassy into the pasture with the other mares, all of the other mares and foals came to investigate. Jeannette was thrilled to see the new Percheron foals. Jacques explained that the colt was named "Buck," short for *Bucephalus,* but confessed he could not decide on a name for the filly.

Meanwhile, the filly was curiously nuzzling Jeannette's hands. Jeannette said, "Oh, what an angel. She's a love!"

"That's her name," exclaimed Jacques, laughing.

"What—what do you mean?"

"Angel Love—just like you said. That's why I couldn't come up with a name. She was waiting for you to name her."

Then they were both laughing and embracing. The mares were sniffing and otherwise investigating each other, but the only squeals came from Sassy, who was really the only new one.

CHAPTER 36

New Beginnings

T HE ROYAL COACHES came up the lane into Newlandia, causing a stir among the servants, which immediately alerted the principals of the Grand House. Rachel saw the grand coaches and remembered seeing them in the lane in front of her parents' home, the night of her escape.

Raleigh, the elderly butler, who had been at Newlandia forever, opened the door to the two footmen who announced the Crown Prince of England and his companion, the Lady Margaret Montgomery. As Raleigh invited the visitors in, the footmen backed away, and the young prince entered with Peggy on his arm. They were led by Raleigh into the parlor, where Darren and Rachel stood up as they entered. Darren extended his hand to the prince, who took it, standing straight as a rod, and looking straight into his eyes. Rachel stood, hesitantly, waiting respectfully, but Peggy let go of the prince's arm and ran to her sister to embrace her. The prince, watching her, laughed gleefully, encouraging Darren to drop the pretense of respect.

The prince began, "My good friend Peggy has been anxious to spend time with her sister whom she loves and misses, so I hope we can all relate to each other as friends. I'm most grateful, Squire Newall, to be a guest in your home. I have heard much good about you, and I hope we might become friends as well."

Darren almost winced at being addressed as Squire Newall, but he recovered quickly to agree with the prince, who continued, "It is my opinion these young ladies have much to discuss, and I have heard much about the quality of the Newlandia stables. Perhaps you would indulge me, to give me a tour while the ladies catch up."

As soon as Darren and the prince headed for the stable, with the ever present footmen following, Peggy turned to embrace her sister again, exclaiming, "Oh, look at you, the Lady of Newlandia! I'm so proud of you!"

"Well, there's still the former lady of Newlandia," Rachel rolled her eyes. "We have to remember she thinks she's still the Lady of Newlandia, and she thinks her husband Will is still running things while Darren actually runs it, with Mr. Breadon's help—and Jules, of course. What would we do without Jules?"

"Like what are we doing without Jules?" Peggy retorted. "Oh, I so missed them all, and you! There's just Mother and Father, and they're always fighting."

"They're fighting? Why?" Rachel asked.

"Because you're gone, and Father's furious Mother let the Duran's go. And he's really upset about Uncle Marshall."

"He's not our uncle! And Father should be upset. He's a murderer and Father wanted me to marry him!" Rachel looked ill.

"Well, the police think he might have murdered those people," Peggy responded.

"He did it! He even told me he did. He probably would have murdered me if Roman and Fidel hadn't gotten me out of that cab."

"Really? Oh, Rachel, I didn't know," Peggy caught her breath. "What happened?"

"He got the police to chase down the ship. He said he was married to me. Uhg! He had Darren thrown in gaol. He even tried to say that Darren stole his horses. Then he told me it was all my fault he killed Aunt Maddie and his brother, just so he could marry me."

"Oh, my!" Peggy was aghast.

"Roman and his father are the real heroes. If they had not gotten me out of that cab—I don't know…"

"Did you really get married with the Gypsies?" Peggy interrupted.

"Oh, yes, it was wonderful. I got to wear Grace's beautiful gown. And all those people celebrated with us like we were family. And Grace and Roman stood with us." Rachel paused, then remembered, "Oh, and Grace had her baby, a little girl. I was there with her when her baby was born. Her mother and Roman's mother helped her."

"Oh, that's wonderful," Peggy agreed. "But Rachel, I pray you'll see Father. He's really sorry for everything. He knows he wasn't fair with Darren. And he feels terrible he didn't know about all what Marshall was doing."

"Well, I don't know—it was pretty bad. I was furious the way he treated Darren. And I was so scared when Marshall made me go with him, and had Darren arrested. But I've missed you," Rachel said.

"Well, I hope you'll forgive Mother and Father, so we can all see you more often. They really miss you and so do I!"

Peggy and the prince and all the entourage were gone, and Rachel and Darren were together in the Grand House.

"Did you have a good visit with your sister?" he asked.

"Yes, but she wants me to forgive Mother and Father," she replied.

"Well, isn't that what we're supposed to do?" he asked.

"I guess you're right, but it's hard. Father should not have treated you so."

"If you want to invite them here, it's all right with me," he suggested.

"Thanks. I'll think about it," she answered, then continued. "Are you sorry we didn't go to Canada with your family?"

"I miss them, but Mother seemed to think I belong here," he shrugged.

"Do we really belong here, or is that just tradition?" she asked.

"What do you mean—you're not happy here?" he asked.

"This place is wonderful, but I was ready to go to Canada with you," she responded.

"Maybe we should talk about it some more," he said.

When the *Bucephalus* was in port for almost a week, Pierre went with Jacques to stand before Judge Harris and testify concerning them finding Harry in Birmingham. Others in attendance were Captain Palmer, Roger Breakfield, Jeannette Newall and her mother, all saying good things about his character, and his relationship with Harry.

The judge asked Jeannette about her intention to marry Jacques, then suggested they plan to finalize the adoption after their marriage, and adopt Harry as a married couple. Everyone agreed this was a good plan. On the way back to the house, Jacques turned to Jeannette, "So when can we get married? I remember Antoine told me we should get married the moment you set foot in Montreal. You've been here almost a week now." He laughed.

Harry was seated between them on the driver's seat. Jeannette looked at the boy and said, "What do you think, Harry? Would you like it if Jacques and I were to be married soon?"

"Would you be my mother, then?" he asked.

"Would you like that—for me to be your new mother?" Jeannette asked.

The boy grinned, shyly, and nodded.

Jeannette looked back at Jacques. "I guess that settles it then. I think we should go ahead and plan our wedding. I know my mother will want to help with that."

Jacques reached around Harry and Jeannette to hug them both, grinning happily with them.

In the weeks that followed the fire, Willis asked Sean to help him with the chores. Sean remembered the man told him to work, so he went willingly with Willis. He still felt responsible for his sisters. He thought if he could work enough, then maybe that would pay for their keep. They gave him new clothes and shoes, and provided wonderful meals, very lovingly and cheerfully, but he reminded himself, *These are not my parents. My parents are dead. I'm responsible for my sisters.*

He felt in awe of all the huge horses, but was drawn to the small black mare. She was not as overwhelming as the big horses. *But she is a horse.* He remembered, *in Ireland, only the rich folks had horses. The tenant farmers, at best, had a donkey.* Sean liked to pet the little mare, but he wanted to be sure Willis did not think he wasn't doing his work. One day when Willis saw him petting the mare, he handed the boy a brush and said, "Here, give her a good grooming."

Sean suddenly grinned, "All right," as he put all the effort of his work ethic into grooming the little mare. Willis went back to grooming his own horses with a smile on his face.

After awhile, Willis gathered up the little mare's harness, and taking it to Sean, he said, "This little mare is my wife's horse, but I want you to be in charge of taking care of her. I want you to make sure she gets her proper feed each day. Let me show you how to check her feet." Willis went around, picking up each of the mare's feet to show the boy. "See if she doesn't want to pick it up right away, just lean a little against her shoulder like this," as he demonstrated. "Make sure

HELENA POORTVLIET

her shoes are tight, and she doesn't have anything stuck in her feet that will hurt her, okay?"

Sean responded, "Okay!"

Willis went on, "If Patricia needs to go somewhere, you are to harness the mare and hitch her to the cart. Come on, I'll show you how." Willis proceeded to harness the mare and hitch her to the cart, then reversed the process, unhooking her from the cart and removing the harness, saying, "Now you do it. I'll watch. Don't worry, if you forget something, I'll help." Willis grinned as he handed Sean the harness.

Willis watched as Sean harnessed the mare, correcting only when needed, nodding approval as he backed her into the traces. Then he moved in to say, "Now you've got her hitched, let's take her for a drive," as he led the mare out of the barn. Outside, he urged the boy, "Get on up there." Then he climbed into the driver's seat along with the boy, taking the reins. He shook the reins gently on the mare's back, until she moved into a trot, pulling the right rein slightly as they turned onto the road. Once they were on the straight road, he handed the reins to Sean, who took them, grinning broadly.

"Now I'm going to coach you a little," Willis began, "while we are together, but only because I want you to do it right when we're not together, okay? This is how I learned to drive. My father showed me and coached me until I learned to do it right."

Sean listened respectfully, but thought to himself, *But you're not my father, but I'll listen because I need to work.*

Darren awoke before Rachel, but refrained from reaching for her as he would like to, knowing she preferred to awaken more slowly. As he lay there, he looked around the elegant room, thinking, *This was my father's childhood home,* trying to imagine what it would have been like. *My father gave up all this to marry my mother.* He remembered his father always treated his mother with the utmost respect. He always referred to her as Madam Newall, both at home and in public, and expected everyone else to as well. Waves of nostalgia enveloped him as he thought of his mother and sister so far away. The longing overcame him, as Rachel rolled over to embrace him, and he responded to her embrace.

"What is it?" she asked.

"My father considered my mother more important than all this," he replied. "He always had so much respect for her."

"You really miss them, don't you?"

"I miss them more than I thought I would."

"Do you still want to go to Canada?"

"What about you?"

"I always expected I would go to Canada with you. It's up to you my love."

Morton answered the door when the messenger came. Taking the note to Lord Montgomery, he waited respectfully for further orders while Arthur read the note. Arthur looked up and said, "We are invited to Newlandia on Saturday for dinner, and will stay over to return after breakfast in the morning. You may tell Lady Montgomery and Peggy. I will be here in my office."

After Morton left, Arthur resumed his self-reflection. He was thankful for the invitation from his daughter and son-in-law, but wondered, *am I still angry? Am I still angry at Rachel? Can I face Darren? How do I feel about my son-in-law? Has he forgiven me? Will he forgive me? What about my wife? This has been terrible for her. At least Peggy will be glad to see her sister.*

The *Bucephalus* was expected to be in Montreal in mid-October. Once Jeannette and her mother started planning the wedding, Jacques realized why they would need at least that much time. First they found a Methodist church which was a relatively new congregation southwest of Mount Royale, and made plans to begin to attend there. Jacques realized this meant he and Harry would also attend. The only church Jacques ever attended was the Catholic Church in France. This was really different. It was more like the Bible reading sessions on the ship, or with the Romani.

As soon as they began to attend, most of their friends began to attend as well. Jeannette and her mother talked to the minister about their plans to marry and when the earliest option was around the middle of October, Jacques thought *maybe the* Bucephalus *will be in port and Pierre would be able to attend.* That made it easier to wait.

The house Roger's company provided for them was just as sparsely furnished as the Caldwells' house had been. Jacques was impressed how Patricia had been decorating and furnishing their home with the requisition provided by their company. He was given the same requisition, but as yet not used it. Now he showed the requisition to Jeannette and invited her and her mother to use it to furnish their house.

Jeannette was delighted, and hurried to show her mother. After the men all left for work, there was a knock on the door. When Jeannette opened the door she found Patricia Caldwell, bearing a still-hot pan of cinnamon rolls.

"I can't stay; I just left Sean in charge of his sisters, but I wanted to bring you some of my hot cinnamon rolls," she explained, as she handed over the pan, wrapped in a towel.

"Oh, thank you," Jeannette answered. "Jacques just gave me this requisition to furnish our house. We're thinking of going shopping today. Harry's with Andrea, so it's just mother and me."

"Oh, Lanier's is wonderful!" Patricia laughed. I got our furniture there! You'll love it!"

Patricia left and Jeannette turned back to the kitchen with the pan of rolls. "We've spent our lives cooking for others, but to have a neighbor bring us a pan of cinnamon rolls in this new land is all about receiving love."

Her mother agreed, as she poured cups of tea to accompany the rolls.

"Oh Mother," Jeannette said fervently, "I so wish Darren could be here with us to share these rolls. I so miss him."

"I do also, Sweetie," her mother agreed.

"I hope he and Rachel are happy. I pray she has made amends with her family." After a moment's pause, she continued, "It's wonderful to know they are both walking with God."

"I'm glad of that also," her mother agreed. "Otherwise, it would have been awfully hard to leave them. But we always continue to pray for those we love, even if we cannot be together."

"I agree, Mother, but I still miss him, and I wish he could be here for my wedding."

Peggy was thrilled at the prospect of the trip to Newlandia with her parents. But she was troubled by what her mother had to say, "I just know my daughter has come to her senses and is ready to come home."

"Mother!" Peggy exclaimed, "Rachel is with her husband. She loves him! Newlandia is her home!"

Arthur rolled his eyes. *I know Rachel will not be coming home, but at least I hope she's forgiven me.*

When they reached the door at Newlandia, Peggy was happy as she anticipated seeing her sister. Lady Montgomery was nervous and emotional. Lord Montgomery was quiet, feeling humbled, not only by the grandeur of Newlandia, but also by his recent self-examination concerning his own actions, and his hope for reconciliation with his daughter and new son-in-law.

Rachel opened the door herself, flanked by the disapproving Raleigh, and her husband. Peggy did not hesitate to embrace her sister. Their mother hesitated, looking apprehensive as her daughters embraced. Darren offered his hand to Lord Montgomery, inviting him in. Rachel pulled her sister inside as Darren led Lord Montgomery into the Great Room. Lady Montgomery stood in the entry looking confused and indignant. Raleigh offered her his elbow. After he deposited her with the others, he disappeared.

Rachel and Peggy were so thrilled to be together, they were almost oblivious of the others. Darren talked to Lord Montgomery as freely as if there had never been an issue between them. Montgomery began calling him Squire Newall, but was quickly corrected with "Darren."

Montgomery then said, "Then in all fairness, call me Arthur."

Then the room grew quiet and they all looked to the entry to see the lady who appeared with Raleigh. Darren quickly arose and went to her, offering his elbow, as he turned to present her to the others. "This is Aunt Melinda," he explained, then turned to introduce the others. "Aunt Melinda, these people are my wife's family, Lord and Lady Montgomery, and Rachel's sister Peggy." Then he led her to a chair and assisted her as she sat down.

"Wil shall be joining us soon," she said quietly, with a faraway look.

"Yes, Auntie," Darren reassured her. As he returned to his chair, Darren explained, "Our family friend and solicitor will be joining us. He said he would be bringing a guest with him. He did not say who, so I don't know. As soon as they arrive, we'll go to dinner." He turned to Raleigh, "You can tell the staff, as soon as our other guests arrive, we'll go to dinner."

After a moment of questioning looks, Peggy and Rachel resumed their conversation. Lady Montgomery attempted to make polite conversation with Melinda, who responded politely, but seemed confused with all the people there. Arthur broke the ensuing tension by asking Darren, "Do you still have that nice bay mare you were riding?"

Darren replied, smiling, "Oh, yes. I would not let her go. She is as important to me as Rachel's gray is to her! We inherited quite a stable, but she is still my favorite. After dinner, perhaps you would like to see our stable."

"Absolutely," was the enthusiastic reply.

Before long Raleigh answered the door, and led the newcomers into the Great Room, announcing them: "Edward, Crown Prince of England, and Master Harold Breadon."

Darren and Arthur both stood as the prince entered the room, followed by Breadon. Arthur remembered Breadon from their interview at the Birmingham Police Headquarters. Lady Montgomery arose quickly when she recognized the prince, but Peggy was the first to greet him.

"Oh, Edward, it's wonderful to see you."

He took her hand, saying, "It's wonderful to see you, Peggy." Heads turned at their use of first names, but they both smiled, delighted. Then Edward turned to Lady Montgomery to take her hand in greeting, before turning to shake hands with Lord Montgomery.

When they went into the dining room, there was a place set at the head of the table, but no one sat there. Melinda Newall sat at the opposite end of the table, saying again, "Wil shall be joining us shortly."

Rachel and Darren sat in the two seats next to the empty chair at the head of the table, facing each other. The prince sat next to Rachel with Peggy seated next to him. Harold Breadon sat next to Darren. Lord and Lady Montgomery were seated on either side of Melinda. Darren recalled to himself the evening his family dined with the Montgomerys. At that time, Lord Montgomery had control, pulling all the strings. *Now the tables are turned.*

Servants quickly brought the first course and Melinda smiled at the others and began to eat, signaling the others. After a period of vigorous eating and talking, and more courses, Harold Breadon stood up and spoke. "His Highness, Prince Edward asked to accompany me here, so he may make an announcement." As the prince stood, Breadon sat down.

"I'm delighted to be here for several reasons. Quite selfishly, I'm glad to be able to visit my good friend, Peggy," said the prince, smiling at Peggy, and glancing quickly at her mother, who smiled proudly. But more importantly, I have some important announcements that will effect both of your families. There are certain titles and honors in England that come automatically according to who your parents are. For instance, I get to be a prince simply because my mother is the queen. I did not do anything I can brag about, I was simply born a prince. But, with the permission of the queen, some titles come easier if a person has been deemed of exceptional service to our country. Several members of this family were recently involved in activities which brought to light injustices which had gone unprosecuted. Some of you were even at risk for your lives in this process. Some of you took great risk to not allow this perpetrator to continue his mischief. Some of you suffered great emotional trauma in doing the right thing. For this, your country is rewarding you. By authority given by your Queen, Lord Arthur Montgomery, you are named Earl of Gloucestershire, and are eligible to be elected to the House of Lords."

Arthur could not hide his surprise, but did not miss the smiles of pride from both his daughters. His wife had the biggest smile.

Then Edward turned to Darren. "Your father was high born, but also gave remarkable service in the Royal Dragoons. But because he loved your mother, he gave up his inheritance and title. But you have inherited the title that would have been his. But now, because of your courageous actions to do what you believed to be right, you have aided in a great service to your country. Squire Newall, you shall now be addressed as Lord Newall, Earl of Hampshire, which also entitles you to be eligible for election to the House of Lords."

Rachel was smiling proudly at her husband. But he looked perplexed and troubled. After a moment, he looked at Breadon, then at the prince. "What if we should decide to leave England, that is, immigrate to Canada?"

Edward looked at Breadon who spoke, "Just as your inheritance is yours, whether or not you stay in England, as far as England is concerned, you are who you are, the title and position are yours. Your neighbors and your government in Canada may not recognize that, but England does. The title may also be passed on. If your son chooses to return to England in the future, he shall be known as the second Earl of Hampshire."

Arthur Montgomery was now looking at Darren and Rachel. "What are your plans? Are the two of you going to Canada?" Darren turned to his wife, who faced her parents. "Mother and Father," she began, "Yes, we have decided to go to Canada." She looked back at her husband as he turned to face Breadon.

"The Durans have agreed to stay here and manage this property. They will be here to be sure Aunt Melinda has everything she needs. The Balansay family, father and son, will be moving here to help manage the grounds. And we will stay in touch, by mail and occasional visits. And I expect you will continue to take care of the legal affairs of the estate."

There was silence all around the table. Then Peggy got up from her chair to go to embrace her sister. "I know this is what you want to do, and my heart goes with you."

The prince and Mr. Breadon were gone, and the others retired for the evening, leaving the new Earl of Hampshire and his Lady to their own company. Darren smiled at his wife, "So now it's official we are going, perhaps we should be making some plans."

Rachel was excited at the future, now the decision was made and announced. "So should we be thinking of just what we shall be doing in Canada?"

"My mother and my sister and I planned on using the capital to purchase another property like our inn in Southampton, and rebuild the same type of business. If we had not inherited Newlandia, I would have been part of building that business."

"And now what?" Rachel prompted. "What would you do differently now?"

"I think we can still be part of that, but with a little more capital from this estate, we'll have a little more freedom to make it what we want," he replied.

"And what else?"

"Well, what do we like the most about this place?" He smiled.

"Well, I love riding every day!" she grinned. "We have to take Misty and Dani!"

"We can do more than that. What is my sister's fiancé doing? He's taking those big black horses to breed and raise in Canada. There's some fine horses here that my family has bred for generations, all the best English thoroughbreds. We could take enough capital from this property to build a nice place in Canada—and also take some good breeding stock." Darren's voice raised as he anticipated what he was saying. Rachel's expression was matching his as her excitement grew. "Oh, my love, I think we shall have a good life!"

"There's something else I would like to do here, before we leave." Darren now was reflective.

"What is it, my love?"

"I want to do something here for the Romani. I want to build a chapel, and open this property to any of them who will come here and work on the property and live here, and worship God here."

"That's a wonderful idea," Rachel agreed. "Where would we be if they had not helped us?"

"That's right. If Roman had not been such a friend, I might not have had the courage to try to win you, my love!" He was laughing.

"Really!"

"I think that when I saw how happy he and Grace were, it encouraged me to try to win you."

Now Rachel was laughing joyfully.

CHAPTER 37

Resolution

B Y THE END of August, Jacques nearly finished the basic structure of the great home Roger assigned to him and his crew. He was amazed at how much he learned in just a few months. In a few weeks, the outside of the house would be finished. They were racing the time left before the weather began to change in late September. By October he expected to be working on inside finishing of homes they raised throughout the summer.

Jeannette and her mother did a splendid job of furnishing their home. In the meantime, Ramon moved to Maude's house, giving them his room. Harry could have his own room once more.

It was an exceptionally warm September in Montreal. Business was booming after the fire. There were still hundreds of homeless, but many were working on the demolition and clearing of debris in the fire zone. Like the proverbial phoenix, newer, better, more modern buildings were rising in the burned out neighborhoods. The birth of the new business district was transforming the face of the city, bringing hope where there was monumental disaster.

All of the children were in school now at the West Sherwood Academy, except for Lizzie, who was still too young. Sean protested, insisting he must work, until Willis took him aside.

"I understand you feel you need to work, for you and your sisters, and that's all right. But if you want the best for your sisters, you'll go to school and learn to be the best you can be, and set a good example for them. There's plenty of time before and after school for you to work. An important part of your work is what you accomplish at school. It will still be your responsibility to get up and take care of the mare in the morning, and have her harnessed and ready to go, so

Patricia can get you and your sister to school." Willis smiled, adding, "You've done a good job these last coupla' months. I really appreciate your help, especially taking care of the mare. That gives Patricia more time to take care of your sisters."

After that conversation, Sean willingly went to school, but was careful to make sure the mare was also well cared for.

On Wednesday, the twentieth of October, it was cool, near freezing, but it had not rained for several days. Work began on the inside of the huge house, which Jacques and his crew finished on the outside. Roger assigned a foreman, Jack Neville, to train Jacques and Ramon together on the interior work of the elaborate structure. Shortly after arriving at the worksite, Jacques was given a note from Roger, indicating the *Bucephalus* was in port, and he was free to leave the worksite if necessary.

Jacques' and Jeannette's wedding was planned for Saturday, October 23. He hoped his friend Pierre would arrive in time to attend. He ran to the stable to get Sassy, the tall roan mare Darren sent him. At times like this, he appreciated having a saddle horse, since it was much quicker to throw on a saddle, than harness and hitch. He hurried through town and around the detour, to the waterfront, anticipating seeing Pierre again, joyful at the prospect of his marriage in a few days.

His excitement was still growing as he reached the pier where the *Bucephalus* was tied. Pierre was on the pier at the foot of the ramp, holding a team for a family who were just getting into their carriage. Jacques tied Sassy and walked toward Pierre.

"Hello, my brother," he called happily, as the team and carriage moved past him.

Pierre turned to see his friend smiling broadly. "My brother, it is wonderful to see you! Is the married life all you thought it would be?"

Jacques laughed, "We will find out soon. Our wedding is on Saturday, and we have been hoping you would be here to share our celebration."

There was something in Pierre's demeanor that told Jacques all was not well. "What is it, brother? Are you not happy to be on solid earth?"

"For that I am happy," Pierre responded, now showing his worry, "but news I have for you is not good."

Jacques stopped still. "What is it?"

"Your bride's brother and sister-in-law are here," Pierre began.

Jacques looked around, "Oh, wonderful—Jeannette will be so happy! She's been wishing he would be here for her wedding. Where are they?"

Pierre looked down, shaking his head. "They're in sick bay."

"Why? What's wrong? What's happened?"

"We had stormy seas coming into the gulf. Lady Newall fell, and it seems she lost her child, and she hasn't been well. We're afraid she's dying. Lord Newall has not left her side." Pierre's voice was shaking, looking very emotional. "They brought a lot of horses with them, and I don't know what to do with them. We had some damage to the ship, so we'll be in port for a while—maybe all winter."

Jacques felt overwhelmed with disappointment. He remembered how Darren was so depressed over his father's death. "Oh, Father," he began to pray, "I pray your hand is on our brother and sister." Pierre stopped to pray with him, reassuring his agreement.

"Can I see Darren and Rachel—or even just Darren?" They started up the ramp, and as they turned toward sick bay they were met by Captain Palmer.

"Pierre, I've got owners waiting for those Clydesdales," he began, as he turned to Jacques. "I guess you know about your relatives. I'll take you to them."

Jacques followed Palmer to the infirmary, where they were greeted by Doc Carlton, the ship's surgeon.

"You remember our former stableman, Jacques," he reminded the doctor. He's related to your patient. You can explain what's going on."

"Yes, come on in," Carlton motioned toward his tiny office. "The young lady took a fall during the storm, just off Newfoundland, I believe it was. Apparently, she did not realize she was expecting a child, but after the fall, she did have a miscarriage. It should not have been critical, since she was early term. However, she lost a lost of blood and we almost lost her. She seems to be hanging on, but we could still lose her."

"Oh, my God," Jacques voice shook. He was so happy, anticipating his wedding. Now, that all seemed to go away. "Can I see them—or even Darren?"

"Come with me." The doctor moved to the door, leading the way.

Darren was on a chair, next to the bed, holding Rachel's hand, his head bowed. Jacques remembered the beautiful young girl back in England, the picture of health and vitality. She lay back, her eyes closed, her skin so white, her hair looked even blacker than he remembered. He noticed her cheekbones stood out sharply.

As Jacques came into the room, Darren looked up, his face wet with tears. When he recognized Jacques he quickly stood up. Jacques reached out his hand to Darren, who started to take his hand, but then collapsed into his arms.

"It's okay, brother," Jacques reassured him. "It's okay!"

Darren was sobbing. "I never should have brought her on this trip. I was so selfish. It was all about me."

Jacques held him until the sobbing began to abate. Then he began to pray, "I pray for my brother and sister. I know you wouldn't have brought them this far to lose them now. I ask for healing in Jesus name."

He pulled away from Darren, saying, "You're home now, brother. Your mother and sister are close by. Your wife is going to be all right. We'll get her home, and she'll be fine." Jacques looked back toward Rachel. She blinked her eyes, looking toward them. Darren turned back to her.

She barely whispered, "My love…"

"I'm here, love."

Jacques was amazed to see the devotion between the two, in spite of the circumstances.

There was a knock on the door, and Jacques turned to see Pierre. "I got the last bunch of horses off the ship—all that's left are theirs." He saw Rachel was awake.

"Praise God, Lady Newall! We've been praying for you!" Pierre exclaimed.

The doctor was coming back in the door. "Go on you two," he said. "This is too much activity for now," he went on, waving Jacques and Pierre out the door, so they went back to the horse deck, where they found nine horses from Newlandia, including Misty and Dani, a stallion and six mares.

"These are all their horses?"

"Every one of them."

"How long can they stay here?"

"We're not going out to sea again this winter, but there's not much feed left. The ship is going into dry dock for repairs soon, so we won't be taking on anymore feed. They have a nice coach, also, so four of the mares will go in harness."

"I'll talk to Darren again, and then I'll head home. I need to let Jeannette and her mother know they are here. I can take at least one horse with me now.

When Jacques went back to the infirmary, Rachel was asleep. Darren looked exhausted. Doc Carlton had examined Rachel and determined she was very weak, but not losing ground, but made it clear she was not out of danger.

Jeannette was in her wedding gown; her mother was making the last adjustments. "You're just beautiful, my darling. That young man will be just captivated when he sets eyes on you"

Jeannette looked over her mother's shoulder out the kitchen window when she recognized the roan mare. "Oh, Mother, he's home. He mustn't see me!" She ran for her room. As she ran, she thought, *That looked like Katy. What is Jacques doing with Katy?*

When Jacques came in, Madam Newall met him at the door. "You're home early," she said.

"Where's Jeannette? I have some news for you," he began.

"She's dressing. What is it?"

"Your son and his wife are in Montreal."

"Where are they?" Madam Newall looked excited, but worried.

"They're on the ship. Rachel is very ill."

"Oh, no!"

Jeannette came in the room in time to hear her mother, "What is it?"

Jacques said again, "Darren is here with Rachel. They're on the ship, but Rachel is very sick."

Jeannette stopped short. "How bad? Can we see her?"

"I'm going to hitch Tounerre, so we can all go back down there. I'm sorry, she's pretty bad. Darren is really scared for her." He went out the door.

The two women embraced and prayed together until they heard the carriage outside the front door. When they went out, they found Antoine and Ellienne in the carriage with Jacques.

When they arrived at the *Bucephalus*, the ramp was still down on the pier, but there were two sailors standing guard on the deck. As soon as they reached the top of the ramp, both Pierre and Captain Palmer were there to greet them, leading them all to the infirmary.

Then Darren was in front of them, embracing both his mother and his sister at once. Jeannette immediately began to pray and Jacques moved in to embrace them all. Then Darren led them into the room, where Rachel lay as if asleep. Jeannette was shocked to see the sharpness of the bones of her face. Madam Newall went quickly to the chair where Darren was sitting earlier, sat down and picked up Rachel's hand. As she did, Rachel opened here eyes and whispered, "Mother?"

"I'm here, Sweetie. You're going to be all right, now. We're all here and we love you," Darren's mother reassured her. Rachel lay back and closed her eyes again.

Madam Newall looked around, "We've got to get her out of here."

"But Mother," Darren began.

"She'll not get better here. I'll speak to the doctor." She got up and found her way to the doctor's office. After a few moments, she was back, the doctor following.

"The night air will kill her," he said.

"When has she eaten last?" asked Madam Newall.

"Not for days. She's only awakened for moments at a time," Darren answered.

"My Lord, Son, You were in a coma for weeks, and I fed you," she retorted. "We'll bundle her up and make sure the night air does not get to her."

Darren's expression brightened. "Mother, we have that nice coach; it's as warm as a house."

His mother looked around at the other men. "How long does it take you to get that coach hitched up.?"

Pierre, Jacques and Antoine all left for the horse deck. In a short while, they had four of the mares hitched to the coach and before long it was on the pier, waiting.

Darren scooped up his wife from the bed, wrapping the blanket around her. His mother helped tuck it in around her. As he carried her down the ramp, Captain Palmer stood watching.

Madam Newall turned to the captain to say, "My daughter is getting married on Saturday at one o'clock at the West Sherbrook Methodist Church. We would be pleased if you would attend."

The captain looked surprised, then said, "I'll be there."

Darren's mother and sister climbed into the coach with Darren and Rachel. Antoine climbed up on the driver's seat. The others went back to Jacques' carriage with him.

Shortly after they arrived at the house, Roger arrived with Harry. "When you didn't come to get Harry, we thought there must be something wrong," he said.

Jacques explained the situation, then looked at Harry. "Sorry, Son, I knew you'd be okay with Andrew. You see, we've more visitors from England, so I hope you don't mind sharing my room again."

Harry rolled his eyes. "All right."

In the next two days, they were able to get the rest of the Newalls' horses and other belongings off the ship, with Pierre's help, then Pierre returned with them, to stay, as it turned out, with Ramon at Maude's house.

Every little while Madam Newall helped Rachel to swallow some broth while Darren watched. She told him, "Now you can see how I brought you back from the dead, my son." Several of the family and friends came to pray for her each day.

On Saturday morning, Roger, Willis, Ramon, and Antoine came to the door to get Jacques. Jeannette had his clothes for the wedding ready and handed them over to Roger. "Come with us," Roger laughed. "This is the last you'll see of that beautiful lady until you see her in the church." Antoine and Ellienne would stand with them during the ceremony, but her brother would walk down the isle with her, to give her away in marriage.

The men all went with Jacques to Maude's house where they all made sure he was presentable for his wedding. Roger gave him an envelope saying, "Go ahead, open it," which he did, finding receipts for a week stay at one of the nicest hotels in Montreal with all the amenities.

"Don't worry about Harry, he's agreed to stay with us while you're on your honeymoon. Darren's agreed to let us use his beautiful coach to drive you to the hotel. You don't need to worry about your horses. These fellas will look after all of them."

The day had an unreal quality as Jacques got ready. Someone hitched Tounerre to his carriage to drive him to the church. When he arrived at the church, he saw nothing of Jeannette, wondering where she was. Antoine went with him to the minister's office. All the paperwork was in order. The minister led them down a corridor into the front of the church.

As he looked out into the sanctuary, he saw a mass of faces, but could not recognize anyone. He followed the minister, was followed by Antoine. As he looked down the center aisle, he waited nervously. Then he saw Jeannette's mother seated with Rachel, still very pale and thin. Then he saw Harry seated on the other side of Madam Newall, grinning at him. He looked down the aisle. *There she is! Jeannette, the love of my life! She's beautiful!* She was standing in the entry. For a moment she and her brother were smiling at each other. Then he saw Ellienne, right behind her, reach out to give her a hug.

The music started, and Jeannette was walking slowly toward him on Darren's arm, with a broad smile lighting her face. He knew this was the beginning of the best of his life.